Milk
and
Murder

Milk and Murder

Frank Barham

Bridgeview Press
Philadelphia

Cover art: a portion of
The *Mortal Comedy* by
Paul Matthews

Acknowledgements

Paul Thayer and Michael Lindlau for their assistance in preparation of the manuscript.

Chapter One

Philadelphia, Pennsylvania
1929

"GET OUT! Get out and don't come back!"
Carol's father shouted. He had always been quiet
spoken, but his recent shouts lingered in her mind. Her
mother usually dominated family conversations, however, that day she stood in a corner, sobbing but saying
nothing.

The trolley, smelling of burned oil, rumbled over
lop-sided tracks, jostling the sixteen-year-old girl.
Crying, Carol blotted tears then stared at the back of the
wicker seat in front of her. *Why didn't I listen to mama?*
I should have listened. She warned me. Does she still
love me? Does anyone?

Carol's eyes burned as she tried to hold back her
tears, but she suddenly burst out sobbing.

"Last stop!" the trolley operator shouted.

Carol felt the operator's gaze reflected in his
rearview mirror as he watched her walk to the front of
the streetcar.

"Are you okay?" the operator asked.

She nodded. Between sobs, she dabbed her eyes
with a lace handkerchief. "I'm okay."

Carol, wearing silk slippers, stepped down onto a
crumbling sidewalk in the outskirts of Philadelphia. She
shivered as she scanned the empty street. Only the
purplish-orange rays of the setting sun illuminated the
pavement. *Remember to mention Rachel.*

Plodding alongside a twisted and broken iron fence,

she dragged her gloved hand over its spindles and watched flakes of rust fall to the ground. Her pace slowed until she stopped at the gate. *Should I go in there? What if I don't? I have to.* She pushed the sagging open. Its high-pitched squeak startled her. She yelped and jumped, then took a minute to calm herself.

Remember Rachel, she thought as she stepped onto a dirt path that stretched along a rundown Victorian house in need of painting.

All day, she had carried a pink silk parasol, but now, she tired of lugging it and allowed it to drag behind her, leaving a groove in the dirt. At the end of the path, she climbed four rickety wooden steps to a sagging porch lit by a dim, dirty bulb. She raised her trembling hand to knock on the door and noted its odd woodgrain poking through peeling and faded paint. "Oh no!" she said, staring at the grain and a brown knot that formed a skull-like image.

Off to the right, a loud noise rattled her already shakened nerves, causing her to jump. Using her hand to block the overhead light, she forced herself to scan the over-grown yard of tall weeds.

Voice breaking from nerves, she asked, "Who's there?" All remained quiet. *Maybe it was a cat.*

Carol rapped her knuckles on the door and waited. No one responded. She tried to swallow, but her mouth felt like cotton. She knocked again.

Seconds later, the door opened an inch, then knobby fingers pulled the door inward. A craggy-faced old woman peered out. "Yes?" she asked in a gravely voice.

Carol swallowed hard. "I'm Carol. Rachel sent me."

"Come in," the woman said grabbing Carol's arm

and pulling her inside.

"What—?" Carol said. *Who is this?*

Still gripping Carol's wrist, the old woman asked, "Does anyone other than Rachel know you're here?"

"No."

"You sure no one followed you?"

"Yes. I was the last person on the trolley."

The old woman pointed a crooked finger toward a chair in the parlor. "Wait there."

Carol sat alone in the only chair in the room. Round and round she turned an amethyst ring given to her seven days earlier, for her birthday. She scanned what she imagined had once been a beautiful formal parlor. Yellowed paper shades covered the windows. Black spots showed through the worn red rose design of the linoleum floor covering. A lopsided table lamp strained to light the space.

What a pigsty.

Smoothing her silk dress over and over, she admired it, the favorite of the fifty-seven she once owned. She crossed then uncrossed her ankles and rubbed the back of her legs. "I hate mohair chairs," she muttered. "They chafe."

Carol picked up a week-old copy of the *Inquirer* newspaper and turned it toward the lamp to read the front page. She stopped at the headline, "Depression Worsens*.*" The paper shook as she tried to read. *Why is everything about the market crash or dust storms in the Midwest?* She half-folded the paper and then slammed it on the end table.

This chair is so uncomfortable. She repeatedly shifted her weight on its sagging springs in an attempt to find a comy spot . *It's so quiet in here. Where is everyone?*

Suddenly, the door to a room behind Carol burst open. Surprised, she jerked her elbow and knocked the newspaper from the table.

A tall, middle-aged woman, followed by the smell of disinfectant, walked in front of the trembling girl.

Startled by the woman's abrupt entrance, Carol thought, *She can't be a nurse. She's not wearing white.*

"Carol," the woman said, sounding like Carol's mother. "My, you're a pretty little thing. I'm Nurse Agnes. I'll help you get ready. Come with me."

Carol sighed and clutched her belly, struggling to get up from the low chair.

"Let me help you," Agnes said, extending her hand. "Thanks."

"Are you alone?" Agnes asked, putting an arm around Carol's shoulder.

Eyes downcast, Carol placed her left hand on her hip and arched her back. "Yes," she said in a soft, shaky voice.

Agnes hugged Carol and pushed her auburn hair from her tear-streaked face. "Your hair is gorgeous."

"Thank you." Carol felt her smile morph into a frown as she stared at the floor and rubbed her aching back.

Agnes tightened her hug. "Back bothering you?"

"It always hurts, but it's worse this week."

"How will you get home? Who's going to care for you?"

"Me," Carol said, hobbling and sniffling as the two women walked down a hall. "I'm on my own. Got no place to go or anyone who cares anymore."

"Where's your mother or father?" Agnes asked, guid-ing Carol into a room.

"Disowned me," she said as tears dripped from her chin.

"They don't want me."

"And your husband?"

"No. No husband."

"A boyfriend?"

"No . . . not anymore. Nobody."

"Well, now. We'll have to find a place for you to stay for a few days."

A sense of calm came over Carol. She looked at Agnes and asked, "Could you?"

"We'll work out something."

"Did Rachel call?"

Agnes squeezed Carol's shoulder. "Don't worry. Rachel has covered the costs."

Carol entered a large room. The odor of mildew stung her nostrils. She guessed the room had once been a dining room. It had wide baseboards and wide but plain doorframes—unlike the carved ones in her old home. Above the beat-up wainscoting, remnants of faded floral wallpaper hung in shreds from two walls.

She stared at the only large item in the room, a long, narrow wooden table. *This is not what I expected. I thought it would be like a hospital, not a dungeon.*

Sensing Carol's anxiety, Agnes said, "Don't worry. We'll take good care of you, but now, you need to get undressed. Take off everything." Agnes held up a clothes hanger and a short white gown with string closures. "Put this on—opening in the back—then sit on the end of the table." Agnes headed for the door. "I'll tell the doctor you're here."

Carol fumbled with the buttons on her lace dress, placed it on the hanger, and then hung it on a hook. She sat on a chair and rolled her right silk stocking to her toes. She stared at it for a second. *God help me.* She pulled the stocking from her foot. Seconds later, she removed the left stocking. She laid one stocking on the other, folded them in half then stared at the floor as she twisted the stockings into a rope. She un-twisted it then twisted it—over and over. *Do I want to do this?* She untwisted and separated the stockings, stuffed each into the corresponding shoe, and then pushed them under the table.

Having folded her silk slip and panties, she placed them under the pillow at the head of the table. *I feel so ashamed.* Carol kneaded her forehead and muttered, "Why did this happen to me? Why me?"

She donned the hospital gown with the opening in the front. *God, what am I doing? The opening goes in the back.* She removed the gown, put it on as instructed, and then struggled to get onto the end of the oak table. *Why don't they have a stool?*

As her butt touched the table, she exclaimed, "Oh! It's cold." She pushed the gown under her butt then scooted toward the middle of the table.

She sat erect, wrung her sweaty hands, and rubbed tears with her wrists as she waited for the doctor.

When the door opened without warning, she shook and yelled, "Uh!"

Agnes and a tall, smiling man in his late twenties entered and extended his hand. "Carol, I'm Doctor Goode. How are you?"

Carol took his hand and then rubbed her belly. "I wish I could say I'm fine, but as you can see, I'm not."

The doctor pushed strands of black hair from his glasses, rolled up his starched, white sleeves, and then pulled on a pair of amber-colored rubber gloves. "I understand how you feel. Have you given your decision serious thought?"

Carol glimpsed her cheerless face reflected in the doctor's black framed glasses. She did not recognize the face staring back at her. "Yes. It's all I've thought about."

From under the table, the doctor extended two metal arm-like things then moved them toward Carol's knees. "Well, let's have a look . . . see if everything is okay." The doctor placed his hand against Carol's shoulder and said, "Lie back and put your feet in the stirrups."

Agnes guided Carol's feet into the stirrups. "Relax, Carol. It's going to be okay. No one is going to hurt you."

"I know you're sixteen," the doctor said, "but have you ever had an examination?"

"No," Carol said biting her lip. She felt her face warm red as she focused on a water stain on the ceiling.

"Try to relax," the doctor said, draping a sheet over her legs. "Now, let your legs relax. I want you to let your knees fall apart. That's it . . . a little more. Good. Hold still. I'm not going to hurt you, but you will feel something cold—maybe a little pressure, but nothing should hurt."

"Please . . . be careful."

Embarrassed, Carol covered her warm, flushed face with her arms. *No one has seen me like this with the lights on.*

"I'll be careful," he said. "Relax. Breathe through your mouth, slow and steady. Concentrate on relaxing your belly and legs, okay?"

"I'll try." Carol hugged her chest with folded, shaking arms. She swallowed hard and squeezed her eyelids shut, forcing a tear from her right eye.

With one eye, she watched the doctor sit down on a stool then adjust a nearby gooseneck lamp. As he examined Carol's vagina, she jumped, winced, and bit her lip.

"Relax, Carol," the doctor said. After a few seconds, the doctor peered over the sheet into Carol's wide eyes. "Everything is fine."

That's a relief, Carol thought and exhaled a long sigh. She forced her knees together and asked, "Is it over?"

"For the moment," the doctor said and looked at Agnes. "She's quite far alon—"

"I know," Carol said, "I couldn't hide it anymore."

Doctor Goode looked Carol in the eye. "Don't worry. We shouldn't have any problems, but are you sure you want to proceed?"

"I've prayed and prayed about it." Carol choked up. "I have to."

"Alright," the doctor said. He dropped his used gloves in a bucket, patted Carol's hand, and then assisted Carol in sitting up. "Agnes and I are going to make sure the equipment is ready. We'll be back in a minute."

Carol bit her cuticle until it bled. She kissed it then rapped her fingers on the table. Moments later, she rub-

14

bed her temples and glanced at the wall clock. Its ticking grew louder and louder. *Calm down*, she told herself. *Calm down. God, help me get through this.*

The clock struck seven. As if on cue, the door opened. Doctor Goode and Agnes entered, carrying trays covered with white towels. An elderly, rotund man with yellowed white hair followed them then walked to the head of the table. His rumpled black suit reeked of tobacco smoke and his breath smelled of alcohol. His stained tie hung loosely around his open collar.

"Carol," Doctor Goode said and nodded toward the head of the table. "This doctor will administer your anesthesia."

"What's that?"

The older doctor patted her shoulder. "It's something to help you relax without pain. It will help you sleep throughout the procedure."

Sensing danger, Carol stared at Agnes. "What's a procedure?"

"Nothing to worry about," Agnes said. "Try to relax."

Doctor Goode eased Carol backward.

"Oh, God. Now what?" she asked in a shaky voice.

"Just put your feet in the stirrups, like before," Doctor Goode said.

For thirty seconds, Carol shifted her feet in the stirrups and drew her knees together. She stared at the ceiling, her lips quivering. "Don't hurt me. Please don't hurt me." *God, don't let it hurt.* "I'm cold."

Agnes covered Carol with another sheet then said, "I'm going to start this liquid in your vein." She hung a bottle of clear liquid from a hook that dangled overhead then untangled the rubber tubing through which the liquid would flow.

Wide eyed, Carol watched Agnes' every move. "What is that for?"

"It's like a drink of water to keep you from getting thirsty while you're asleep. "Straighten your arm," Agnes said, tying a tourniquet above Carol's elbow. Agnes slapped the ashen-blue forearm three times then fingered it for a suitable vein. "Ah, here's a good one."

Carol raised her head and stared at the needle moving toward her skin. She held her breath and shuddered as it drew closer.

"Hold still," Agnes said. "There will be a little stick."

Carol dropped her head back and sucked air as the needle pierced her arm. "Ouch!" she yelled, staring at the puncture site. Once the needle settled in place, she exhaled and went limp. Agnes placed tape across the needle to secure it then started the flow of liquid.

Carol watched with fascination and less trembling as the liquid flowed through the tube. Still wide eyed, she stared at her arm. "Is it supposed to feel cold in my vein?"

"It's alright," Agnes said. "Don't worry."

Doctor Goode uncovered the trays revealing a multitude of shiny surgical instruments. Carol swallowed hard as she glimpsed the implements, looking like tools of torture.

"Doctor, please don't let it hurt." *Please, God, don't let it hurt.*

Doctor Goode busied himself with several instruments on another tray. He then turned to Carol. "Before we start the anesthesia, I want to ask again. Do you want to do this?"

"I do," Carol said, a tear running down her cheek. "I thought I'd be saying 'I do' at my wedding—not here. I wished I didn't have to say it now—here, but I do."

"Very well," Doctor Goode said, patting her hand. He looked at the other doctor and said, "Let's get started."

The older doctor touched Carol's shoulder. "I want you to count backwards from one hundred to fifty."

Carol watched tobacco-stained fingers lower a black triangular mask over her nose and mouth. At first, she held her breath but then counted, "One hundred . . . ninety-nine . . . ninety-eight . . . ninety-seven . . . ninety-six . . . ninety-five . . . ninnnneeety-four . . . nin . . . "

"Is she's under?" Doctor Goode asked the older doctor.

"Yes. You can start."

Doctor Goode extended his hand toward Agnes and said, "Speculum."

"Speculum," Agnes said.

The sounds of steel instruments slapping against the doctor's gloved hand echoed around the room.

"Too bad she has to go through this alone," Agnes said.

"Dilator," the doctor said, without looking at Agnes.

"Yeah," he said, steading the speculum in Carol's vagina.

Agnes slapped the handle of the dilator in his hand. "Dilator," she said.

The egg-shaped steel dilator, with its long, rounded

point and six-inch handle, settled into the doctor's grip.

Agnes said, "I'm going to let her stay here for a few days until it's medically safe for her to move on."

"Okay, but steady the speculum, Agnes."

The doctor inserted the dilator into the mouth of Carol's womb. Under gentle pressure, her cervix dilated. The doctor removed the dilator. "Hook number two," he said.

The requested tool resembled a long-handled shoe hook used to close high top shoes.

"Hook. Number two," Agnes said.

It clinked against the speculum as the doctor inserted it into Carol's womb.

"Okay. I'm in," he said. "Is the bucket in place?"

Agnes toe-nudged a rolling bucket to the foot of the table. "It's in place.

"Here goes," Doctor Goode said. A gush of blood-tinged liquid flowed into the bucket. "Hmmm. That wasn't as much as I had expected. Well, let's get started. Curette, please."

Agnes slapped the scraper into his hand. The implement disappeared into Carol's vagina. The doctor pulled the sharp edge of the curette against the lower wall of the uterus and then withdrew it. A lump of flesh dangled from its end. The doctor had just removed the tissue when his elderly assistant, working in the front of the house, yelled, "Doctor!"

Suddenly, the house filled with the deafening sounds of whistles and running. The operating room door burst open. Four cops rushed in. Three brandished pistols.

"What the hell?" the astonished doctor asked, his

gaze darting around the room.

"Stop everything!" the sergeant yelled, waving a brown envelope. "I have a warrant for your arrest. You're *ALL* under arrest. Wake her up!"

"What!" Doctor Goode said. "We can't stop! I just started to empty her womb. She could bleed to death."

"Stop—this instant!" the sergeant shouted, waving his gun. "You up there. Old man, wake her up."

"We can't wake her up like turning on a light," the elderly doctor said, anger chopping his words.

Doctor Goode shouted at the sergeant. "Damn it, man, have you any idea what we're doing—what we're in the middle of?"

The sergeant glared at Doctor Goode. "You heard what I—"

"Damn it, Sergeant," Agnes said. "Do you know what you're asking?"

"I don't give a damn what you think!" the sergeant said, knocking over the surgical trays and sending sharp instruments flying.

Doctor Goode and Agnes dodged the instruments as they fell to the floor, sounding like cheap wind chimes.

Waving the warrant, the sergeant shouted, "I order you to stop every goddamn thing you're doing and *wake her up. Now!*"

"Wake her up," Doctor Goode said, covering Carol's pelvic area. Staring at the sergeant, he said, "She's your responsibility now. God forgive us all if she dies."

The doctor at the head of the table removed the ether mask. "Sergeant, it may take up to three hours for her to regain consciousness."

"Then, we'll take her asleep," the sergeant said.

Slumping against the wall, Agnes gasped then said. "This can't be happening."

"She's going to Memorial Hospital," the sergeant said, scanning the faces of the professionals. "You scoundrels, you're going to Central Station. *You're* out of business. None of you will *ever* practice medicine again."

Chapter Two

After the interrupted abortion, Carol gave birth to her unwanted infant in the hospital. She surrendered the baby to the Department of Family Services (DFS) for adoption then left the hospital without seeing the child or knowing its sex.

Hospital supervisor Sister Mary Savanah entered the newborn nursery and asked, "Where is she? The miracle baby."

"Bassinet number 3, Sister," Sister Mary Cecelia said.

The baby lay with the right side of its face exposed.

Sister Savanah picked up the baby and exclaimed, "Blessed Mother! What happened to her face?"

"The result of the abortion attempt," Sister Mary Cecelia said.

"Poor thing. Look at her face and lip . . . and her heel. With that lip, shs's going to have trouble breast *or* bottle feeding."

"And taunting when she's older," Sister Mary Cecelia said. "She won't fit in."

"She's a child of God and therefore beautiful," Sister Savanah said. "At least her soul is. She deserves a name. Let's call her Mary—the miracle baby."

After thirty days, Mary was transferred to a Catholic hospital in Baltimore for long-term care.

A month later, the DFS placed her in the care of Josephine, a black foster mother and wet-nurse.

"Josephine," the social worker said, "you will have to care for Mary much longer than most babies because of the difficulty she has breastfeeding. Her scarred lips require pinching so she can suckle."

Josephine was to care for Mary until she could switched from breastfeedings to bottle feedings. Orphanage placement would follow.

A jollyand rotund woman, Josephine, had short nappy hair. She said, "I keep it short, 'cause I can't afford them beautifying parlors." Her oily skin shined like the patina of a bronze bust. She had an ever-present bead of sweat between her eyebrows and always smelled of baby powder. She often said, "Powder is cheaper than soap and water."

Located on the poor side of Baltimore, Josephine cared for eight children who shared sparse meals and little love. Two of the six black children were her own. The other four and two white children were wards of the state. The children's ages ranged from nine months to seven years. Each wore clothing equal to the shabbiness of the house in which they existed. Nevertheless, everyone related well—except for Mary.

Due to a lack of bedrooms and heat, the foster children slept three to a bed—except for Mary.

Carol's attempt to abort Mary resulted in the loss of fat in the pad of her heel. Her face and lip were so scarred and contorted that she frightened her peers. This caused her to not only sleep alone but sleep in a make-shift bed on the windowless former back porch. During the winter, she slept bundled in her clothes, coat, and heavy quilts.

After a year of Josephine's care, the DFS believed

Mary's scarred lip and her emotional attachment to Josephine were so strong a new caretaker would have trouble coping with Mary's needs.

"I'll leave Mary with you for another year," the DFS worker said.

1935

"I don't want to!" Mary said when informed she had to enter a first-grade class at a nearby public school.

"All children gotta go to school when they turn six," Josephine said. "You'll meet some nice people."

That did not happen. Mary kept to herself in the segregated school. Her limp and an ill-fitting shoe, along with her facial scar, set her apart.

Her response to being taunted by classmates caused several fights on the playground. One day, a clutch of well-to-do girls gathered around the playground drinking fountain. As Mary walked by, the girls snickered. Theresa laughed.

"What are you laughing at, Theresa?" Mary asked through clenched teeth.

Theresa yelled, "You, scar face!"

Mary tightened her fists and limped toward Theresa. A teacher, fearing a fight would ensue, escorted Mary to another part of the playground. Mary glared at Theresa, and Theresa glared back.

"What are you staring at?" Mary asked.

"Your hair!" Theresa shouted. "Nice!"

Mary felt an unexpected tinge of pride.

"Nice that it covers your ugly face!" Theresa shouted.

Mary's temper boiled. Her flushed face glowed hot as she set her jaw. She wanted to pummel Theresa and struggled to free herself from the teacher's grasp, but the teacher tightened her grip and escorted Mary, crying, to the nurse's office.

Just wait, Mary thought. *I'll get you Theresa.*

Two days later, Charlette, the DFS officer said, "Mary, your grades aren't good, and you've had a lot of fights at school. I think it best if you went to the Saint Anthony Orphanage here in Baltimore. They give special help to lots of children. I think you'll like it there, *and* your grades will improve. That's very important."

Silent, Mary stared at the floor. "When?"

"Day after tomorrow—Wednesday. Josephine will help pack your things."

The next day, Mary watched Josephine pack her three dresses, a pair of shoes, two pairs of underwear, three pairs of socks, one light coat, a mirror, a comb, a hair ribbon, a book satchel, and a thin pillow.

Wednesday, Charlotte took Mary for her second ever car ride as they made their way to the orphanage. Mary stared out the windshield fascinated by the snow building up on the glass.

Thirty minutes later, the car stopped in front of a tall edifice. Mary scanned the brick building—her new home.

Its twelve-foot-tall wooden door opened and a giant of a woman, dressed in a long black dress with a funny looking white cover on her head, stepped onto the porch. She smiled and opened her arms in greeting.

Mary crept toward the woman.

"Come," the woman said, embracing Mary. "I'm the mother superior who runs this place, and we're happy to have you join us. Come, let's get you register-ed."

In her office, Mother Superior asked Mary her name.

"I'm Mary"

"And your last name?"

"I don't have a real one. I'm called Mary . . . Doe."

"Well, you need a proper last name." The nun thought for a moment. "How about Snow because of the snowstorm you came through. So far, it's the worst of 1935. I'll speak with the court and the DFS to see if we can get you named Mary *Snow*.

Mary expected to live with other children whom she feared would mock her, but the nuns gave her a private room. For her first three days, she remained in her room, soaking her mattress with tears, refusing to go to the dining room, school, or mass. She kept saying, "I want Josephine.

It took three weeks for Mary to drop most of her defenses and interact with her teachers and classmates.

"Mary, that's a wonderful looking cow," Sister Mary Jacob said, scanning the drawing Mary did in art class. "I put your last drawing of the tree on the hallway bulletin board. Now, everyone knows how good an artist you are."

"Thank you," Mary said in a flat voice.

Mary dreamed of the day when someone would adopt her. For that and other reasons, she worked in the nursery. She tried to make herself desirable to the many couples who visited the orphanage, looking for a child to adopt. She covered her facial scar with her long hair and always had her drawings nearby to show visitors, but the would-be-parents were only interested in babies

As each set of adoptive parents left the orphanage without her, she retreated into her shell, feeling more unwanted.

Always a loner, Mary learned to play solitaire with old cards and listened to a radio the nuns put in her room. Preferring to study alone, she buried herself in a world of mistrust and fantasy.

A few days after her seventh birthday, Mary shook with excitement as she prepared for her first communion. She had never felt happier than when Sister Mary James helped her pull on the first white dress she had ever worn.

"The dress is beautiful," Sister Mary James said. "We have to send a thank you note to Mrs. Blackburn for donating it." The nun straightened the white silk bow at its waist. "Did you remember to put a wad of toilet paper in the heel of your shoe? The church has a very long aisle and you don't want to walk it without something to cushion your heel bone."

"I did, Sister," Mary said, admiring and fingering the lace on the bodice of the dress. She looked at the nun and smiled. "It's beautiful. Is it mine?"

"Yes, it's yours—for today. Another girl will wear it next year when it's time for her first communion."

Mary lifted the lace hem of the skirt, admired its fullness, and then twisted her body, causing the skirt to swirl outward as if she was pirouetting at a grand ball.

She giggled. "It's dancing."

"Calm down," the nun said, "let's get your veil on."

The nun positioned a doubled over layer of the white veil to cover the jagged scar that stretched from the outer corner of Mary's left eye to the left edge of her lip and onto her chin.

"My! You look angelic," the nun said, fluffing Mary's skirt. "Maybe one day you'll wear a veil as a bride of Christ. You'd make a wonderful nun." The sister gave Mary a hug. "Now, let's get ready for the procession. Can't keep the bishop waiting."

Mary followed her catechism group of ten girls and twelve nuns along the gothic aisle of Saint Mary Church. The white marble altar blazed with six tall candles for a high mass.

The group stopped at the first two rows of pews. First, the nuns and then the children genuflected, filed into the pews, knelt, crossed themselves, and then prayed. The young communicants sat behind the nuns. Mary, as usual, took the last seat.

Time came for Mary's first communion. Head bowed, Mary templed her fingers, crossed her thumbs, walked to the altar rail, and then knelt. Her lips moved little as she prayed, *Jesus, forgive my sins. Bless me. Help me be a good girl. May the Blessed Mother protect me and help me get good grades. Amen.*

Mary kept her head bowed until the bishop pproached. He pushed the sleeve of his chasuble back from his wrist, took a host from the ciborium, and then held it in front of Mary. She raised her head, stuck out her tongue, and then lifted her veil, revealing her long, jagged facial scar.

The elderly bishop recoiled. "Blessed Jesus!" His words echoed throughout the church. He dropped the host on the floor and shook the red zucchetto cap from his head.

Those parishioners who saw the host fall to the floor gave a collective gasp.

Mary looked toward the rear of the church. A few people had jumped to their feet apparently thinking something bad had happened.

Mary's classmates tittered. She heard one snicker. "Look what scar face has done now." She saw several students pointing at her with one hand while using the other hand to stifle giggles.

She felt humiliated and cried. *No, no,* she thought, her face awash in tears.

The nun in charge of the class rushed to Mary's side and tried to hug her, but she struggled free of the smothering embrace. In doing so, she exposed her face. The congregation muttered their shock.

"They hate me!" Mary screamed. "They hate me!"

"Shhh. Shhh," the nun said, trying to console Mary.

The bishop regained his composure then offered another host, but Mary, sobbing, hobbled toward the exit as fast as she could.

A skinny boy in the last pew stared at Mary as she limped by. "Look, Mommy," he said, "she's ugly."

Those words embedded themselves in Mary's memory. *The sisters lied!* Mary said to herself. *I'm not beautiful. I'm ugly. Ugly! Everyone's making fun of me. They hate me.*

At the age of nine, and a year after Mary's transer

to the orphanage, her biologic mother had learned her miracle daughter lived in the Saint Anthony Orphanage.

Carol did not want to see her daughter, but she sent a letter to the orphanage along with a note for Mary. The note was to be given to Mary on her twelfth birthday.

On that special birthday in 1941, the elderly mother superior invited Mary to her office. There were several nuns to lend their support to the mother superior during the upcoming difficult conversation.

Mary felt she had been summoned by the mother superior because of something to do with her mother. Mary was happy when she saw five nuns crammed into the small office, fingering their waist rosaries.

"Is my mother coming for me?" Mary asked, twisting her scarred lip into a smile.

The mother superior shook her head. "No. Your mother had to move far away many years ago." Holding out a yellowed envelope, the nun continued, "But she sent this. She asked that I give it to you today—your twelfth birthday."

Mary extended her hand but paused before taking the envelope. *I hope it says when she's coming for me.* Mary stared into the faces of the nuns then opened the envelope. Her heart raced, hoping to read that her mother loved and wanted her. Mary glanced at the nuns then removed the letter. She mouthed the note's words.

> Mary,
>> You were an unexpected baby. Your father and I were sixteen when you were born. We couldn't care for you. Not with things the

way they were. Your father was Jewish. I
was Catholic. We couldn't get married. I
had no choice. I had to give you up. The
nuns will give you a good home. Listen to
what they say. Mind them and grow up to be
someone very special.

                                Carol

Mary's hand dropped, and the letter fell to the floor.
She stood motionless for a moment, bunched her face,
and then sobbed. "She didn't want me. My mother
didn't love me."

The nuns embraced the heartbroken girl in a group
hug.

"That's not true," Mother Superior said. "She loved
you, but she wanted you to have a life she couldn't give
you."

Between sobs, Mary said, "No she didn't."

One of the younger nuns picked Mary up. "Shhh,
Mary. We have a surprise for you in the dining hall.
Let's go see, okay?"

"I hope you like your birthday cake" mother
superior said as she picked up the letter and replaced it
in its envelope.

The fat pad of Mary's right heel had been missing
since birth. A thin layer of scarred skin covered her heel
bone, making walking and engaging in physical games
painful. Now, she waited for a prosthetic and its longed-
for relief from her painful condition.

For the occasion, Mary wore her black velvet
Sunday dress. She wore lace topped white socks and
secondhand black patent leather Mary Jane shoes, gifted

to the orphanage by a wealthy family. Their daughter hated the fit of the shoes.

Mary fidgeted on a tall wooden office chair from which her legs swung back and forth.

"Mary, be a good girl and wait here," Sister Mary Albert said, "I have to get the doctor. He has a special shoe for you. It has special cushioning that will substitute for your heel's lost fat pad and let you walk and run without all the pain you've been having."

Doctor Goode waited in Sister Mary Albert's office. "Well, Sister, I have good news for Mary," he said. "Are we ready?"

"We're ready. Please follow me," the sister said.

Sister Mary Albert and Doctor Goode entered the room where Mary waited.

Apprehension filled her eyes as the young doctor approached her.

He felt his face blanch when he saw Mary's face. *Oh my! You poor child. What a scar!*

"Mary, meet Doctor Goode," sister said.

Mary sat motionless, staring at the floor.

"What do you say?" sister asked, lifting Mary's chin. "Mary is a little shy, Doctor."

Mary slid from the chair, stood tall, curtsied, and then extended her chubby hand. "Nice to meet you, Doctor Goode."

Doctor Goode squatted and shook her hand.

"Nice to meet you, Mary. My, your dress is beautyful, and I like the purple ribbon in your hair."

"Thank you, Doctor Goode." Mary said, pressing her forefinger against her disfigured lip while twisting her torso back and forth.

"Do you remember the plaster cast my nurse made of your foot three months ago?"

"Uh huh. It was wet and cold, and then it got hot and the white stuff got hard."

"Well, we used that cast to make a special shoe for you." Doctor Goode held out a green box. "It's right here—made special just for you." He opened the box, removed a brown shoe, and then placed the box on the floor. "You're the only person in Baltimore who has one of these."

"For me?" Mary asked, offering a twisted smile. "I have never had anything just for me."

"Well, let's see how it fits. Would you take off your right shoe and sock, so I can see your heel?"

Sister Mary Albert grunted as she picked up Mary and placed her on the tall chair. The motion of her habit released the fragrance of frankincense and myrrh that lingered from the morning mass. She unlaced Mary's right shoe. A compressed wad of toilet paper fell from the shoe as sister removed it. The nun then removed Mary's lace topped sock.

"Thank you, Sister," Mary said, staring at her deformed heel.

Doctor Goode felt his eyes widen on seeing the heel. He stifled a gasp and handed the new shoe to Mary for examination while he pulled sister aside. "I heard she had a birth defect of her heel, but that's no birth defect. That's scar tissue—trauma caused that—not God."

"We'll talk later, Doctor."

Doctor Goode slipped the shoe onto Mary's foot and inserted his finger between her heel and the inside back of the shoe to check for fit. "Good," he said then laced the shoe.

Mary smiled, moving the shoe through a ray of sunlight streaming through a pane of clear glass in a stained glass window.

"I like it," Mary said, beaming. "Do I get the other one?"

"Of course," Doctor Goode said, smiling at her happiness. "Let's try it on, but first let's get your right sock on."

Having replaced the sock, sister removed Mary's left shoe and Doctor Goode slipped the new shoe onto her left foot then laced it. He then replaced the right shoe.

"Those are much prettier than I had expected," sister said, caressing the soft, shiny brown leather.

"Well, Mary, let's see how they feel," Doctor Goode said. "Walk around the room."

Mary slid from the chair and for a second stood still. On the verge of giggling, she stared at the new shoes. "I can wiggle my toes, and it doesn't hurt."

"Good, but I want to see how they feel when you walk."

Mary took a tenuous step, stared at the right shoe, and then looked at the doctor. She giggled, took a few more steps then giggled again. "They tickle," she said, stomping over the hardwood floor. After walking a few seconds, she looked at the doctor. "Can I jump rope?"

Doctor Goode glanced at the nun. "Sister, we have a winner. She should wear them all the time. If she can jump rope without pain, let her do it."

"Oh, goodie," Mary said, shaking her hands with

glee.

"I don't know how to thank you, Doctor," the nun said, touching his head. "May God bless you." She made the sign of the cross over him.

Sister asked, "Mary, what do you say to Doctor Goode?"

Mary curtsied. "Thank you, Doctor Goode." She giggled and extended her arms to embrace him. Doctor Goode picked her up, and they exchanged a hug. She kissed him on the cheek.

"Doctor, you are the first person I've ever seen Mary hug."

"God, bless her. Well, my work is done, Sister. The shoes will need replacing as she grows. Let me know when she needs the next pair, and I'll have new molds made." He placed Mary on the floor and said, "Mary, I have to be going."

"Thank you, Doctor," sister said. "I'll walk you to the door."

Sister patted Mary on the head. "Go put on your regular clothes and then you can play but don't scuff your new shoes."

Mary rushed away to show off her shoes while Doctor Goode and Sister Mary Albert walked along the cloister-like hall toward the orphanage's main entrance.

Smiling, Doctor Goode asked, "Did you notice that she ran?"

"It's a miracle. She'll have a much happier life, thanks to you."

They walked past several statues of saints and flickering prayer candles. In the distance, nuns could be heard singing in the chapel.

"Sister, how did Mary get those scars?"

Sister tugged at her wimple and scrunched her plump, rosy cheeks. She looked around then whispered, "We were told she was being aborted, but the devilish procedure was stopped at its beginning. It's a miracle she survived." Sister crossed herself. "Seems God had a plan for her."

Doctor Goode felt dizzy. For a moment, he thought he might pass out. *Oh God! It can't be her. Not her. I remember dad talking about an interrupted abortion, but Mary can't be that baby. She couldn't have survived. Don't tell me he did this.*

"Doctor Goode, are you alright?" sister asked, supporting the stumbling doctor.

"I'm fine. Don't know what came over me. Guess a cold is coming on."

"Sit on that bench beside the blessed mother," the nun said, guiding him to a bench. "I'll get you some water."

"Thanks, Sister. I'll be okay. I have to get to the office." Staring at the nun, he asked, "How do the children react to her?"

Fingering her rosary, the nun said, "Over time, most have accepted her, but there's no doubt her scar causes them, and her, concern. She sits in the back of the classroom. In public, she wears a headscarf. As you might imagine, she's last to be chosen for everything. She can't run—couldn't run, but now, with the new shoe, that might change." Sister crossed herself. "May God watch over her."

"I'm sure the shoe will give her loads of pleasure. Let me know if she needs anything else."

Sweating, Doctor Goode walked to his car. *I can't believe she survived, and I met her. It's a miracle.*

Mary and the other orphans attended a Catholic school one block away. Mary didn't like school. She preferred to be alone. Isolation helped her avoid bullies' ridicule and allowed her to devote herself to studying.

She chose not to have contact with private-paying students whose wealthy parents could afford the school's tuition, fancier uniforms, shoes, and jewelry—none of which she had. The popular pretty girls in her class were always discussing boys, experimenting with makeup, and showing off their fancy clothes.

Mary and the other orphans wore second-hand clothes—except at Christmas when the city donated money to buy one new piece of clothing for each orphan.

One day on the playground, Mary and her ill-fitting donated dress became the butt of a classmate's joke. The dress had belonged to the bully.

Mary felt humiliated and sobbed. *I hate them. I hate them.*

The nun in charge of the playground rushed to Mary's side and tried to console her, but she broke free and ran to the orphanage. She refused to leave her room for twenty-four hours.

Mary's seventh grade homeroom class met to plan a Mother's Day celebration party. The plan had secular and religious elements. Catholic students and their mothers would attend mass before a special luncheon.

The orphaned students received encouragement to

think of the Blessed Virgin as their surrogate mother and celebrate her presence in their lives.

The nun, who taught the sixth grade homeroom class, took Jenny and Mary to a meeting of the Mothers' Day Planning Committee.

Looking at Evelyn, the committee chairperson, the nun said, "I'm here to ask the members of the committee to let Mary and Jenny join your group?"

"But, Sister, all the spots are filled," Evelyn said, sarcastically.

"No one wants me!" Mary shouted and ran from the room. "I don't need them! I don't need anybody."

Chapter Three

Mary's intelligence and dedication to her studies throughout junior high and high school earned her a college scholarship.

During her first years of college, she had no friends and never thought of dating because of her facial scar.

In her junior year, Mary thought she had attracted the attention of Tony, a handsome calculus classmate. He came on to her in a strong way, causing her to wonder why.

One day, Tony phoned Mary and asked, "How about if I come over to your dorm tonight, so we can study together?"

"You really want to?"

"Sure. I'll bring snacks so we don't have to interrupt studying to go out to eat."

"Sounds great," Mary said. "Harvey Hall, room 405. See you at seven."

Mary didn't need help with calculus, but she did not mind helping Tony because of his attention.

Sometimes, they studied in locations free of bothersome people. Mary thought the chosen locations were to spare her ridicule. Despite her fear of being mocked or hurt, she lowered her emotional guard.

Late one evening, she and Tony shared an ice cream soda in the back corner of an empty student hangout. Another student entered, called and waved to Tony. As the student approached the couple, Tony rose and greeted him fifteen feet from the table where Mary pulled her hair over her face.

"How goes it?" Mary heard the student ask Tony.

"Okay. How about you?" Tony asked, shaking the student's hand.

"Are you . . . dating that . . . ugly girl?"

Dropping his voice, Tony said, "God no. She's the brain in my calculus class. I need her help to pass the damn course. Hell, I'd have sex with a pig if it would get me a passing grade. This gal will help me get the "A" I need to get into grad school."

Mary had heard enough. She stood, grabbed her soda, and then walked to Tony's side.

Tony turned and said, "Mary—"

Mary dumped her soda on Tony's head. "No one uses me, you creep! Don't you ever come close to me again. Never! You could rot in hell before I'd help you."

Mary stormed out heart broken. *I'll never get close to another man again.*

Despite her handicaps, feeling unloved and unwant-ed, Mary graduated college in May, 1952, *summa cum laude* and received a scholarship to medical school.

In the third year of medical school, Mary got to experience the joy of being a doctor-in-training. As a student-doctor, and with a mentor standing by, she assisted a mother deliver her eighth baby. Mary had little to do—just prevent the baby from falling to the floor.

Mary delivered the baby. The mentor smiled and said, "Great job, Mary."

As Mary moved through the obstetrical program, she acquired the skills to perform an uncomplicated delivery.

*That's the fourteenth baby I've helped deliver. I
love sharing the mother's elation when she holds her
baby for the first time. I can feel the love flowing between them. I wish my mother had wanted and loved me
like that.*

In her third year of medical school, Mary added a
lot to her knowledge about the discipline of plastic
surgery. She witnessed the transformation of facial
disfigurations into beautiful visages through surgery.
She told herself that when she had earned enough
money, she would have surgery to rid herself of her scar.
She wanted to be beautiful, but most of all, she wanted
love.

Mary's desire for love and acceptance became a
driving force, for she had neither. Her childhood experi-
ences blocked her receptivity to love. The world had
been cold toward her because she had been cold toward
it. Deep inside, she felt she didn't deserve love otherwise her mother would not have abandoned her.

July, 1956, Mary received her MD degree and
began a residency program in obstetrics and gynecology
at Johns Hopkins Hospital. She chose this field because
of her long-time interest in babies. As a child, she often
visited the orphanage nursery to see the new arrivals.
She liked to feed them and often changed their diapers.

The overwhelmed nun in charge of the always filled
nursery welcomed Mary's assistance. She once overheard the nuns discuss her interest in infants.

One sister said, "I think Mary's love of, and attention to, the babies makes her feel wanted. Babies don't

care about her face."

Working in the nursery helped Mary forget about her deformities and the fact she had been an unwanted baby. While she felt love for the infants, she could not give or accept love from adults.

One nun had been overheard to say, "Mary's love for babies is Mary loving herself. Her plight mirrors each orphaned baby she cares for."

"Doctor Green," Mary said to her mentor, "I want to invite you to join me and three nuns from Saint Anthony Orphanage to celebrate the completion of my residency program. We're going to have a celebratory dinner at the Lord Baltimore Hotel. This 1959 group is the sixty fifth for the school and should be a big affair."

"I'll be there," the doctor said.

The Lord Baltimore Hotel had hosted politicians, actors, opera stars, and gangsters. Its large public spaces made it a favorite venue for parties and conventions. Its grandeur still showed, but like an aged grand dame, it had wrinkles and few diamonds.

Doctor Green, Mary and three nuns sat at a round table in the hotel ballroom converted into a dining venue.

"May I pour you a glass of champagne," Doctor Green asked Mary.

"Why not." she said. "It's a special occasion. Thanks."

"Sisters, would you join us?" Doctor Green asked.

"A little," Sister Immaculate said, "if you'll put it in a water glass. I don't want anyone complaining to the bishop."

The doctor poured a round of champagne.

"Congratulations," everyone said, raising their glasses in a toast to Mary.

A band played new music called Rock and Roll. A few feet from the group's table, Mary watched couples dancing to the music's fast tempo. After much coaxing, Doctor Green got Mary onto the dance floor for her first ever dance. Mary flailed her arms for a minute and then gave up when she overheard snide remarks about her dancing.

"Don't let those people bother you," Doctor Green said.

"They don't. I just can't dance."

Always smiling, Doctor Green a man of sixty with a round angelic face and pleasant disposition, led Mary back to the table where the nuns clapped. He pulled out a chair for Mary to sit down.

"Mary, I have something for you," he said and handed her a folded paper.

Doctor Green knew of Mary's patient dedication because he had been her mentor. Despite her disfigurement, he saw patients liked her and demonstrated their affection with hugs, kisses, and gifts.

The Baltimore suburban town of Towson, where Doctor Green practiced, had no female doctors.

In the past, he had told her that adding a female physician to his practice might attract more patients than if he added another male physician.

Mary unfolded the paper then scanned a contract. "You're kidding. I remember you mentioning my joining your practice, but I didn't expect a contract—not today."

"I don't want someone signing you up for another practice before we can get you to Towson," he said, flashing his endearing smile.

"Well thank you," Mary said, covering her reddening face with her long hair. "Let me discuss this with my attorney. Can we talk in a week?"

"Of course, but I want you to start the first of the month."

"That's possible," Mary said, beaming with pride.

"Come now," the doctor said. "Have some more champagne."

"We have more than your graduation to celebrate," Sister Wilma said, "Now, you have a *real* job."

Everyone laughed at the joke.

1961

The time had come for Mary to consider whether she would renew her two year contract with Doctor Green, join another group, or start a solo practice.

Late one afternoon, after the last patient had left the clinic, Mary knocked on Doctor Green's open office door. "John, got a minute?" she asked, putting her hands in the pockets of her white lab coat.

"Of course, Mary. Come in. Have a seat."

Mary sat in a chair beside John's large mahogany desk.

"You look troubled," he said. "What's on your mind?"

"I've had two wonderful years working here, and I think we get along well. I've discussed the new contract with my attorney, and . . . This is what I've decided."

John held his breath and put down his pen.

Mary thought, *He looks worried. Is he thinking I'll ask for an unreasonable salary or worse—announce I'm leaving for greener pastures?* "Your salary proposal is reasonable," she said. "I'd . . . like to stay on—with the proviso I have four weeks off, with pay, starting next week." She sat very erect and shook her head. "You know I've wanted to have cosmetic surgery. Well, I've scheduled it for Monday, and I'll need time to recover."

Looking relieved, John sighed and leaned back in his chair. "God, Mary, you have no idea how relieved I am—knowing you'll stay." He walked to the side of the desk and hugged her. "I thought you might say you were leaving or wanted double your compensation. Of course, you can have four weeks. Believe me, I and the other doctors want you to stay. You're family. I'll have the secretary revise the work schedule as soon as we finish here.

"Thanks, John. Here's the signed contract."

Mary felt like skipping out of the office, knowing she would have paid time to recuperate from surgery. She looked back at John and said, "See you after my surgery."

Ten days later, Mary fidgeted in her hospital bed as she awaited her surgeon. Looking out the window, she stared past the hospital campus to the highway and the slow-moving traffic. *I'm going to see the most beautiful woman in the world when these bandages come off.*

Mary twiddled her thumbs then tried reading a magazine while she listened to the sounds of her doctor and his entourage of medical students and residents as they visited other patient rooms before heading to hers—their last stop.

Doctor Mack, in a buoyant mood, entered Mary's room. "Well, Doctor Snow, are you ready to get those bandages off?"

"You bet." Mary tried not to smile for fear of pain.

Doctor Mack turned to a nurse. "Scissors, please."

Mary's outer bandages yielded to sharp scissors. Next came the ones covered with dried brown blood. They required careful teasing from the underlying gauzes.

God, let me be beautiful, Mary thought.

Everyone, including Mary, held their breath waiting for the removal of the final layer of gauze and "the reveal."

"Well!" Doctor Mack said, smiling as he removed the last gauze. "What a beautiful sight." He observed Mary's face, tilted his head to the left and nodded to the junior doctors gathered around the foot of her bed. "There's the usual swelling and bruising, but I'm pleased as hell with my work." He raised his hands, spread his fingers, and said, "Voila! Beautiful."

Doctor Mack looked at the youngest of his trainees. "Doctors, look at the placement of my sutures, the wound edges, and the lack of mottling." His smile broadened to reveal most of his teeth. "That is the work of a talented surgeon even if I say so myself."

"Dennis, you're so full of yourself," Mary said, thwarting a chuckle. *Let me be beautiful, God. Please, let me be beautiful.*

At Doctor Mack's invitation, several members of the entourage moved closer to inspect Mary's face and his handiwork.

"Nurse, would you please hand Doctor Snow a mirror?"

Mary's hand shook as she took the mirror. Eyes closed, she raised it to face level then opened her eyes. "Oh my God!" she screeched, dropping the mirror on her lap. She stared at Doctor Mack then picked up the mirror. "It can't be. No! It's horrible!" She turned her head right and left then stared into the mirror. "Horrible! *What* have you done to me—to my face? Oh God! No!"

"Mary. You're a *doctor*," Doctor Mack said, patting Mary's arm. "You had to know there would be swelling and bruising. Yours is normal. I assure you it *will* subside. I don't think I, or anyone else, could have done a better job. Give it a few days."

Mary took a deep breath, exhaled, and then let her shoulders sag. "I'm sorry," she said, blotting a tear with the sheet. Her hands shook. "It's just that swelling looks worse when it's yours . . . uh, mine. I know better, but I hoped the results would be immediate—not weeks." She chuckled, "Please, forgive me and my unrealistic expectations."

"Glad to see you can laugh," Dennis said. "The dressing is to remain off. I'll see you tomorrow."

Three weeks after her surgery, Mary went to her office at 7:00 a.m. Monday morning to catch up on mail and then present her new face to her colleagues and patients.

She waited in her office until the last minute before going to the staff meeting. The group emitted a collective gasp as Mary entered the conference room.

She took her seat and placed a pad and pencil on the table. She felt the gaze of everyone in the room as they

scanned her face.

The group broke out in applause.

"Hello everyone," Mary said, smiling as never before while pushing hair from her face.

"Welcome back," Doctor Green said. "What a wonderful outcome. Beautiful."

"You look fantastic," the receptionist added.

"Had I not known about the surgery, I would never have recognized you," nurse Ela said.

I'm so glad to hear that, Mary thought.

"Mary, we're glad you're back," Doctor Smythe said. "We and your patients have missed you. Doctor Mack did a great job. Given a little time, no one would ever guess you had surgery. Wonderful work."

The group applauded, and Mary beamed with self-satisfaction.

They like it! She said to herself. *They think I'm beautiful.*

Mary acted as if nothing had happened, except when she looked in the mirror each morning to put on makeup. *Your face is beautiful,* she told herself, but despite the surgery, her sense of unworthiness had not been expunged with her scar's removal.

1964

Mary registered for the Annual Meeting of the

American College of Obstetrics and Gynecology to be held at the Americana Hotel in Bal Harbour, Florida.

The grand hotel stood a block from the ocean and was surrounded by masions, elaborate condominium buildings, and moored yachts.

A tall, blond-male peer caught Mary's eye as she crossed the expansive and lavish lobby to pick up her registration pack for the convention. *Now, there's a handsome man. Electric blue eyes, looks fit, dresses well, and he's not wearing a wedding band. I hope he's not queer. He could be the father of my children.*

Everywhere Mary went in the convention center, she saw the same tall, blond doctor. Once, he sat in front of her during an hour of boring presentations. After the lecture, he stood, knocking his chair against Mary's knees.

"I'm so sorry," he said, lifting the chair and staring into her eyes.

Rubbing her knee, Mary said, "No problem. I'm as anxious to get out of here as you. What a boring presentation."

"You disliked it too?"

"Yes, but not enough to destroy furniture."

"Please, let me apologize for my clumsiness by buying you a cup of free coffee in the lobby."

"Apology and coffee accepted," Mary said. *I can't believe I said that! What has come over me?* She placed a notebook on her chair and walked with the doctor to the lobby.

In the refreshment area, he said, "Please, wait at this table. I'll get the coffee. No need for both of us to wait in line. How do you like yours?"

"Black, one sugar." Mary sized him up as he walked away. *He certainly has a nice butt. Looks like he works out. Cute!*

Minutes later, the doctor returned with Styrofoam cups of coffee. "Hope I mixed it properly."

"Shaken or stirred I don't care as long as it's not bruised."

"I'm David," the doctor said, extending his hand. "David Horowitz."

"Nice to meet you, David." Mary extended her hand and smiled. "Thought you were going to say you were James Bond. I'm Mary. Mary Snow."

"Where're you from?" David asked, shaking her hand.

"Towson. Near Baltimore."

"Love Baltimore. I spent a year at the *John*, with Doctor Reynolds. Know him?"

"I knew him," Mary said. "Unfortunately, he died, a year ago. His death left a void in infertility research. Is that your specialty?"

"Yep," David said then sipped his coffee. "It is. And you?"

"Just bread and butter ob gyn," Mary said.

"That's a tough business." David said and put his cup down. "Medicine *ain't* what it used to be." David looked at his watch. "It's time for the next presentation. May I join you?"

"Surely," Mary said. "Maybe this one will be more interesting."

Mary reclaimed her seat, and David sat beside her. After the presentation, they had another cup of coffee then sat through more lectures. At the close of the business day, they left the room together.

Just outside the door, David said, "I have to meet some friends, but will you have dinner with me?"

Mary hesitated for a second. *Wow! I didn't expect that.* "Surely."

"I'll meet you in the lobby. Eight o'clock? Think about what kind of food you'd like, and I'll see if the concierge can recommend a restaurant."

"Great. See you at eight." *I can't believe I've met such a handsome, easy going guy who shares my profession. I've got to get something special to wear.*

For the first time in her life, Mary felt exhilarated because of a stranger's attention. *I can barely wait until dinner.*

Wearing high heels, with a special heel pad, and a curve clinging dress, Mary felt regal walking through the lobby. For the first time, she liked having men stare at her. *This feels good.*

David smiled and eyed her from head to toe. "You are looking lovely."

The compliment and a sudden release of adrenalin set Mary's heart racing. "Thank you." She smiled and forced back a tear.

"Have you decided what kind of food you want?"

"How about French? The Le Mar?"

"Great!" David said. "I like French. I've seen Le Mar's advertisements. Supposed to be a five-star place."

"Then, let's do it.

For Mary, dinner proceeded at the right pace. She allowed herself three glasses of wine, which no doubt added to her sense of wellbeing and jovialness. She and David laughed often, talking about medicine, movies, music, and sport cars.

"Don't laugh," Mary said. "I'm thinking about buying a sports car. An MG-B."

"A British 'B,' eh?"

"Know anything about them?"

"I used to own one," David said, "a few years back, but I sold it."

"Oh. Why?"

"It twenty-dollared-me-to-death." David fingered the top of his wine glass. "Every time I turned around, it cost me twenty dollars—something broke. Damn car was always in the shop. Had lots of problems with the oil hoses. They ruptured three times. No one could figure out why. Once they blew right in the middle of the street between marching bands at a Saint Patrick's Day parade. What a mess. I'm lucky I didn't get a ticket."

"Thanks for warning me. Guess I'd better forget about that one."

David smiled. "It's rare and nice to meet a woman who appreciates sports cars."

Mary glanced at her watch. "I hate to break up the party, but it's getting late. I have to be up early to attend a breakfast lecture. Mind if we get our checks?"

David waved to the waiter. "Check please and call a taxi for us—"

"*Separate* checks, please," Mary said.

"Please," David said, "be my guest. We discussed business therefore it's a write off."

"Then I should get the taxi."

Sitting beside David in the taxi, Mary had a deep feeling of warmth. *I've never had such a good time! He's a great guy.*

In their hotel lobby, they waited for an elevator. Inside, David pushed a button for the sixth floor. Mary asked for the eleventh floor. They rode in silence in the otherwise empty car. At the sixth floor, the door opened and David stepped out, holding the door open. "Thanks for a wonderful evening."

Mary smiled. "Thank *you*. I enjoyed the evening more than I don't know when. See you tomorrow."

Chapter Four

Mary scanned the convention hall, looking for David, but she did not see him. The ten o'clock coffee break had come and gone, still no David. *Is he avoiding me?*

She stood in the back of the conference room as a presentation on pregnancy testing ended. To her delight, David entered the left side of the room. She waved until she caught his attention.

'Hi,' he mouthed and walked to her location. "Good morning," he whispered.

"Morning," Mary whispered. "Enjoying the morning lecturers?"

"I slept in. Nothing of interest for me except the upcoming lecture."

"Look. The new panel members are coming," Mary said. "Let's get a seat."

David and Mary sat through several lecturers. Her feigned interest became a reason to remain beside him. *I hate this stuff, but I'm glad he showed up.*

After the last lecture, Mary turned to David. "May I invite *you* to dinner? I'm buying." She laughed then said, "I'll write it off."

For Mary, dinner had been a success. The restaurant's soft lighting and pale-pink décor lent a sophisticated air to the dining room. Being with David made her feel warm and comfortable, and he appeared at ease with her. Several times, their hands touched as they passed condiments. Conversation flowed and time stood still.

Scanning the empty restaurant, Mary said, "We're the last customers. We should leave so they can close."

"Gosh, the time flew."

David took Mary by the elbow and escorted her to the door where the *maitre de* waved for a taxi. The couple's conversation continued, unabated.

"Driver, take the beach road, please," David said. "I enjoy seeing the moon over the ocean."

"Me too," Mary said.

David continued to talk while Mary stared at the sky as the cab passed wide lawns and gardens interspersed among tall buildings.

"Let's take a walk on the beach," Mary said.

"If that's what you want," David said. "Driver, stop here please and wait for us?"

"Will do, but the meter is running," the driver said.

"We won't be long," David said, helping Mary out of the cab.

Mary removed her shoes, wiggled her toes in the sand and walked toward the water. The sand conformed to her missing heel pad and helped hide its absence.

David followed her.

"It's beautiful," Mary said, looking at the moon.

"Yes. It's . . . beautiful."

Except for the soft crunch of dry sand short of the water's edge and the soft lapping of waves riding the receding tide, quietude prevailed.

"I don't know when I've seen such a large, bright moon," Mary said.

"This is a special time for the moon. It's close to the earth, which causes very high and low tides."

"I admire a person who knows a lot about many

things."

David laughed. "I wouldn't have known that stuff except that a morning TV show had a long spiel about this moon."

"You could have fooled me. Think we should get back to the taxi?"

David looked at his watch."Yeah. It's getting late."

David stood beside Mary, holding her elbow while watching the changing red lights track the elevator's descent to the posh lobby. Once inside the levator and the door closed, he continued to hold her elbow.

What a gentleman, she thought. *Wonder what he has in mind?*

At the sixth floor, David left the elevator and thanked Mary for a great evening.

"Thank you for a wonderful evening—and moon," Mary said holding the door. She kissed him on the cheek. "See you tomorrow."

David grinned as the door closed.

The next morning, Mary ignored her unspoken rule about not wearing makeup during the business day. She took a long time applying powder, rouge, and lipstick.

Entering the convention hall, she caught David's eye as he spoke to a group of attendees. He left the group to greet her.

"Good morning," he said. "How are you?"

Mary rubbed her forehead. "Got a bit of a headache. I had too much wine last night."

"Well, I'll have to monitor your intake this evening when we attend the pharmaceutical reception."

"Is that an invitation?" Mary asked.

"Certainly. Will you join me?"

"How about dinner afterwards?"

"Of course."

The promising relationship with David warranted Mary purchasing another sexy dress. The proverbial little black dress revealed everything she wanted revealed.

Thirty minutes late, Mary entered the room hosting The Association of Pharmaceutical Manufacturers reception for doctors attending the conference.

She felt buoyant on seeing the hotel's largest party space decorated with fragrant fresh flowers, soft pink lighting from crystal chandeliers, and hearing smooth jazz played by a live band. The room reeked of charm, class, and sophistication.

With new confidence, she exaggerated her motions as she crossed the event room, looking for David. In a far corner, she saw him talking to a group of male doctors. She turned on her repressed, innate sex appeal and slinked toward him.

He and his colleagues interrupted their conversation to share their obvious admiration of her.

The closer she got, the more David smiled. "You look beautiful," he said as she extended her hand.

"Thank you. Sorry, I'm late."

"No worry. I want to introduce my friends." David turned toward his colleagues. "These guys and I were in the same training program at Columbia."

This is the kind of acceptance I've been looking for, Mary said to herself.

David introduced Mary to each doctor then asked

her, "What do you want to drink?"

"Hmmm. How about a Chardonnay?"

"Be right back." David smiled and winked.

Mary and the group discussed a few medical presentations and favorite mentors in their residency programs.

David, ever attentive to Mary's needs, made sure her glass never went empty.

Waiters, in white tie, tails, and white gloves, served canapés, but Mary refused them. The more the group ate, the more they drank. Mary had had three glasses of wine when she asked David for a fourth.

"Are you sure?" David asked, frowning.

"Yes. It's the last night of this darn conference, and I want to enjoy myself."

"Fortunately, you're staying in this hotel. You don't have far to go when you leave."

"What? No dinner?" Mary asked, with slurred speech.

"We could go for dinner if you want, but with all the canapés I've had, I'm stuffed. I don't have room for more food."

"Well then, let's have another glass of wine. See if it stimulates your appetite."

"Not a good idea," David said.

"Oh, come on," Mary mumbled and jiggled her empty glass toward David. "Don't be a party pooper. Pleeeease, get me another Chardonnay."

"One more but no more after that."

Mark, a friend of David's, whispered in his ear, "You trying to get *lucky* tonight?"

"Hadn't planned on it, old buddy. Besides, sex with a drunken woman is not my idea of fun."

"Then *you* need a drink," Mark said, leering at Mary. "You don't ignore a woman that hot."

David walked to the bar, looking over his shoulder to confirm Mary hadn't toppled over. He ordered a glass of sparkling water for himself and a Chardonnay spritzer for Mary.

"Thank you, hon," Mary said as David handed her the drink.

As the group conversation continued, Mary hung onto David's arm. One woman, who had joined the group late, inquired about having dinner.

"I'm not sure," David responded. "What do you think, Mary?"

"Sure. Dinner will give me more time to get acquainted with your friends."

"Well, group. Where to?" David asked.

"Let's eat in the hotel," Mark said. "The food is good." He whispered to David, "And it's closer to her bed."

"Will you quit?" David whispered.

During dinner, Mary drank two glasses of Chardonnay and two after dinner drinks. As dinner concluded, one of the female doctors asked, "Mary, do you want me to help you to your room?"

"Thanks, but no," Mary replied. "David and I are in the same tower. He can see me to my room—won't you, David?"

Stifling a chuckle, Mark tapped his shoe against David's shoe and winked. "David, you'll help Mary to her room, won't you?"

David looked at Mark, frowned, and mouthed, 'Stop it.'

The group called for the check which they divided its total into equal parts.

David said, "I'm indebted to Mary for a dinner, so I'll pay for her."

"How chivalrous," she said and put her hand beneath the table and slid it along David's leg. "You're such a gentleman."

David held his breath as Mary's hand settled near his crotch. *This gal is looking for action.*

"Okay, everybody," Mark said after collecting the money. "It's late. Let's get out of here."

After a round of continental cheek-kissing, the group split up, heading for their respective tower.

David helped Mary stay upright while waiting for the elevator. Inside, he pushed the button for the eleventh floor. Mary rested her head on his shoulder and hummed the melody of *Ebb Tide* that wafted from overhead speakers. When the elevator stopped, David assisted Mary to her door.

She fumbled in her purse, searching for her key. Having found it, she failed two attempts at inserting it in the lock.

"Let me," David said, taking the key.

"Thanks," Mary slurred, rubbing David's lower back.

David unlocked the door and pushed it into the dimly lit room. "After you."

"Aren't you coming in?" Mary asked. "I need help with one more thing."

"What's that?"

"My zipper."

"You can't do that by yourself?" David asked, disbelief tinging his words.

"Oh come on, David. You've seen lots of women undress."

Mary pulled him into the room.

"Uh, turn . . . around," he said, sounding perturbed.

After kicking off her shoes, she turned her back, lifted her auburn hair, and tilted her head. He kissed her neck. She moaned her approval.

David unhooked the neck of her dress then pulled its zipper to her hips.

Mary swayed like a rundown top and needed assistance to stand. "Oh God, my head is spinning."

David placed a hand on each side of her bare waist as her dress fell to the floor.

Attempting to step out of her dress, she had difficulty freeing her feet from the crumpled garment.

David left one hand on her waist and knelt to help. "Lift your foot," he said.

Mary placed her hand on David's head as if to pull his mouth against her crotch. "Mind if I steady myself?" she asked, fingering his hair.

David pulled the dress free of her feet. He stood then tossed it onto a chair.

Mary attempted to turn around but almost fell.

David caught her. "Let's get you to bed before you kill yourself."

"Such a gentleman," she mumbled and pulled him close. "Let's make love. I want you inside me."

"Mary. It's not the time."

"Yes it is," she pouted. "Make love to me. Please."

Mary fumbled with his zipper.

David thought, *I shouldn't . . . but . . . Why not? I'm not forcing her. She's begging me.*

Mary had fumbled with his zipper for a while when David interrupted and unzipped his fly himself.

Mary pulled her bra catch to the front of her chest then unhooked it. With one hand inside David's fly, she used her other hand to remove her panties. She offered a smirked smile.

As David grew in her hand, he removed his jacket, tie, and shirt. He used one foot to remove a shoe and then the other. He then unbuckled his belt and stepped out of his trousers.

"What a man," Mary muttered, releasing his crotch long enough for him to shed his underwear. Mary slid to her knees and uttered a loud hmmm as she mouthed David's manhood.

He held her head as if to keep it on course. "Atta girl."

Mary took David's hand and pulled him toward the bed. She fell onto the fluffy duvet, pulled him between her legs, and then guided him inside while he tongued her nipples. Mary moaned, bit his ear, and clawed his back.

I can't believe this is happening, David thought.

Although alcohol might have dulled David's pelvic nerves, Mary didn't seem to mind that he took longer to climax than he had expected.

"David," she said, "Faster! Faster! Oh God! Oh . . . ooohhh!" Slick with sweat, her breath came in short bursts between crescendos of moans of pleasure.

David increased the pace of thrusting and climaxed

just after Mary.

David collapsed onto her breast. For a moment, she lay motionless then caressed his head. In a strange, detached way, she said, "Good boy. Good boy."

What's this good-boy stuff about? David asked himself.

Exhausted, he rolled onto the bed and stared at the ceiling. "That's the first time I've had sex with an obstetrician."

"Ditto," Mary mumbled, stroking the hair on David's lower abdomen.

"You going to be okay?"

"Yep . . . peeerfeeeect."

"I'd better be on my way." Once dressed, David said, "See ya on campus."

"See yaaaa."

"Are you sure you're okay?"

"I'm fine. Just a little drunk."

"Better take something.

The next morning, Mary rubbed her forehead as she waited for the elevator. *God, I've got to watch my drinking.*

She made her way across the lobby then stood at the end of the long checkout line. She saw David at the checkout desk and searched her purse for a business card on which she scribbled her home number and waited for him to pass by.

David finished checking out and then walked toward the end of the line where Mary waited.

"Good morning," she said, smiling.

"Good morning." David put his receipt in his

satchel and said, "How's the head?"

"As you might guess, I had a headache, but two aspirin and it's gone." Mary held out her card. "Here's my number. If you're in Baltimore let's do lunch."

"Thanks," he said, taking the card. "I'd love to. Sorry, but I gotta run or I'll miss my flight. See ya."

"Have a great flight."

Mary watched David exit the hotel. *God, I want to see him again!*

Chapter Five

Mary arrived at her office before anyone else. She wanted to go through her mail, before seeing patients.

Doctor Green knocked on her door. "Welcome back. How was Bal Habour?"

"It's a wonderful beach city, and the conference was great. Met some nice people and had a good time. There were a few presentations about new research findings that will change the way we care for patients." She waved a sheath of papers. "I saved the presentation summaries for you guys."

Four weeks after the convention, Mary had not heard from David. *He probably doesn't want to reconnect. Maybe he thought of our time as a onetime fling? Maybe he's busy with his practice. I don't have his number, but I'm sure I could find it. Should I call him? Nah, I don't want to appear desperate. God, I hope he calls.*

Two more weeks passed and David had not called.

Men! Who needs them? Who wants them? What are you thinking, Mary? You want him, but he doesn't want you. Shit! Nobody does. They never have.

Mary created a racket, rummaging through the office medical-supply closet.

"Looking for something, Doctor," a nurse asked.

"Where are our pregnancy kits?"

"Top shelf. In the back. I'll get the ladder and get one for you."

"Thanks. I'll be in my office."

The next morning, Mary went to the bathroom, opened the pregnancy kit, and collected the day's first urine. She labeled the container Sandra Kurp.

Later, she took it to the hospital lab. "Please do a pregnancy test on this specimen," Mary said to the lab's secretary.

Two days later, Mary stopped by the laboratory and waited while a technician killed the rabbit injected with her urine. The technician opened its abdomen.

"The ovaries are inflamed," the technician said. "It's positive. Your patient is pregnant."

Mary covered her mouth to mask a gasp. *Can't say I'm surprised.* Mary headed for the parking lot. *Missing my period should have told me. Shit!*

This couldn't have happened at a worse time for Mary. Her patient load, the heaviest it had ever been, continued to grow. She could not stop her practice to have a baby.

What the fuck do I do now? Maybe I should go away, have an abortion.

About to start her car, Mary thought. *Should I have an abortion? I had better give this careful thought.*

Over the next few weeks, Mary stuck to her routine, but she began experiencing morning sickness. One morning, she excused herself with a patient and went to a bathroom where she threw up. *Other people get morning sickness—not me. Not a doctor.*

A nurse heard her retching and knocked on the bathroom door. "Doctor, are you alright?"

"I'm fine, thank you."

Mary rested a few minutes then returned to her

patient and the morning's work.

Having seen the last of her patients, Mary went to her office to rest. She sat at her desk, head in her hands.

Rose, one of the office nurses, walked by Mary's half-opened door. "You okay?" she asked.

"I'm okay," Mary murmured without looking up.

"Are you *sure*?"

Mary started to say yes but cried.

"For heaven's sake, what's wrong?" Rose asked as she entered the office then put her arm around Mary.

"Rose . . . I'm pregnant."

"What?" Rose pulled back and stared at Mary. "Are you sure?"

"I'm sure," Mary said, nodding.

"How far?"

Choking back tears, she said, "Six or seven weeks. It happened in Bal Habour."

Rose covered her face with both hands. "Oh goodness. Does Doctor Green know?"

"I've told no one. Hell, I'm having trouble admiting it myself."

Rose shook her head. "Oh, honey. What are you going to do?"

"I'm going to have the baby."

"Are you *sure*?"

Staring into Roses' eyes, Mary said. "Yes. I can't abort my baby *or* give it up."

Rose patted Mary on the back. "Why don't you see a doctor in the Kelmer practice? Let Doctor Green know right away. He'll understand you not wanting your partners delivering you."

"Thanks, Rose." Mary sighed and then smiled. "Guess I'd better tell Doctor Green."

Doctor Green had just taken a bite of a sandwich when Mary knocked on his door.

"Want a bite?" he asked, looking over his black framed glasses and flashing his famous smile.

Wringing her hands, Mary said, "No, thanks. John, I have a problem . . . a personal problem."

John laid his sandwich on the desk. "Want to talk?"

"Yeah . . . I do."

He gestured toward a chair, "Please. Have a seat."

Mary sat down, looked at the floor and gripped her palms. She looked at John and said, "I'm pregnant."

John leaned back and sat motionless for a second.

"Are you sure?"

"For God's sake, John. I'm an obstetrician—remember?"

"Sorry, Mary. For a moment, I saw you as a patient. As you know, they're often wrong about being pregnant."

"It happened at the meeting in Bal Habour. I didn't use protection. Had too much to drink and met a wonderful guy. It just happened."

"Does he know?"

"No. I haven't heard from him. Haven't told him."

"What are you going to do?"

Mary sighed and bit her lip. "I'm going to have the baby."

John took a deep breath. "Do you think you're *ready* for motherhood?"

Mary smiled. "Who's ever ready for motherhood?

I'm *not* having an abortion, and I won't give up the baby. I've been there. I don't want that to happen to my child."

"What can we—I mean what can *I* do to help?"

"Thanks for asking. I think I'll see Jerry Schmidt in the Kelmer practice. Our relationship has been remote enough that I'd be comfortable having him deliver me."

John sat upright. "He's a good doc. You do whatever you need for yourself and the baby. Promise you'll let me know if I can help in any way."

"Thanks for listening, John. Glad I got this off my chest."

"The staff will know sooner or later, so let me and Helen plan a baby shower. That should make your announcement a matter of routine."

"Thanks. That would be nice."

Mary placed herself and her unborn baby under the care of Doctor Schmidt. Her morning sickness abated and her pregnancy proceeded as expected.

Several times, she considered calling David to let him know he would be a father, but she didn't. *I don't want to complicate his life with unplanned fatherhood,* she told herself. *Hell, he could have a wife and six kids. No, this is my baby—mine alone.*

As the pregnancy progressed, Mary planned what she and the baby would do together. *I'll teach him, or her, to toss a ball, ride a bike, help with homework, help decide what to wear to the prom, visit colleges, get involved in wedding plans, and prepare myself for being a grandmother. My child will have the best that money can buy. He or she will be loved, respected, and feel part of a family. We'll have a home . . . maybe a dog or a cat or both. I'll have a car and plan family vacations and maybe take along his or her friends. He or she will love me, and I'll love him or her.*

Mary had always lived in apartments, but now, she felt she should buy a house and make a home for herself and her child.

Barbara, a real estate broker, assisted Mary in her search for a house. They visited twenty-seven houses before Mary found *the* house—a grand Tudor-style home with large rooms, a basement, backyard, and a garage.

Someday, my child will enjoy this yard. We'll get a swing set and have lots of fun running, playing, and getting hosed down on hot summer days. God, we'll have fun.

"I forgot to tell you," Barbara said, "the furniture stays, including the antique Duncan Phyfe living room and dining room furniture.

Barbara visited Mary's office two days before closing on her house. "Mary, I want to tell you about some unusual happenings in the house you want to buy."

"I hope it's nothing dreadful," Mary said. "No deaths? No murders?"

"Oh no. Nothing like that." Barbara took a deep breath. "Your house belonged to John McCloud, a dignitary from a well-heeled, local family. After his wife died, he took a fancy to call girls. He became interested in a dominatrix and converted his wine cellar into a dungeon—for sex games. Seems he liked to get tied up and whipped and . . . Well, one day, his *girlfriend* tied him up, beat him—something awful—and left him tied in the dungeon. She emptied the house of valuables and fled. Two days later, the housekeeper found John, naked, bound, and unconscious. Thank God the dungeon door was open."

"He didn't die?" Mary asked.

"No, thank God, but John spent a week in the hospital."

"What happened to the girlfriend?"

"She's in prison. The cops retrieved many of John's things, but the mess hit the newspapers. Poor John left town—disgraced. That's why his house is for sale. It's been on the market a long time."

"Why didn't you show me the dungeon when we toured the house?" Mary asked. "I should know what I'm buying."

"I apologize, Mary, but I didn't want to scare you from considering the house. It had everything you wanted, but now that you're buying it, I have to tell you. I could lose my license if I don't."

"Don't worry," Mary said, ignoring a blinking light on her phone. "The story adds to the character of the house."

"Then you'd better get used to strange looks when you tell locals where you live."

Mary laughed. "It might be fun to let them know I'm the owner. See you at the closing."

Following the closing, Mary asked Barbara to go with her to the house she had just bought. Mary had been in the basement during her first visit but had not thought much of the dark oak door in the basement's dimly lit south wall. She had thought it led to the backyard.

Mary now sensed a mystery in the silent, empty house. The echo of hers and Barbara's footfalls on the hardwood floors lingered in the vacant rooms as the women walked toward the basement door. Mary opened it then flipped the switch for the basement light. "My, that's a dim bulb."

She hesitated at the top of the stairs. *Spooky,* she thought. *Glad Barbara's with me.* Mary took the first step down the steep, squeaky basement steps. She paused on each step and cocked her head as if listening for God knows what. Once in the basement, she looked back at Barbara who had moved halfway down the steps.

Mary inched toward the dark oak door. She reached for Barbara's hand. Barbara took it then followed Mary. Except for the sound of their shoes abrading grit on the concrete floor, the basement had the sound of a funeral home at midnight.

"Okay, here goes nothing," Mary said, confronting the dungeon door.

She gave Barbara's hand a squeeze, and with the other trembling hand, she gripped the rusty doorknob. She turned it to the right until it stopped then pulled.

"Nothing, damn it," Mary exclaimed. "Now what do I do?"

"Let me try," Barbara said. She tugged at the knob, but the door refused to budge. "Maybe it's locked. Let's look for a key. There has to be one somewhere."

Mary and Barbara searched for the key, pushing

aside spider webs and disturbing aged dust in the process.

"There." Mary pointed above the door. "There's a key on that nail."

She jumped to grab the key, inserted it in the lock, and then turned the knob. "It worked," she said, her voice cracking. *Hope there's nothing bad in there.*

She took a deep breath, turned the knob and pulled, but the door refused to budge.

"Barbara, help me open this damn thing?"

They tugged at the door. Its hinges emitted a weak squeak as they pulled on the knob, but the door failed to open more than a quarter of an inch.

"Damn it!" Mary said. "Hinges are rusted."

She gave the door a sharp kick and then pulled the knob. Suddenly, the door swung toward her. "What—?" She stumbled backward but regained her balance. Something darted out of the room, sounding like a screaming child, and struck Mary's chest. "Get it off!"

The thing fell to the floor.

"What the—?" Barbara yelled in shock.

"What the hell?" Mary asked, looking past her shaking hands to the floor. A gush of cold, moldy air engulfed the women as spider webs fell on Mary's face. Yuk," she said, picking at them.

A narrow beam of sunlight, streaming through a broken windowpane at the back of the dungeon, illuminated an emaciated Tabby cat lying at Mary's feet. It took a shallow breath.

"Ugh!" Mary exclaimed, still swatting at spider webs. "That's what hit me. How the hell did it get in?"

Barbara clutched her chest and caught her breath.

Pointing, she said, "He probably got in through that broken window. Must have fallen to the floor and couldn't get out."

"From the looks of the poor thing, he hasn't had food or water in a long time."

"What do we do with him?"

"I'll give it some water in a minute," Mary said, feeling inside the doorway. "I found a light switch."

After three attempts to turn on lights, three fluorescent bulbs flickered on.

Staring into the room known as the dungeon, Mary said, "Oh, my God! Look at all this . . . *shit*. Pardon my French."

With her toe, Barbara nudged the cat. "I think he's dead."

"Guess there's no need to worry about feeding it."

They scanned the circular room and its two bed-like tables with attached chains and mildew covered leather restraints. A wall rack held chains and several leather whips covered with mold.

"What am I going to do with all this shit?" Mary asked.

"Give it to a charity for a tax deduction," Barbara said straight faced and then chuckled.

"Which charity?" Mary chuckled. "The one for spousal abuse?" She continued to scan the room. "What the hell is a bathtub doing in here?"

"Maybe old John liked water sports."

"Maybe I should keep this stuff for historical purposes. Show it off during house tours for the Junior League."

Barbara chuckled.

Mary took a dust-laden towel from a nail and picked up the dead cat by its tail. "Sorry kitty. You're headed for the trash bin."

"Let's get out of here," Barbara said.

"Yeah. This place gives me the creeps."

Nine days before Mary's due date, she went into labor at home. "God! Now I know how my patients feel."

"Missy," Mary yelled to her maid. "Call Doctor Green. Let him know I'm in labor, and . . . Oh, God it hurts. Tell him I'm on the way to the hospital. I'll phone Doctor Schmidt. Car keys are on the kitchen table—you drive?"

Missy, a twenty-three-year-old Native American, sat alone in the father's lounge, waiting for someone to tell her Doctor Snow had delivered her baby and both were well.

Missy had waited twelve hours and heard nothing. She went in search of someone to ask about Mary.

"Are you family?" the nurse asked, without looking up from a chart.

"No, I'm Doctor Snow's maid. She has no family."

"Have you spoken to Doctor Green or Doctor Schmidt about her?"

"No. I've never met them."

"Doctor Snow is having a hard labor. You stay in the waiting room. I'll let you know about her progress."

Missy went to the last seat in the row of chairs in the waiting area, rested her head against the wall, and fell asleep.

"Miss. Wake up," a nurse said, shaking Missy's shoulder. "Doctor Snow had a C-section. She's in the recovery room, but her baby is in the newborn nursery. You may see him if you want."

"She had a boy?" Missy asked.

"Yes. He's down the hall to the right, next to the large window."

"Thank you," Missy said, rushing to the nursery.

Behind the nursery window, she saw a baby wrapped in a blue blanket, wearing a blue skull cap. An ID card on the basinet, read SNOW.

He's so red, she thought, scanning the baby's face. *His ears look funny, and his eyes seem kinda far apart.*

Missy rapped the window to get the attention of a nurse at the back of the room.

The nurse approached the window, and Missy pointed to baby Snow. The nurse picked him up and smiled as she held him close to the window.

Missy shook her head and pointed to the nurse. "No. I want to talk to you."

The nurse placed the baby in his basinet then left the nursery. A moment later, she stood beside Missy. "How may I help you?"

"Is that baby okay?"

The nurse shook her head. "The doctor said, 'the baby will have problems as he gets older.'"

"What kinda problems?"

"Mental issues."

"Oh no!" Missy wrung her hands. "Doctor Snow is going to be so upset."

Chapter Six

Mary woke from her anesthetic fog to confront the chaos of the recovery room. "How's my baby?"

"He's fine," a nurse said, wiping Mary's brow with a cold cloth. "He's in the nursery."

"A boy?" Mary asked, her voice filled with excitement. "Oooohhh, I want to see him."

"Just as soon as he is cleaned up, and you're recovered."

"Why can't I see him? Surely, he's cleaned up by now."

"Okay. I'll get him in a few minutes, but first, let me straighten your bed covers."

"No! I want to see him now. Now!"

"Doctor. Please, you don't have to yell."

The nurse frowned then scurried away.

Despite the post-op pain, Mary pushed herself toward the head of the bed. She clasped her belly with both hands. *Where the hell is my baby?*

Minutes later, the nurse returned with the baby swaddled in a blue blanket. She cradled it in Mary's arms. Her heart raced, and she smiled as she raised the corner of the blanket covering the baby's face.

At first, she cooed, then smiled, and then held her breath.

"Oh, God! What's wrong with him?" Mary held the baby toward the nurse and stared into her face. "This isn't my son! What have you done with *my* baby? This isn't mine!"

"Doctor Snow, please, quiet down. That *is* your

son."

"No, he's *not*! Can't be! Look at him. He's not . . .
normal! God . . . *look* at him."

"Doctor Snow, he *is* your son."

Mary stared at the nurse, then the ceiling, and then
she cried. "Oh, God, what have you done? Is this some
kind of punishment? Why did this happen to me? To
us . . . to him? Why God? Why?" She held the baby
toward the nurse. "Take it away!"

The nurse left with the baby. Another nurse, attracted by Mary's emotional outburst, tried to comfort her.

Mary wept, saying, "No, no, no . . ." She clutched
her aching belly and muttered, "What did I do to cause
this? I gave up cigarettes—didn't drink. What have I
done? This can't be! I know what it's like to be different. How could I have caused this? How? Why me God?
Why me?"

"Doctor Snow," the nurse said, "you're a mother
now. You *will* get through this. You can do it. You
must." She squeezed Mary's hand, kissed her on the
forehead, and then left the room saying, "You're
stronger than you think, Doctor."

Mary sat alone, crying. Over a few hours, she realized that no matter her son's problems, he belonged to
her. *God, what am I going to do? He's my son, and he
needs a mother . . . and care—mine. God, help me.*

Mary composed herself then called to a passing
nurse and asked for her son. "I want to breastfeed him.
He's got to have my milk to get my antibodies." She
closed her eyes and prayed, "God, help me be the best
mother I can be."

Mary had decided if she had a son, she would name

him Timothy. As the nurse placed the baby in Mary's arms, she beamed with elation. "You are *my* son, and your name is *Timothy*." Mary sobbed for a minute, stroked his red, chubby cheek and said, "Tim."

With the eyes of a physician, she examined Tim's face, puffy eyelids, his hands, fingers, arms, feet, and toes. *Thank God. Everything is here.* She asked the waiting nurse, "Will you help me with my gown? I want to breastfeed him."

Mary's hand shook as she rubbed her nipple over and between Tim's lips. At first, he resisted, but after several attempts, his innate, sucking reflex kicked in and he suckled. Tim opened his eyes for a second and stared into her face. A warm wave of love swept over her. *Oh God! He's accepted me. He loves me.* She smiled as a tear streaked her cheek. "Look," Mary said with pride between sobs. "He's nursing. What a strange, wonderful sensation."

She glanced at the nurse. "He wants me."

"Of course, he wants you. You're his mother."

Mary looked into Tim's face. "Yes, I'm his mother, and I'm going to be a good mother."

Tim made a feeble attempt to extend his clenched fist but could not coordinate his movements. Excited, Mary said, "Look, he's trying to touch my breast." Mary lifted his arm and placed his open hand against her breast. In cog-like motions, he closed his hand, gripping the breast.

"Doctor Snow," the nurse said, "your face is beaming like the sun after a storm."

Tim fed for a few minutes and then fell asleep in her arms. Mary caressed his head and thin black hair

then sang to him of her love. She said to the nurse,
"He's asleep. Please, take him to the nursery?"

Mary felt well and happy. Her post-operative period
had gone well, and Tim had no trouble breastfeeding.

Mary felt they were bonding because he often stared
into her eyes while he suckled and gripped her breast.

I never thought being a mother would feel so good.

Mary looked forward to feeding Tim because she
gave and felt love during those precious minutes.

"Look at him," Mary said to the nurse carrying Tim.
"He's so beautiful. Well, to me he's beautiful. I know
he'll have problems, but we'll get through them. I'm
determined to give him everything he needs or wants. I
know how it feels to be denied a mother's love. He will
never be unwanted or unloved."

"You will be a wonderful mother," the nurse said,
helping Mary bare her chest.

Mary placed Tim against her breast. "Mommy loves
you, Tim. She loves you very much." Mary trembled
with love as they melded, causing her to hum and rock
him while he suckled.

"Do you know the nurses call you the cooer?" the
nurse asked.

"Guess I do coo a bit." She smiled. "Can't help it. I
love him."

Mary saw positive changes on Tim's face when she
held him. Even more so when she returned his smile.

Three weeks after delivery, Mary left the hospital.
She had to decide whether to continue breastfeeding
Tim or switch to bottle feedings and return to her

practice. If she returned to fulltime practice, Tim would need day-care services and bottle feedings. She weighed the pros and cons of her options and chose breast-feedings.

For the first time in her life, Mary felt needed and loved by someone—someone with whom she could share her love. Their bond grew stronger each day. After each breastfeeding, she hugged him, caressed his back, kissed his forehead, and sang to him. Each song ended with "and mother loves you."

I'll breastfeed you for as long as it takes. To hell with the office. I'll cut back on patients. I'm sure John will allow it for a while.

At twenty-eight months of age, Tim still wanted to breastfeed.

How long do I continue breastfeedings? Mary asked herself. *Maybe I should try again to wean him, so I can start solid foods.*

To Mary's dismay, Tim rejected a long list of pre-pared foods.

Maybe I should add small amounts of sugar or salt, Mary thought. *The taste might be more acceptable.*

They weren't. She added small amounts of breast milk to Tim's foods and found he accepted more solids, but took too little to thrive.

She discussed the problem with the office secretary who had five children. "I've tried substituting cow's, mare's, and goat's milk for breast milk, but Tim refuses them."

"Perhaps, you should consult a pediatrician," the secretary advised.

Mary had Tim seen by Doctor Schmidt. He told her,

"It's not good for you *or* your baby to continue breastfeedings. Tim needs more and better nutrition. He also needs to move beyond his fixation on breasts. He has developed a specific taste for human milk. That's a good thing—to a limited extent, but he has an emotional addiction to breasts and breast milk."

Doctor Schmidt walked to the window and stared beyond the parking lot for a moment then faced Mary.

"Your career is being compromised by your absence from your practice. I'm sure Doctor Green wants you back as soon as possible. The longer you're away from patients the rustier your skills will become."

"What am I to do?" Mary asked.

"I recommend you offer Tim only solid foods. If he refuses them, wait until he's hungry. When he's hungry, he'll eat."

Mary considered the recommendations but resisted starving Tim until he ate. She told herself, *Maybe it's selfish of me, but Tim is the calmest when he breast-feeds. When he does, I . . . no, we feel connected. We're one. He loves me, and I love him. I'm wanted, and he's wanted. I can't destroy our bond by starving him. I'll breast feed him as long as he wants.*

At the end of each breast feeding, Mary hugged Tim, kissed him on the forehead and then said, "Mother loves you very much. Don't you worry. Nothing is going to separate us. I'm here for you." She caressed his back and head and then sang of her love.

Doctor Taylor, a pediatric consultant, told Mary, "There's no hard and fast rule when a mother should stop breastfeedings. I'd recommend you continue feeding Tim solids *and* breastfeed him for a few more weeks—a few months *if* you have to—but *no* longer."

Mary though, *In time, I know he'll take solids—like a normal kid. I just have to give him time.*

Every other day, Mary force fed Tim solids, but he often spat them out or vomited. She now worried he had an obstruction at the emptying end of his stomach that caused his vomiting. She consulted a pediatric gastroenterologist who suggested a gastroscopy to rule out a blockage.

Mary paced the waiting room as Tim underwent a gastroscopy. She worried the doctor would find something bad, or Tim would suffer an adverse reaction to the anesthetic.

Ninety minutes later, the gastroenterologist entered the surgical waiting area. He wore not even a hint of a smile. *What the hell?* She asked herself, *Why should I worry? This guy is always stern faced.*

"Mary, all went well. I found nothing unusual."

Mary's heart skipped a beat. "Thank God. I'm glad you didn't."

"Tim's vomiting has nothing to do with his stomach. It's probably psychological. Give him time."

Mary hugged the doctor. "You have no idea how happy I am."

"He's in recovery if you want to see him."

Mary rushed to the recovery room. She blotted a tear, smiled and stroked Tim's head. "Everything is going to be okay."

His lids parted half an inch and he smiled.

Seeing Mary cry, a nurse put an arm around her. "You alright?"

"I'm okay. These are tears of happiness."

Mary continued to feed Tim solid foods blended with breast milk but his acceptance of the mixture was unpredictable. As he grew, he required larger amounts of breastmilk but took decreasing amounts of solids.

I can't keep this up, Mary thought. *My breasts are going dry. Soon, I'll have no milk. What the hell am I going to do?*

Mary continued to supplement Tim's mixed diet with breastfeedings. *I can't change everything about his diet. He wouldn't like it. Hell, I wouldn't like giving up our breastfeeding time.*

Mary's milk production and checking account were shrinking. She asked for an extension of time to pay past due electric and water bills.

She knew the best way to reverse her financial situation required she return to her medical practice. Not only would she generate income, she could contact new mothers who might sell their breast milk or donate it. It would supplement, and later replace, her breasts dwindling milk production.

Two weeks after Mary returned to work, she heard a doctor in her group had delivered a woman of a still-born baby.

This might be my opportunity to buy breast milk for Tim.

Mary's partners often rotated seeing each other's hospitalized patients provided they were recovering as expected.

On Mary's day to make hospital rounds, she visited the woman who had lost her baby. Mary needed to evaluate the woman's physical condition, but she also wanted to ask about buying the woman's breast milk before it dried up.

Chapter Seven

The patient rested in bed, eyes closed as Mary knocked on the open door.

"It's okay. I'm not asleep," the woman said.

"Sarah, I'm Doctor Snow, Doctor Hellman's partner. He's involved with another patient and asked me to look in on you. How are you doing?"

"Mentally, I'm a wreck." Sarah picked at the cuticle of her left index finger. "My husband isn't doing so well either." Sarah stared into Mary's eyes. "Why do you think I lost my baby?"

Mary sighed and shook her head. "There could be many reasons." She placed Sarah's chart in the rack on the foot of the bed. "I don't think we'll ever know what caused your loss."

"We were trying so long to get pregnant."

"Did you have prenatal care?"

"Didn't think I needed any," Sarah said, appearing confused. "I didn't see a doctor until I went into labor."

"Were you and your husband having sex prior to labor?"

Sarah had a puzzled look. "Yes, but what's that got to do with it?"

"Having sex during the weeks prior to your *expected* delivery date can be dangerous. Perhaps that had something to do with your loss."

Sarah's face blanched. Her mouth fell open as if in a silent scream. She dropped her head and muttered, "Oh, God. I . . . no, we . . . might have caused the loss of our baby." A tear dripped from her cheek and then she wailed. The room filled with the sorrow of the heart-broken woman.

"I'm sorry about your baby," Mary said and hugged her. After a moment, Mary pulled away. "How are you physically? Had any bleeding? Any pain?"

"No bleeding," Sarah said between sobs. "I hurt when I walk, but I'm able to get through that. I'd say I'm doing okay—considering everything else."

"Good," Mary said andn began examining Sarah's abdomen. "Would you be willing to help another mother?"

"How?" Sarah asked, drying tears. "What's her problem?"

"Her breasts are dry. She can't make enough milk to feed her baby. Since you can, and you don't need to feed a baby of your own, would you allow your milk to be taken and given to another baby?"

"Never heard of such a thing."

"Happens all the time," Mary said, speaking with authority. "It's even mentioned in the Bible. A wet nurse."

"Oh, yeah. I remember." Sarah stared at the wall for a moment. "I'd need to ask Jonathan, my husband, but I don't see why I couldn't."

"In your case, we would pump, or you would pump, your breast and store the milk in your home refrigerator until needed. How about I come by tomorrow to see what you and Jonathan have decided?"

Sarah bit her lower lip. "Sure."

Mary made her rounds at the hospital then went to hear Sarah's decision.

Sarah sat in a chair flooded by sunlight. She seemed to glow as she read a book.

"Good morning, Sarah," Mary said, knocking on Sarah's open door. "How are you?"

Sarah looked up and smiled. "I'm fine. Just want out of here and eat my own food."

Mary chuckled, "Glad to hear that. What have you and Jonathan decided about your breast milk?"

"He wasn't sure I should do it but left it to me." Sarah shifted on the chair then stared into space. "If I was that mother, I'd want someone to help me. Who knows. *I* might need help someday."

"Is that a *yes*?"

"Yes. I want to help. When do we start?"

Thank God. "I'll be back this afternoon to teach you to use a breast pump and how to store the milk. If it's not processed properly, it can't be used."

"I'm up for it as long as it doesn't hurt."

Mary shook her head. "I assure you, it won't hurt, but we need to discuss payment. How much do you want?"

Sarah looked surprised. "I hadn't thought about money." She paused for a moment. "No. I don't want money. Just knowing I'm helping a baby and its mother is enough. Could I meet them?"

Mary's heart skipped a few beats. "Sorry. Rules don't allow that."

Mary pushed a sheet-covered cart into the room. A nurse elevated the head of Sarah's bed while Mary busied herself with a small pump, tubing, and a glass funnel. The nurse helped Sarah expose her left breast.

"This is rubbing alcohol," Mary said, cleaning Sarah's left nipple. "We need to let it evaporate before we start." Mary waved at the alcohol vapors until they dissipated then held up the funnel. She taught Sarah how to use the equipment, patted Sarah's hand, and then asked, "Are you ready?"

"Ready as I'll ever be," Sarah said, moving her long hair aside. She exhaled and dropped her head onto the pillow.

Mary glanced at the nurse. "Let's get started."

The nurse started the pump. It emitted a hushed whir. All eyes were fixed on the glass funnel.

Suddenly, Sarah glared at her breast. "Oh! That pulls."

"Don't worry," Mary said, patting Sarah's hand. "The suction has started, but it won't hurt."

"Yeah. It's not painful . . . just strange."

"We'll let the pump run until the flow stops," Mary said. "Then we turn it off, remove the funnel, and then place it on the other breast. Afterwards, we'll place one of these covers over the top of the bottle to protect the milk from contamination."

Sarah and Mary watched the funnel fill as the process proceeded to conclusion.

"Now, that wasn't so bad was it?" Mary asked.

"Not at all," Sarah said then smiled.

"Glad to hear that." Mary placed a cover on the bottle. "Now, we date this label, stick it on the bottle, and then refrigerate the milk. That's it."

"What do I do with this stuff?" Sarah asked, pointing to the apparatus.

"After pumping, you need to boil the funnel and

tube for five minutes. I'll provide sterile bottles and covers once a week. Anymore questions?"

"Who picks up the milk?"

"Don't worry. I'll stop by once a week."

"Good," Sarah said, "because I'm not going to be driving for a while."

Mary gave Sarah a business card. "Here's my private number. If you have any problems, don't hesitate to call."

Sarah gripped Mary's arm and looked into her eyes. "Thanks for letting me help that poor mother."

"Thank you for helping. She's most appreciative, knowing her baby will have antibody-rich breast milk."

Mary left the room with a bottle of breast milk and a sense of relief. *Tim now has a source of milk.*

Over the next five years, Mary felt less and less sure about Tim's future.

He grew at the rate of a normal child. However, he had difficulties with cognition and coordinating his legs, hands, and fingers. Nevertheless, with the help of therapists and Mary's care, Tim overcame some of his problems, but Mary's work with Tim caused her to spend less time with patients.

Mary believed Tim needed socialization with children his age. After a long search, she located a center that would accept him. She hoped he could relate with other similarly challenged children.

Her hands shook on the steering wheel as she drove to the center for Tim's first encounter with peers.

Outside the modern stone and glass building, Mary took a deep breath and kept repeating, "Everything will be fine. Everything will be fine."

Anxious to see how Tim and other children might relate, Mary saw several of the center's staff waiting just inside the entrance. They made a great fuss over Tim as introductions proceeded.

The director introduced Tim to Johnny, a boy of similar disposition. Mary held her breath as the boys played with rubber balls on the floor. At first, Tim stared at them as if wondering what they were. Mary rolled a red one toward him. He smiled and struck at it with his fist.

"No, no," the director said, kneeling beside Tim. "Pick it up." She handed the ball to Tim, and after a few attempts, he took it and smiled. "That's a good boy," she said, hugging and kissing him on the forehead.

Mary rolled another ball toward Tim. He picked it up and held it. "Roll it back," Mary said.

"Give him time," the director said, patting the air. "Try this." She rolled another ball to Tim. It stopped just short of his reach. Tim began to cry.

"Now see what you've done," Mary said. "Roll it *to* him."

The director dropped several balls near Tim.

"Doctor Snow, please wait to see how he reacts."

Tim screamed and looked at his mother. He crawled toward the balls as fast as his uncoordinated limbs allowed.

"Give him time," the director said, blocking Mary's hand from pushing the balls toward him. After five minutes, he had collected two of the five balls.

"Okay," the director said, "time to share one with Johnny." She rolled a ball toward Johnny who sat four feet in front of Tim. Tim screamed his displeasure and reached for the ball.

Mary set her jaw, stared at the director. "Roll it *back* to Tim."

"Doctor, he has to learn to share," the director said.

"He does not," Mary yelled. "If he wants the ball, he gets it."

"Pardon me, Doctor, but that's *not* the way to train Tim. He must learn to share."

"You're wrong, *woman*. If he wants the ball, he gets the ball. Now roll it to him."

"Doctor, you shouldn't indulge him so."

"Don't tell me what I can do. I give my son whatever he wants. He's to be happy no matter what."

Standing erect, the director said, "Doctor . . . I don't think this school is for Tim. I'm sorry, but I think it best if you found another center."

Mary didn't want Tim confronting bullies in a public school for challenged children so she chose to home school him. She set up a special corner of a room in which she placed several toys and teaching tools for her to use with the assistance of visiting teachers and therapists.

Three months after starting the home school program, Mary's head swirled on hearing Linda, the therapist, say, "Tim hasn't accomplished a single therapeutic task." Linda looked Mary in the eyes. "I can't go on taking your money."

"What do you mean taking my money?"

"Doctor Snow, you *have* to know Tim is making no progress. We have spent hours and hours trying to

95

get him to do the simplest things. He has no concept of any of the things we've tried to teach him. I can't continue trying to get him to do things he can't do. I've done as much as I can. I doubt he will ever do more than he does now. To continue taking your money would be unethical. I can't do that. I'm sorry."

Mary felt dumbfounded. *I can't believe this.* "Quitting? You're giving up? Well, I can't. I'm his mother. You can leave, but I'm continuing. I'll never give up." Mary started crying. The therapist tried to comfort her, but Mary pushed her away and yelled, "Get out! Quitters aren't welcome here. Get out."

Every few days, Tim had raucous temper tantrums often triggered by removing him from his mother's breast or interrupting his rare episode of bottle feeding.

At other times, he had emotional outbursts, without identifiable causes, and often became inconsolable. He yelled a screech while flailing his arms and legs and crying. At those times, Mary spent hours pacing the floor, cuddling him, trying to comfort him, but her efforts often went unrewarded. She had to wait until he exhaused himself and fell asleep.

Tim's crying often became so intense he stopped breathing and became as cyanotic as a corpse. Mary worried the seizures were a form of epilepsy and feared he might die during a tantrum.

He underwent a neurological evaluation. The exam and brain wave tests were negative, but the good news did nothing to answer Mary's quandary. "How do I control or terminate Tim's tantrums?"

Mary consulted pediatricians and several mothers

about Tim's problem. The consultants suggested various things to quiet Tim, but none worked—at least not for long. One doctor suggested codeine.

"Codeine could lead to addiction," Mary said. "I can't risk that."

One day, Mary reached her wits end during one of Tim's tantrums. Missy, the Native American maid, heard Tim and knocked on his bedroom door where Mary paced. "Doctor Snow. Sorry to bother you, but maybe, you could try an old Indian mother's remedy for Tim."

Exhausted, Mary shook her head and pulled Tim against her chest. "I'll try anything. What is it?"

Missy blushed. "Rub his pee wee," she said.

"What did you say?" Mary asked, frowning in disbelief.

"Rub his pee wee."

"Missy! That sounds awful, even pornographic. I can't do that. I'm his mother, for God's sake."

"Old Indian mothers say it works."

Exhausted, Mary stared at her screaming son. "Thanks, Missy. I'll think about it."

Missy returned to her housework as Mary watched Tim thrash about in his bed and scream.

What do I have to lose?

Mary unpinned Tim's diaper then rubbed his penis. Seconds later, the penis became engorged, and Tim quieted.

"My god, it worked." Mary yelled, "Missy! Missy, come here!"

Missy ran to the nursery as if she thought something terrible had happened. "What's wrong, Doctor Snow?"

Excited, Mary said, "Your Indian remedy worked. It really worked."

"I told you." Missy smiled and then hummed as she returned to work. "I told you so."

The unusual therapy became a mainstay in controlling Tim's tantrums.

Although disabled in mind and body, Tim grew to be a young man, but his fixation on breasts and breast milk persisted into his twelfth year.

Despite Mary's repeated attempts to feed him solids, he spat them out. Once, she tried to starve him into taking solids, but he rejected them for four days. She worried he would starve to death if she persisted, so she tried energizing her breast by using every known milk-stimulating therapy. None were satisfactory.

Mary met Tim's nutritional needs through donated breast milk, but childless, lactating mothers, became more and more difficult to find because of advances in pre and postnatal medical care.

Tim preferred his mother's breast to bottles, even if she made too little milk to sustain him. Nevertheless, she permitted him to continue to suckle because it strengthened their emotional bond. During those times, she hugged him, rubbed his back, kissed his forehead, and sang to him. Each session ended with profuse expressions of her love, causing Tim to smile. She then asked, "Can you say mama loves me?"

It had taken Tim several years to speak a few words, but with much prompting, he learned to say, "Mama loves me." With each declaration, Tim smiled. Mary smiled back, feeling an emotional surge of love. "You are so beautiful, and momma loves you so much."

Over the years, Mary had tried various alternatives to breastfeedings, but now, she needed to change her feeding routine and weighed the options. She extrapolated the concept of a bottle made into a more human-like container. In order to meet Tim's nutritional needs and demand for breastfeeding, she purchased a custom made, double walled, black latex brassiere made by a Baltimore sex shop. The space between the overlapping cups held sixteen ounces of breast milk that Mary augmented with protein powder and vitamins. The outer cups had functioning, nipples that permitted her to simulate breastfeeding and continue the mother-son-bonds she and Tim cherished.

Mary glanced at her watch. *Time to feed Tim.* She strapped the milk-filled bra over her breasts and waited for the bra, and its milk, to reach skin temperature. She then climbed the stairs to Tim's second floor room.

Tim's room contained a double bed and a chair anchored to the floor. Padded walls provided protection for Tim during his temper tantrums. An open shower filled one corner of the room. It allowed Mary to bathe him without restrictions. In the opposite corner stood a toilet. Non-opening, impact-resistant windows prevented injuries on those occasions when Tim banged his head or fists against the panes. Rubber covered floors protected them from biological accidents.

"Tim, Mom's here," Mary said, entering the room. "Ready to nurse?"

"Mommy. Yum," Tim mumbled, waving his hands. In a gurgled voice, he repeated the word "Yum" and crawled to the edge of his bed and puckered his lips.

"Be patient. I'm almost ready."

Mary, wearing only panties and the rubber bra, climbed onto the bed and prepared to nurse Tim. He lay in her lap and suckled the bra's nipple. He turned onto his side as he suckled. After Tim emptied the first bra cup, Mary moved it aside, so he could grip the uncovered breast while he nursed at the other cup. He stared Mary in the eye as a smile crossed his lips. Mary smiled back. "I'm happy you're happy."

Mary knew acquiescing to his desire for her breasts and milk would be considered strange by society, but she found the arrangement psychologically and emotionally rewarding. He had become addicted to the structure and warmth of her breasts and she to his touch and the emotional connection that touch produced. She provided Tim with sensory input that maintained their love-bond and nurtured their mutual feeling of attachment.

By age twenty, Tim had grown to be a five foot-eleven-inch tall man of slight build. Despite his age, he required diapers for occasional accidents. He continued to have behavioral problems beyond his fixation on breasts and breast milk. His outbursts could last for hours unless Mary quieted him by injecting sedatives in order to avoid penis stimulation.

Tim, however, had learned to masturbate to compensate for his mother's denied stimulation. Sometimes, he found his way into different parts of the house, sans pants, pleasuring himself. Several maids resigned because of his behavior. He often chased them and attempted to fondle and suckle their breasts. These acts caused Mary's first maid, Missy, to resign when Tim, age fourteen, became aware of other women's breast.

Once, Tim attacked Theresa, a large-breasted Mexican maid. He ripped her dress open and licked her breast as she struggled to get away. During the tussle, she phoned police then grabbed a fireplace tool and struck him on the head, creating a gash requiring thirty sutures. She refused to press charges but demanded Mary pay her five thousand dollars for psychological trauma. Mary paid the hush money, and Theresa never returned.

Over the years, Tim had several intelligence evaluations. The IQ scores averaged sixty-two. This indicated a borderline idiot / moron level of intelligence. His mental age equaled that of a three and a half-year-old child and was not expected to change. His primary drives were pain, pleasure, and fear.

Mary knew Tim would require lifelong care, and she needed to plan for this. She did not want him to live in a public institution and knew private care could cost thousands of dollars a year, so she established a trust fund for his future care. She added several thousand dollars a month to the fund often leaving little money for herself.

Late one evening, Mary sat in her home office staring at her checking account balance then bills for electricity, gas, and water. *What am I going to do?* She began to cry then knocked the bills to the floor. "Shit." Mary picked them up and stared at her balances. *I have to. I have to cut back on what I'm adding to Tim's account. We won't survive if I don't.*

She quit the obstetrical part of her practice, so she could provide for Tim's physical and emotional needs. Giving up the care of pregnant women saddened her, but she wanted to care for Tim. She continued office-based-care of women having non-obstetrical problems. This type of practice earned more money per hour than obstetrics and allowed her to feed Tim three times a day with the rubber bra.

The years of searching for sources of breast milk, driving between office and home, caring for patients, managing the obligations of living, and caring for Tim took its toll on Mary.

One morning while brushing her teeth, she paused and scanned her face. *Mary, you look like an old woman. You've got to take better care of yourself. You can't keep this up.*

Mary's office staff knew nothing of her "breast-feeding" routine. She had been too embarrassed to discuss it even though it created a source of personal stress manifested as fatigue and failure to maintain a profess-sional appearance.

Close contacts advised Mary to place Tim in an institution or hire aides to help care for him at home, but she always replied, "They cost too much," or "He's my responsibility, and no one would care for him like me. Other people wouldn't understand him. He needs *me*."

On several occasions, Mary had overheard partners and nurses speak about the toll Tim's care had taken on her.

Once, Mary overheard a nurse say, "Mary's looking more and more disheveled. She's stopped going to the beauty parlor, and her personal hygiene is getting more and more offensive."

Mary chose to ignore the comments, but she acknowledged that her parting her graying hair in the middle and letting it hang loose on her shoulders was not attractive.

Doctor Green had discussed Mary's personality changes with his wife, Helen. During a late dinner, the doctor said, "I'm very concerned about Mary, the care of her patients, and her appearance."

"Really?" Helen asked.

"Yes. I'm worried about her mental and physical health."

"Sounds like she's overwhelmed. Taking care of that disabled son and patients may be too much for her. What are you going to do?"

"I'm too close to the situation to do much, but . . . maybe, you can help."

"Me? I'm not a psychologist. What could I do?" Helen asked.

"Bake some cookies. Take them over . . . talk to her. You were a psychiatric nurse. See what's going on. Look around."

"That's not something I'd like to do, but if you think it'll help, I'll do it."

"Thanks, Babe." John kissed her on the cheek.

Sunday morning, Helen stood at Mary's front door waiting for her to respond to the ringing doorbell.

Mary's mouth fell open as she opened the door. "Helen. Why are you here?" Mary adjusted her bathrobe, pushed her hair from her eyes, and said, "Come in."

"I guessed you'd be home. I haven't seen you since God knows when. How are you?"

"I'm fine, thank you."

Helen held out an aluminum foil covered tray. "I made a batch of your favorite cookies."

"White chocolate Macadamia nut?"

"You guessed it."

"Thank you so much." Mary took the tray. "Come in. Have a seat. I'll put these in the kitchen." *Why did she have to come now? The house is a mess.*

Helen moved several books, a towel and a crumpled blanket from the Duncan Phyfe sofa and sat down. She looked around the living room and shook her head. "Hmm, hmm, hmm." *What a mess. Trash everywhere. Mary and the house smell awful.*

Mary returned to the living room and sat in a wing chair. "Forgive the mess." She pushed her unkempt hair from her eyes with shaking fingers. "I've been busy."

"That's part of the reason I'm here. I haven't seen you at any of the hospital socials, medical society socials or office parties. I hope you aren't angry with us."

Mary adjusted her chenille robe over her knees. "Oh, God, no. I'm just . . . very busy. Tim's a handful and there are the patients and paperwork. Keeps me busy."

"I know what you mean." Helen forced a chuckle. "How about we do lunch Tuesday. I'm buying."

Mary squirmed on her seat. "That's so nice of you, but I have to be here . . . to feed and care for Tim." *Is she planning to have someone sneak in and spy on Tim while she and I eat salads?*

"How's he doing?" Helen asked. "Any favorable changes?"

"I wish there were but no." Mary shook her head. "That's just the way things are."

"Could I say hello to Tim?"

Mary's breath caught. "He's sleeping now, but I'm sorry to say he wouldn't remember you."

"Oh. Well. How would you like to join me at the spa some weekend? They have the best masseuses and do the most refreshing facials and pedicures. It would do you good to get out. I'm buying."

"Sorry, I can't." *Even wish I didn't have to sit here talking now.*

"Too bad," Helen said, frowning. "Well, I had better let you get back to doing whatever you were doing. Sorry you can't do lunch. If you change your mind, let me know. I'll buy."

Getting up from her chair, Mary said, "Helen, thank you for your kindness—and the cookies."

"You're welcome. Let me know if you want more." *How am I going to explain all this to John?*

A week after Helen's visit, Mary received a phone call from an emergency room nurse at Saint Mary Hospital. The call concerned one of Mary's patients who insisted on being seen by Doctor Snow.

"Please, tell her I can't see her tonight. Tell her I recommend she be seen by Doctor Taylor, the duty doctor."

"I'll try, Doctor, but I don't think she will accept that answer."

"Just tell her of my recommendation."

Mary hung up the phone then tried to go back to sleep. Five minutes later, the phone rang. "Oh God, who's calling now?" Mary reached for the phone. "Doctor Snow."

"Sorry to bother you again, Doctor, but your patient is having a hissy fit. She won't let anyone examine her. She won't be seen by anyone but you."

"God, I guess I'd better get in there. Give me thirty minutes."

Mary dressed, looked in on Tim and closed his door.

He could not open it from inside.

The fastest route to the hospital passed through, Swamp Town, a seedy part of Baltimore that Mary always avoided. However, to save time, she drove through the area. Its streets were quiet, and most of the street lights did not function. With the aid of moonlight and her high-beams, she saw sparkling broken glass strewn everywhere.

Gusting wind caused her to dodge debris and a garbage pail rolling toward the gutter. A red traffic light meant she had to stop at the largest intersection in the most hellish part of town. *I'm not waiting for a green light.* She looked left then right. *No one's around. I'm out of here.*

Suddenly, Mary saw three women move from the shadows to stand under the only functioning street light on the block. *Hookers*, Mary thought, looking at her watch. *At this hour, they have to be. Their skirts are short and blouses too open.*

At the hospital, Mary saw her patient then settled her in the intensive care unit.

#

Back home, she checked on Tim, and then went to bed. "God, I'm exhausted."

The next morning, Mary poured water into the coffee maker then sat at the breakfast table. A minute later, she glanced toward the coffee pot. "For God's sake, hurry up."

She ran her finger over the handle of her empty cup and stared out the window. *What a weird dream. Maybe I should pursue it. Hell, Mary, think about it. A lactating woman—here—all the time.*

All day, Mary replayed her dream, verbalized its pros and the cons, argued with herself, and then decided to implement her dream-inspired plan.

Chapter Eight

I must have fallen asleep, Mary thought, uprighting her lounger chair.

The only light in the den came from the TV, which displayed a test pattern accompanied by the sound of static. *Better get on with the plan.*

Mary drove to Swamp Town where she had seen the prostitutes. She scanned every nook and doorway along the deserted Main Street. She saw no one. *Maybe they're taking care of customers. I'll drive around the block. Maybe they're working another corner.*

She drove five miles per hour, peering into the shadows of boarded up buildings, searching for any movement. *No one on this block.* Mary turned the corner and continued to search for the hookers. Two black women stood under a pawnshop sign. *They must be working girls, look at those short skirts. Who wears fishnet stockings in cold weather? No wonder they seem so tall. They're wearing six-inch platform shoes.*

As Mary approached their location, the women stepped into the street, gawking at her Cadillac.

Mary stopped the car, looked around, then lowered the passenger-side window six inches. "Evening ladies," Mary said, in a shaky voice, leaning toward the window.

"Hello, honey," the taller black woman said, pushing her matted, blond wig into place while walking toward the car. "Lookin' for girl-girl fun?"

"Not me."

"You wanna watch us—together?" the other woman

asked, pointing to her friend and raising her own skirt to show she wore no underwear.

"Nah. Not that."

"Well, whattcha want, honey? You ain't vice are ya?"

"Far from it. Have you ladies ever heard of surrogate lovers?"

"*Suck gate* lovers?" the shorter woman asked, scrunching her face.

Mary chuckled. "Nooo. *Surr . . . a . . . gate* lovers. A woman who stands in for another woman—a substitute."

"Oh, yeah. Heard 'bout that shit," the taller woman said. "Seen it on TV. All kind of problems with that shit. Sometimes the woman don't get paid or falls in love, or tries to get settlement money when the guy don't want her no more. Know what I'm sayin'?"

"Well," Mary said, "I'm looking for a woman to be a make-believe lover for my son."

"Your son?" the shorter woman asked. "That's going to cost money, honey—a *lotta* money."

"What's your name?" Mary asked.

"I'm Quickie Nikie. Most people just call me Quickie. Who you?"

"I'm Mary."

"Nice to meet ya, hon," Quickie said, extending her fingerless, white lace gloved hand through the window. "This here is my friend, Kashandra," Quickie pronounced her friend's name with a faked English accent and pouted lips, "*Kă shăn' dră.* She thinks she be English royalty."

"Nice to meet you Kashandra," Mary said, extending her hand over the lowered window.

"Likewise, I'm shor," Kashandra said, popping pink bubble gum.

"You always chew bubble gum?" Mary asked.

"Sho do. Keeps my jaws in shape for . . . whatever."

"Would either of you ladies be interested in discussing the work I mentioned?"

"Hon, we got nothin' to lose," Quickie said, looking up and down the street.

Mary motioned toward the passenger door. "Please. Get in, so we can talk?"

"Only if we sit in the back, baby," Kashandra said.

"Surely, get in." *Do they think I wanted to slip a feel without paying?*

The women slid across the back seat and scanned the car's interior.

"Nice car," Quickie said. "You rich, hon?"

"Far from it," Mary replied. "Just live comfortably."

"So, Mary, baby, how do this shit work? What we gotta do, baby?"

"I've heard of men taking a kid to a prostitute to have his first sexual encounter. Has that ever happened to either of you ladies?"

"About three times a year," Kashandra said, smiling. "I'm known for my technique, baby. I'm a great teacher. The kids love me. Oh God, I mean the young *men* love me . . . *it*."

"And you Quickie?" Mary asked, looking at her via the rearview mirror.

Quickie smiled then said, "A couple of times a year, but I charge more for beginners, honey. They take time. You don't want 'em gettin' off on the wrong foot, or should I say gettin' off with the wrong lady?" Quickie burst out laughing and slapped her thighs.

"Oh, calm down," Kashandra said, glaring at Quickie.

"Have you ladies ever had sex with men who have . . . problems?"

"What ya mean *problems*, honey?" Quickie asked.

"Handicapped guys," Mary said and looked away from the mirror.

"Honey, I done had sex with guys who got no legs, no arms and one guy who had nothin' down there," Quickie said. "He wanted to lick me while I used a dildo on him."

"Wow, and how about you, Kashandra? Anything unusual?"

"Yeah. I've had my share of weirdoes, baby. No arms. No legs. Even had one of those mongo guys. One dumb shit, but girl, he could fuck. He almost got *me* off."

Scrunching her face, Quickie touched Mary's shoulder and said, "A working girl don't want that to happen, honey. Makes it hard to work afterwards."

Mary said, "Well, I have a son—"

"I hope he ain't fifteen," Quickie said.

"No. He's older."

"Shit, girl," Kashandra said, "what's wrong with your boy? By that age, baby, all of 'em are gettin' it on at school. It's like there's a course in gettin' laid."

"He's had a sheltered life because he's a little like that mongo kid you mentioned. How do I say this? He has mental problems."

"Hell. That ain't no problem. Not for me, honey,"

Quickie said, "as long as he's not dangerous."

"Me neither, baby," Kashandra added. "But I'm better with kids than Quickie—plus, she charges more."

"And worth every dollar," Quickie said, leaning over the front seat and shaking her finger to make her point.

"How often do you ladies get checked by a doctor? A pelvic exam? Blood tests?"

"We use conums, baby," Kashandra said, looking at Quickie who nodded agreement. "We ain't got no problems."

"You ladies would have to have a complete medical evaluation if you are to have sex with my Tim."

"Baby, that medical stuff costs money. Quickie and me ain't got no money for doctor stuff."

"What if I paid for it?" Mary asked.

"If you payin', you can have anything ya want, baby," Kashandra said.

"You got it, honey," Quickie said. "Anything."

"You ladies meet me tomorrow night. Same time same place. I'll have some papers and appointments for you to see a doctor. He'll examine you and do blood tests. When I get the results, I'll pay you for your effort. By the way, don't mention to the doctor that you are working for me."

"It's goin' to cost fifty dollars for us to use our time havin' all that doctor stuff," Quickie said then held her breath apparently waiting for an answer.

"Okay," Mary said. "Do we have a deal?"

"Yep. A deal," the women replied.

Suddenly, bright light filled Mary's car. A police car had pulled up behind it.

"Oh my God," Kashandra said. "Damn coppers. Ain't seen them assholes in these parts for a while."

Squinting, Mary peered into the rearview mirror to see if she could see who had arrived. *This can't be happening. God, I hope they don't know me from the hospital. I can't be arrested with prostitutes? My practice, my life could be ruined if it hits the papers. Shit! What do I do now? Think girl, think.*

The women in the back seat busied themselves straightening their clothing then sat still, hands in their laps.

"Don't say nothin', baby," Kashandra said, tapping Mary on the shoulder.

"Ladies, let me handle this," Mary said, shielding her eyes from the light reflected in the rearview mirror.

Two burly policemen approached Mary's car. Each carried a flashlight with a bright beam. One walked to the driver's window and one walked to the front passenger window.

Mary lowered her window. "Evening Officers."

The beams of light moved about the interior of the car, pausing on each face, the seats, and then the floor. Each cop kept a hand on his holstered revolver while scanning the car.

"Alright *ladies*, everybody, out of the car," the sergeant ordered. "Get out and put your hands on the top of the car—now!"

The women hesitated.

"Let's not take all night, *ladies*," the sergeant yelled. "Move it!"

Mary exited the car, facing away from the lights. "What's the problem, Officer?"

Mary's new friends moved to her side and stood erect, their chins in the air.

"I said hands on the car," the sergeant said, waving his gun. "Pat 'em down, Sam. See if they got enough drugs to be dealers."

Sam patted down Quickie. Her raised arms had hiked her short skirt, revealing her bare ass. She glared at Sam. "Don't ya put your hand where it ain't supposed to be."

The sergeant chuckled. "Drafty, eh?"

Mary worried the cops might find drugs on one or both of the prostitutes. *What would I do if they find anything illegal?*

"She's clean," Sam said, finishing Quickie's pat down.

"Arms down, *Missy,*" the sergeant whispered in Quickie's ear, "and cover your ass."

Quickie smoothed her skirt.

"Check the other one," the sergeant ordered, drawing and waving his gun toward Kashandra.

After a quick pat-down of Kashandra, Sam said, "She's clean."

"I told ya. I ain't hiding nothin' baby," Kashandra said, staring at the sergeant.

"Now the white one," the sergeant said.

After an even faster pat down of Mary, Sam said, "Nothing here."

"What's the problem?" Quickie asked. "We ain't hurtin' nobody."

"What are you *ladies* doing out here this hour?" Sam asked.

"We's havin' a church meeting. A meetin' of the

Lady's Missionary Aid Society," Kashandra said, with sarcasm.

"Yeah? And I'm Saint Peter who just stopped by on my way to a pilgrimage to Rome," the sergeant retorted. "This area is known for drugs and prostitutes." He nodded toward Quickie and Kashandra. You two look familiar. Where's your pimp?"

"You must be mistaken, Sergeant," Mary said, with authority. "As you can see, I'm not a *John*." She moved her bare forearms into the light and said, "See any needle marks on my arms? No. Nada. I don't do drugs. I'm Mary from the mission. I'm interested in these ladies' souls. I'm trying to get them to give their hearts to Jesus. I hope you noticed that they were in the back of the car and *fully* clothed. There's nothing illegal here."

"Driver's license, please?" the sergeant ordered, putting his gun in its holster and then extending his hand toward Mary.

"Certainly. It's in my purse—on the front seat."

"Watch her, Sam," the sergeant said, "make sure there's no weapon."

Mary retrieved and opened her purse, so the policeman could look inside. "See. No gun." Mary removed her driver's license and handed it to the sergeant.

"Search the car, Sam" the sergeant said while looking at Mary's license. "ID seems okay," he said, scanning the license with the aid of his flashlight. "Got any ID from the mission?"

Oh God, Mary thought. *What am I going to do now?* She cleared her throat. "Not in this purse. Call Pastor Jim at the mission if you want. He'll vouch for me."

"That won't be necessary," the sergeant said. He turned toward the black women. "Got any ID?"

"I don't, and I don't have ta," Quickie said.

"Yeah, we not required to have no ID," Kashandra added.

"You're wrong," the sergeant yelled. "Both of you! You gotta carry ID."

"Yeah," Sam repeated, "you gotta carry ID. It's the law."

The sergeant holstered his flashlight and tipped his hat. "Have a nice night, *ladies*. As for the black *sisters*, if I see you on the streets again, I'll take you in so fast your skirts will catch fire."

"Nite officers," Quickie smirked, curtsied, and waved goodbye with a middle-finger salute.

Mary slumped against the car. "God! I'm glad that's over?"

"Baby, you're one cool bitch," Kashandra said, nodding toward Mary.

"I couldn't have done better," Quickie said, tugging at her too short skirt.

"I don't know about you gals, but I need a drink," Mary said. "Anyone interested?"

"Yeah, Honey, but it's gonna cost you for our time," Quickie said. "Otherwise, we'd be working . . . makin' some 'doe re me.'"

"Get in, ladies," Mary said, sliding behind the steering wheel. "Where to?"

"Honey, we goin' to the Humpty Dumpty," Quickie said. "I'll tell ya how to get there."

Chapter Nine

Mary stood just inside the door of Kashandra's and Quickie's "watering hole," the Humpty Dumpty Bar. She scanned the seedy, dimly lit space. A twenty-foot-long bar crowded the left side of the small room. Ten neon signs displaying the logos of different beers hung over the bar. The six dilapidated bar stools, in front of the iridescent Formica covered bar, leaked their dirty-cotton stuffing.

Worn red and green checkerboard tiles, reminiscent of a classless Christmas-sale item, covered the floor. The air, and many of its customers, reeked of cigarette smoke, urine, and stale beer.

A jukebox, encircled by dimly lit neon bubbles, droned a whiny Tammy Wynette song of lost love to complement the depressing environment.

Oh, God, what have I gotten myself into? This is right out of a "B," movie, Mary said to herself. *No, it's a "D" movie.* "What den of iniquity have you ladies brought me to?" Mary asked, pulling out a rust-pitted, chrome framed chair. Its torn blue vinyl cover had exposed brownish padding. Nevertheless, she sat on it.

"Baby, this is a *fine* place," Kashandra said. "You should see the others around here. Nothin' but bums and clap spreaders. Some got lice."

Mary asked herself, *Who the hell do these hookers think these customers are?*

"Here, the glasses are cleaned—ever once in a while," Kashandra said then chuckled. "This place gets acceptable license from the health people. Besides, the owner treats Quickie and me like ladies."

"And they don't water our drinks or short change us," Kashandra added.

I never thought I'd be in a place like this, Mary thought, dragging a fingertip over the table top.

Kashandra tilted a chair and brushed its seat before sitting down.

"Atta girl," Quickie said. "Wipe before ya sit, honey. Never can tell what you'll find."

Mary squirmed on her uncomfortable, worn chair then peeked under the table to see what had stuck to the sole of her shoe.

"Baby, you want a *shot* of somethin' or a *bottle* of somethin'," Kashandra asked Mary.

Mary thought, *I'm not going to drink from a glass.* "I'll have a *lite* beer—in a bottle."

"Hey! Puss," Quickie yelled to the barmaid. "Bring three *lites*. We watching our figures tonight. Don't want that fattening stuff."

"Bottled," Mary yelled.

Puss, a short, rotund black woman, looked tired and weathered—well past her prime. She waddled like a woman suffering failed hip surgery. She carried three beer bottles by their necks, one between each of the four fat fingers of her left hand.

"Quickie. Kashandra," Puss said, "how you ladies doin' tonight?" She looked at Mary. "A new girl? Is she competition?"

"This here's a new friend," Quickie said, tilting her head toward Mary. "Mary's her name. She's not working. At least not yet. We don't need no competition."

"The name's Puss," the barmaid said, extending her

coarse hand toward Mary.

"Nice to meet you, Puss," Mary said and offered her fingers. "I'm Mary." *God, her hand feels like sandpaper.*

Under cover of the table, Mary rubbed her shaken hand on her slacks as if wiping off plague.

"Puss used to be a workin' girl," Kashandra said. "Then she became a *highclass* madam. Saved her money and bought this place. She's always looking out for us street girls. Nothing gets by her . . . and don't mess with her. She's one tough bitch. Ain't ya Puss?"

Puss pulled a bottle opener from her cleavage and removed the caps from the women's beer bottles. "Yell when you're ready for another," she said, waddling back to the bar.

Mary used her blouse to wipe the neck and top of her bottle then took a sip.

"Now, baby," Kashandra said, "let's say our doctor test is okay, and we got none of them diseases you so worried 'bout. What you want us ta do for your boy?"

Quickie blurted, "Kash, it sounds like she wants us ta teach him to fuck."

Mary sat motionless for a moment, frowned, and then nodded as she swallowed a gulp of beer. "That's about it, but he needs somebody caring and patient."

"Sound like it's gonna take time," Kashandra added. "Time costs money, baby. I think we oughta get paid—hourly. A hundred dollars."

"Yeah, hourly," Quickie added. "This ain't gonna be wham-bam-thank-ya-mam work, honey."

"That might be true," Mary said, "but first we need a doctor to give you ladies a clean bill of health."

"Honey, that's easy," Quickie said. "Just tell us when and where."

"How can I reach you girls—by phone?" Mary asked.

Kashandra dug into her fake looking Gucci purse and pulled out a stub of a yellow lead pencil and a fragment of a utility bill. She wrote something on the back of the bill. "Here's the number," she said.

"Thank you," Mary said and took the scrap. "I'll call as soon as I set up the appointments. Now, I need to get home. May I give you a lift?"

"Thanks, but no thanks, honey," Quickie said. "It's late, and I wanna finish this beer."

"Me too," Kashandra added. "But thanks, baby."

Mary dug in her purse and pulled out some large bills. "Here's the money for your time."

During the previous month, Doctor Green had delivered ten babies in a thirty-day period. The deliveries had kept him at the hospital for hours on end, allowing him little time with his wife, Helen. She had threatened him with divorce if he didn't take a couple of nights off and treat her to dinner. He took the hint and made a reservation at Baltimore's famous Hausner's restaurant.

During dinner, he said, "Babe, I hate to ask about the matter now, but what did you think of Mary's situation?"

Helen sipped her wine. "You're right. We shouldn't talk shop. Enjoy your snails."

"I wanted you to talk to her because I worry about her. What did you think?"

Helen put her fork on her plate and said, "She's a mess. She greeted me at the door wearing a dirty robe. She had unkempt hair and BO. The house looked as if it hadn't been cleaned in months . . . piled high with . . . stuff—everywhere."

"That bad, huh? How did she sound? Was she coherent?"

"It's been thirty years since I did a nurse-type, mental-health evaluation, but I thought she was disturbed. She had a faraway look even when she looked right at me. Her speech was halting, and I got the feeling she was hiding something."

"Like what?"

"Not sure. She seemed evasive and standoffish. I felt she wanted me to leave. I don't think she does anything, out of the house, other than medical office work."

"A problem, eh?"

Helen nodded. "I'd say so, but I don't think you'll be able to get her to talk to anyone. Hmmm. There might be a way."

"What's that?"

"Tell her you're concerned about the changes you've noted in her personality. Tell her she is not to return to work until she has been seen by a psychologist or a psychiatrist."

"God, babe. You know Mary. Do you think I could do that? Or if she'd follow through?"

"Well, you wanted my input. That's it."

"Yeah, I did, didn't I? This is not what I wanted to Hear, or something I want to get involved in, but I guess I have to." *God help me.* "Let's have some champagne."

A week after meeting the prostitutes, Mary called Kashandra. "I have the information I wanted. When can we meet to discuss it?"

"How about tonight, baby . . . before we hit the streets?"

"Could I meet you at that bar?"

"Buy us a beer?"

"Okay. See you at eight."

Mary parked in front of the bar—the only intact building on the block. She squeezed the steering wheel and sighed. "Okay, Mary, let's get this over with."

She entered the saloon, allowed her eyes to adapt to the dim light, and scanned the room for her hookers.

"Over here, baby" Kashandra called from a corner booth.

Mary pushed her way between tables occupied by male patrons who were either passed out or dead. Some hung backwards in their chair, arms swinging like pendulums when struck by passing customers. Two men, resting their heads on a table, sat so close to the edge of their chair they were in danger of falling.

"Those two guys must have had the good stuff," Mary said, sliding onto a banquette opposite the two women.

"Honey, don't pay no never mind to dem guys," Quickie said. "They could be drunk, but they probably didn't sleep last night. You know how cops chase po folk outta doorways and parks."

Sitting down, Mary asked, "Have any problems, with the doctor, or the lab testing?"

"Baby, that doctor, he's real nice," Kashandra said.

"Cute too. I made him laugh during my down-there look. For a minute, I thought he put his thang in me but it turns out it's something like a duck's bill but got no quack."

"You mean a speculum," Mary added.

"Yeah, a duck's specum," Kashandra said, seemingly lost in her unintended humor.

"I kept my mouth shut," Quickie said, "but he's a nice man. I know I ain't had no problems."

"Well, I'm happy to tell both of you that both of you got a clean bill of health. There's nothing for me, or my son, to be worried about *provided* you don't catch something between now and the chosen time. To minimize the risk, I want you ladies to stay away from other men until you visit my Tim."

"But baby, I done schedule my regular man for tomorrow," Kashandra said.

"Guess you'll have to disappoint him," Mary said. "You'll be the first to visit Tim and then Quickie the next night? I want to see how he reacts to each of you."

"When do we report for work, baby?" Kashandra asked.

"Tomorrow night? I'll pick you up at eight, outside this bar. You know my Cadillac."

"I'll be here, baby," Kashandra said, waving to the barmaid then pointing to her empty beer bottle.

"One more thing," Mary said. "Wear something nice—long and loose. If anyone sees us, I want them to think you are society ladies—not hookers."

"Honey, we ain't hookers," Quickie said then laughed. "We're street secretaries. Know what I'm saying—we be *professionals.*"

Kashandra stood in the shadows outside the Humpty Dumpty Bar. She wore a frumpy, long green satin dress that billowed in the breeze.

Mary pulled to the curb, lowered the passenger window, and tooted her horn. *Hope she doesn't think she's wearing a ball gown.*

"Evenin' Miss Mary," Kashandra said. "I wasn't sure you'd come, baby."

"I'm a woman of my word, but I wasn't sure *you* would show up. Get in."

They rode in silence as Mary dodged pot holes, a dead cat, and blowing trash. They crossed the railroad tracks, leaving Swamp Town and the nearby trash dump behind.

"Glad we're past that smell," Mary said.

"Ya get used to it, baby" Kashandra said. "I don't smell it no more."

"Nice 'hood," Kashandra said as Mary drove on to an alley street that provided access to the garage in the back of her house.

"Thanks," Mary said in a dry tone of voice.

Kashandra watched as Mary pushed a button on the remote garage door opener. "One of them fancy doors, eh?" Kashandra said.

Mary turned off the engine. "Okay. Let's go meet Tim."

Bumping into a bicycle that half blocked the door to the kitchen, Mary said, "Shit. Got to get rid of that or get new tires."

They entered a dark hall covered with an oriental

carpet. Mary stopped at the foot of a flight of stairs and said, "Remember, my son's mind is not normal." Mary wrung her hands as she spoke. "That's not to say he doesn't deserve the same sexual satisfaction as normal people, but his reactions are going to be . . . different." As Mary spoke, Kashandra eyed the room and sniffed the air.

"Tim has never seen a naked woman. However, he *is* familiar with women's breasts. In fact, he's obsessed with them."

"Hell, baby, he's no different than most men."

"Tim isn't like most men," Mary said, her voice trailing off. "Don't be surprised if he sucks your breasts for an hour."

"He don't bite do he?"

"Never. But he does like to suckle. I doubt he'll become sexually aroused on a visual basis. He'll require manual stimulation. He responds to that." Mary folded her arms over her chest. "Sometimes, he calls everyone mama, so don't let that bother you." Kashandra looked up the stairs as Mary asked, "Ready?"

"Let's go."

At the top of the stairs, they stepped into the middle of a long, bare hall. It had a wall phone and long, narrow blue oriental carpet. Mary pointed to one of four bedrooms. "You should undress and leave your things in there. While you do, I'll get Tim ready. Wait here in the hall until I open this door behind me."

"Naked?" Kashandra asked.

"Everything," Mary said.

Mary left Tim's door ajar and tiptoed to his bedside. He had curled up on his bed, facing away from the door.

"Are you asleep?" Mary asked.

"Mama? Tim asked, turning over.

"Yes, it's Mama. I need to take off your diaper."

"Bath?"

"No. No bath. You're going to have fun."

"Fun?"

"Yes, new fun."

Tim smiled. "I like fun."

Mary removed Tim's diaper. "You wait in bed."

"Here?"

"Yes, here."

Mary returned to the hallway where Kashandra waited. "My, your body is more curvaceous than I had expected. Nice."

"Thank ya, baby. You bought the best."

"I hope Tim appreciates it. Come with me." Mary motioned for Kashandra to follow her into Tim's white room. "Did you lubricate yourself? Mary asked. "I put a tube of KY on the dresser."

"Don't worry," Kashandra said, "I know how ta prepare myself." Stepping into the room, she said "Girl, I ain't never seen a room so white and bright." Artificial light beamed from recessed ceiling fixtures, twelve feet overhead. She looked around and inhaled. "I like the smell of pine oil. It's clean."

"The room is padded, so Tim can't hurt himself. The floor is covered with rubber for easy cleaning. That's a water drain in the middle of the floor. That's a shower in the corner you can use if there's a need. The knobs are high on the wall. Shower water runs to that floor drain."

Mary pointed at Tim's bed. "His footboard and headboard are padded for protection. The side boards are padded and the mattress is screwed to its supports. All this is to prevent him from hurting himself."

As Kashandra listened, her eyes grew wide. She seemed nervous. Barefooted, she moved toward Tim as if trying to avoid stepping on broken glass.

"When talking to him, speak calmly," Mary said, "use simple words, and speak slowly."

Kashandra stood tall, took a deep breath and moved from behind Mary into the naked Tim's field-of-vision.

"Tim, this is Kash," Mary said, turning to her guest. "Okay if I call you Kash? Short names are easier for him to remember."

"That's fine." Kash moved closer and half squatted to look Tim in the eye. "Tim, my name's Kash. How you doin'?"

"Kash?" Tim asked.

"Yes, I'm Kash. My, you're a big boy. How old are you?"

Tim held up ten skinny fingers and said, "Old."

"That's not his age," Mary whispered.

"Honey, I can tell. Look at him. Ten-year-old kids ain't got dongs like that."

Tim stared at Kashandra's large breasts as she approached the bed.

"Yum," Tim said, reaching in their direction.

"Let him fondle your breasts," Mary said, moving to the side of the bed.

Tim took Kashandra's left breast then kneaded it. He smiled. His head moved forward until his open mouth captured the targeted nipple.

Kashandra wanted to scream from shock.

"Lordie, he's trying to suck me inside out, baby. No man ever sucked me like this."

"Lie on the bed. You'll be more comfortable."

"Is this all I'm supposed ta do, baby?" Kashandra asked, climbing onto the bed while Tim continued to suckle her breast.

"No," Mary said. "See if you can get him interested in intercourse."

"Inna—what?"

"I hate saying it, but see if you can get him inside you," Mary whispered.

"Oh, baby, I got no problem with that, but he's not interested. Seems all he wanna do is suck."

"You'll have to help him."

"Whatta ya mean, baby?" Kashandra shifted her head on the pillow while Tim continued his breast feast. "Shouldn't he have a 'conum'?"

"Can't. He's allergic. Stimulate him with your hand. If he responds, see if you can get him inside. If you can't do it while he's sucking, let me know."

"That's a first, baby," Kashandra said, struggling to stimulate Tim.

Tim glanced at his crotch without interrupting his sucking Kashandra's breast.

Mary asked, "Can you move your left leg under his hips?" Mary pulled on Kashandra's foot. "Good. Now, get him inside."

"I'm tryin', baby. I'm tryin'."

Kashandra slid down the bed, trying to situate her pelvis under Tim's crotch, but she couldn't make the alignment. He did not appear to have any innate interest in copulation. She tried twice to guide him inside, but he missed the target.

"For God's sake," Mary said, feeling frustrated by Kashandra's failures. *Can't you do anything right?* "Let me help."

Mary grasped Tim's hips and moved him over Kashandra's crotch then pushed down on his buttocks.

"Uhh . . . He's in," Kashandra said, wiggling her hips.

"Bounce your hips, otherwise he won't enjoy this."

"God, baby, I ain't never had ta do *all* the work for nobody."

"Well, you do this time. Now, move it."

Kashandra bucked her hips as Tim suckled her breast. "Baby, my breast is getting' sore."

"If you stop him, he will throw a tantrum."

"Then what we gonna do, baby?"

"You get the other nipple ready, I'm going to move his head from this breast to the other. Ready? On one . . . two . . . three."

Mary pulled Tim's mouth from Kashandra's breast. He started to yell, but she pushed her right nipple into his mouth. Tim had no time to utter a sound. He latched onto the nipple and suckled like nothing had happened. Kashandra rocked her hips and gyrated her pelvis like she wanted to finish, collect her money, and leave.

Mary remarked, "From the look on his face, I think he's about to climax."

"Seems he's moving his ass for cumin', baby. He's movin' different than before."

"Let's hope," Mary said, waving her hands and

smiling. "I hope he enjoys this."

Until then, Tim's had said nothing but utter "Yum," but now, he moaned as he tried to swallow the breast.

"Something is happening," Mary said, watching Tim's face.

Kashandra increased her gyrations. "Baby, I think he's ready."

Suddenly, Tim grunted. His body became as rigid as someone having a grand mal seizure. He bit Kashandra's breast, shuddered, and then collapsed as if dead.

"Ouch!" Kashandra yelled, half sitting up. "He bit me! The son-of-a-bitch bit me!"

"Sorry," Mary said, "but he climaxed. That's good." Mary pulled Tim's head from Kashandra's breast and examined her nipple. "The skin isn't broken. There's no blood."

"Thanks God, baby. I don't want no rabies." Looking perplexed, Kashandra asked, "Is he in a coma? He's awful still and sweating."

"He's just exhausted."

Kashandra pushed Tim's body off hers. "I heard of men dying in the saddle, but this is the first time I almost seen it. Look at him. Baby, he's like a dead man."

"He's like most men after sex. I know he enjoyed it. Thank you."

"Baby, Kashandra always gets her man—leaves 'em *satisfied*."

"Let's let him sleep. Come, I'll show you where you can shower."

Mary led Kashandra to the bedroom where she had

undressed. Mary pointed to the *en suite* bath. "Shower in there." Mary then picked up an envelope from a table. "This is your money."

Chapter Ten

Mary pulled her car to the curb in front of the Humpty Dumpty. She tooted her horn just as Quickie exited the bar.

"Miss Mary, how you doin'?" Quickie asked as she opened the car door then slid onto the front seat.

"I'm fine, thank you. Are you ready?"

"I guess so, honey. Kashandra and me talk about your boy. He's a little . . . weird. Sorry, I mean he's not right."

"I thought I had explained my son's condition the other night."

"Ya kinda did, but Kashandra say yo Tim bit her titty, said almost nothin', and she thought he died when he finished."

"He bit her breast . . . slightly, but the skin wasn't broken. Tim has limited mental abilities. He didn't know what he had done. I told you about that. I hope you're not going to back out. You're not getting cold feet are you?"

"No, Miss Mary, but, honey, I charge more for weird sex."

Mary stomped on the brake. She glared at Quickie. "I assure you there is nothing *weird* about what I want for my son—no whips, no chains, no pain. Nothing weird."

"Well . . . okay" Quickie said. "Let's do it, honey."

Mary sniffed the air. *"What's that smell?"*

"Ya like my new perfume?" Quickie asked then smiled.

Mary shook her head. "I'm allergic. Please don't wear it again."

Mary left Swamp Town feeling perturbed. She kept her cool and listened while Quickie hummed "Nobody Knows the Trouble I've Seen" for the sixteenth time.

"Quickie, please hum something different. Humming the same thing over and over gets on my nerves."

"Sorry, Miss Mary. I'll give ma throat a rest."

Seconds later, Quickie hummed "Jingle Bells."

"Quickie, I thought you were going to rest your throat. Are you *nervous*?"

"Gotta admit I is—a little. I'll be okay, honey. Don't ya worry none. I'll take care of your boy."

"I don't want you feeling you *have* to do this," Mary said. "You shouldn't feel I'm pressuring you."

"No, I wanna do it, honey. I need the money. I'm ready ta get started."

"We're almost there," Mary said, turning onto the alley-street providing access to her garage, which she opened with her remote.

"Nice place ya got here, honey," Quickie said, scanning the rear of the house.

"Thanks."

They entered the house from the garage. Quickie followed Mary along a hall, stepping over strewn clothes. Stopping at the foot of the stairs, Mary repeated the information she had given Kashandra.

"Any questions?" Mary asked.

"No? Then let's go upstairs." At the top of the stairs, Mary pointed to a bedroom. "You can undress in there. I'll get Tim ready while you undress."

With everything ready, Mary addressed naked Quickie who stood in the hall. "Come in and meet Tim."

Tim stood at the foot of his bed, naked and masturbating.

"Stop that!" Mary said, moving Tim's hand away.

Oh God, Quickie thought. *What've I gotten myself into? This is the palest, skinniest, white boy I ever seen. Oh Lordie, look at that thing. That could hurt.*

"Tim, this is Quickie," Mary said.

"Qik," he said.

"Yes, Qik," Mary said. "You and Qik are going to have fun. You remember Kash? Well, Qik is going to make fun like Kash."

"Kash. Fun."

Tim stared at Quickie's breast as she extended her hand in greeting. She must have thought Tim would return the gesture, instead he grabbed her left breast.

"Oh Lordie!" Quickie yelled. "This kid is really into titty ain't he?"

"Yes, he has a fascination with breasts, but he has never seen a tattoo before, and I've never seen one so large it covered the breast. He just wants to suck on your breast so let him."

"Well, I guess so."

His mouth open, Tim's head shook as it moved toward the breast. Suddenly he yelled, "Yum!"

The shrillness of Tim's voice so startled Quickie that she backed away.

Tim must have thought Qik wanted to deprive him of her breast, so he screamed his displeasure.

"Oh, God," Mary said, "rub his penis. That's the only way to quiet him."

"Honey, I ain't never given a hand job to a screaming man."

"Just do it!" Mary said, grabbing Tim's arms from the rear. He screamed and struggled to get free.

Quickie stroked him as if getting a "John" off before his wife came up the stairs.

"Slow down!" Mary said. "Just slow and easy."

Quickie slowed her hand and seconds later, Tim quieted.

Mary released his arms. "There. That's better."

When Quickie removed her hand, Tim grabbed his penis and masturbated.

"Stop that," Mary said and grabbed his hand. "Let's get you two to bed." She turned to Quickie. "Let him suckle your breast then get him to mount you."

"Honey, I ain't no animal. I ain't hanging on no wall, and I don't do trapezes."

"No, no. I meant get him on top of you, for intercourse."

"You want us ta fuck?"

"That's one way to put it," Mary said.

"Then why didn't ya say so."

Quickie moved to the middle of the bed then lay on her left side as instructed.

Mary restrained Tim while he stared at Qik's jiggling breasts

"Stay close, honey," Quickie said, "in case he goes all crazy."

"Jiggle your breast more," Mary said. "That will hold his attention."

Qik's moving breast caught Tim's attention. He hurried to the bed where he stretched out, facing her, then attached his mouth to the right breast.

"Yum," he mumbled over and over.

"He sho is a titty man, ain't he, honey?" Quickie asked, staring at Mary.

"He's still erect. See if you can guide him inside."

"Honey, it's your money." Quickie soon got Tim inside.

"Now, slowly roll onto your back," Mary said. "I'll help get him on your belly, so he can stay connected."

Quickie grabbed Tim's head and held it against her breast as she rolled onto her back.

Mary pushed on Tim's hips, aligning them over Quickies. "Okay, Quickie, do your thing,"

Quickie planted her feet on the mattress then gyrated her hips. "Want it to happen quick?" she asked as if doing nothing more than filing her nails.

"Do what you do best," Mary said. "Nature will dictate what happens."

"Honey, my titty is gettin' sore. He's gotta switch."

"Okay," Mary said, gripping Tim's head, "Are you ready?"

Quickie squeezed her free nipple, causing it to protrude. Mary pried Tim's mouth from Quickie's breast and moved his head to the waiting nipple. He attacked it like a leech.

"He slipped out down there," Quickie said.

"For God's sake, get him back in," Mary yelled.

"I'm tryin'. . . but it ain't easy, hon. He's humping my belly."

Mary got onto the bed, stood over Tim, and pulled

his hips upwards. "See what you can do now."

Quickie grabbed Tim and, despite his pelvic thrusts, guided him. "He's in."

Mary got off the bed and sat in the chair as Tim continued sucking on Quickie's breast.

"Hey, kid. Take it easy," Quickie yelled. "Take it easy!"

"Sorry if he's a little rough," Mary said, getting out of the chair to monitor the situation. "Rub the back of his head. Sometimes that calms him."

Suddenly, Quickie slapped Tim. "Hey! Easy on the tit!"

Tim released her breast, stopped thrusting his hips, screamed, and then cried.

"What the hell have you done?" Mary yelled, rushing to Tim's side. She pulled him off Quickie then slapped her.

"You son-of-a-bitch. No one slaps my son." Mary climbed onto the bed and cradled Tim in her arms. "Mama's here. It's going to be okay. Shhhh. Mama's here. Okay."

Quickie stood on the floor holding her slapped face.

Mary rocked Tim and stroked his head. He sucked his thumb and whimpered.

"Get out of here!" Mary yelled. "Nobody treats my baby like that. Get your clothes on and get out of here."

Quickie hurried from the room. "Honey, I don't need this shit. No white boy gonna bite me and get away with it."

Oh, God. What have I done? Still rocking Tim, Mary thought, *I need that woman. I'd better*

140

apologize. I've got to get her back.

Mary helped Tim into a fetal position, put his thumb in his mouth and stroked his head as he continued to cry.

"Momma will be right back. Stay here, okay."

Rushing from the room, Mary yelled, "Quickie! I'm sorry. I'm sorry. Please, let me apologize."

Mary entered the bedroom as Quickie pulled her dress over her head. "Honey, I ain't never been treated like that! Never!"

"I'm sorry," Mary said, hugging Quickie. "I lost my head. I apologize. It's just that no one, not even me, has ever slapped him."

"He *needed* slappin'." Quickie's voice shook with anger. "Honey, I told him ta take it easy, and he didn't. I don't take that shit from *no* man!"

"He's not responsible . . . not like other men. Please, forgive him. He likes you."

"Honey, I can put up with about anythin' but this is gonna cost money."

"We'll work out something. Will you come back?"

"Honey, I'm a workin' girl. I need the money. Get me at the bar. At eight. In three days."

"Okay, but right now I need to spend time with Tim. Got to see if I can calm him. I'll get your money, but would you mind calling a taxi?"

Mary continued to bra-feed Tim, see patients at the office, make periodic trips to pick up breast milk, and chauffeur Kashandra and Quickie. The stress extracted a physical, emotional, and psychological toll. She grew tired and anxious but gained no insight into her problem or how to lessen her stresses.

After a busy day at the office, she had seen her last patient and sat at her desk, feeling wilted.

Her fellow physician and practice owner, John, knocked on her door. "God, Mary, you look worn out."

Mary wiped a tear away. "Oh. It's you. Come in, John."

"How are you doing?"

"I'm fine."

"Mary, I've known you for a while, and I'm aware of the concerns you have for Tim, but—"

"But what?" Mary said, sitting upright and glaring at him.

"I'm concerned. A lot," John continued. "You've changed over the years. Something serious is happening to you."

"What the hell are you talking about?" Mary said with a tinge of anger.

"Like that. The tone of your voice. You're always angry, on edge. The nurses, and a few patients, have made comments about changes in your personality. And look at yourself. You've lost weight. Your hair's a mess, and your clothes are rumpled. You're not professional looking *or* acting. You look tired."

"Sorry, if I'm not up to your standards. Yes, I'm tired. I work hard."

John reached across her desk and patted her hand. "You can't go on like this. You need a break. Time for yourself."

Weepy eyed, Mary said, "You know I have to keep working. I'm not a wealthy woman. My hours are limited and that limits my income."

"As a part of your employment contract, you have

disability income protection."

"Yeah but I'm not disab— Oh. I get it. You think I'm cracking up. Going crazy."

"No. But I'm concerned you have more on your shoulders than you can carry. I want you to take some time, with pay, but . . . you have to see a therapist. You choose who you talk with, but you have to see someone—right away.

Mary burst into tears. John moved to her side and tried to hug her.

Mary jerked back. "Get away from me! You talk about stress and now you pile it on by suggesting I'm going crazy." Glaring, she said, "Thanks for nothing."

"Mary. You know that's not what I meant. You're like family. I'm worried for you, your wellbeing, and Tim's wellbeing. You need help."

Gladys, an office nurse, walked by the open door and heard Mary shouting. "Doctors, is everything okay here?"

John nodded. "Gladys, would you drive Doctor Snow home?"

"I don't need Gladys or anyone else to drive me."

"Mary, you're in no shape to drive," John said, looking at Gladys. "Please see that Doctor Snow gets home safely. Mary, give me a call tomorrow and let me know your plans."

Mary picked up Quickie at the bar on a regular basis.

After three months of monogamous sexual interludes with Tim, Quickie announced, in the middle of a car ride, "Miss Mary, I think I'm pregnant."

"You can't be!" Mary yelled, stopping the car and feigning outrage. *I'm so happy!* "Didn't you know when you were vulnerable?"

"Vul what?"

"Didn't you know the time of the month when you could get pregnant?"

"Kinda, but a woman can't be sure, honey."

"Fuck!" Mary said, striking the steering wheel and thinking, *This is good.* She patted Quickie's hand. "Don't you worry. I'll take care of you."

"Seein' you're a baby doctor and all, I'd hope ya would."

"How did you know I'm a baby doctor?"

"First time in your house, I saw yo diploma or whatever they call that paper thing. You an Ob doc."

"Yes. I am."

Mary continued the drive, thinking of ways she could capitalize on Quickie's pregnancy.

"Honey, guess this means I can't work no more?"

"You're wrong. You can work all you want," Mary said, driving her car onto her alley street. "The more the better."

Quickie stared at Mary. "You mean that?"

"I do."

"That's good 'cause I need the money."

"Then get upstairs and get to work," Mary said, pulling into her garage. "Tim is expecting you."

Mary consulted psychologist Doctor Miller because Doctor Green had demanded it. However, she did not admit to the specialist, or herself, that she had trouble dealing with her circumstances. She remained in total denial. She could not admit she needed to improve her personal appearance in order to present a professional facade.

Mary told Doctor Green she had seen a psychologist, but she did not tell him she had had only two visits before she returned to part-time practice.

Mary saw fewer and fewer patients after their first visit. If it hadn't been for the system of assigning new patients to doctors on a rotating basis, she would not have any patients.

Kashandra and Quickie continued to service Tim, but Mary noted that Quickie's large belly interfered with Tim's ability to copulate.

"Quickie, you're getting big," Mary said, "and you're close to delivery time. I want you to stay here, until the baby comes. I wouldn't want you to go into labor at home and have an ambulance take you to a hospital where I don't have admitting privileges. I couldn't care for you."

"Mighty kinda you, Miss Mary."

"Why don't you move into the room where you've been undressing? It has everything you need."

"That would be easier on me . . . and you too, honey. I'll bring my things when I come next time."

"Does Kashandra know you're pregnant?"

"Not sure, honey. We don't see each other since we ain't working the street anymore. She lives blocks from me."

That's good, Mary thought. "I'll tell Kashandra that I won't need her services for a while. That is if you don't mind working every day. Your money should add up quickly."

"Thanks, honey. Money's good."

"Does the sex bother you?" Mary asked. "If it does, put a pillow under your hips."

"I'll try it, but Tim being on ma belly ain't good, honey."

"Maybe you two should do it lying on your sides? He could still suckle your breast."

"Okay wit me," Quickie said. "I'll give it a try."

One day while watching Quickie and Tim, Mary said, "Tim has had his mouth on your breast so much I hadn't noticed that he's drinking your milk." *That's good.*

"But shouldn't I be savin' it for the baby?"

"Don't you worry. You'll make all the milk the baby needs and more." *Oh, God. She's concerned about the baby. My son can't have a half-breed child, and I don't want a grandchild—not this one. Neither I nor Tim needs it. The only thing he needs is her milk.*

Quickie had trouble walking. Twenty days before her due date, she complained of back pain that caused her to spend most of the day in bed. However, four times a day, she waddled to Tim's room to provide breast-milk meals. Once a day, they had intercourse.

Quickie thought, *What would mama say if she saw me doing this shit. This ain't normal but neither is working the streets. On the other hand, the money's good. Very good and there's no pimp to pay and no gettin' beat up. Besides, I'm gonna have a baby in a rich family. We oughta live well after it's born.*

After months of intercourse, Tim's sexual thrusts became deeper and more rapid. One day as he climaxed, Quickie felt wet. She experienced a short, sharp pain in her pelvis and yelled, "Mary, come here. Quick! Miss Mary. Somethin' happened."

Mary rushed into Tim's room. "What's wrong?"

Quickie clutched her belly and moaned. Tim continued to suckle her breast. "Honey, I'm wet . . . down there."

Mary pushed Tim away. "The sheets are wet and bloody, and Tim, you need a shower. You have blood all over you. Go sit in the shower. I'll give you a bath in a few minutes." Tim hesitated. "Now!" Mary yelled.

Tim surrendered Quickie's breast and rolled onto his back.

"Don't you worry, Quickie," Mary said. "Your water broke. The baby will be here soon."

"Oh, Lordie! When?"

"Can't be sure. Could be one to four days. Come. Let's get you to your own bed."

As Quickie stood up, a gush of placental fluid flowed across the floor. With a look of horror, Quickie asked, "Is the baby here?"

"Not yet," Mary said. "That's just womb water."

Mary pulled the sheets from Tim's bed, dried Quickie, and then helped her to her bedroom.

"You rest," Mary said. "You could start cramping anytime. Is this your first baby?"

"Number one."

"Cramping episodes will get closer and closer as you get close to delivering," Mary said. "Stay in bed, except to go to the bathroom. I'll look in on you often, but right now, I have to bathe Tim."

"Honey, ya not gonna leave me alone are ya?"

"I'm going to give Tim a shower, and then I have to go to the office—just for an hour. Nothing will happen during that time."

Mary bathed Tim, put him to bed, and then returned to Quickie's room.

"Quickie, I'm going to the office. You'll be alright, but call my direct line if you need me."

"Honey, I don't wanna be alone. Please, stay wit me 'til this shit's over."

"I assure you, you'll be okay for an hour, but I want to have a feel of your womb's opening before I leave."

Mary went to Quickie's dresser where she had stored equipment for Quickie's home delivery. She watched as Mary opened a white cloth-covered tray and removed a shiny speculum.

"On your back, bend your knees, and open your legs," Mary said as she inserted the speculum and inspected Quickie's birth canal. "So far so good. Now, I'm going to use my gloved finger to examine your womb. "Hmmm . . . Everything's okay. You'll be fine, until I return."

"You sho, honey?"

"You're going to be alright. Your water broke. That's all. It could be several days before labor starts."

"Doctor Mary, I'm scared."

"Relax. I'll be back in an hour."

Quickie began to cry. "Mama, if you up there in heaven, watch over me.

You gonna have a grandbaby."

Chapter Eleven

Two days after Quickie's water broke, Mary asked her how she felt.

"I've been feeling hot."

Mary touched Quickie's forehead. "Have you been sweating?"

"Sweatin'? It comes and goes, honey. Once I had a chill, but it didn't last long."

"Had any discharge . . . down there?"

"Some. Mostly when one of them cramps hits me."

"When did the discharge start?"

"Yesterday. Why ya asking, honey?"

"I need to examine you."

Mary examined Quickie's birth canal.

"Uh oh," Mary said, peering through the speculum.

"What ya see, Doc?"

"An infection. You'll need antibiotics. I have to get the medicine from the hospital, but I'll be back in an hour."

Mary had just left the house when Quickie had a chill. She and the bed shook, frightening her. Since she did not know the name of Mary's hospital, she could not phone Mary. "What am I gonna do?" she muttered through chattering teeth. She held out her hand to note its shaking. "Jesus, help me. Don't let me die. Please, don't let me die."

Quickie forced her shaking body out of bed to search for a blanket. She rummaged through several dresser drawers but found none. In the closet, she found several blankets on a low shelf. After selecting one, she stood up and felt dizzy. She fell against a shelf then slumped to the floor unconscious.

Minutes later, Quickie regained consciousness.

"Oh, God. What happened?" She rubbed a painful lump between her eyes. "Hallelujah. No blood." She looked at her painful right leg, twisted under her body.

Her extended left leg had been buried under items that fell from the shelves she struck as she fainted. She rubbed her aching right knee and moaned. After a minute or two, she straightened her right leg. The knee had swollen to twice its normal size.

"I gotta get outta here." Taking a few seconds, she got on her left knee. She wiped sweat from her brow then tried to put weight on the right leg. "Lordie, it hurts!" She cried, clutched her knee, and fell back on the floor.

Between the pain in her swollen knee, the size of a cantaloupe, fever, and a shaking chill, she failed three attempts to stand. "I can't do it! I can't." *Oh God. What am I to do?* Filled with fear, rage, pain, and sorrow, Quickie sobbed. She rolled onto her side, curled up as much as possible, and pulled the blankets over her shaking body. Her teeth chattered as sweat rolled from her pained face awash in tears. *Hope I ain't dying.*

Tim walked into Quickie's bedroom and sat on the floor beside her. For a moment, they stared at each other. He then attempted to pull her breast to his lips.

"I can't fight ya off, boy."

Tim lay beside Quickie and got a nipple in his mouth. He licked his lips then spit. He acted as if he did not like the wet breast or the taste of sweat. Appearing perplexed, he returned to his room.

After what felt like a year in prison, Quickie heard the front door open. "Up here!" she yelled. "Help me!"

Mary ran up the stairs.

Quickie lay half inside the closet, crying and sweating.

"Poor baby," Mary said, kneeling beside her. "Are you hurt?"

"I passed out, hurt my head, and twisted my leg, honey.

"Knee hurts like hell, but I don't think I broke nothin'."

"Let's get you up," Mary said. "Hold onto the doorframe, and on the count of three, I'll pull you up. Are you ready? One. Two. Three."

Using all her strength, Quickie rose to her feet.

"You're drenched," Mary said. "Been sweating a lot?"

"Like a pig, honey. Had one of dem shaking chills. That's why I looked for a blanket. Blacked out when I stood up."

"Let's get you covered. Sit on the edge of the bed while I get you a gown."

Once Quickie had donned the gown, she went to bed while Mary prepared a bottle of intravenous antibiotics.

This won't save the baby, Mary thought, *but it will protect Quickie. She needs to keep making milk.*

After a quick stick, the IV needle settled into Quickie's vein. Mary taped it in place. She opened the valve on the tubing and watched the antibiotic flow into Quickie's vein.

"There," Mary said, smiling. "You should feel better in two hours. Now rest. I'll get dinner ready."

Mary mixed everything needed for dinner and placed it in the oven. *Now it's time to feed Tim.* She filled the latex bra with breast milk, strapped it on, and waited for the milk to warm.

She climbed into bed with Tim and nursed him with the bra. As he suckled, she hugged him, caressed his back, and kissed his forehead. He smiled. Mary felt a warm sense of love. "Yes, mother loves you very much." She caressed his back and head then sang Tim's favorite song of motherly love.

"Mommy loves me."

Mary smiled and glanced toward the door to make sure she had left it ajar, in case Quickie called for help.

Tim emptied both bra cups and then suckled one of Mary's breasts while kneading the other.

Mary told herself, *I need a rest, but I don't know when I'll be able to get it, so why not rest here for a while?*

Startled, Mary sat up. "What?"

"Mary!" Quickie yelled.

Mary looked around the room. *God, I must have fallen asleep.*

"Something's burning, honey," Quickie yelled.

"Shit. It's the meat loaf."

"Mary," Quickie yelled again. "Something's burning."

"Heard you, Quickie." Mary sat on the side of the bed, shook sleep from her head, and glanced at Tim. "Thank God he's asleep. I couldn't handle a tantrum now."

Still wearing the latex bra, Mary rushed from Tim's room.

Quickie stood in her doorway holding her abdomen. "What the fuck you wearin', honey?" Quickie asked, staring at the black bra.

"We'll talk later," Mary said, dashing down the stairs. "Got to save the house and the meatloaf." *Shit! What am I going to tell her about the bra?*

Minutes later, Mary, dressed in a bathrobe, returned to Quickie's room and presented to her a tray of salvaged meat loaf. Mary placed the tray on Quickie's lap then Mary sat down in a chair.

"Sorry. It's a little burned," Mary said, "but I fell asleep."

Taking a bite, Quickie said, "I've eaten worse, hon." Suddenly, Quickie yelled and grabbed her belly. "Oh God!"

"What's wrong?" Mary asked, moving the tray aside.

"My belly." Quickie winced from pain. "It's my belly, honey. Crampin' something awful. Oh, God! It hurts."

A tear trickled down Quickie's face, twisted from pain.

"Hang on," Mary said in a calm voice. "Let's get you settled in bed." Mary helped Quickie lay flat in the bed then felt her belly. "Your womb is contracting. It's very hard."

Quickie scrunched her face. "Oh, God! It hurts. It hurts!" She stared into Mary's face. Don't dem cramps ever let up, honey?"

"A little," Mary said. "Lie back."

"I gotta have something for the pain."

"Can't give you anything yet," Mary said, pulling the sheet to Quickie's chin. "It would slow your labor."

"Honey, I heard of that natural birth shit, and I want nothin' ta do with it. Me and pain ain't friends."

"When you're farther along, I'll give you a spinal. That should relieve you."

"Oh shit! Another one's coming," Quickie yelled, clutching her belly. "Oh, God! Oh, God!"

"Those contractions are close. I'd better do an exam." Mary pulled on a rubber glove then pushed Quickie's legs apart. After examining her, Mary said, "Your cervix is fully dilated *and* thinned."

"What the fuck does that mean, Hon?" Quickie asked through her pain.

"Your baby is coming faster than I thought. The next time you have a contraction, bear down—like you were having a hard bowel movement. Understand?"

"Gottcha, honey. Oh, God! I think another one's startin'."

"Bear down, Quickie. Push! Push with all you have!"

"I'm tryin', Damn it! I'm . . . trying. Uhhhh!"

Between grunting and panting, Quickie yelled with pain.

"I'll get the spinal kit ready," Mary said, patting Quickie's arm. "Be right back."

"Don't worry, honey. I ain't going nowhere. Oh, God! Oh, God! I'm crampin'. Shiiiiittt! That's one determined baby."

Mary returned with a surgical tray and placed it on

the dresser. "I want to explain what I'm going to do before you get too far into labor."

"I don't need no medical sermon, honey. Do what ya gotta do but kill the damn pain. Oh, God! Another one's startin'. Oh, God! Oh . . . God!"

"Bear down, girl. Push! Push!"

Mary sat at Quickie's side, offering moral, physical, and emotional support. Every ten minutes, she replaced a cold cloth on Quickie's forehead.

After four hours of labor, Mary said, "I need to do another pelvic exam. Let's see if it's time for a spinal."

After the exam, Mary said, "It's time. Let's get you on your side."

Mary's arranging instruments on a metal tray did not break the tension.

"Something cold," Mary said, wiping antiseptic on Quickie's mid-back.

"That stuff smells awful," Quickie said.

"You'll feel some pressure, but it's from my finger. I'm feeling for a spot to insert the needle."

"Do it quick, honey."

"Okay. You'll feel a little stick. I'll be injecting some Lidocaine to numb you."

"Damn!' Quickie exclaimed. "That hurts, honey. For God's sake, get it over wit!"

"There . . . that's done. Now, the spinal needle." After a second or two, Mary said, "The anesthetic is in." She dropped the used needle onto the tray. "You should feel relief now. Your legs may get numb, but don't let that bother you."

"Hope it works quick."

"It will."

Mary informed Quickie about how labor and delivery would proceed. "You have to bear down when you have contractions," Mary fluffed Quickie's pillow. "You won't be completely pain free, but there will be much less."

"Honey, shouldn't you be boilin' water or tearin' sheets?" Quickie asked, grimacing at the onset of another contraction.

"Why? You want a boiled baby?" Mary chuckled. "That boiling stuff happens only in the movies. It keeps the expectant father from under foot."

"Another cramp's startin'!"

"Push girl! Push."

Quickie had labored off and on for thirty minutes when she had a particularly strong contraction. "Oh, Jesus!" she yelled.

Mary pushed Quickie's legs apart and examined her birth canal. "It's crowning. I can see the head."

"Does that mean the baby's comin', honey?"

Quickie squeezed her eyelids shut then grunted.

"Yes! The head is out. Push . . . Push with all you got, girl."

Semi-upright, Quickie grunted and pushed her baby out of the birth canal. A gush of amniotic fluid followed, and she slumped onto the bed.

Without flourish, Mary clamped then cut the umbilical cord. She wrapped the baby in a blanket and left the room. Moments later, she returned.

Resting on the bed, Quickie panted, eyes closed.

"We need to deliver the placenta," Mary said. "I'll be massaging your belly—hard." She firmly rubbed her fist from the top of Quickie's abdomen toward her pelvis. "This may hurt a little and might take a few minutes. Try to relax."

"When can I see my baby?" Quickie asked, staring at Mary.

"When we get the placenta out."

Quickie let her legs fall flat on the bed, forced the back of her head into the pillow and closed her eyes.

"It's out," Mary said. "I know you're tired so rest."

Mary sat in the bedside chair and closed her eyes. *Glad that's over.* A moment later, she jerked herself awake. *I can't go to sleep. Not now.*

She reexamined Quickie, massaged her abdomen, and felt the uterus contract as it should.

"Can I see ma baby?" Quickie asked as Mary dropped Quickie's placenta into a plastic bag.

"Quickie . . . I need to tell you something . . . something unpleasant."

"Don't tell me my baby has two heads or web feet."

"Worse than that," Mary said.

"He's not missing arms or legs?"

"Quickie . . . he didn't make it."

"What you talkin', honey?"

"He's . . . dead. Your infection got into his lungs."

"No! Can't be! Let me see him. Let me see!" Panting and puffing, Quickie pushed herself upright in bed, her eyes filled with fear and horror. "No. No."

Mary left the room and returned with a blanketed bundle in her arms. "Here," she said, cradling the bundle in Quickie's arms.

Quickie stared at Mary as if asking what she should do. Mary raised a corner of the blanket.

Quickie stared at the baby's bluish-grey tan face, stared at the ceiling, and then cried. "Lord, why you gotta take my baby before he even sees his mother's face? Before he took one breath? He didn't get to see his aunties or cousins. Why God? Why?" She wiped her tears with the sheet then smiled. "He's beautiful." She looked at Mary. "He's got Tim's hair."

A wave of anger flowed over Mary. *How dare this whore think this baby has anything of Tim's.* "We have to notify the police . . . of the death," Mary said, in a monotone. "Then we can have him cremated."

"No!" Quickie yelled. "My baby's not gonna be burned like garbage. He's gonna get a Christian funeral at the mission. Kashandra's gotta see my baby."

Chapter Twelve

Mary knocked on Quickie's bedroom door.

"Quickie, it's been three days since the funeral, and Tim needs you. Go, let him have your milk or it will dry up."

"Miss Mary, I don't know if I can do that . . . not five or six times day."

"Remember, you're paid double your fee each time he's fed. If your baby had lived, you would have fed him more often than you're feeding Tim."

"I need the money, but . . . I don't wanna keep doing this."

"Shut up!" Mary yelled at the top of her voice. "Tim needs your milk."

Quickie appeared stunned and speechless on hearing Mary's outburst.

"We've discussed this long enough," Mary yelled. "Get your ass in there and feed him!"

"Don't ya yell at me, *bitch*! This girl ain't gonna be bossed around. Not by you. Not by nobody—especially a white bitch."

Mary grabbed Quickie's arm, twisted it behind her back and yelled, "You heard me. Get your ass in there. Now!"

Resisting Mary's physical and psychological pressure, Quickie tried to stand her ground, but Mary's yelling and arm-twisting caused the terrified woman to relent. She undressed and sulked into Tim's room.

"Now get on the bed!" Mary yelled.

Tim stopped playing with himself and stared at

Quickie's breasts as she moved to the center of the bed then took her feeding position. "This gotta stop," she mumbled.

"I heard that," Mary said, waiting for Tim to settle in before she left. From the hall, she said, "We'll talk later."

Despite trying to quietly lock Tim's door, Quickie surely heard the loud lock's dead bolt slide into place. Mary leaned against the hall side of the door. *I've got to do something, or she'll leave. Can't let that happen. She's making milk now.* Mary struck the door with her fist and mumbled, "Shit! What do I—?" She thought a moment. "Desperate times require desperate things."

Tim had had his fill of breast milk and slept.

Quickie stared at the ceiling, contemplating her situation. Befuddled, she crept to the door and tried the knob. "Shit. That bitch done locked me in."

She paced the cold rubber floor, glancing at the clock, high on the wall. "Shit. It ain't working." She guessed at the hours of her captivity "That woman has been gone a long time."

Tired of pacing the cold floor and hating the firmness of the straight back chair, Quickie sat on the edge of the bed, awakening Tim.

He must have thought feeding time had arrived and attached himself to Quickie's breast.

What the hell do I do now? Shit! It's near his feeding time. Might as well feed the idiot. I can't get out, and I don't wanna run around this room until his mama comes back.

She closed her eyes for a minute then fell asleep.

Two hours later, Quickie awoke. She felt something cold and heavy on her right wrist. Drowsy, she tried moving her right arm to determine the cause of the strange sensation, but her arm would not move. "What the fuck?" She bolted upright, staring at her wrist. "That bitch done handcuffed me to the fuckin' bed! "Mary! Where the fuck you at, woman? Get in here, now! Damn it. I said *NOW*!" *Why did she do this?*

Quickie tugged at the handcuff as if it might fall away. She pushed Tim from her breast and yelled for Mary. Tim fought Quickie's physical assaults, but she pushed him away. As expected, the denial of her breast caused him to scream at the top of his voice.

"Scream. I don't care. Now you'll stay away from me."

Quickie yelled, "Mary, you bitch. Where you at?" Getting off the bed, she had to stand in a hunched position because of the handcuff. "Mary! Get your white ass in here and undo these fuckin' cuffs!"

Attracted by Quickie's dangling breasts, Tim crawled across the bed and targeted a nipple.

"Get away, ya white bastard!" Quickie screamed, striking him with her free hand. "Get away from me!"

Tim ignored several punches, grabbed her left breast, and squeezed it hard.

"Son-of-a bitch! Stop, ya bastard!" She slapped Tim's face while trying to free her squeezed breast. "That hurts damn it."

Tim cried but got a nipple in his mouth, sucking with the force of a sand dredger.

"Shit! He's going ta suck it off," Quickie yelled, pummeling him. "Mary!"

161

Suddenly, the door opened. "Stop yelling," Mary said, almost in a whisper. "You'll wake the dead."

"Get this off!" Quickie yelled, pulling at the cuff. "And get this honkey off me. Now!"

"Sorry; I can't do that. He needs you and your milk. I can't risk having you run away."

"Ya can't do this." Quickie said, attempting to kick Tim off the bed. "I ain't no slave. Let me the fuck go!"

Mary grabbed Quickie's kicking legs. "Get used to it. This is where you'll be living now."

"Bitch, this ain't legal. It's illegal ya hear. *Illegal*!" Quickie sobbed and slumped to the floor, her tethered hand high in the air.

Dodging Quickie's spittle, Mary said, "I have your dinner in the hall."

Tim retreated to a corner and masturbated. This gave Quickie's sore breast a respite.

Mary went to the hall and brought back a plastic tray holding a Styrofoam plate with boiled frankfurters, a fried hamburger patty, an apple, and a Styrofoam cup of milk.

"Everything here is nutritious and will help you make milk. Sorry, but you'll have to eat it out-of-hand. Can't risk giving you a knife or fork."

Mary placed the tray on the bed and turned to leave.

Quickie hurled the tray at Mary. Food and milk splattered across the floor.

"My, my," Mary said. "You missed. I hope you don't get hungry."

"Let me loose!"

"Yelling doesn't help. See you in the morning."

"I gotta piss," Quickie yelled, shaking her cuffed

hand. "Get this off me."

"Use the floor drain. The cuff stays on."

"I gotta shit!"

"Good night."

Mary closed the door, and from outside, turned off Tim's lights.

Curled on the bed, Quickie awoke with bright light pouring through the window at the foot of the bed. Tim slept beside her. She tried not to wake him while she slid off the bed, squatted on the floor, and relieved herself. A long trail of urine inched across the floor and disappeared into the floor drain.

Moments later, Mary entered, carrying a tray of food. "Hello, Quickie. I see Tim is still asleep. Hope you had a good sleep."

"Not with a damn cuff holding me like a June bug on a string."

Mary placed the tray on the bed. "Enjoy." As she left, she said, "Better eat it because there's nothing more for hours."

Hungry, Quickie sat upright on the bed. She tried not to spill the milk as she reached over Tim for the food. About to bite into a piece of toast, Tim grabbed her breast. "I don't give a fuck what you do kid. I'm eatin' my breakfast."

Quickie refused to lie on the bed, despite Tim's efforts to pull her down. She gulped milk, then grabbed Tim by the wrist and pulled him to her side of the bed where she kicked him to the floor. He landed with a thud. "Shit! He landed on his head. Hope he's dead."

Within a second or two, Tim rose to his feet. As if nothing had happened, he reached for her left breast.

Still sitting on the edge of the bed, Quickie pulled Tim between her knees, guided his head toward her right breast and continued eating. "Fuck you kid! I'm hungry, and I'm gonna eat no matter what."

Mary stood at the edge of the bed. "Glad to see you two getting along so well. If you've finished with the food, I'll take the tray."

"Take it, but I gotta shit."

"Use the floor," Mary said. I'll hose it down. Besides, I need to clean up the mess you created when you threw dinner at me last night."

"What's come over you, woman?" Quickie asked as a look of confusion crossed her face. "Why you treat me like this? I ain't no *animal*. I'm Quickie—a human. People don't treat people like this—even if they black. Not no more."

"My, my," Mary said. "How unappreciative you are. You have free room and board, paid utilities, you earn money, and you perform a service just like in the old days, but the pay is better and your client is safe. There are people who would kill for a job with these benefits."

"But they don't piss and shit on the floor. They got their freedom."

"Yes, but there's someone to cook for you and clean up after you," Mary said. "You have a maid. No, *you* have a *servant*. *I'm* your servant."

"You full of shit, honey. You a kidnapper. They send people like you ta jail—or the loony bin."

Mary reached across the bed and removed the tray. "Keep Tim happy."

Quickie remained cuffed to the bed for seven days. Each day began and ended the same way—eat, sleep, nurse, fuck, poop, and pee. "Now, I know what it's like ta be one of them breeding dogs—always caged. Used and tormented. God, I gotta get outta here!"

Mary placed Quickie's breakfast tray on the bed and watched as she ate and Tim suckled. "Glad to see you aren't so angry anymore," Mary said.

"I've always been a clean woman," Quickie said, wiping a crumb from her breast. "I ain't had no bath for a week. Please, I gotta clean myself. You don't want Tim havin' sex with an unclean woman do ya?"

Mary stared out the window. "I'll arrange something at lunch time."

At noon, Mary returned with the usual tray, but this time, she insisted Quickie drink her milk before eating. With no reason not to, she drank it as Mary nudged the bottom of the cup upward.

"There. That wasn't so bad was it?" Mary asked.

"Now, can I eat?"

"By all means. Enjoy it."

After taking a few bites of food, Quickie said, "Strange. My head feels light. *God,* I'm feeling dizzy. You drug me?"

"Don't worry. It's something to help you relax, so we can get you showered."

"I can barely stay awake," Quickie said, slurring her words.

Mary pulled a pair of handcuffs from her pocket.

She placed one new cuff around each of Quickie's wrist then removed the cuff attached to the bed.

She pulled Quickie to her feet and led her to the shower, where she guided Quickie's butt onto Tim's bath chair in the middle of the shower. Mary turned on the preset valve, sending water through an automatic soap dispenser. Suds soon covered Quickie's body.

Tim walked to the shower and attempted to suckle Quickie's breast.

"Go play," Mary said, grabbing Tim's arm and pushing him toward the bed where he sat and pleasured himself.

Quickie complied with Mary's request for various body parts to be moved to expedite showering. Once completed, Mary dried Quickie then took her to the bed. Mary cuffed Quickie's right wrist to the bed rail, then removed the other cuffs.

"Now, sleep it off," Mary said, and headed for the door as Tim crawled onto the bed to suckle Quickie's breast.

The next morning, Mary heard a knock at her kitchen door. Looking through the door window, she saw Joan, the neighbor who lived across the alley from Mary's house.

No matter her destination, Joan, a slim woman, always dressed as if she were a model and president of the Junior League. Her makeup and hair looked as if she had just left a beauty parlor.

Opening the door, Mary said, "Good morning, Joan. What has you up so early?"

"Sorry to bother you, but may I borrow your bike?"

"Having a problem, are you?" Mary asked, opening the door wider.

"Yeah. I want to ride with the girls, but my bike has a flat, and Hank can't get it fixed until tomorrow, so I thought of your bike."

"Hope mine isn't flat too. I haven't used it in while. Why don't you go around to the garage, and I'll open its door from inside? Meet you there in ten seconds."

Mary opened the garage door. "Here it is," she said, rolling the bike outside. "It's old, but it still works, and the tires aren't flat."

"I love these old Schwinns," Joan said. "I had one years ago . . . until Hank went into the bike business and insisted I get a new one."

"Yeah. This one's an oldie but a goodie. Enjoy your ride."

"What do you want me to do with it when I return?"

"Just lean it against the deck. I'll take care of it later."

Two months later, Mary noted Quickie appeared depressed. She often cried even though Tim slept.

I should do something for her, Mary thought, *or the stress is going to stop her milk production. I can't risk that.* After a minute of reflection, Mary said, "TV! I'll get her a TV. That should help her pass the time."

Mary arranged for the installation of a TV in Tim's room.

What am I to do with Quickie while the set is being installed? Ah. The dungeon. I'll keep her there while the man works.

Mary placed a breakfast tray on Tim's bed and

stood by, shifting her weight while watching Quickie scarf down the food.

"A man will be here today to install a TV set in this room. It will help you pass the time, but I need to move you to another place until the work is completed. I trust you'll cooperate. Don't make things difficult for either of us."

"You gonna drug me?"

"Should I?"

"You decide, honey. You know I got no say."

"I'll let you know."

At lunch time, Mary placed Quickie's food tray on the bed and took Tim from the room.

"Eat your lunch," Mary said, closing the door behind her.

Mary escorted Tim to the dungeon, which she had cleared of everything dangerous. As a makeshift bed, she placed pillows and blankets on one of the torture tables. She then locked him in and returned to the padded room with a pair of the former homeowner's leg shackles.

Quickie lay on the bed, eyes closed.

"Good," Mary said. "The drug is working."

Mary placed the shackles on Quickie's ankles, freed her cuffed wrist, and then rolled her onto her side. Mary cuffed Quickie's hands in front of her belly as Quickie opened her eyes.

Mary shook her. "Wake up." She slapped Quickie's face.

"Huh?" Quickie mumbled.

"Stand up. We have to go downstairs."

"Where . . .?"

"Come. I'll show you. Stand up."

Mary pulled Quickie to her feet. The shackles let her take twelve inch steps.

With her head bobbing, Quickie stared at her feet. "Mo cuffs?"

"Yes. Special ones. Hang onto my arm. We're going downstairs. Be careful." Mary shook Quickie. "Open your eyes, woman; watch where you step."

Accompanied by the sounds of clanging ankle chains, Quickie lumbered toward the top of the stairs.

"Don't step on the chain," Mary said, grabbing the handrails at the top of the stairs. "I'm going to back down the stairs so I can guide your feet down each tread. Let's go, girl. One step at a time."

Quickie hobbled down the stairs. On reaching the last step, she tried to descend a nonexistent step and fell on the floor.

"You okay?" Mary asked.

"Yep," Quickie mumbled. "But that's noooo fun."

"Let's get you up."

Mary helped Quickie to her feet then pulled the limping woman toward the basement stairs.

"My . . . ankle . . . hurts," Quickie mumbled.

"Okay. Okay. Let's get you down the steps."

"My . . . ankle . . . hurts."

"Sit," Mary said, easing Quickie to the kitchen floor just inside the opened door at the top of the basement stairs.

"Let me see your ankle."

Mary pushed the shackle above the part of the ankle to which Quickie had pointed. She noted a slight swelling. She pushed on the ankle causing Quickie to wince.

Maybe it's sprained. It'll do what I can now and worry later.

Propping Quickie against the kitchen doorjamb, Mary went to a room in the basement where she stored paint and several eighteen-inch-long wooden paint stirrers. *I can use these and electrical tape to splint her ankle.*

Minutes later, Mary said, "There. It's done." Mary examined the makeshift splint on Quickie's ankle. "Okay, let's get you to the basement. Slide down on your butt one step at a time."

The drowsy woman raised her head and mumbled, "My butt?"

"Yes, on your butt. Slide down one step at a time."

Mary backed down the steps while pulling Quickie's legs but avoiding the painful ankle. "Scoot, damn it . . . one step at a time."

Taking a minute per step, Quickie butt-bounced down each step. When she reached the bottom step, she said, "My back hurts . . ."

Mary pushed Quickie forward and examined her back. "Nothing bad. Just some abrasions. Nothing to worry about. Okay. Stand up."

Mary pushed her head under Quickie's cuffed wrists, snuggled her shoulder into Quickie's arm pit, and then helped the drowsy woman to her feet.

"Let's walk," Mary ordered, pulling Quickie for-ward.

Quickie whined. "Ankle . . . hurts."

"We'll take care of it later. I've got to get you to your new bed."

"Hurts!"

"Damn it! I said walk. Move your ass, woman! You are going in there no matter what."

Chapter Thirteen

Mary hustled Quickie toward the dungeon. Her splinted right ankle lagged behind as she hopped and limped. Despite sedation, pain registered on her face.

"Shit, this can't be happening," Mary murmured, "Not now."

"What . . .?" Quickie asked.

"I'm not talking to you. Move it!"

"Cold . . . ," Quickie said.

"Yeah, the basement is cool, but once we get where we're going, I'll get you a blanket. Now get the lead out!"

Mary lugged Quickie toward the dungeon. When Mary opened the dungeon door, she saw Tim pacing and masturbating.

"Qik," he said, approaching the drowsy woman.

"Give her a minute," Mary said, pushing Tim away. He returned causing Mary to yell, "Wait a minute! Damn it!"

Mary helped Quickie onto the bed-table and cuffed her wrist to the rail that encircled the periphery of the table.

"Cold . . .," Quickie mumbled. "Ankle hurts . . ."

"This should keep you warm," Mary said, covering Quickie with a wool blanket.

Mary got Tim onto the bed and helped him and Quickie onto their sides. Tim pulled the blanket off Quickie and suckled her breast. As he repositioned himself, he bumped Quick's injured ankle.

"Ow . . .!" Quickie moaned and stared at her ankle.

"Ankle . . . hurts!"

Her moaning did nothing to dampen Tim's interest in her breast. He continued to suckle while Quickie moaned in pain.

Mary noted the odd angle of Quickie's ankle. *Shit! It's broken!*

Mary adjusted the splint and covered Qik and Tim with the blanket. She watched Tim for a minute and then closed and locked the dungeon door.

Upstairs, she waited for the TV installation man. Half an hour later, the doorbell rang.

"Coming!" Mary yelled. She opened the door thinking, *Goodness. Blue eyes, blond hair. I thought this kind of guy existed only in romance novels.*

"Doctor Snow?" the serviceman asked.

"Yes."

"I'm Joe, from Cable Land.

"Come in, Joe." She scanned his tight, white shirt and snug grey slacks. "I've been expecting you." *I can't believe they sent you. Wow!*

Looking around, Joe asked, "Where do you want the TV installed?"

"My son's room." Mary pointed to the stairs. "Follow me, but don't get upset when you see the room. My son is handicapped and needs certain protections."

"Won't be disturbing him will I?"

"No. He's away while the TV is being installed."

"My older brother had problems. I know how stressful that can be. How old is your son?"

"Oh, God. Let's see . . . he's going on nineteen . . . maybe older." Mary led Joe into Tim's room. "Hope the room's padding doesn't appear cruel, but it's for his protection."

"Believe me, I understand. My brother lived in a room like this for most of his life—until he died."

"Sorry to hear that." Mary pointed to a spot, eight feet above the floor and to the right of the window. "Can you mount it there? Out of reach."

"Sure. Do you already have TV in the house?"

"One set. In the den. I use rabbit ears."

"Do you know if there's cable or where it enters the house?"

"Sorry, I don't."

"Mind if I look around . . . to see if there's a cable that could be used for the new set?"

"No. Go ahead."

"I'll start outside . . . maybe the front of the house. Can I get to the backyard from the front yard, or do I have to come through the house?"

"No. There's a walkway on the northside of the house." *God, I can't get over how good looking he is.*

"Great! See ya in a minute." Joe exited the front door to search for a cable entry site.

Mary closed the door then pulled its curtain back to watch Joe as he walked around, looking up at trees, light poles and the front of the house. He must have found nothing of interest because he walked toward the front of the house and gestured he would go around the house.

Mary moved room-to-room, watching Joe's head bob up and down as he passed several windows, still searching for a cable's entry point. *I can't get over how hot looking this guy is.*

Nice house, Joe thought. *This gal must have big*

bucks.

He examined the foundation stones and basement window frames for possible points of cable entry. He looked under the deck. *Strange. Why paint a basement window black and then break a pane to let light in? Just scrape off the paint. Oh well. No cable here. Let's see what's in the backyard.*

After scanning the backyard, he noted a dangling wire on an old lamp pole at the rear edge of the property. *That has to be the old cable. It's no good now. Wonder what kind of cable or connection boxes are in the basement?*

Mary peered out a kitchen window as Joe walked toward the kitchen door.

He waved and smiled.

Not only is he cute, he's friendly.

As Joe approached the steps to the back deck, he squatted and shined his flashlight under the boards. He stood, nodded, and then climbed the steps to the deck.

Mary opened the kitchen door. "Find what you were looking for?"

"Cable entry," he said. "The old cable probably entered the basement through a hole drilled in a basement window sash. From there who knows where it goes."

"What do you need to do now?"

Pointing toward the old lamp pole, he said, "I'll have to run new cable from there through the existing hole in the sash, across the basement then up the walls to your son's room."

Gripping her hands to hide their trembling, Mary

asked, "Can't you run the cable up the outside wall and into his room?"

"Sorry. I can't do that. Company policy. I have to run it the most direct, *protected* route. Cable is expensive. You don't want squirrels chewing on it or have it weather and fail."

"Well then, where do you start?"

"First, I have to make a connection on the pole then to a splitter-box in the basement. Sometime in the future you'll want to add more TVs. Hopefully, there's already a box there. If not, I'll install one. That'll cost a bit more, but *if* the original cable is intact, *and* it runs in the direction of the upstairs room, I might be able to use it. Otherwise, I'll install new cable."

"Okay. Why don't you start outside? Ring the back-door bell when you need to go to the basement."

Mary worried about what Joe might discover in the basement. She hadn't planned on the installer going there. *What if he needs to go inside the dungeon?* After a few minutes, Mary thought, *I'll have to postpone the installation. I'll tell him that Tim is in there—out of the way—and can't be disturbed. He knows about these things. He'll understand.*

Peering out a window and biting her nails, Mary watched Joe climb the lamp pole. She then moved to the kitchen door window for a better view. *Nice butt. Wonder if he's married? Mary, stop this! What the hell are you doing? He's probably all of twenty-five and not interested in an old woman like you.*

Mary poured herself a cup coffee and sat at the kitchen table where she watched Joe connect the cable. *Wonder what he looks like naked? Hairy? Hung? God!*

177

Mary, you're horny.

Joe completed the cable connections, shimmied down the pole, and then stretched cable behind him as he walked toward the back of the house. *I think I'm being watched.* At first, he felt uncomfortable. *She's not bad looking. A little old for me, but she might be a good lay. She might even want sex. Think I'll have some fun with her—string her along—see what happens.* He looked at his watch. *I'm due a lunch break after this job, so I'll use it for a nooner—if I'm lucky.*

Joe faked the need to scratch his chest. He scratched the spot repeatedly as he walked toward the back deck. Making it appear the shirt interfered with scratching, he opened its three top buttons, inserted his hand and scratched. The open shirt exposed much of his hairy, muscular chest. *Hope she likes this.* Joe pulled his shirt forward, looked at his chest, and scratched again. *This is fun.*

Mary opened the kitchen door. "How is everything?"

Scratching his bared chest, Joe said, "This place is filled with mosquitoes."

"They can be a bother. If the itch doesn't go away, let me know. I'll give you some cortisone cream."

"Thanks," he said. "I'm going to *push* the cable through the hole in the basement window sash. Would you mind going to the basement and *pull* it?"

Mary froze for a moment. *I hope he doesn't mean the dungeon window.* "Which window?" she asked.

Joe looked down. His gaze stopped for a split

second at his crotch. He then pointed to the deck. "The one under the deck."

Did he say dick? "Okay," Mary said, feeling relieved. "You start pushing and I'll start pulling." *Thank God!* she thought. *The cable is not going through the dungeon window. Can't believe I said that pushing, pulling stuff? It sounded suggestive.*

Joe's smile faded. He crawled under the deck then yelled, "Go to the basement and get ready."

Mary grinned. "I'm ready for whatever." *Girl, you are so brazen.*

Mary went to the basement and waited for the end of the cable to be pushed into view.

"Give it a minute," Joe yelled. "See it yet? I'm pushing it."

"Not yet," Mary yelled. *I wish he was pushing it.*

"Are you looking?" Joe yelled.

Mary glimpsed the cable at the right corner of the window sash. She grasped it, and yelled, "I have it!"

"Good! Pull it!"

Mary pulled on the cable, until she had pulled five or six inches through the hole. "How much more?"

"Lots more!"

Mary's phone rang in the kitchen. "Hey! I have to answer my phone. Can you finish without me?"

"Okay! You go ahead!"

"Let yourself in! The kitchen door's open!"

Mary ran to the ringing phone.

Rose, a nurse from Mary's office, had called. While they spoke, Joe walked into the kitchen shirtless. Dirt covered his chest and back.

"Sorry," he whispered. "It's dirty down there.

Didn't wanna get my shirt dirty."

Mary covered the handset mouthpiece. "Okay, Joe." She went back to talking to Rose but continued to eye Joe's chest and then his back muscles as he walked in the direction indicated by Mary. At the top of the basement steps, he looked back at Mary. She covered the mouthpiece of the phone and said, "It's down there. Window is on the left." As he descended the basement steps, Mary continued her conversation while ogling Joe's muscular back.

After the business part of her conversation, Mary said, "Rose, you wouldn't believe your eyes if you saw the serviceman working here. He's quite a hunk. He's shirtless and looks like one of those guys in a romance novel."

"Are you safe there . . . alone?" Rose asked.

Mary chuckled. "Maybe you should ask if *he's* safe."

Rose chuckled. "Don't do anything I wouldn't."

"From what I've heard about nurses that leaves me lots of wiggle room."

"Doctor Snow! *What* are you saying? Who's been talking?"

"Just gossip."

"Well, be careful," Rose said. "Sure you don't want company until the man—I mean the work—is finished?"

"I think I can handle myself. See you tomorrow."

"Can't wait to hear the whole story."

Mary hung up then went to check on the progress of the installation.

With a hand over her breast, she thought, *Should I do a little titty exposing? Hell. Why not?* She unbuttoned two buttons on her blouse, widening its opening and then crept down the basement stairs.

"Glad you're here," Joe said. "Would you pull while I coil up the excess cable?"

"Surely," Mary said, moving ahead of Joe, then grasping the cable where he pointed.

"Pull hard," he said, coiling the excess cable behind Mary.

She tugged and grunted.

"Not doing too well, huh? Let me show you." Joe moved behind her, extended his arms under hers and overlapped his hands on each of her cable-gripping hands. For a split second, his crotch rubbed her ass as he adjusted his stance behind her.

Mary's breath caught. *What a crotch.*

Joe gripped her hands. "Pull the cable up. If you pull down, it'll bind."

"I see," Mary said, pulling as instructed.

Joe maintained his grip on her hands.

Mary yanked the cable, faked a foot slip, and then fell backwards. The top of her head struck Joe's chest as he caught her.

"Glad I caught you," he said, staring at her exposed breasts.

"Me too," she said, staring at his cleavage. "I could have cracked my head on the floor."

"Let me help you up," he said, lifting her shoulders.

She grabbed each of his forearms and pulled herself up as he assisted. For a moment, they gazed into each other's eyes.

Joe smiled and picked up the coiled cable from the floor. "Guess we had better get back to work."

"Good idea," Mary said. "You'll have to continue without me? I have things to do upstairs."

"Yeah. I'm good."

You can say that again. "Yell if you need anything," she said, climbing the stairs. "What was I thinking?" she mumbled to herself. *I'm as bad as those hookers, but . . . Maybe he likes me. Shit, Mary, he may want you, girl.*

Chapter Fourteen

Joe installed a cable connection box to a wooden beam on the basement ceiling. As he worked in the dimly lit space, he fanned away a shower of debris that fell onto his face, hair, and shoulders. Next, he connected the cable to carry the TV signal to Tim's room, humming as he worked.

"Doctor Snow, did you say something," he yelled.

"What?" Mary answered, from the top of the basement stairs.

"Did you ask me something?"

"No."

Strange, Joe thought. *I could have sworn I heard voices.*

Joe returned to work then heard strange sounds from the dark side of the basement. *What the hell?* He dropped the cable and walked toward the odd looking door.

"Anyone there?" Joe asked. "Anyone back there?" Joe listened for a moment then said, "Shit, I did hear something." He brushed dirt from the door and placed his ear against it and heard a distant sounding voice.

"Help me. Get me outta here."

Shocked, he stepped back and stared at the door with puzzlement. *What the fuck? There's somebody in there.* He tried the rusty door knob. "It's locked. Who's in there?"

"Help me. Help me."

The sound of gritty footfalls on the basement floor startled Joe. He turned to see Mary holding a hammer across her chest. He jumped back, putting his arms over his head to fend off a blow.

"What?" Mary said.

"There's somebody in there," Joe said, lowering his arms. He pointed to the door. "It's locked."

"Relax," Mary said, in a calm voice. "It's my son. I wanted him out of the way while you worked, but I didn't want to tell you I had put him here—in the basement. Don't worry. He's fine."

Joe stared at the hammer now at Mary's side.

She glanced at the hammer. While turning it in her hand, she said, "Oh. Hanging pictures—upstairs."

"Thank God. I thought you were going to hit me."

"God *no*. Well, let's both get back to work."

Mary turned to leave when she heard a thud on the other side of the dungeon door.

"What's that?" Joe asked.

"Sounded like something hit the door," Mary said. "I'll check. Just keep working."

Mary unlocked the door, opened it three inches and peered inside. She then looked at Joe. "This is a private matter. No need to get involved, just do your cable thing." She opened the door another three inches then picked up a three-inch bolt from inside. She showed it to Joe and said, "Tim threw it."

Mary started to close the door when the person inside said, "Help me. Get me outta here."

"That sounds more like a woman than a boy," Joe said while Mary locked the door.

"That's Tim. He has a high-pitched voice. Despite his age, he never went through puberty."

"You're sure he's okay in there?"

"Don't worry. He's fine, but the faster you get the

cable installed, the sooner he can get back to his room."

"I'll be finished in an hour."

"Glad to hear that . . . the hour I mean. Then where?"

"Next job is in Hunter Park."

"No. I meant what else here," Mary said.

"Tim's room."

"Great. I'll get things ready upstairs."

Having completed the basement work, Joe walked into the kitchen and yelled, "Doctor Snow! I need to get to Tim's room."

"Come upstairs. I'm in his room, tidying up a bit."

Joe entered Tim's padded room where Mary stared, wide eyed, at his bare chest. "My, you got dirty down there didn't you?"

"Sorry," he said. *She's staring at my chest.* "A ton of dirt, dead spiders, ants, and God only knows what else fell from the basement ceiling."

"If you want, you can use Tim's shower when you finish."

"Thanks. I might do that."

Joe mounted a metal TV support high on the wall as Mary sat on Tim's bed observing the work.

Joe thought, *I'll pretend I need to test the strength of this thing. Maybe these muscles will turn her on. Hell, it's worth a try. Who knows, maybe she wants me.*

After installing the TV mount, Joe hung from it then did a few chin-ups.

"Just testing the strength of the hardware," he said, flexing his chest muscles. "Don't want it pulling out of the wall after the TV is attached."

Joe bolted the TV to the wall mount, connected the

cables then plugged in the power cord. He turned on the set and adjusted the cable box.

"There," he said. "That's channel 10."

Suddenly, music blared from the TV, and the flickering picture revealed a fleeting glimpse of a soap opera scene.

"Sorry!" he yelled, turning down the volume. "I didn't know I had it on high."

Mary chucked. "I'm glad it works, but I have things to do." She pointed to Tim's shower. "You can shower there if you want."

Looking at his chest, Joe said, "Yeah. I'd like ta get this dirt off."

"I'll get you a towel." Mary exited the room, leaving the door ajar. From outside, she said, "The valve is preset for ninety degrees. Just turn it to the right. It has an automatic soap dispenser."

Joe stripped. *Is she going to peek around that door?* He lathered up, using lots of hand action over his chest and crotch. *I hope she's peeking.*

He rinsed the suds from his hair, his chest and then his crotch. He turned off the water then, with the sides of his hands, scraped water from his torso.

"Hey! I need a towel."

"I have one for you," Mary said through the half-opened door. "Don't worry about the floor. It's nonslip, and water drains away in no time."

Suddenly, a clap of thunder rumbled in the background.

"Better get away from the metal in the shower," Mary said. "You don't want lightning striking the plumbing and killing you."

"Don't worry. I'm out of the shower. I need that towel."

With the sounds of Joe's wet footfalls nearing the half-opened door, Mary thrust a towel through the opening. Her arm struck the door's edge, causing it to swing open as Joe reached for the towel.

"Oops," Mary said, staring at Joe's glistening naked body.

"No need to apologize," he said, taking the towel.

Mary stood frozen like Lot's wife.

"You're a doctor," he said, drying his hair and face. "Nothing here you haven't seen before."

Blushing, Mary said, "Yeah. Give me the towel. I'll dry your back."

"Thanks." Joe turned his back and held his arms away from his body. *Now, we're getting somewhere.*

Mary dried down Joe's back to his butt. He flexed his glutes.

"You obviously work out,' Mary said. "Spend lots of time exercising your Gluteus Maximii?

Joe flexed his glutes. "You talking about my butt?"

"I didn't want to be so crude."

"That's okay." Joe looked over his shoulder at Mary. "Guys refer to their butt as glutes."

"So do women, but when men aren't around, we call it ass."

Joe flexed his glutes. "How's mine? My butt?"

"You mean on a scale of one to ten?"

"Okay."

"Mary squeezed his flexed ass through the towel then said, "Eight and a half."

"What!" Joe exclaimed, turning to face her. "Not a

ten?"

Mary raised the towel to dry Joe's chest, but dropped it, leaned against his torso, and reached her hands around his waist and squeezed his butt. "Could be a bit larger, rounder, firmer, and stronger," she said.

"How's that?" he asked, flexing his glutes.

"Not bad," she said, staring into his eyes.

"How's this?" Joe pulled Mary's right hand onto his pride. She gripped it. He pulled her close and kissed her hard on the mouth. She kissed back, cradling his balls in her left hand and then tugged them.

Joe unbuttoned her blouse and pushed it off her shoulders. She surrendered his crotch long enough to let her blouse fall from her arms. He kissed her neck as she shed her jeans, letting him push her underwear to her knees. She wiggled them to the floor and then kissed him.

He picked her up then took her to Tim's bed. He kissed her as she opened her legs, allowing him entry. Moaning, he kissed her neck and breasts then they kissed. He pinned her arms against the bed and wiggled against her pelvis. *Lady, I'm going to give you the fuck of your life.*

Mary sucked air in appreciation then nibbled his ear. Joe's thrusting grew in vigor as Mary moaned, joining his crescendo of excitement.

Dampened by padded walls, their vocals of fulfillment filled the stark space.

"Do it!" she yelled, over and over, louder and louder.

"I'm close," Joe said. "I'm . . ." Joe stiffened then became quiet except for a long exhaled "Uh . . ." He thrust a last time, moaned, and then fell onto Mary's writhing body as she climaxed.

They caught their breath and rested for a moment, reconnecting to reality.

Joe's heart pounded as his air-starved lungs sucked oxygen from a deep breath.

Suddenly, the room filled with a flash of lightning followed by a clap of thunder.

"What the hell?" Mary asked, looking over Joe's shoulder.

"What?" Joe asked.

Mary stared at the door. "Oh, God!"

"What the fuc—" Joe said. He stared at a naked black woman wearing a handcuff and ankle shackles. She appeared drugged as she held onto the doorframe, struggling to stand. Electrical tape and several strips of wood dangled from her lower leg, and a tall, naked white man sucked her breast.

"Help!" the woman mumbled. "Get me outta here."

Joe got off the bed. "What the fuck?"

"I can explain," Mary said, trying to pull Joe to her side. She sat up and yelled, "*Quickie*! Go to your room. Tim, go with her. Go! I said go!"

Joe watched as Mary rushed past him and grabbed Quickie and Tim by their arms. Mary struggled to get them into the room across the hall, but Quickie slumped to the hall floor.

"Get in there!" Mary yelled.

Joe asked, "Is that your son—"

"Help me," Quickie pleaded, extending her cuffed wrists toward Joe. "Get me outta here. I'm a slave."

"Who the fuck's that black woman?" Joe asked.

"She's a patient," Mary yelled, pushing Tim and pulling Quickie toward a bedroom.

Joe rushed to the door and helped Quickie to her feet. "Who are you?"

Mary plowed into Joe, knocking him to the floor. She grabbed Quickie's arm and pulled her across the hall.

Joe grabbed Mary's arm and swung her around. "What the hell's going on here?"

Quickie said, "I'm bein' held against my will. I ain't crazy. I'm a prisoner."

Mary wrested her arm free of Joe's grip and rushed Tim into a bedroom then closed the door.

"She doesn't know what she's saying," Mary said. "She's mentally unstable."

"I'm not crazy!" Quickie said, in a weak voice. She slumped into Joe's arms. "I'm forced ta breastfeed that stupid son. I'm a prisoner. Kidnapped!"

"I don't know what's going on here, but it's weird." Joe pushed Mary aside. "I'm calling the police."

Joe headed toward the wall phone in the hallway.

"No!" Mary yelled, grabbing his arm. "No! You can't. This woman doesn't know what she's saying. She's crazy. That's why she's here. She can't take care of herself."

"This is too weird. Let the police decide if this is crazy."

Pulling Joe's arm, Mary yelled, "No! You can't call the police. They won't understand!"

Shaking Mary's arms, Joe stared her in the eye. "That woman says you're holding her against her will. Did you kidnap her?"

"She's insane I tell you. Listen to me. I'm a doctor."

"Maybe you're the crazy one. You have an idiot kid sucking a woman's tit while she's begging me to get her out of here. And she's wearing chains. Chains! Did you drug her?"

Shaking her head and waving her hands in the air, Mary pleaded, "You can't call the police! You don't know what you're doing."

Joe pushed Mary to the floor. "The fuck I don't. I'm calling the police."

Mary reached toward Joe. "You want me to go to jail, leaving a sick son alone?"

Bending over Quickie to evaluate her condition, Joe glanced at Mary and shouted, "What have you done to this woman?"

Mary leaned against the wall. "She has to be sedated. She's dangerous."

Quickie half-opened her eyes. "Help me. She makes me breast feed that mongo son. Get me outta here."

Helping Quickie to her feet, Joe said, "Let's get you up."

Quickie mumbled, "My ankle hurts."

Mary rushed at Joe but knocked Quickie to the floor.

Standing between Mary and Quickie, Joe shouted, "You're the one who's crazy. I'm calling the police."

"No. You'll ruin everything."

Shaking his fist, Joe said, "Lady, I don't give a damn about you."

Mary dropped her arms to her side. "Don't you love me anymore?"

Joe froze in place and stared at Mary not believing

what he had heard. "What did you say?"

"Don't you love me anymore?"

"Lady, you're crazy."

Mary slumped to the floor as Joe headed for the hall phone. He had just dialed the police when he heard bare feet running toward him. He turned to see Mary waving his pliers over her head. He had no time to defend himself. She struck him on the left side of the head. A sound, similar to a cracking coconut, filled the hallway.

Joe fell. His head hit the floor with an echoing thud and opened a gash in his scalp. He appeared unconscious.

"There, you son of a bitch."

Mary watched as blood streamed onto the floor.

Joe's curled fingers still clutched the handset. "This is Sergeant Michels. How may I help you? Hello. Hello. Is everything okay there?"

Mary pried the phone from Joe's hand. "Sorry, I dropped the handset. Wrong number."

Mary had just put the handset in its cradle when Quickie forced her cuffed wrists over Mary's head and around her neck.

"I'll kill ya," Quickie mumbled.

Mary jabbed her elbow into Quickie's ribs, but she maintained the pressure around Mary's throat. Mary swung the pliers backwards, over her head, striking Quickie on the head. Quickie and Mary fell to the floor. Quickie lay still and unconscious.

Mary pulled her head from between Quickie's bound wrists then stood up, staring at the two naked bodies sprawled in the hallway.

With an empty, claw shaped, hand held skyward, Mary said, "What have I done? What have I done? Oh, my God, where's Tim? Shit! I put him in Quickie's room."

Mary opened Quickie's bedroom door and saw Tim sitting on the floor, sucking his thumb, babbling.

"Baby, I'm sorry," Mary said, dropping the pliers and sitting down beside Tim and hugging him. Mommy is sorry." She cradled and rocked Tim for a minute then said, "Let's get you to your room."

Tim reached for his mother's breast.

"Not now," Mary said, pushing Tim's hand away. "Later."

She took Tim to his bed, placed his thumb in his Mouth, and covered him with a sheet.

Mary picked up Joe's toolbox, making sure she had left nothing behind that could harm Tim, then carried it to the hallway and closed Tim's door.

Chapter Fifteen

Mary stared at her victims and hammered the wall with her fists. "Shit! What do I do now? Think, Mary, think."

Feeling Quickie's neck for a pulse, Mary sighed then said, "Thank God, I didn't kill her." She struggled to drag Quickie into Tim's room where she left the unconscious woman beside Tim's bed.

Mary returned to the hall. *Damn, his wound has bled a lot.* She knelt beside Joe to examine his scalp. Near a jagged bloody laceration, she pressed her index finger on his skull and felt something crunch as if she had squeezed Rice Krispies. "Damn. It's fractured." She sat back on her heels and felt Joe's left carotid artery and then the right. "Shit! He's dead! What the fuck do I do with his body?"

Pacing the hallway, she stepped over his body. *I've got to ditch him but how? How?* She closed Joe's eyelids. "Can't stand that death stare." She continued to pace. *What do I do? I know! Drive his van to the back of the house and put him inside. Then drive to Murphy Park and ditch him.* "Got to make it look like he was mugged . . . robbed. That's it, but first, I have to dress him." *Oh, God, I've got to collect his blood . . . That's the key. I can't let it clot. Not here.*

Donning a bath robe, Mary rushed to the kitchen where she rummaged through a kitchen drawer then pulled out a turkey baster, squeezed its red rubber bulb to make sure it did not leak, and then rushed upstairs. From her medicine chest, she got a bottle of aspirins, shook out a tablet, and then crushed it in a drinking glass. Adding a small amount of water, she stirred the mixture with her finger then held the glass to the light to examine the liquid for clarity. "Good. It dissolved."

Back in the hall, she poured the liquid into the pool of Joe's blood. She stirred the liquid and blood with the baster. *There. That should keep it from clotting.*

Using the baster, she collected Joe's treated blood and transferred it into the glass. With her hand over the top of the glass, she ran to the kitchen and got a piece of plastic wrap. She secured it over the glass with a rubber band then placed it on the counter. *Now, I don't have to worry about it spilling.*

She picked up Joe's shirt from the rear deck then thought, *Shit! I can't dress him now. I can't risk having anyone see me driving his van to the garage. I have to wear his work clothes.*

Mary shook dirt from his shirt then took it upstairs. There she donned the shirt, Joe's pants and shoes. "God, these pants are baggy." Mary snugged the belt around the too large waistband. "I hope no one sees me dressed like this. Now, the keys? Where are the van keys?" She patted the pants pockets. *Not there.* She felt the shirt pockets and the pants pockets again. *Nothing.* "The tool-box! Maybe they're in his toolbox." After a frantic search, she found the keys under some tools.

Mary opened her front door a few inches and peered outside. A flashy sports car passed. She narrowed the opening and continued to watch. *All clear.*

She hurried to the driver's side of the van and pulled the door handle. "Shit! It's locked!" Mary fumbled with the key ring then tried a random key in the lock. "Not that one." She tried another key. The door didn't open. "Shit!" She tried another key. "Thank, God!" The door opened.

A black car raced by. The driver blew his horn and waved.

Mary dropped her head and waved. "Shit! Hope they didn't see my face."

Hands shaking, she jumped onto the driver's seat and pushed the largest key into the ignition and started the engine. "Oh, God. It's a manual transmission." She struggled to put the van into first gear. *For God's sake, get in there*. The gears made a loud, grinding sound. "Shit!" She scanned the neighborhood to see if anyone had seen her or maybe heard the noise. "Thank God no one is around." She took a deep breath and pushed the gear shifter hard. The transmission resisted moving. For a moment, it sounded like a thrashing machine but then it connected. "Thank God. Now, take it easy, Mary."

She let the clutch out and the van lurched as if driven by a teenager on her first drive. She turned on the windshield wipers, clearing the rain that had fallen while she and Joe were in bed. The van jerked as she "ground" gears and headed for her garage.

From the alley, Mary backed along her driveway, until the van's rear doors were close to the garage door. She put the van in neutral, applied the emergency brake then walked to the garage door. "Damn, I'm too close to the garage to let the van's doors open all the way."

She moved the van forward two feet.

Using a wall mounted key pad to open the garage door, she then opened the van's rear doors. They would shield her actions from neighbors while loading Joe's body into the cargo space.

Back upstairs, Mary shed Joe's clothes.

She pulled Joe's body away from the remaining pool of blood. Using a hand towel, she cleaned blood from his body and the floor then dressed him. She had dragged the body to the stairs when she realized he had no underwear.

"Shit! Where are they? *He took them off in Tim's room, but where are they? In the toolbox? No. Didn't see them when I got the pliers. On the bed? No. He was naked when he got on the bed.*

Mary inched open Tim's door. *Good. Quickie's still out.* Mary scanned the space under the bed. "Ah. There they are." She grabbed the briefs and returned to the hall. She removed Joe's pants then pulled the underwear onto his limp body. She then replaced his clothes, socks and shoes.

Mary struggled to drag the body down the stairs. "Shit! He's heavy. Now, I know where the expression 'dead weight' comes from." She mustered her strength and tugged at his ankles. He moved a few inches.

"Shit! I'm leaving a trail of blood from his head." *Can't have that. Got to wrap it.*

Mary rummaged through her closet until she found a plastic blanket bag. After placing the bag over Joe's head and half closing its zipper, she turned her attention to cleaning the last of the blood from the floor.

Tossing the bloody towels in the washing machine, adding bleach, and then starting the wash cycle, she donned her work clothes.

Mary aligned Joe's body with the stairs then pulled his ankles with all her strength. The body inched down one step. Mary rested for a moment then continued.

Joe's head made a loud thump as it bounced step-to-step. After ten minutes, the body neared the last tread. Mary placed an oriental rug against the bottom riser then pulled the body onto the rug. It would help her slide the body over the hardwood floor.

Exhausted, Mary lugged Joe's body into the garage. *Now, how do I get him in the van? Its three feet off the ground.* She looked around the garage for anything to hoist the body. *Ah. TV Cable. I'll get some from the van.*

Mary got an old towel from a garage storage box then wrapped it around Joe's ankles. It would prevent skin damage from the cable tied around his ankles.

She dragged the body, bound ankles first, to within a few inches of the closed garage door. Mary reasoned that if she tied the ankle cable to the bottom handle on the outside of the door and then raised it, the body would follow. After making the attachments, she pushed the up button on the hand-held remote and raised the door. Joe's lower body rose twenty inches off the ground as the door stopped. Mary lifted Joe's head and laid it on the edge of the van floor. *How the hell am I going to get the rest of him inside? Damn. I have to back the van a little closer to the garage.*

Mary crawled through the van's storage area to get to the driver's seat then inched the vehicle backwards.

Joe's neck bent to the left at an sixty degree angle as the van moved backwards.

"Shit! I hope I didn't break his damn neck."

Mary crawled to the storage space and lifted Joe's head. She straightened his neck, then tugged at his shoulders. She managed to pull a few more inches of his upper body inside. *Now what do I do?*

After thinking for a moment, she grasped the remote in her right hand then placed that hand in Joe's right armpit—her left hand in his left armpit. As she tugged on the body, she activated the remote. The garage door closed, allowing her to pull more of the body inside the van. However, she did not react fast enough. The garage door moved too far down, dragging the lower part of Joe's body from the van.

"Shit!"

Pushing on the remote, Mary stopped the door and prevented the total extraction of the body. She tapped on the up button of the remote. The door inched upward, raising the legs and body to a horizontal position. With an all-out effort, she pulled Joe inside the van then removed the cable from Joe's ankles and the garage door, storing the cable in the van.

Exhausted and anxious, she sat in the van catching her breath, hands shaking from fear. *Calm down, girl. Relax. Take a deep breath.* Having caught her breath, she pondered her next move. *Shit! I forgot the toolbox and blood. Got to get that!*

Mary ran upstairs and got Joe's toolbox. She braced the glass of blood in the box then took both to the van's passenger seat. She removed a rag from the toolbox and used it to wipe her fingerprints from the box handle and tools.

Damn! Got to get the bicycle.

Mary loaded her bicycle in the cargo space and prepared to leave. Glancing in the rearview mirror, she said, "Better sit him up. Can't have blood pooling on his backside, otherwise the police won't buy him being killed while sitting at the steering wheel." She wedged Joe's back against one wheel well and his feet against the other. "Shit, he's slumping at the waist." Mary used a length of cable to secure Joe's uprighted torso to wooden slats attached to the van walls. She got another towel then placed it under the cable to prevent marks on his chest.

Okay. Time to go.

Mary drove to the far side of Murphy Park. She had explored the locale months earlier while on a Sunday drive. The remoteness of the area would provide cover for her mission.

She left the pavement then drove down a bumpy, unpaved road, splashing through rain puddles and weedy tire ruts as she headed for the lake. The crude road caused the van to rock from side to side. After a severe shaking of the van, the bicycle fell onto Joe.

"Oh shit!" Mary yelled. *Hell. He's dead. Can't hurt him now.*

At the lake, she scanned the area but saw no one. She lowered a window then parked at a picnic spot with a covered sitting area. Near the shed, hanging from a post, hung a rusty fifty-five-gallon oil drum. Its blackened surface and smoky smell suggested it had been used to burn trash in the past few days. *I can use that to burn Joe's things.*

Mary took a book of matches from the ashtray then placed them in her blouse pocket. She removed the glass of blood from the toolbox and placed it on the passenger seat.

Pulling another rag from the toolbox, she wrapped

it around the handle then carried the toolbox to the edge of the lake. One-by-one, she wiped the tools with the rag then hurled each into different parts of the lake. She placed the toolbox on the ground then jumped on it, splintering its handle and sides. She dumped the pieces in the oil drum. Using the trash inside, she started a fire that spread to the remnants of the toolbox.

One down. One to go.

Mary got into the van and watched the flames consume the wood before she drove away.

In another remote part of the park, Mary parked the van and lowered the right front window as though the driver might have stopped to enjoy the fresh air.

She leaned the bicycle against the outside of the van so she had room to work in the cargo area.

After twenty minutes of tugging and pulling, Joe's body had been moved into the driver's seat. Mary took forty-seven dollars from his wallet, wiped it clean, and threw it on the ground. She placed his watch in her slacks pocket then scattered the contents of the glove box in the cab. She repositioned the driver's seat to where it had been before being moved to accommodate her short legs.

"Now, what have I forgotten?" *Better scatter the stuff in the back. Make it look rifled for valuables.*

Mary threw the contents of the storage area about the van and the ground. She then scanned the van for anything that might be out of place. *Does this look like a real robbery?*

A small amount of blood clung to the van wall, where Joe's head had rested. Mary wiped it off with spit and an old rag.

Fringerprints needed to be removed from everything she had touched then Joe's prints added. With a rag, she wiped the surfaces near the driver's seat then pressed Joe's fingertips on the front door, various handles, steering wheel, radio knobs, gearshift and every thing else within a driver's reach.

"Shit! What am I going to do about the rear doors?" *Can't risk moving him just to put his prints on the handles so . . . I'll put mine there but smudge them so they can't be read.*

Mary let Joe's left arm hang beside his seat. She placed the right hand on the seat beside Joe's leg then removed the blanket bag from his head. After positioning his head, right side against the steering wheel, she positioned his feet near the brake and clutch.

"Now, what else, Mary? Think!" *If he had been struck while sitting behind the steering wheel, where would his blood have splattered?*

After flicking a few drops of Joe's treated blood on the cab ceiling, the sun visor, passenger seat, windshield, instrument cluster, and interior surfaces, Mary wiped her brow. *The blood should clot in an hour or so. Have I forgotten anything?* "Shit!" *The ankle wrap and blanket bag. I'd better burn them.*

Mary left the driver's door and rear doors open. She walked around the van looking for anything that might be unrelated to a mugging. She found nothing.

She mounted her bike and rode away.

Farther down the road, she stopped at another isolated picnic shed. She tossed the ankle wrap and bloody blanket bag into a hanging oil drum, set them on fire, and then threw in the matches. As the items burned,

Mary picked up a rock and used it to crush Joe's watch on the concrete floor of the picnic hut. She gathered the pieces then tossed them into the lake. She dropped the watch's leather strap into the fire then sat on a bench, watched the flames and sighed. "Well, time to head home."

The bike ride home provided time for Mary to consider what she would do with Quickie. She knew she could never release the hooker as long as Quickie produced milk and nursed Tim.

Twilight time provided enough light for Mary to see the keypad and enter the code to open her garage door. As she stored her bicycle, she heard the phone ringing in the kitchen.

Who the hell is that? Mary rushed to the phone then said, "Hello."

"Is this Doctor Snow?"

"Speaking."

"This is Ari, dispatcher for Cable Land. Was Joe, our installation man, at your house today?"

"I don't remember his name, but yes, your service-man arrived around noon to—," Mary cleared her tightening throat, "to install my TV."

"Do you remember when he left?"

"Not sure. Why?"

"He hasn't reported in since twelve thirty."

"That was near the time he arrived," Mary said. "He was prompt, efficient, and left here around one thirty."

"One thirty you say?"

"Around that time. Hope he shows up."

Mary hung up the phone and then slumped onto a

kitchen chair. *I didn't expect a call so soon.* "Shit!" *The police will be calling as well.*

Three days later, a ringing phone awakened Mary at 8:00 a.m. She rubbed sleep from her eyes, cleared her throat, and answered the phone. "Hello."

"Is this Doctor Snow?" a man asked.

"Speaking."

"Doctor, I'm Detective Harry Jackson with the Towson Police Department. We've had a report of a missing person who was last seen three days ago at your house. I'd like to come by . . . ask a few questions."

"When?"

"Could I come at one o'clock."

"Fine. I'll be expecting you."

Mary's hands trembled as she hung up the phone. "Shit!" *What do I do now? I'd better scan the entire house. Can't overlook anything suggesting a crime.*

Mary used bleach water to wash floors, furniture, walls, and the hall phone—anyplace Joe's blood might have touched. After cleaning everything, the house reeked of bleach. She didn't want the smell to raise Jackson's suspicion, so she opened the windows to rid the house of the odor.

Watching her favorite soap opera on the den TV, Mary fiddled with the TV remote while she waited for the detective.

At one o'clock, the doorbell rang. Mary forced herself to the living room where she took a deep breath then opened the door. She forced a smile on seeing a man display his badge.

"Doctor Snow, I'm Detective Jackson. May I come in?"

Mary scanned the detective's stern looking fiftyish year old face. *From the smell of his clothes, he smokes a lot.* "Come in, Detective." Mary pointed toward her left. "Please, have a seat in the living room."

The detective looked around the room as he sat down. "You have a nice collection of antiques."

"Thanks." Mary sat opposite him and gripped her hands. "Now, how may I help you?"

The detective took a pad and pen from his jacket pocket. "Let's start at the beginning?"

"Well, the man arrived around twelve thirty . . . and that's all I know. I worked in my office while he did his thing outside, in the basement, and then in Tim's room."

"Where did he park?"

"In front," Mary said, pointing toward the front door.

"Mind if I look around?"

Mary swallowed and gripped her hands tighter. *What would he want to see?* "Not at all."

"Where did the cable enter the house?"

"The basement. May I show you?"

"Please."

Mary had anticipated this request. She had drugged Quickie and locked her in the dungeon then pushed an antique highboy dresser in front of the dungeon door. After covering the dresser with a dirty sheet, she knocked debris from the overhead beams onto the sheet, making it appear as if it had been there for years.

Mary led the way to the basement and pointed to where the cable entered. The detective noted the course of the cable to the second floor. He shined a flashlight beam along the cable then made notes on his pad. He scanned the dimly-lit floor and shined his flashlight on the web-covered overhead areas. At the dark end of the basement, his beam paused on the sheet-covered dresser.

I hope he doesn't look too closely, Mary thought, trying to swallow cotton.

Jackson walked to the dresser, lifted the sheet, examined the furniture with his flashlight, and then looked inside a drawer. "Hmm," he said and dropped the sheet.

Mary's heart pounded. Her mouth so dry her tongue stuck to her palate. She felt her gut tighten as if she would vomit. *Please just leave.*

"Everything is in order," he said, "but how did you know where the cable entered if you were upstairs while he worked?"

Mary's heart stopped. *Think Mary. Think.* She felt her face warm with a blush and swallowed hard. "Sorry. I forgot. He asked me to pull on the end of the cable while he fed it inside from under the deck."

"Okay," the detective said. "May I see the place where the cable ended—where it connects to the TV?"

"That's on the second floor. The TV is in the room of my disabled son. He's mentally challenged. That's why the room is padded, and he wears diapers."

"Thanks for the explanation," Jackson said in a gruff voice. "Let's take a look."

Mary led the way to the stairs. She noted Jackson looked at everything around him as they walked through the house and then up the stairs.

Outside Tim's door, Mary said, "Please, wait here. Let me prepare Tim."

She tiptoed inside then nudged his shoulder. "Tim.

A man wants to see your room. His name is Har."

"Har?"

"Yes. Har."

Mary returned to the door. "Detective, you may come in."

Jackson entered the white room as if he might be attacked. "I see what you mean about him being disabled. Ah, there's the TV. Everything's okay here. Thank you."

"Go back to sleep," Mary said, patting Tim's head.

The detective waited in the hall as Mary closed Tim's door.

"Is that blood on the ceiling?" the detective asked, staring upward.

Shit! I missed that. Mary hid her trembling hands behind her back. "I killed a bug there—with a fly swatter a few days ago."

"Uh huh," Jackson said, making a note on his pad. "Looks like I have everything I need. Thanks for your cooperation."

"You're welcome, Detective. Hope he shows up."

The detective walked down the stairs, saying, "I'll be in touch if I need anything else."

"Goodbye," Mary said and closed the front door. "Glad that's over. Hope he bought my bug story."

Chapter Sixteen

Mary peered out a front window and saw Detective Jackson sitting in his unmarked black car. He wrote on a pad, and then he left his car and walked to a neighbor's house to the north. Out of sight for a few minutes, he came back into view then walked to the house south of Mary's and spoke to that neighbor. He took notes, returned to his car, and then drove away.

Mary thought, *Hope that's the end of that.*

She lugged a stepladder to the second floor then cleaned the ceiling with bleach water to remove the blood splatter. "No one's going to test that."

Four days later, Mary busied herself clearing unwanted items from her garage. Joan, the neighbor who lived across the alley from Mary's house, walked into the open garage.

"Morning, Joan," Mary said, opening a box of household goods.

"What's going on in this neighborhood?"

Mary sorted through a third box of clothing without looking up. "What are you talking about?"

"A detective asked me if I had seen a TV guy at your house."

"Did you see him?" Mary asked, holding up a leaf rake. "Should I keep this thing?"

"No," Joan said. "Hire someone to rake leaves. I told him I was cooking at the time—looking out my kitchen window—when I saw a youngish, blond guy working on the pole in your backyard."

"What did the policeman say about that?" Mary

asked, shaking dust from an old coat.

"He asked about the man's van."

"What about it?" Mary asked, hands shaking as she rummaged through another box. *Shit. Why would he talk to her?*

"He asked if I had seen it, or when did I see it. I told him I saw the guy on the pole around one o'clock. Then later, I saw his van parked in your driveway."

Shit! Hope the cop didn't pick up on the time or the truck outside my garage. "Thanks for letting me know about the cop," Mary said, trying to look unconcerned. "That TV guy has been missing since he left my house."

Joan smiled while smoothing her dress. "He was quite a hunk. Saw him without his shirt. Wouldn't want anything to happen to that. I thought about calling him to install a cable for me just to get him in the house."

Mary chuckled. "I know what you mean. I saw him up close."

Two weeks later, Mary was cleaning her coffee pot when the phone rang.

She looked at the clock. "Who's calling this early? Hello."

"Doctor Snow?" the caller asked.

"Speaking."

"This is Detective Jackson. Remember me?"

"Yes, Detective. How may I help you?"

"May I stop by, say . . . ten o'clock?"

"Make it nine? I have an appointment at ten."

"Nine it is."

Right on time, the detective rang Mary's doorbell. "Come in, Detective."

Entering, he said, "When we last spoke, I asked about the installer's van. I couldn't remember where you said he parked. Can you refresh my memory?"

Mary thought for a moment. *I know I saw him write "front of the house" when I told him.* Rubbing her temple, she said, "He first parked in front but later said he didn't want to keep running through the house, getting it dirty. He moved the van to the back, so he could go in and out through the garage with his equipment."

"How did he park?"

"Gosh. Let me think." After a moment, Mary said, "As I remember, he backed in. Yes, he backed in."

"May I see the garage?"

"Certainly. Follow me."

Mary led the detective down the hall toward the garage. She opened the hall door to show him the garage but let the door swing too far into the garage, knocking over her bicycle.

"I'll get it for you," the detective said, picking up the bike.

"Thanks. I need to find a better place to store it."

"A Schwinn! My daughter had one like this . . . years ago. This has to be an antique by now."

"It was a birthday gift . . . from when I lived in the orphanage."

"You sure have taken good care of it."

"Thanks. I have, but I don't ride much anymore." *Shit, I should have cleaned the mud off the tires.*

Jackson looked around the garage, operated the door lift, and made some notes. "Thanks. That's all I need."

"Glad to be of assistance." Mary forced a smile. "Have a great day.

Quickie's milk production had begun to dwindle, and hormonal stimulation had failed to boost its production. This changed Mary's primary daily task to one of locating lactating women.

Ten days after being interviewed by the detective, Mary found just one woman, out of eighty-one phone calls, willing to sell her breast milk.

Later that day, Mary slumped at her desk. "What the hell am I going to do?" She pushed away from the desk and stared into space. "I need a break."

That evening, Mary spent time reading medical publications. In the back of one journals, she saw an ad for an upcoming lecture about breastfeeding. The lecture would start at 8:00 p.m. in a nearby hospital.

I should go. I might meet doctors who know of some women willing to sell their milk.

Mary attended the lecture held in a charity hospital located in an economically depressed part of Baltimore. She queried several obstetricians but found no one who knew of a woman willing to sell breast milk.

The area around the hospital looked less threatening on her way to the hospital, but now that the sun had set, Mary felt uneasy about driving home.

On her way out of the doctor's parking lot, she stopped at the guard house and asked, "What's the safest way to Towson?"

Smiling, the guard said, "There isn't one, Doctor, but there is a *safer* route."

"I don't know if I'm happy to hear that or not."

"Follow the working street lights," the guard said, pointing to the left. "They'll lead you out of town."

"And the lights that are out are—"

"Out because gangs knock 'em out. The hospital keeps the others going so our doctors can see to come and go. If you have to stop for a traffic light, make sure your doors are locked."

"Thanks."

Mary followed the trail of working street lights. *These streets have got to be safe. They're deserted— eerie.* She stopped at the third traffic light as it turned red. She looked in all directions. *No one's around. I'm running this damn thing.* Driving away, she had a second look around and noted movements in the shadow of a doorway in a boarded building on her right. *Hope that's not a carjacker.*

A tall black woman walked into view. She wore a neon-pink short skirt and white patent-leather platform high heel shoes. Her white blouse, tied at the waist, revealed generous love handles. She carried a leopard print shoulder bag the size of a suitcase.

Mary drove around the block and came back to the spot where she had seen the prostitute. Mary pulled to the curb near the shadowy doorway and lowered the passenger window.

"Looking for some fun?" the woman asked.

"Kinda."

The woman sauntered to the car, exaggerating her hip movements. "What kinda fun you looking for, girl?"

"*I'm* not the one looking for fun. I want some fun for my son."

"Your son?" The woman popped gum. "That's a first for me. Some kinda initiation?"

"You might say that. I'm in a hurry tonight, but may

I call you later?"

"Girl, you can call, but don't 'less you can pay hundred dollars—an hour."

"Maybe. What's your number?"

The hooker dug in her purse and pulled out a writing pad and pen. As she wrote, she said, "Don't call before two o'clock. I sleep 'til then."

"What's your name?"

The hooker handed the paper to Mary. "Wonderful. I'm called *Wonderful*."

"I'll bet you are. I'm Mary. I'll be in touch."

"Nite, girl."

A week later, Mary phoned Wonderful to set up an appointment to meet in a restaurant for an exploratory talk.

Despite Mary's request that Wonderful wear conservative clothing, she wore a tight, white blouse with a plunging neckline, a short yellow and black plaid skirt and red spike-heeled shoes, all of which identified her as a hooker.

"You call that conservative clothing?" Mary asked, shaking her head.

Wonderful smoothed her too-short skirt and popped a wad of gum the size of a plum. With her head bobbing like an East Indian dancer, she said, "Girl, I don't get no more conservative than this. Besides, I'm always working. Never can tell when I might run in ta somebody needin' something *Wonderful*."

"Don't forget, we're here to discuss *my* business," Mary said in disgust, "Not yours."

"Don't get a wedgie, girl." Wonderful's head continued to wobble left and right as her words trailed off. "I'm here to hear yo *prop po zish un*."

Mary took a deep breath and explained how she would do a physical examination and blood tests. In exchange for Wonderful's monogamy and steady work with Tim. Mary would provide room and board and cash every week.

"Sounds good, girl."

"Do you have any children?"

"Not really. Gotta nephew. Mama keeps him when I work."

"How old is he?"

Wonderful's smile almost engulfed her head. "He's twenty months."

"Bet he's beautiful."

"Girrrrllll, you know it."

"Now, back to *my* son. His name is Tim." Mary sighed. "He's a young man who is mentally disabled, but I want him to have a life as close to normal as possible to his peers, and that includes sex."

"What ya mean *pears*?"

"*PEERS*—not pears—boys his age."

"Girl, I've heard about this comin' of age shit." Wonderful crossed her fishnet covered leg at the thigh. "I'll fuck anythin'—if the money's right. You can watch if you want."

Wonderful spit her gum wad into her hand then stuck it on the underside of the table.

Mary watched with horror. "Pull that off and wrap it in a piece of paper!"

"Sorry, girl. I forgot where I is." Wonderful took a small notebook from her bag, tore off a page, then used it to wrap her spent gum. "This sho is an uppity place."

"Well, you've heard my terms. What do you think? Oh, one more thing. No rubbers. He's allergic."

"No rubbers?"

Mary shook her finger to make the point. "Noooo rubbers! You have to watch for your risky time of the month."

"Girl, money's money. When do we start?"

Handing Wonderful a business card, Mary said, "Meet me at my office, tomorrow night at nine?"

"See ya there."

Mary rapped her fingers as whe waited in her darkened office. At 9:08, she watched Wonderful exit a cab and walk toward the office front door and then knock on its glass.

"Come in," Mary said, opening the door. "Let's go to an exam room."

"So you is a doctor. Got a fancy office, but girl, can't ya turn on some lights?"

"Not yet. Don't want anyone to know I'm here."

The women entered the exam room. Mary closed the door then turned on a light.

"Get undressed and sit on the table," Mary said. "Ever have a pelvic or breast exam?"

"Had one of them down-under exams once. My men friends examine my breasts all the time. They must be okay, girl. They ain't complaining."

"I meant by a doctor."

"Nah."

"Okay," Mary said, pulling on rubber gloves. "Put your feet in the stirrups and spread your legs. First, you'll feel my fingers then the speculum. It might be a little cold, but it won't hurt."

Wonderful let her legs fall apart. "Do what ya gotta do, girl. I ain't gonna cry."

A minute later, Mary tapped Wonderful on the knee. "Okay. Now, I need to examine your breasts. Okay. . . Everything is normal. You may get dressed."

While Wonderful, dressed, Mary took the used equipment to a room across the hall.

"Come in here," Mary called. "I need to take some blood."

Wonderful followed the sounds of things being moved about until she found Mary.

"Please, sit in that chair," Mary said, "and straighten your arm. First, I'll tie a tourniquet around your arm, clean it with alcohol, and then you'll feel a needle stick." Mary took Wonderful's blood then said, "Now, that didn't hurt did it?"

"I can take it, girl. I'm tough."

"Well, let's get out of here. I'll call you when the test results are back."

"Can ya call me a taxi?"

"Sure. Here's $10.00 for the fare. We'll talk soon."

Chapter Seventeen

Wonderful answered the phone as she played ball with her nephew on the living room floor. "Hello."

"Is this Wonderful?"

"Yeah."

"This is Mary. Your lab tests are normal. I'd like to pick you up tomorrow afternoon—late. Can you get a bus to Towson? If so, I'll pick you up at the bus station."

"Sure, girl. Make it six o'clock. That way I can feed my nephew and put him ta bed."

"Fine. Tell your mother you will be gone for a week. Pack enough clothes."

Prior to going to the Towson bus station, Mary had drugged Quickie then shackled her to a dungeon table-bed.

As Wonderful and Mary arrived at her garage, Mary pushed the button on the remote and opened the garage door.

"Stay in the car until the door closes," Mary said, putting her hand on Wonderful's knee. "Never can tell when someone might be watching. I don't want my neighbors seeing us."

"You wanna play with me?" Wonderful asked, putting her back against the passenger door.

"What?" Mary asked shocked.

"Yo hand on my knee. You wanna play with me?"

Mary jerked her hand away and shook it. "Hell no. Let's go in. Tim's waiting."

Inside, Wonderful said, "Girl, ya got a nice house."

"Thank you. Hope you enjoy staying here."

Mary led Wonderful to the foot of the stairs where Mary spieled her instructions as she had for earlier consorts. Upstairs, Mary showed Wonderful where to undress.

"Wait here when you're naked," Mary said pointing to the hall floor. "I'll get Tim ready."

Minutes later, Wonderful called out, "I'm ready."

Mary opened Tim's door and saw Wonderful standing naked in the hall. She folded and unfolded her arms and shifted her weight several times.

Mary thought, *My, this one is plumper than Quickie. Hope Tim appreciates her larger breasts.* "Come in."

Mary walked to Tim. "Tim, this is your new friend, Won."

Mary turned to Wonderful. "He has trouble with long words like *Wonderful*."

"That ain't no boy, girl. He's the whitest man I ever seen, but that thang—that's a big one!"

"Won?" Tim asked.

"Yes. Won," Mary said, turning toward Wonderful. "Tim likes breasts. Why don't you lie on the bed? Let him suckle."

Wonderful obliged, positioning her breasts so either one would be available. She trembled as Tim climbed onto the bed.

"Are you alright?" Mary asked.

"He looks like he got rage in his eyes. Am I safe?"

Mary chuckled, "You are but your breast may not be."

Wonderful closed her eyes, dropped her head onto the pillow, and waited for the unknown. "What the hell I get myself into?"

"What?"

"Nuttin."

"That's it," Mary said, watching Tim crawl to the middle of the bed. "He'll want to fondle your breast."

Mouth open, Tim stared at Wonderful's breast.

She stared back as his opened mouth neared its target. She squeezed her eyes shut and moaned, "Uhhh."

Just then, Tim locked his lips on the targeted breast. "Yummmm."

Noting Wonderful's wide-eyed look of shock, Mary said, "Relax, Wonderful."

"Girl, he got a vacuum cleaner for a mouth. I ain't never been sucked like this. Does he think there's milk in there?"

"Please, just let him suckle," Mary said, sitting in the bedside chair. "Whatever you do, don't pull your breast away quickly. He doesn't like abrupt interruptions."

As Tim had his fun, Wonderful glanced at the wall clock and pointed toward her involved breast. "Girl, this startin' ta hurt."

"Okay, but let me show you how to make a switch."

Fearing a temper tantrum, Mary held her breath during the swap, but all went well.

"See if you can get him inside," Mary said.

"Ya want him to fuck me?"

"Yes, but help him get inside."

"Girl, I ain't never had ta show a man where to put it or how to get it in."

"Just do it," Mary said, aligning Tim over Wonderful as she grasped and guided him inside.

Mary watched from the bedside chair as Tim enjoyed himself at Wonderful's breast. *I'm so happy he can have sex like other boys his age.* "Okay, Wonderful, move your hips. You know what to do."

"Ya think he'll notice? He seems more interested in sucking than fuckin', girl."

"He will. Just give him time. You do your thing."

Wonderful rocked her hips and raised her butt off the bed. "This is work, girl, and he ain't helpin' none. I gotta lift me *and* him, and that's work."

"Just keep at it. He'll start thrusting."

After a minute of Wonderful's hip actions, Mary knew something in a primitive part of Tim's brain had clicked. Tim began thrusting his hips.

"It's working," Mary said. "I know he likes it. Just keep at it."

"Girl, he got a long one. Feels like it's going right through my back."

"Get ready. When he's close, he makes deep thrusts."

"Oh Lordie, I ain't that deep, g irl. Not since they sewed me up after my last baby."

"Just letting you know."

Tim's thrusts became rhythmic, but his mouth never moved from Wonderful's breast.

"I think he's ready to splod," Wonderful said, staring at Mary. "I can tell by the way he's acting."

"Just keep rocking him." Mary watched Tim's buttocks contract with each pelvic thrust. His moans morphed higher in pitch, speed, and volume. "Get ready," Mary said. *That a boy. That a boy.*

"Eeeehh!" Tim screeched. He raised his mouth from

Wonderful's breast and threw his head backwards. His body curled and then straightened while his flared toes dug into the mattress. He did a partial pushup then emitted a moan that morphed into a screech so loud Wonderful covered her ears. He then fell on her like a dead man.

"You did it!" Mary said, clapping. "You gave him a *great* ride. I know he's happy, and I'm happy for him."

"Girl, I don't know when I been rode like that. He may not be bright, but he sure knows how ta fuck."

"He'll go to sleep now," Mary said. "Let me help get him off of you."

Wonderful stood at the bedside. "I feel like one of them horses at that big-ta-do race in Kentucky."

"The Kentucky Derby." Mary chuckled. "I don't want you rode hard and put away wet. There's a shower off the bedroom where you undressed. Oh yeah. There is a bathrobe behind the door. Put it on."

"I can't get dressed?"

"Not yet. He may want to suckle again."

"Girl, how many times does he do that?"

"Six times."

"*Six* times a *day*?" Wonderful asked.

"Six, but you get him inside only once a day." *That should be enough to get you pregnant.*

Wonderful sighed. "Thanks God, it's only once, girl."

"But the titty stuff is every four to six hours."

Wonderful rubbed her breasts. "O Lordie. I'm not sure they can take it, girl."

"You were told about this before you got here. That's why I pay what I do."

"Yeah, but now I know how hard he sucks. Girl, I could lose a nip."

"Don't worry," Mary said," if it comes off, I'll sew it on."

"Ain't no jokin' matter, girl."

Wonderful headed for her bathroom.

"You'll be all right," Mary said. "Want something to eat or drink?"

"I could use a stiff one," Wonderful yelled from the bathroom. "What ya got?"

"You like hard or soft stuff?"

"A beer would be good."

"Fine. Come down to the kitchen, after you've showered." *Got to be very good to this one if she's to get pregnant.*

Wonderful sat at the kitchen table while Mary searched a drawer for a "church key" to open the beer bottle.

"Here's your beer," Mary said, holding out the opened bottle.

Wonderful took a sip. "When do I gotta go back?"

"Maybe tonight but definitely in the morning— about seven. I'll wake you."

"Good! My tities need a rest." Wonderful took a sip then said, "Must be gonna rain."

"What did you say?"

"Must be gonna rain."

"Why do you say that?"

"I heard a moan, like the wind blowing."

Shit! That's Quickie. Mary walked to the window and peered out. *Nothing, but I can't say that.* "Trees are moving about . . . Guess it could rain."

Mary turned toward Wonderful. "Well, I have work to do. Why don't you go up to your room? Get some sleep. By the way, close your bedroom door. I bring Tim down at night for exercise. Don't let our noises concern you."

Wonderful picked up the beer and headed for her bedroom.

Mary followed her then waited at the foot of the stairs, listening for Wonderful to close her door.

"Good night," Mary yelled then headed for the basement stairs. *I have to sound proof that dungeon. Can't have Wonderful hearing moans and wonder who is making them. That could be disastrous.*

Mary opened the dungeon door. Quickie appeared to be awakening from her drug induced sleep.

"Waking up are you? Good. I'll bring Tim in. You're making little milk, but every little bit helps."

Quickie tried to sit up. "I can't . . . do it . . . any . . . more."

Her eyes closed and she slumped onto the table.

"Go to sleep." Mary said. "Tim won't mind."

On the way to Tim's room, Mary thought, *What would happen if Quickie woke up and yelled? I can't let that happen. I'd better cuff and gag her.*

Standing outside Tim's room, Mary spoke toward Wonderful's room, "I'm going to take Tim downstairs. See you in the morning. Sleep well."

"Nite, girl."

Mary helped Tim downstairs then into the dungeon.

"Okay, Tim. Get on the table. Qik is waiting."

Quickie half-opened her eyes and muttered, "No . . . no . . .."

"Shut up," Mary said. "Tim needs your milk."

Quickie tried to fight Tim off but failed because of her stupor.

Mary handcuffed Quickie's hands to the table, stuffed a gag in her mouth, and then placed a strip of duct tape over the gag to prevent it being dislodged.

She hugged Quickie's kicking legs, to prevent Tim from being bucked off her chest. Using duct tape, Mary bound the kicking legs then taped them to the table.

Quickie drifted off to sleep, allowing Mary to shackle her legs and lock the shackle to the rail at the edge of the table-bed. Fatigued from the day's activities and her tussle with Quickie, Mary sat in a chair and monitored Tim's activities. After her head bobbed a few times, Mary fell asleep.

Startled, Mary was awakened by Tim shaking her shoulder.

"Baf room," Tim mumbled. "Hurrrrry!"

He must really have to go if he's saying hurry. We won't be able to get upstairs fast enough. Where can he go in here?

Mary scanned the room for a small container or jar but saw nothing. "Hang on, Tim. There has to be something you can use."

Mary's gaze fell on the claw-foot tub. "Hell. Why not?" *It was a big urinal for that old man's girl-friend.* Mary led Tim to the tub where he relieved him-self. *I can imagine the old man lying in this tub waiting for his girlfriend to piss on him. "Ugh!"*

Tim finished and turned to his mother. "Hungry."

"Shit! Quickie isn't making enough milk." *What*

the fuck am I going to do? I can't just let her go. She'd go to the police . . . tell them everything. Everything! My ass would be fried and Tim would end up God knows where. People wouldn't understand him. Our bond . . . shattered. He wouldn't understand. I can't let that happen! "Let's get you to bed."

Mary pulled Tim toward the basement steps. "There's breast milk in the frig. I'll fill the bra and feed you." Mary shushed Tim's babbling and led him to his room.

In the kitchen, she filled the rubber bra with breast milk, mixed in a small amount of cow's milk, and then strapped on the bra. When the milk had reached body temperature, Mary returned to Tim's bed.

While gripping Mary's uncovered left breast, Tim suckled at the right side of the bra until empty.

Mary reveled in Tim's attention and their emotional bond. "Mommy loves you. She loves you very much." Mary caressed Tim's head and sang to him of love. She covered her sated son with a sheet, kissed him on the forehead, and then left the room.

In the kitchen, Mary cleaned the rubber bra. *I've got to get rid of Quickie. There's no way around it. She has to go, but how?*

Mary went to the den and sank into her lounger. She sighed, turned on the TV, and watched the eleven o'clock news. A reporter detailed how police had found a missing girl. Her body had been placed in an oil drum and covered with acid.

That's it, Mary thought. *That's it. I have that tub.*

Mary went to the office, unlocked the safe and re-moved a vial of sleeping medicine she had used to sedate Tim. She drew 10 ccs of the fast acting barbiturate into a syringe then locked the bottle away. "Quickie could ruin everything I've worked for." *Tim and I could wind up in separate places. I have to do this. There's no question about it. I have to protect him.*

Over and over, Mary said, "I have to do this."

In the dungeon, she walked around the table, staring at Quickie. "I've got to do this. There's no other way. I've got to."

Mary's voice grew in volume and anger. She slapped Quickie's face.

Quickie winced and moaned.

Mary continued, "You can't ruin our lives. I won't let you. Neither you nor anyone else is going to separate Tim and me."

Mary searched Quickie's forearm for a vein large enough to take an injection.

"I have to do this, Quickie. I have to. Can't have you going to the police . . . telling them I kidnapped you . . . forced you to nurse Tim. If I was taken away, who would care for him? Who? No one! Not like me. No one would love him like me. I'd never nurse him again. I'd never look into his loving eyes again. *No one* is going to take him from me. No one. I won't allow it. He needs me."

Using her left hand as a tourniquet, Mary gripped Quickie's bicep, causing her forearm veins to bulge. Mary poked an engorged vein with her right forefinger. "Good." She inserted the needle, pulled back the syringe plunger, and watched blood flow into the syringe. "Ah, that's good."

Watching the dark-red blood mix with the clear

liquid in the syringe, she steadied the syringe then pushed the plunger toward the needle. "Careful, Mary. Don't rupture the vein," she said, emptying the syringe then withdrawing the needle. A trickle of blood leaked from the puncture site. "Done."

Mary sat in a metal chair and watched Quickie's chest rise and fall. *Did I give her enough? Be patient, Mary, be patient.* She looked at her watch. "I'll give it a minute more."

Seconds later, Quickie's respirations slowed then became shallow. *It's working.* Mary shifted her weight on the chair, watching Quickie's life ebb away. Two minutes later, her breathing stopped.

Mary took a deep breath. *It's done! No one will hear you moan, and you won't tell anyone anything.*

Mary felt relief as she removed the shackles, cuffs, and gag. She unlocked the wheels of the table-bed and rolled it toward the tub. Once parallel to the tub, she locked the table wheels then pushed and pulled Quickie toward the edge of the table. It took several minutes of struggling with the body before it fell, head first into the tub, causing a thud that echoed around the dungeon. Quickie's right foot, however, remained on the table. Mary pushed it toward the tub. It struck the tub edge and then fell beside the other leg, creating another thud. Quickie's dead eyes appeared to scan the ceiling.

"Now," Mary said, "I need some acid."

The next morning, Mary glanced at her watch then placed her coffee mug on the kitchen table. *The supply houses should be open now.* She dialed the first supplier listed in the chemical section of the yellow pages.

"Direct Labs, Manny speaking."

"Manny, this is Doctor Snow. I'd like to order two gallons of technical grade, forty percent hydrochloric acid. We're about to run out."

"The strong stuff, eh? Well, you're in luck. It's in stock. It's good you called early. We can deliver today if you live in Towson."

"Great. Didn't expect you to deliver so soon. Can you deliver it to my house?"

"No problem. We'll have it there by noon."

"May I give you my credit card number?"

"We accept American Express."

"Great."

Mary called six more suppliers in the Towson area, requesting two gallons of acid from each. She didn't want to arouse suspicion by ordering larger amounts from one source.

The following morning, she ordered more acid from suppliers in surrounding cities.

As each order arrived, she poured it over Quickie's body. Mary watched a thin trail of smoke rise from the body as the acid reacted with the skin. She fanned the acrid smoke and fumes from her face. *I hadn't expected such a foul odor. Got to do something about this smell, or I won't be able to enter the house. Can't have Wonderful suspecting anything.*

Two days later, Mary poured another container of acid into the tub. The bloated body floated on the frothy, foul smelling liquid. *I had no idea it would take so long to dissolve her.* Mary picked up another container and emptied it on the body. The mouth of the container struck the bloated abdomen causing its taut skin to split. The room filled with a putrid smell.

Mary gagged, held her breath, rushed out the basement door, and took a deep breath of fresh air.

"Shit." *I have to do something about the smell, or the neighbors are going to complain. I can't open a basement window, and I can't leave the kitchen's basement door open . . . not while Wonderful is here, and I can't leave the dungeon door closed forever. "*What the hell am I going to do?"

Mary scanned the dungeon for an answer. "Ah! The fireplace." *Wonder if the flue is open?* She moved boxes of the former owner's sex toys from in front of the fireplace then peered up the flue. She hoped to see daylight but didn't. "Damn! Everything's black, but I feel a draft." *The flue has to be open, or I wouldn't feel a draft. Got to get more air moving up the chimney but how?"*

Mary sat on a chair and stared at the fireplace. "A fan. *I need an exhaust fan.*"

Chapter Eighteen

The next day, Mary walked up and down the aisles of a home store, looking at fans: box fans, floor fans, table fans, window fans. They confronted her at every turn.

They're all too large.

"You look perplexed," a salesman said. "May I help you?"

"I need a window fan, but a small one."

"Please. Come with me." The salesman led Mary to aisle five. He pointed to a box on an upper shelf. "See the picture on that box. If that's what you need, I'll get it down."

"I'm sure that's it. Please, get it down."

The clerk placed the box on the floor then opened it.

Mary examined the fan. "It's 24" x 12" x 5". That's perfect. I'll take it."

Mary carried the boxed fan into the kitchen where Wonderful sat at the table drinking a beer.

"Damn," Mary muttered under her breath. *Why is she here now?*

"What ya got there, girl?"

"A fan," Mary said, placing the box beside the basement door.

"You must be havin' hot flashes, girl? It's not hot enough for a fan."

Mary took a deep breath. "Got a dead rat. It's in a place I can't get to so I need to ventilate the basement until the odor is gone."

"I wondered what smelled so bad."

"The odor should be gone soon." *Damn it. She did notice the smell. Hope this fan works quickly.* "Try to ignore it, but stay out of the basement."

Wonderful shrugged and shook her head. "Baby, I ain't goin' in no basement. Got locked in a dark one for two days when I was little. I hate all them spiders and bugs. Ugh! Never wanna go in another basement as long as I live."

Glad to hear that. Mary closed the basement door behind her and headed down the steps with the box wedged under her arm. She unpacked the fan then placed the fan in the fireplace and plugged it in. The fan whirred, but the room filled with soot, dust, and bug debris. Much of it blew back onto Mary.

"Shit!" *Bet the damn flue hasn't been cleaned since the house was built.* "Now what?" *Can't call a chimney sweep. He'd want to come in here, and I can't have that. Shit, think Mary. Think. If I can't blow stuff up the chimney maybe I could suck it out. That's it. A vacuum cleaner. I'll use it to clear the flue.*

Mary ran up the basement steps, pushed the door open, almost knocking over Wonderful as she crouched to peer into the refrigerator.

"Sorry," Mary said, running past Wonderful and then up the stairs to the second floor.

Three minutes later, Mary returned to the kitchen with a canister vacuum cleaner and extra bags.

Wonderful chuckled. "You gonna suck up something—like take over my job?"

"Very funny," Mary said, descending the steps. *If she only knew.*

Mary filled four vacuum bags with debris from the firebox and the flue.

She installed and started the fan. "Thank God it's working. No blow back." Mary struck a match the former homeowner had left behind. The flame bent toward the fan. "Yeah." She smiled. *There's definitely more draft. The damn smell should soon be gone.*

After two days of air extraction, the fan had done its job. Mary smelled nothing beyond the dungeon and even that odor had faded by fifty percent.

Once a day, Mary examined the decomposing body. The skin on the fingers, toes, heels, elbows, and back had dissolved, but gas forming bacteria still functioned inside the torso, causing it to bloat and float. The more gas the bacteria made, the higher the body floated, slowing its dissolution.

Mary considered her choices. Should she turn Quickie over? That might hasten the acid's work on her front side but at the expense of the back. *I've got to get the acid working on all sides. I need to sink her.* She looked around the dungeon for something weighty. *Hell! There's all that iron stuff left by old John.*

Mary lugged leg irons, neck irons, chains and lead weights, used for God knows what, to the side of the tub. After balling up a handful of rusted chain, she placed it on Quickie's bloated belly. Shocked, Mary watched as the skin ruptured and the chain fell inside Quickie's abdomen. The hole allowed foul smelling gases out as acid flowed into the cavity.

The body sank a few inches. Large bubbles gurgled from Quickie's nose and mouth. Smaller bubbles formed at the edges of the eyelids and the thin skin of the lips.

With morbid fascination, Mary watched the chains dissolve almost as fast as the newly exposed flesh. *That chain wasn't enough. I've got to get the gas out of the chest.*

Mary searched her mental inventory of the dungeon contents and remembered seeing several fireplace tools. She searched the storage boxes and found a log hook.

Back at the tub, she held the log hook perpendicular over Quickie's chest. *Okay, Mary. Don't splash acid on yourself.* She pushed the point of the hook through a half-dissolved spot between the right, front ribs. The flesh collapsed, and a gush of foul smelling gas filled the room. Mary held her breath, pushed the hook deeper into the chest cavity, forcing the body to the bottom of the tub.

The body settled there as acid flowed into the chest cavity. Several loops of bloated bowel floated out of the rent in the abdomen. Mary poked them with the hook, ripping them open. Another torrent of putrid gases mingled with the room's wretchedness.

Over the following days, Mary tended the decomposing body until all the flesh had dissolved. She noted, with surprise, the bones were dissolving. *Good. There will be less of a disposal problem.*

After two months of servicing Tim, Wonderful had not become pregnant. Mary had no choice but to let her go on her way.

"Thank ya, Miss Mary, for the work," Wonderful said and took her pay envelope. "I gotta care for my nephew for a while."

"Thank you. I know you need a rest. Are you interested in future work?"

"You bet, girl. I always need money."

"Good. We'll be in touch."

For two weeks, Mary fed Tim with the rubber bra.

She felt exhausted from everything the bra's use entailed. *I can't keep this up. Maybe I should call Kashandra. Get her back.*

"Ya want me to work again?" Kashandra yelled into the phone.

"If you're available, but you would have to undergo another examination, testing, and remain monogamous while you're working."

"Sho, baby. Mono. I can do that."

"You remember that Tim has an allergy to latex, so he can't use condoms."

"I'll be careful."

I hope you aren't, Mary said to herself. *I want you pregnant.*

Medical testing completed, Mary told Kashandra she had a clean bill of health and could start work the following day.

"Kinda missed the place," Kashandra said, looking around Mary's kitchen.

"We're happy to have you back. Remember how to get to your room?"

"Yeah, baby. Upstairs, across from Mister Tim's."

"Go ahead, do your thing. He's waiting. I'll be up in a minute."

Kashandra undressed then opened Tim's door.

"Tim, it's me, Kash. Remember me?"

Tim quit sucking his thumb. "Kash?"

"Yes. Kash."

Jostling her breasts to attract him, Kash walked toward the bed where Tim propped himself up on one elbow. His lips parted, halfway between a smile and a pout, ready to attach them to a nipple.

As Kashandra reached the bed, Tim attached himself to her "E" cup breast. She maneuvered herself to the middle of the bed then stretched out. There, he suckled. *He sure ain't forgot how to suck. Just gotta endure it.*

The room filled with Tim's soaring sounds of pleasure.

Mary entered the room and observed Tim for a moment then asked, "Has he shown any interest in getting inside?"

"Not yet, baby. You want him ta fuck me?"

"See if you can get him inside. Having good sex keeps him calm."

"He ain't up, baby. Can't get it in if it ain't up."

"Then get it up."

"Ya gotta move him off my titty if I'm gonna do that." Kashandra groped for Tim's crotch. "Help me, will ya, baby? Lift his butt."

Mary straddled Kashandra's legs and pulled Tim's hips upward while Kashandra grabbed his crotch and stimulated him.

"Hurry, Mary said. "I can't hold him forever."

"Okay, baby. It's gettin' there."

"Then put it in for God's sake."

Kashandra sighed. "It's in."

Mary pushed down on Tim's butt. "Hope this gets him started. Kash, move your hips, woman."

Kashandra bucked him. He must have liked the bucking because he started humping her.

Satisfied with the situation, Mary sat on the bedside chair and watched the action.

"What the fuck?" Mary yelled as a screeching sound filled the house.

Kashandra pushed Tim off her hips. "Sounds like a fire alarm, baby!"

"Shit! It is. Don't tell me the house is on fire."

"We gotta get outta here, baby," Kashandra said, pushing Tim's mouth from her breast.

Mary pulled Tim, screaming, from the bed. "Where is his damn robe?"

Kashandra ran to her room, hands covering her ears. "Lordie, Lordie, don't let us burn ta death!"

The mattress, Mary thought. *His robe is under the mattress.*

She put the robe over Tim's shoulders and led him downstairs. Kashandra followed, wearing her dress but carrying her shoes and underwear.

"Take Tim outside," Mary yelled. "I'm going to look for the fire.

She ran upstairs to search the second-floor rooms. *Nothing here.* She ran downstairs to search the first floor. "Shit. The fire truck is going to show up soon*."* *I've got to settle this now. Can't let the firemen search the basement.* She searched the first floor and found nothing amiss. "Better check the basement."

The basement search revealed nothing, but the dungeon reeked of an electrical fire. After searching the room, Mary discovered the fan's electrical cord had

239

shorted out and smoldered.

Gotta pull that damn plug.

Grabbing the electrical cord, Mary yelled, "Damn! It's hot!"

Better pull on the fan housing. She yanked the metal frame away from the socket. The electrical cord strained, but the plug did not budge. "Shit." *The heat must have welded the plug in the socket.*

Mary thought for a moment. *I need something to pull the plug out. Pliers. I need big ones—with insulation. Wish I had Joe's.*

The thin smoke that fouled the air caused Mary to cough. She rummaged through the boxes of John's sex toys until she found a pair of log tongs. *Wonder what old John did with these?*

She wrapped a towel around each tong handle then closed their nipping end on the burned, sparking plug and pulled. The plug moved a fraction of an inch then stopped. She put her fingers in her ears for a second, muting the screeching alarm mounted over her head.

Work it up and down, Mary.

A hard tug sent her falling backwards, striking her head against the rim of the tub. She jumped up, rubbed her head, and peered into the tub. *Gotta get rid of those bones.* "Shit!" *How the hell do I get the stopper out?* She rubbed her aching head. *I can't put my hand in that acid. It would be destroyed in a flash.* She stared at the drain hole in the bottom of the tub and noted the makeshift glass plug she had used as a stopper had no handle. "Shit!"

Mary paced for a few seconds. "I have to dilute the acid."

She opened the tub's hot and cold faucets and watched the diluting acid mixture flow out the overflow drain. "Hurry damn it. Hurry!"

A slimy glob of undissolved fat wedged itself against the overflow screen almost stopping the flow. She used the log hook to squash the glob. It not only refused to move but got pushed into the screen further obstructing the flow of acid. "Shit" She continued to rub at the glob until she pushed it through the screen, allowing maximum outflow of the acid.

Hands over her ears, Mary squinted. "Damn alarm. It's driving me crazy!"

She used the tongs to mix the water and foul smelling liquid. The heavier acid at the bottom of the tub swirled as water and acid mixed. *Careful, Mary. Don't splash yourself with this shit.*

Bubbles developed along the length of the tongs, indicating their dissolution. After a minute or so, bubble generation slowed—indicating the acid strength had waned. Mary checked the faucet for maximum flow. "Come on, come on," she muttered, scanning the submerged tongs for bubble formation. "Good! No more bubbles." *It must be diluted. Got to pull the plug. I can't risk not doing it.*

Mary placed her left hand on the tub rim for support then took a deep breath. She plunged her right hand to the bottom of the tub where she forced her fingernails under the makeshift plug. After tugging at it for a moment, it yielded and the diluted acid flowed out the bottom drain.

She stared into the tub. "What the hell do I do with the bones?" She scanned the room and noted a pillow.

I'll hide them in the pillowcase. She dried her arm with the pillowcase then placed the bones inside.

Within seconds, she noted a burning sensation on her right hand and arm. "Shit! It's burned." Without thinking, she rubbed her arm then screamed when she saw her skin shred and fall away. "Oh God!" She stared at the discolored, sagging fat and the exposed muscles. "Shit! It hurts."

Dropping the bag of bones, she plunged her arm and hand under the flow of the fresh water. In pain, she gritted her teeth. *Thank God, it hurts. I'm lucky the nerves are still intact.*

Chapter Nineteen

The scream of sirens blared in the distance.

"Shit!" Mary said. "Fire trucks. Gotta move fast. Think girl, think."

She placed the pillowcase containing Quickie's bones in the bottom drawer of the old dresser that had been pushed to the right of the open dungeon door. Using her uninjured hand, she labored to recover the dresser with the debris laden sheet.

Everyone knows about this dungeon. No need to hide it. Just use it to my advantage.

"Damn, those sirens are close." Mary scanned the dungeon for anything to help explain her injury. She grabbed the second pillow and removed its case. Using a match, she burned one corner of the cloth and then threw the blackened case into the tub and doused it with water then rubbed it against her sweating brow.

Exhausted and in pain, she sat on the floor and rested her head against the edge of the tub. *Guess I'm as ready as I'll ever be.*

Moments later, the fire trucks' sirens sounded as if they had stopped four feet from the dungeon door.

Mary heard Kashandra outside, yelling to the firemen. "Doctor Mary's inside."

In seconds, t he house filled with the sounds of firemen running room-to-room, searching for smoke or flames and her.

"Doctor Snow, where are you?" the firemen yelled in various parts of the house.

The thud of heavy boots over Mary's head meant

the firemen would soon come to the basement.

"Down here," Mary yelled.

A heavy-footed fireman made his way to the open basement door. He shined his flashlight into the dimly lit space and yelled, "Hey guys, the smell of smoke is in here. Anyone there?"

"It's me," Mary answered. "Doctor Snow. I'm here. I'm burned."

The fireman rushed into the room where Mary sat on the floor. "You okay?" he asked, moving to her side.

"I guess, but I'm a nervous wreck." She held out her arm and hand. "I'm burned."

The fireman shined his flashlight on her forearm. "I'll say. Everything else okay?"

"Yeah."

The fireman raised his radio to his lips and said, "Chief here. I'm in the basement. There is no fire now. Send the EMT in with something for burns." Turning to Mary, he asked, "What happened?"

Mary pointed to the fan. "It developed a short in the plug, and the cord caught fire. I tried to pull the plug with a rag, but the burning cord got wrapped around my arm along with the rag and burned my arm. Rag is in the tub. I ran water on it."

The chief looked in the tub. "Yeah, it's out." He moved his light around the room. "So, this is the in-famous dungeon. Heard about it over the years, but never thought I'd see it."

"It's something, isn't it? I've thought about dis-mantling it but haven't gotten around to doing it. It does add something to the ambience of the house, doesn't it?"

"I'll say."

An EMT entered the basement.

The chief said, "Here's your patient. Arm's burned pretty bad."

"You're Doctor Snow, aren't you?" the EMT asked. "I've seen you at the hospital."

"What's your name?"

"Mike. Mike Allen," he said, opening his first aid kit.

"Nice to meet you, Mike."

"Sorry we meet under these circumstances, Doctor. Let's have a look at your arm."

Mary held out her arm and winced. The chief shined his light on the burned area.

"Nasty burn," Mike said. "I'm going to wrap it, but you need a doctor. Should we take you to your hospital or Saint Luke's?"

"Mine. I know the doctors."

"There's nothing more here for us," the chief said. "Mike, you get the doctor to the hospital, and we'll close out this case. I'll take care of the alarm."

Weeks later, Detective Jackson threaded his police car through rush hour traffic and yelled into his two-way radio. "Who found the body?"

Shredding the air, the siren mounted behind the car's grille made it difficult for Jackson to hear his partner, Tom, who sat beside him.

"A group of Cub Scouts found the body while out for a day of hiking," Tom said, scanning a map of Murphy Park.

"Sometimes, I wish I was still a beat cop," Jackson said. "I hate murder scenes. Hope the scouts didn't disturb the site."

"Fortunately," a policeman announced over the radio, "the scout leader is a crime-movie nut. He knew to keep the kids away from the van. They didn't touch anything."

Jackson turned off the siren as his car bumped its way over the last few feet of the dirt road leading to the Murphy Park crime scene. The car came to a stop at a small clearing, buzzing with police activitys.

"Who was first on scene?" Detective Jackson asked the nearest policeman.

"Park Officer Jones," the policeman said, pointing toward an elderly man standing in the shade of a picnic hut. "He's kinda shook up—his first decomposing body."

"Tell the crime scene guys to do their thing," Jackson said. "I'm going to look around."

Detective Jackson walked to the driver's side of the van and looked at the body slumped over the steering wheel. "Skull's crushed. Blunt trauma means a blunt weapon." Jackson turned to a nearby officer. "Anyone find a hammer, ax, piece of pipe? Anything?"

"Sorry, Detective. Nothing yet. We're still searching the area."

"Anyone search the garbage cans or that hanging fire can?"

"Still working on that," a crime scene investigator said.

"Don't forget the lake," Jackson yelled, walking toward the park officer.

The elderly, overweight park officer's brown short-sleeve shirt appeared soaked with perspiration. Using a handkerchief, he wiped his bald head and fanned himself with his sweat-stained cap.

"Officer Jones, I'm Detective Harry Jackson. I've been working this case a while. I'd like to hear what you and the scouts know, what you and they saw—"

"Worse thing I've ever seen." Officer Jones began a ten-minute download of information and impressions, ending with, "I noticed some unusual shoe imprints. They're quite clear. Must have rained the day of the murder. Made the ground soft. The crime scene guys just took casts of the imprints and bike tracks. Happy to show you if you want to see them."

"Detective Jackson," a crime scene investigator yelled, "Let the morgue guys get the body out before you go back to the van. Might be something under the body we need to photograph or tag."

"Okay," Jackson yelled then turned to the park officer. "Would you show me the imprints?"

The park officer pointed at the imprints. "Think they have anything to do with this dead guy?"

"Who knows. I've got your phone number. Why don't you go back to your post? I don't think there's any more you can do here. You've been very helpful. Thank you."

"My pleasure, Detective." Officer Jones headed for his park-patrol car.

Forensic attendants removed the body from the van, and the crime scene techs photographed the back of the victim's clothing and the driver's seat.

Another tech and Jackson searched the victim's clothing and seat cover for evidence then did a cursory examination of the body. Just then a tow truck arrived.

"Detective Jackson," a crime scene tech said, "The van's all yours."

"Good, but I don't want the tow truck moving it over those imprints until I can get a better look at them. I hate looking at plaster casts."

Jackson knelt on the ground then pushed the weeds away from the imprints. "Hmm. Strange impressions. One letter on each instep." *Who puts an "L" on shoe soles?* The detective chuckled as he remembered the Broadway show *Nunsense*. He chuckled again. *Guess I'll save the question for the lab guys.*

Jackson moved to the areas marked by small, yellow plastic cones numbered one through ten. "So these are the bike tracks?" He pushed weeds away from the tire imprints then spoke to a policeman. "Interesting. The "V's" of the front and back tires point in the same direction, presumeably the front . . . could be toward the rear but how the hell did they get here. There are no tracks leading in—just out." *Did someone walk or carry the bike here? Did the bike get here inside the van . . . with someone known by the driver? Did he . . . they . . . come here for a private tryst? A jealous woman? A gay lover? A hustler cruising the park on a bike?*

Jackson looked around then yelled to a policeman. "Have the techs stop whatever they're doing and search for more bike tracks. If they find any, block off the area and call the lab guys for castings. And call me! I'll be downtown."

Detective Jackson had just walked to his desk when a policeman said, "This call is for you, Harry." The officer took his feet off his desk and waved the receiver toward Jackson.

"Who is it?"

"The state crime lab. Jim Bonavista. He has something he wants you to see."

"Tell him I'll be down in an hour."

Detective Jackson pushed open the lab door then spoke to a tech staring into a microscope. "Where is Jim Bonavista?"

"Desk is in the far corner, on the right," the tech said, without looking from the microscope.

Jackson walked to the far corner. "Which of you guys is Jim?"

"That'd be me," Jim said. "Are you Detective Jackson?"

"That's me."

"Got something to show you about the park case. Seems those bike tires are old—very old. I'm surprised they still hold air."

Jackson stared at side-by-side photos of the tire castings and catalog images of tire treads from the mid-1900s.

One-by-one, Jim compared the photos. He paused at one image with the "V" markings found on the imprints in the park. "It's a match," Jim said, smiling at Jackson.

"Who made the tire and for which company?"

"Only one manufacturer, the Victory Tire Company. They were in business for a hundred years. Made tires for many bike manufacturers, but the "V" tire was made only for Schwinn. They'll be hard to trace, but we'll contact all the dealers on the east coast."

"See if some mom and pop company makes them or

if there is a source for 'new' old stock. Good work," Harry said, slapping Jim on the back. "Got anything on the shoes?"

"They're custom," Jim said, opening a reference book. "Made by the Liberty Shoe Company in Baltimore. They've been in operation since 1928. Almost went out of business during the depression but hung on by the skin of their teeth. They're going over their records to see if they can identify the shoe owner. Liberty isn't computerized, so it'll take time to search files. Said they'd call in a few days."

"Excellent work, Jim. Let me know as soon as you hear anything. By-the-way, who's doing the blood research?"

"That'd be Rich Clark. He's next door."

"Thanks."

Jackson went next door and spoke to a woman leaving the blood lab. "Where does Rich work?" The woman held the door open and yelled, "Rich, someone to see you!"

A young, black-haired man, wearing black framed glasses and a lab coat walked to the door and extended his hand. "I'm Rich. How may I help you?"

"I'm Detective Harry Jackson. You must be new. I don't recall seeing you before."

"Yeah. Been here four months."

"Well, welcome. I'm working the Murphy Park case. Wondering if you have anything on the blood samples taken from the van or victim?"

Rich went to his desk, picked up a folder, and then folded back a page. "I don't know how this fits in, but samples from the cab, seat, floor, and door belonged to the victim, but they contained something we don't see often in a young man—anticoagulants."

"Yeah? I don't remember the medical examiner's autopsy report mentioning anticoagulants. The anticoagulant had to be added post mortem."

Harry rubbed his chin and stared at the floor. "Why would anyone anticoagulate blood *after* its owner is dead?"

"More importantly, how would anyone get the driver's *clean* blood?" Rich asked. "The medical examiner's report makes no mention of needle marks anywhere on the body."

Feeling confused, Harry asked, "Why would anyone take his blood, mix it with anticoagulants, and then kill him? Seems like a lot of trouble just to get the guy's money and a few tools."

Rich shrugged. "Perhaps the perp took blood from the scalp wound. That would explain the absence of needle marks or the blood was taken days before the death, but in either case, why?" Rich raised his palms to the ceiling. "Somebody would have had to take a lot of blood if I read the crime scene report correctly, but why would the victim let someone take so much blood?"

"Does sound weird," Harry said.

"Could it be the dead man had been a donor at the Red Cross, and the murderer, somehow, got the man's blood there? It all sounds like a cover up for something but what?"

"I like your thinking, Rich. We'd better check if he had been a local blood donor, but who has anticoagulants in the first place?"

"Could be a host of people," Rich said, putting his

hands in his lab coat pockets. "Doctors, pharmacists, nurses, vets, podiatrists, researchers, nurse's aides, and technicians in a clinical lab . . . The list goes on."

"Any way to find out who manufactured the anti-coagulant?" Harry asked.

"Nah. The drug's too generic. It's made by lots of pharmaceutical companies."

"Well, thanks for your work, Rich. Give a call if you get anything else."

Detective Jackson spent a few days contemplating the relationships of the evidence from the park case.

One day while riding his own bike, Jackson thought, *So many things keep pointing to Snow. The victim was last seen at her house, and his blood in the cab had anticoagulants, which could have been added by her . . . but why? Why would she kill him? Damn it, why kill a cable guy?*

Harry watched a jet's contrail as he tried to clear his mind of lingering questions about motives for killing the cable man.

Snow didn't need his money or his tools. Blackmail maybe? For what? She's busy taking care of her disabled son, her patients . . . doing routine stuff. She doesn't date. No ex-husbands. No known boyfriends. What's the motive? The detective rubbed his forehead.

Shit, better look into the victim's private life. Is he gay? Was he into hustlers or prostitutes? Did he have a jealous boy or girlfriend? A bookie or loan shark?

Chapter Twenty

Five days after the fire, Mary's arm wound show-ed signs of healing.

"Damn it, woman!" Mary yelled. "You're killing me. Be careful!"

"Miss Mary," Kashandra said, removing the dressing from Mary's arm. "You know I ain't no nurse,"

Mary turned her arm for self-examination. *There's less redness and new skin is growing. Should be healed in three to four weeks.*

She handed Kashandra a tube of salve. "My doctor wants me to use this new stuff." Mary unwrapped a sterile tongue blade then spread the new salve over the burned area. "Ugh. It smells bad."

She held the wooden depressor toward Kashandra. "Spread it on the back side."

Kashandra started to spread the grey cream when Mary screamed and jerked her arm aside. "For God's sake, woman, be careful. You're not spreading con-crete."

"Sorry. Here, read this newspaper while I wrap your arm. It's not new, but it'll take your mind off your arm."

"Geeez," Mary said and took the paper. "Maybe reading will take my mind off the torture you're putting me through." Mary placed the paper on her lap and, with her free hand, unfolded it to the front page. "Oh, my God," she yelled and dropped the newspaper on the floor.

Startled, Kashandra said, "Baby, I ain't done nothin' to make ya yell like that."

"Sorry." *Police found a body in Murphy Park. Joe?*

"Would you hand me the paper again?" Mary asked.

She silently read, Missing cable man's body found in Murphy Park. The article mentioned robbery as the motive for the murder.

Mary reread the article, searching for any mention of clues found at the site. *Nothing. I hope this means they found nothing suspicious. What if they did and aren't saying so? Oh God I hope not!*

"What ya reading, baby?"

"They found the body of that missing cable man. The one who installed Tim's TV. What a shame. He was such a nice young man."

"Yeah. That death. It gets us all in the end," Kashandra said, putting the last piece of tape on Mary's dressing. "But that murder stuff, that's something else."

"Kashandra, I want you to help me with something."

"Sho, baby, if I can. What ya want me ta do?"

"Would you make some phone calls for me? After I've dialed a few numbers, my arm hurts—a lot. I'd appreciate you making the calls for me."

"Callin' for what?"

"I have to supplement Tim's diet with breast milk. He needs the antibodies found only in human milk." *She won't know I'm lying.* "I have to get milk from women willing to donate or sell their breast milk. It's a constant search, and I need your help calling prospective donors. Of course, you'd be calling on my behalf."

"Sure, baby. I can do that."

"I'll give you a script to read when you call. That

way you'll know exactly what to say."

"When do I start?"

"I'll write the script tonight, and you can start in the morning."

"Let's go over the script," Mary said, handing two typed pages to Kashandra. "Make sure you read it *exactly* as written. I can't have you talking to women in your southern fake English drawl, *understand*? Okay? Let's get started, just as it's written."

Kashandra stood erect and cleared her throat. She looked like a third grader about to recite her lines for a school play. "Dear --insert name--"

"No! Don't read that insert name part. That's where the name of the woman you are calling goes. Her name is on the second page. You're supposed to insert one name per call, in place of the words 'insert name.' *Understand*?"

"Alright, baby, but ya don't have to yell. Here I go. My name's Kashan—"

"No, no," Mary said. "Say my name *is* Kashandra."

"Okay. My name *es* Kashandra."

Feeling frustrated, Mary said, "Never mind. Go on."

"I am callin' on—"

"*NO*! Can't you read, woman? It's *calling* not *callin'*. There is a 'g' at the end of the word!"

"That's what I said," Kashandra murmured. "You white folk sure particular when it comes ta talkin'."

"I know . . . you're tired, Kashandra, but . . . This is *not* going to work. I'll make the calls. Just have to use my good arm to hold the receiver *and* dial. You go take care of Tim. Make sure he gets a good ride. Keeps him calm the rest of the day."

Mary called the listed names and found two women willing to donate milk.

She took a taxi to each woman's house, so she could spare her arm the pain of driving.

With each donor, Mary went into great detail, discussing the process of collecting milk and demonstrating the process. In neither case did the woman want money.

Before leaving each home, Mary thanked the donor several times. "You have no idea how helpful you are to the mother and her new baby. Each baby depends, one hundred percent, on human milk for its sustenance. Without your generosity, the baby would die. *You,* my dear, are a life saver."

Sometimes, a woman would write a note to be given to the needy mother. They contained well wishes for the desperate mother and hungry baby.

Two women sent small gifts or flowers for the alleged mother. One woman sent a basket of fruit. Kashandra enjoyed the oranges.

After six weeks of servicing Tim, Kashandra said, "Miss Mary, I don't mind the fuckin', but my titties can't take all Tim's sucking. I need a rest."

Mary gave Kashandra a three week break. This required Mary to find other prostitutes to fill in.

Two weeks after Kashandra's departure, Mary got a call from her. "Miss Mary. It's Kashandra, baby, I'm pregnant."

"Are you sure?"

"No doubt about it, baby. I'm late. Got no flow."

Thank God. "Come by the house and let me examine

you?" Mary thumbed through her appointment book. "What about Thursday, ten o'clock?"

"Baby, I'll be there."

Mary pulled off her rubber gloves. "You can put your legs down and sit up, Kashandra. No doubt about it. You are pregnant. I'd say about eight weeks."

"Baby, I told ya."

"Have you told anyone?"

"No, baby! Ya think I'm crazy. No street woman wants to admit she's pregnant. It's suicide in my profession. Them Johns would say, 'If she can get pregnant, she can get the clap or worse.' Word like that would put a girl outta business. No, baby. No way I'm gonna tell folks I'm pregnant."

Thank God, Mary thought. *A woman who can keep her mouth shut. Tim's milk is on its way.* "Why don't you plan on living here until the baby comes? I'll care for you through the delivery. I doubt you have insurance. Do you?"

"Nope. Can't afford none, baby. I use the clinics."

"Well, don't worry. You can continue to work here, and when the time comes, I'll deliver you . . . here. No charge."

"I heard that women with a baby can't have sex, so how can I do it with Tim?"

"What you've heard is half true. If you're having certain problems, you should not have sex. Otherwise, you can. That's why I'd like you to stay here. I'll make sure you don't have problems."

"That's mighty kinda you, especially since I ain't got no insurance, and I don't like them clinics."

"Why don't you tell your family you've landed a traveling job—with a rich family? You'll be travelling with them for eight months and care for their children. Tell them you'll send money home. That should stop them from worrying. Of course, you can stay here for free. No one else will know you're pregnant."

"I likes ya thinking, baby, 'cause I don't want nobody ta know."

Neither do I.

Five weeks after the fire, spring arrived and the weather warmed. Because Mary's yard had no color, she decided she would plant flowers. She purchased seventy pots of flowering plants that now waited in the garage.

"Kashandra, I'm going to plant some flowers in the front yard. Yell if you need me, otherwise take care of Tim."

"I'm going in his room now, baby," Kashandra yelled down the stairs.

Mary planted the flowers in long-neglected flower beds on either side of the front steps. She stood and wiped sweat from her brow as a UPS truck stopped at her curb.

"Wonder what that is," Mary said as the truck driver approached and handed her a box. "Thanks." Mary glanced at the shipping label. "Ah. My new shoes." She tucked the box under her arm and went inside.

Much to Mary's delight, Kashandra had reached that time in her pregnancy when she had begun to produce small amounts of breast milk. This meant Mary did not have to search much longer for lactating women willing to donate their breast milk.

Kashandra and Mary had discussed the process of delivering a baby, but Mary became concerned when Kashandra said, "After the baby comes, we goin' to live with my auntie for a while—until I can get about. You and Tim can come and visit us anytime ya want."

Damn! Mary said to herself. *She can't leave.*

As Kashandra approached her due date, Mary encouraged her to engage in vigorous intercourse. Mary wanted the sex to cause a complication in the pregnancy, but nothing happened.

A week before Kashandra's due date, Mary awoke at 1:27 a.m. to the sounds of Kashandra's calls for help.

"Mary, help me. Come here! Mary!"

Mary ran to Kashandra's bedside. "You having labor pains?"

"Can't be sure. Ain't never had this feeling before, but baby, it don't feel like I just need a shit."

"I'd better do a pelvic exam," Mary said, pulling on rubber gloves. "Relax. Let your belly go loose. Breathe with your mouth open."

Kashandra winced, held her breath, and bit her lower lip as Mary began the exam.

"What's wrong?" Mary asked.

"Hurry up down there. There ain't room for the baby and your hand at the same time."

"Try and relax." Mary patted Kashandra's knee. "Okay. I'm done." Mary placed the used instruments on a tray.

"What is it, baby?"

Shit! "Looks like you'll soon deliver your baby." *We*

don't need a baby now.

Chapter Twenty-one

Kashandra's labor lasted forty-seven hours before the baby's head could be seen in the birth canal.

Thank God, Mary thought. *I won't have to take her to the hospital for a C-section. That would require too much explaining.*

With a sheet covering Kashandra's elevated knees, Mary controlled the delivery of the baby's head then delivered its right shoulder followed by the left.

"It's a boy!" Mary said, placing the baby on the bed between Kashandra's bent and covered knees. At this point, a rubber suction bulb should be used to suck mucus from the baby's nose, mouth, and throat to clear its airway.

Mary stared at the infant. *Nobody needs you, but Tim needs your mother's milk. Mary, do what you have to do.*

She squeezed the suction bulb a few times in view of Kashandra to confirm it worked. *You have to do this, Mary. It's for Tim. Get on with it.* Instead of sucking mucus from the airways, Mary used the bulb for the opposite effect. Every few seconds, she used the bulb to make sucking sounds outside the baby's mouth and then shook the bulb in full view of Kashandra as if emptying mucus sucked from the baby's airways.

"My baby ain't crying," Kashandra said, trying to see the baby which lay out of sight between her legs. "Ain't you supposed to slap his ass?"

"We don't do that anymore. I could break some-thing. We stimulate the baby's back with our knuckles."

"Ya better rub it harder," Kashandra said, moving

onto her elbows. "Baby, he ain't crying."

Out of Kashandra's view, Mary rubbed the bed as if she massaged the baby's back. The baby made some gasps but did not breathe.

Looking anxious, Kashandra propped herself higher on her arms. "Hurry, Miss Mary, or my baby ain't gonna make it."

After several minutes of rubbing the bed instead of the baby, Mary stopped the pretense.

"Rubbing isn't working," Mary said, trying to sound concerned. "I'd better slap his butt."

Mary held the bluish baby high in the air by its heels. "He's making no sounds," Mary said. "No attempts to breathe." She slapped the baby's butt. *I'd better slap it again. Kashandra has to believe I'm doing everything possible.*

Seeing her baby, Kashandra cried out, "Oh, Lordie, he's blue. He ain't dying, is he?"

"I'm trying everything I know," Mary said, slapping his butt again.

"Do something, baby. Don't let him die!"

Mary placed the baby on the bed and blew into its mouth—without squeezing his nose shut as she should. The baby's belly rose and fell with each faked resuscitation effort. Mary knew air entered his belly—not his lungs.

Mary slapped his butt again and then moved the baby beside his mother. *Kashandra has to believe I'm doing all I can.* Mary continued fake CPR.

"My baby's mighty blue," Kashandra said, sitting up and staring in disbelief at the failing activity. "You're doing that resuscitation stuff ain't ya, baby. My boy dying?" Kashandra templed her hands and looked toward the ceiling. "Lord, please don't let him die."

Mary stood and shook her head. "Kashandra . . . I'm sorry. It wasn't meant to be." She forced a frown and sat on the bedside chair.

Kashandra lay still, unable to speak.

Mary said to herself, *There is nothing to worry about now.*

After a few seconds, Mary picked up the dead infant, wrapped him in a blanket, and placed him in Kashandra's arms.

Kashandra stroked the baby's face and cried. "Why did ya die on me, baby? Did the Lord need ya back with the angels?" Kashandra used her trembling hand to wipe tears as they fell on the baby's chest. "You ain't never gonna know yo daddy, your granny and a lotta aunties."

Mary stared out the window and shuddered as she thought of her son fathering a mulatto. *But I have milk for Tim.*

"What do you want me to do with the baby?" Mary asked.

"We gotta bury him, baby."

"I have to contact the police before we can contact a funeral home."

"I understand."

"When the police come, don't say anything about your work here."

"I know, baby."

Two hours later, the doorbell rang. Mary rushed downstairs, pushing her hair from her face then smoothing her clothes before opening the door.

God, he's a tall one, Mary said to herself.

The policeman removed his cap. "Doctor Snow, I'm Officer Gary King."

Gary stood about six feet, eleven-inches tall. A man of about thirty. His blue eyes and auburn hair glistened.

"Thanks for coming, Officer." *My*, is *he giving me the once over. He's awfully neat . . . good looking too.* "Please, come in. Bet you played basketball in high school didn't you?"

"You guessed it. Also played a year in college."

"From which college did you graduate?"

"Didn't. Got married in my freshman year and had a baby."

Mary closed the door. "I know how demanding children can be. Sorry we have to bother you, but there has been an unfortunate incident."

"Hope I can help," Officer King said. "What happened?"

"Let's go upstairs. I'll introduce you to Kashandra." Mary and the officer climbed the stairs. "She's a poor black woman who couldn't afford private care. She had some serious problems with her pregnancy. Through the grapevine, I heard about her and offered to deliver her here. Unfortunately, the baby was stillborn."

Mary knocked on Kashandra's door. "Kashandra, Officer King is here. He wants to talk to you."

"Come in."

Kashandra still cradled her blanket-covered son in her arms. She wiped a tear.

The officer stared at the bundle in Kashandra's arms. "Kashandra, sorry to meet you like this." He scanned the bucket at the foot of the bed, the instruments, the sheets, and bloody towels. "What is your full name and address?"

"Kashandra Smiley. I live at 202 Leonard Street, Towson."

"Thank you. Now, tell me what happened."

"Officer, I had the high pressure with my baby. Miss Mary and I had a heap of trouble gettin' it where it oughta be, but we did."

That's good Kashandra, Mary thought. *Keep it up.* "Officer, Kashandra had a dangerous condition known as preeclampsia several weeks ago. Her blood pressure became extremely high and was difficult to stabilize, but I finally got it in check."

"It was scary," Kashandra added. "First I had bad headaches then almost faintin' spells."

"Everything went well after controlling her blood pressure until delivery," Mary said. "The baby never breathed. Not even a gasp. I tried to resuscitate him, repeatedly suctioned his airways, stimulated his back, and slapped his rear, but he wouldn't breathe." Mary sighed and shook her head. "Would you like to see him?"

"Please," Gary said.

Mary took the baby from Kashandra's arms and laid him on the bed. She unfolded the blanket and held up the limp baby.

"He's a beautiful baby," Gary said, scanning its body. "May I see his back?"

Mary turned the baby over.

The officer shook his head. "Beautiful but sad. Thank you, Doctor Snow. Kashandra, I'm sorry for your loss. I had two sons. Lost my second son at birth, just like you. I think I have an idea about how you feel right now."

The officer turned to Mary. "I don't think there is anything here warranting an autopsy. You may contact your funeral home. If you don't have one in mind, I know Watson's Funeral Home does free funerals for babies—if the parents can't afford one. Give them my badge number and my name."

Gary wrote his name, badge number, and the number of his police report on a pad then gave the page to Mary.

"Thank you, Officer. If there's nothing else, I'll see you out."

"Nothing more," he said and nodded to Kashandra. "My condolences."

"Please, follow me," Mary said.

Pausing in the living room, Officer King opened his billfold, removed a photograph and stared at it for a moment. "This is a picture of our baby that died." He turned the photo toward Doctor Snow and then choked up.

"I'm sorry for your loss," Mary said. "Thank you for coming."

Mary returned to Kashandra's room. "Shall I call Watson's?"

"Please. I ain't got no money for a proper funeral."

"I'll do that, but while we wait, I'd like to pump your milk so Tim is fed without you having to take on that physical activity now."

"Now, baby?"

"Sorry, but Tim needs milk. Want me to take the baby away?"

"No." Kashandra rocked the baby then looked at

the ceiling. Between sobs, she said, "I wanna hold him as long as I can."

Mary attached a glass funnel to Kashandra's left breast and pumped her milk while Kashandra rocked her dead son and muttered a broken song.

Kashandra continued to nurse Tim and have sex with him for four months. However, the volume of her breast milk declined. After several more weeks, production tapered to almost nothing. While Tim seemed content to suckle Kashandra's breast and have sex, Mary had to search for donor milk.

The portly sixty-year-old, gray haired police chief paused chewing his cigar butt to yell out his office door. "King, where is your report for this month? I expect it this afternoon."

"Have it on your desk in fifteen minutes," Officer King yelled.

Twenty minutes later, the chief yelled, "Gary, where the hell's that damn report?"

"Coming right up, Chief!"

Minutes later, King rushed into the chief's office and placed the report on his desk.

Snarling, the chief asked, "What took so long? Been copying the Gutenberg Bible by hand?"

"Nah. Just cogitating about this case."

"Which case?"

"The dead baby I told you about."

Putting down some papers, the chief asked, "Wanna talk about it?"

"Not much to tell. I just feel uneasy about it. I don't know why, but I do."

"Maybe it's because your son died under similar circumstances . . . but it was malpractice if I recall. You and Betty sued—right?"

"Yeah."

The chief dropped another pile of papers on his desk and leaned back in his squeaking swivel chair. "What the hell? Tell me about the baby."

King gave a brief summary of his report and waited for the chief's response.

"Not much to go on, son. Sure you have all the facts?"

"As far as I can tell, I . . . We have the facts."

"If you're uneasy about the case, see what you can find out about the doc and the mother. Let me know if you find anything. If not, don't bother me and don't waste anymore time.

King went to the archives and searched for information about Kashandra. He found several entries for the surname Smiley. He dragged his finger down the list of entries, looking for a Kashandra Smiley.

While searching names, King spoke to another officer, Mike, working beside him. "Here it is. Kashandra Smiley. Oh my God. One, two, three, four, five . . . thirteen arrests for soliciting and prostitution."

"Glad you found something," Mike said. "I can't find any of the stuff I need."

"Sorry, Mike. Why the hell would a doctor take a prostitute like Kashandra into her home and give her free care? Better see what I can find on Doctor Snow."

King began a new search of police records. "Here it is. Snow, Mary. Hmm. A case of death at birth. Better check on the mother of that baby."

King found Quickie's name and nine cases of arrests for soliciting and prostitution. *That's strange. Both prostitutes had dead babies at Snow's house. Better tell the chief.*

"You back again?" the chief asked, peering over his half frame glasses.

"Yeah," King said, dropping a printout of his information on the chief's desk. "Like to have your take on this. It's about that dead baby. I did some checking. That Doctor Snow has reported two dead babies delivered at her house. Get this. Both mothers were prostitutes."

"So?"

"Don't you think it's strange a doctor would treat prostitutes in her home?"

"It's unusual, but someone has to care for prostitutes, even pregnant ones. Especially if they don't have money or insurance." The chief propped his feet on his desk. "One reason women get prenatal care is to improve the chances of having a live baby. Seems like these hookers didn't have proper care and their babies died." The chief sat upright. "You said this Kashandra woman had high blood pressure problems. So, where's the crime?"

"I don't know, but this case bothers me. I'll keep digging. Let you know as soon as I find anything."

"Son, don't waste time on this! There are lots of other cases, you know."

King retrieved Detective Jackson's report on his visit to Doctor Snow's house and scanned it for clues Jackson might have overlooked, but nothing stood out. *Maybe I'll snoop around the doctor's neighborhood.*

King drove to Mary's home. He took photographs

of the front of her house and the houses of neighbors. He then drove to the back of the house where he took more photos. He noted the garage entrance and the houses across the alley from Snow's property. He took several photos of the back of those houses as well.

Everything looks straight forward here, except for pregnant women. Better do some neighbor interviews.

Officer King knocked on the door of the neighbor to the north of Mary.

The door opened, and a woman in her mid-fifties pushed at a headscarf intended to hide her hair curlers. "Yes?"

"Good morning," King said. "I'm Officer King. I'm investigating a complaint we've had about happenings in the neighborhood. May I come in?"

"By all means," the woman said, pointing toward the living room. "I'm Martha. Please, have a seat. How may I help?"

King sat down then pulled a note pad from his shirt pocket, along with a yellow pencil. He scanned the living room, noting the owner's antique furniture. "You have some nice looking Victorian pieces."

"Thank you."

"My wife likes antiques. Is your whole house furnished with similar pieces?"

"Everything except for mattresses." Martha chuckled. "Don't like sleeping on horsehair."

"Know what you mean. Now, let's see. Where was I? Have you seen any black women coming and going to any house in the neighborhood?"

"Hmm. Let me think. There's Rula, my maid, who comes twice a week."

"How about neighbors' houses?"

"Barbara has a maid once a week. That's the house on the other side of Doctor Snow."

King wrote some notes. "How about the houses behind you?"

Martha shook her head. "No. Can't say I have."

"Have you noted any unusual activities late at night or early in the morning?"

"Nothing unusual, except the garbage truck. Well, maybe a garbage truck. I've heard vehicle sounds in the alley a few times, around midnight, but I thought it was a garbage truck—coming early."

"Did you see the truck?"

"No, I didn't look. Had no reason to."

"How many times did you hear those sounds?"

"About nine or ten . . . several weeks ago. None since. Oh, I almost forgot. I also saw a black woman in Doctor Snow's side yard just before a plumber showed up. Mary must have had a plumbing problem. I saw his truck parked on the street, but he didn't stay long."

"Did you notice anything unusual about the black woman? Tall, short, pregnant?"

"No. Nothing. But I only saw her for a second or two."

"Had you ever seen her before or since?"

"No . . . can't say I have."

"Do you know if Doctor Snow has a maid?"

"No . . . I don't."

"Would you mind if I had a look out your bedroom window . . . from where you heard the night sounds?"

"Not at all," Martha said. "It's upstairs. Come with me."

Martha led the way to her bedroom.

King looked around the room and then out its only window. It overlooked Doctor Snow's backyard and a small corner of her front yard. He noted Mary's driveway with its broken concrete, her wooden deck, garbage cans, and two unkempt backyard flower beds.

"You can't see in Doctor Snow's kitchen or garage door from here."

Martha shook her head. "No, not from here."

"When you heard the garbage men, did it sound like they or their vehicle was in that alley or possibly in the doctor's driveway?"

"I can't be sure," Martha said, "but the sounds were close."

Gary wrote on his pad. "Do you live alone?"

"No. Just my husband and me."

"What's your husband's profession?"

"He's a patent attorney."

"Does he ever leave home at night for business?"

"Definitely not. That's why he's a patent attorney. It's day work."

Officer King closed his pad. "Guess that's it. Here is my card. Call me if you recall anything. Anything at all." King pulled down on the front of his jacket and said, "Thanks for your time."

"Glad to help."

Officer King visited the neighbor to the south of Mary's house. He asked the same questions he asked Martha, but he received no new information and no mention of the night sounds. The neighbor's husband managed the day shift of an atomic reactor not far from home, and he never worked at night.

King went to the house at the rear of Mary's home and knocked on the front door.

The door opened a few inches and a middle-aged woman peered out.

"Afternoon, Ma'am. I'm Officer King. I'm investigating a report of unusual happenings in the neighborhood. May I come in?"

"Please. I'm Joan. Sorry I'm still in my bathrobe." She pulled her robe closed and pointed toward the living room. "Have a seat. Give me a minute to get dressed."

Joan left, leaving King free to look around the living room. From there, he could see through the kitchen to Mary's house and up to the second floor and her garage.

Minutes later, Joan returned, dressed as if going to a fancy party, fluffing her hair. "Now, how may I help?"

"Have you noted any unusual comings and goings over the last few weeks?"

"There's lots of comings and goings in this neighborhood but nothing unusual."

King stopped taking notes. "Could you explain?"

"Lots of doctors and lawyers live in this neighborhood. They come and go at all hours, delivering babies, taking care of the sick, getting clients out of jail . . . That kind of stuff."

"Who's delivering babies?"

"Doctor Snow I guess," Joan pointed to Mary's house, "and there's Doctor Lowery. He lives two houses down."

"Have you seen any black women coming and going in the neighborhood . . . other than known maids or domestic help?"

"No."

"Any unusual night sounds?"

"What kind of sounds?" Joan asked, tilting her head and leaning forward in her chair.

"Anything out of the ordinary."

"There were a few times when I thought I heard a vehicle—garbage men—coming early."

"When was that?"

"Last time . . . several weeks ago. Maybe three or four times before that."

"Did you see the garbage truck?"

"No. I didn't."

"Did you look outside?"

"No. Just rolled over and went back to sleep," Joan said, shaking her head.

"What time did the sounds occur?"

"I'd guess around one o'clock, but I'm not sure."

"Did the sounds seem far away or close?"

"Mostly outside my window—close by."

"Was it a garbage day?" King asked.

"Can't say I remember, but I guess so, or I would not have thought of garbage men."

"Mind if I ask if you are married?"

"Twenty-five years to Hank."

"What's Hank's profession?"

"Years ago, he won the Tour de France. You know, that big European bicycle race. Now he owns a chain of bicycle shops called Spinning Wheels. There's a shop here in Towson."

"I know that store. Bought my son a bike there a few years ago. Nice shop."

"Thanks." Joan smiled. "Is it time to get him a new one?"

"Not yet," King said. "I can't afford the new ones. Well, Joan, thanks for your input. You've been helpful."

Officer King sat at his desk, dialing the phone number of the sanitation department.

"Sanitation, Larry Moore speaking. How may I help ya?"

"Larry, this is Officer King, Towson Police. I'm working a case that hinges on your department's schedule for collecting garbage in the 1200 block of Mulberry Street. Could you fax me the schedule for the last six months?"

"I could, but it's not necessary."

"Why not?"

"Schedule hasn't changed in years. We pick up on that street on Wednesdays—except holidays"

"About what time?"

"Mornings, between seven and nine."

"Ever arrive early?"

Larry chuckled. "Somebody complaining we're making too much noise?"

"No."

"What then?"

"Just want to know if your men might have ever been early?"

"We get complaints only if we're late or noisy. Which is it?"

"Just tell me if they might have been in the neighborhood around one o'clock in the morning?"

Larry laughed. "Now, that would be early. No. Never at that hour."

"Thanks Larry. You've been very helpful."

King searched the state bar attorney database and located the names of lawyers living in Mary's neighborhood. He cross referenced cases where the attorneys might have seen clients at night but found no relevant cases.

So, no reason for those lawyers to be out in the middle of the night. I should check on the doctors.

Joan said there were two obstetricians who lived near her.

Gary first investigated Doctor Lowery's practice. His office closed at 6:00 p.m., and he almost never went to the hospital at night. His hospital provided resident physicians to help with his patients. Resident coverage eliminated the need for him to make night visits to the hospital.

Hmmm. That leaves Doctor Snow. Guess I'll call her office.

Snow's receptionist answered, "Obstetrics and gynecology. Please hold."

King listened to music for a while. *God, she's taking a long time.* He considered hanging up, but the receptionist came back on line.

"Hello. This is Helen. Sorry for the wait. How may I direct your call?"

"Helen, I'm Gary calling for my wife, Sherry. Does Doctor Snow have evening hours?"

"Not for a long time."

"Pardon?"

"She hasn't had evening hours since she gave up her obstetrics practice. She only does office gynecology three times a week."

"Oh, I didn't know. When did she start that?"

"Two years ago."

"Do you know if she sees patients at home?"

"I doubt it. She has her hands full taking care of a son."

"Then, where does she admit patients or have admitting privileges?"

"She has privileges at Memorial Hospital, but she doesn't admit anymore—not for the last two years. Sorry, but how may I direct your call?"

"Nothing more. Thanks." Gary hung up. *Guess I'd better check with Memorial.*

King called the administrators of the two city-owned hospitals and the private Memorial Hospital. He requested the names of doctors who had delivered babies between 11:00 p.m. and 3:00 a.m. over the previous six months. In every case, he heard it would take a month to collect the requested information.

Chapter Twenty-two

Four months after Kashandra's baby's death, Mary placed scrambled eggs, a waffle, and coffee on the kitchen table then called to Kashandra from the foot of the stairs. "Your breakfast is ready."

Kashandra moped downstairs and then to the table.

"Not feeling too well this morning?" Mary asked.

"Not very. Got sick waves in my belly."

"Try eating. I've made waffles—your favorite breakfast."

"I can't, baby. Not this mornin'."

"Not even juice?"

"No, baby. If I do, I gonna puke."

"Well. We don't want that. Go upstairs and rest. You can try again at lunchtime."

Kashandra had been upstairs for ten minutes when Mary heard her vomiting. *I hope that's what I think it is. She's pregnant.*

Mary went to Kashandra's bedroom. "You alright?"

"No, baby. I'm sick."

"Have you missed your period?"

"You think I'm pregnant, baby?"

"It's possible." *I hope so.* "I'll do a pregnancy test."

"Oh, Lordie," Kashandra said. "That can't be. Not me, baby. Not again. Not now."

"Wait here. I'll get something to make you feel better."

Mary returned with washcloth and a glass of water. She held out her hand. "See if you can swallow this pill. It'll make you feel better. I'll get a pregnancy kit tomorrow when I'm in the office."

Mary placed a damp cloth on Kashandra's forehead. "Feel better soon. Tim is expecting you. I've got to pull weeds from the flower beds so they will be ready for planting. Yell if you need me."

In the garage, Mary strapped on kneepads, forced her hands into stiff work gloves, and then headed for an unkempt flowerbed in the backyard.

While pulling weeds, Mary's neighbor, Joan, walked into the alley separating their properties. Despite the fact she carried a bulging garbage bag to the trashcan, she wore a blue silk dress.

"Morning, Mary," Joan called.

"Morning, Joan. How are you?"

Joan dropped her garbage into the can, replaced the lid, and then walked to Mary's side. "Police are asking more questions about the neighborhood again."

A chill climbed Mary's back as she continued pulling weeds. She did not look up but asked, "What did they ask *you*?"

Joan placed her hands on her hips. "Things about strangers in the neighborhood, husbands, maids, night noises. That kind of stuff."

"Did you speak to the same policeman who was here a few weeks ago?" Mary asked, still weeding.

"No. A different man," Joan said then smiled. "But much younger. Good looking too."

"He was, wasn't he," Mary said, hoping Joan would believe she too had been questioned. "What did he ask about the most . . . with you?"

With her ear tuned to Joan's every word, Mary pulled a clump of crabgrass from the flowerbed and tossed it into a bucket.

"Night sounds," Joan said. "Definitely wanted to know about night sounds."

"Yeah, night sounds," Mary repeated. "Have you heard any?"

"I told him I thought they were made by the garbage men, coming too early." Joan shook a finger at Mary. "Careful, I think you pulled up a tulip bulb."

Mary looked at the ball of dirt in her hand. "Oh, I did didn't I. Better put it back. Did the policeman ask you about anything else?"

"Just what my husband did for work and whether or not he worked at night. Did he mention a husband to you?"

"Yeah," Mary said, replanting the bulb. "Told him I didn't have one." Mary removed her straw hat and wiped sweat from her brow with the cuff of her glove. "It's getting hot out here."

"Yeah," Joan said. "Summer heat builds quickly. Well, gotta go. Don't get a heatstroke."

"See you, Joan. Give my regards to Hank."

Tamping the dirt around the replanted tulip bulb, Mary thought, *Wonder if other neighbors were questioned by that policeman. Think I'll ask.*

Mary phoned her neighbors and inquired if they had been questioned by police as she had. She felt shock on hearing they had.

What is going on? Why would police question my neighbors and not me? Were the questions related to the cable guy? I admitted he was in the house. Joan saw him and told the detective she had seen him. Did someone see one of Tim's whores and suspect I ran a house of prostitution? Mary chuckled, "Me running a house of ill repute." *Maybe that's it. I thought I was careful, especially with Kashandra. Maybe someone saw Quickie. I wasn't as careful getting her into the house. I'd better tell the neighbors I've been interviewing maids.*

Mary phoned the neighbors interviewed by police and told them she had been interviewing maids after they got off their day jobs. So far, she hadn't hired one. She asked neighbors to let her know if they knew of a maid looking for work.

One neighbor, Irene, said she knew of such a maid.

Six days later, Irene phoned Mary about an available maid.

"Wonderful," Mary said. *Shit! This is the last thing I need.* "I appreciate your interest. What's the woman's name?"

"She goes by Yolanda. Sorry, but I don't know her last name. I gave her your phone number. Told her to call you in a few days."

"Thanks, Irene. I'll let you know what happens." *Hope the hell she doesn't call.*

The next day, Yolanda called and received an interview appointment.

Responding to her doorbell, Mary opened the door.

A tall black woman, about thirty-five-years old, stood at attention. She wore a straw hat and her hair in a bun held in place with a red band. Her white, starched dress had sharp creases.

"Hello," Mary said. "You must be Yolanda."

"That's me."

"Please. Come in. Let's go to the kitchen. I'm washing dishes. That's why the house smells of lemon detergent." Mary pulled out a chrome kitchen chair. "Have a seat."

"I could do those dishes for ya if you want, Doctor Mary."

"Thanks, but I can manage." Mary pulled a soapy dish from the sink and rinsed it. "Tell me about yourself."

Mary dried her hands and took a seat opposite Yolanda.

"Well, Ma'am, I'm from Alabama. Been livin' in Baltimore eight years." Yolanda moved her shiny white purse onto the table and fingered its strap. "Moved to Towson ta help care for my Auntie May."

"Is she ill?"

"Not sick, just old. She's been fallin' a lot. We're fraid she's gonna break somethin'. My mama, Auntie May's youngest sister, didn't want her living alone."

"Ever work as a maid?"

"Yes, ma'am. In Birmingham and Baltimore. I got references." Yolanda pulled a folded white envelope from her purse and handed it to Mary. "These are them."

"My. You came prepared. I like that."

"Yes, Ma'am. I'm good at everything I do."

"Let me show you through the house. Don't want you taking on more than you can handle."

Mary showed Yolanda the first-floor rooms then took her upstairs. Mary pointed to a closed door. "That's my son's room. He's disabled. You wouldn't be cleaning in there."

"What's wrong with your boy?"

"Sorry to say so, but he has the mind of a four-year-old. Can't care for himself. Sometimes, he's difficult to handle. That's why he stays in this padded, sound proof room."

"I feel for ya. A friend's daughter is like that. Had ta put her away."

As Mary started to show Yolanda the second floor rooms, Kashandra stepped out of her bedroom, wearing her bathrobe. "Sorry, baby. Didn't know you entertaining."

"Not a problem," Mary said. "Yolanda, meet Kashandra. Yolanda is interviewing for a maid's job."

"Miss Yolanda," Kashandra said. "Pleased ta make your acquaintance."

"Pleased ta meet you," Yolanda said, shaking Kashandra's hand.

"Me too, baby." Kashandra returned to her room and closed the door.

"Kashandra is a pregnant patient of mine," Mary said. "She can't afford a private doctor. She's staying here until she delivers."

"That's mighty nice of you, Doctor Mary. It's Christian charity."

"Yes. It's the Christian thing to do. We have to help those in need."

"I like ta work for God-fearing people."

Mary nodded. "Now that you've seen the house, think you could handle the work?"

"Doctor Mary, I've taken care of houses bigger than this one. Ain't no problem for me."

"Good. I'll check your references and get back to

you."

Mary escorted Yolanda to the front door and bid her farewell.

Heading to the bus stop with a certain lightness to her steps, Yolanda thought, *I sure hope I get that job. She'd be a fine person ta work for.*

Yolanda heard footsteps behind her. At first, she thought nothing of them. However, they became louder, and faster.

I hope that ain't a pervert set on dragging me in these bushes.

She stopped and faced the person behind her. "Who you followin'?"

"I'm Officer King," he said, holding up his badge.

"I ain't done nothing wrong?"

He pointed to the Snow house. "Why were you in there?"

"What she done wrong?"

"I didn't say she had done anything wrong but answer my question."

"I interviewed for a job—a maid."

"What did you see in there?"

"It's a big house. Lotta work ta clean it. She seems like a nice lady. A Christian woman taking care of a poor, pregnant black sister and a crazy son."

"A pregnant woman?" the officer asked.

"Yes, sir. A pregnant woman. Her name Kashandra."

"Kashandra? Hmm. That name's familiar. Could you tell how far along she was?"

"Can't be sure. Didn't see no baby bump."

"Would you mind coming to the station? I'd like to

hear your full story."

Why he wanna talk with me? Better cooperate. Don't wanna be jailed for doing nothing. "If ya promise to take me home before five o'clock."

"Deal."

At police headquarters, Yolanda sat in a small room with a large mirror. She squirmed on a hard wooden chair, clutching her purse on her lap. She had finished answering all the questions thrown at her.

"Yolanda, will you excuse us for a minute," Officer King said. "I want to have a word with a detective."

"Sure, Mista King."

Outside the interview room, King spoke with the detective who had been watching King and Yolanda. "I think we should encourage her to take that maid's job. Be our eyes and ears inside the house. I'm afraid the pregnant woman might be in danger. She's already lost one baby."

"Gary," the dective said, "do you really believe Doctor Snow is killing babies? For what? Witchcraft or some other evil purpose? It doesn't make sense." The detective scratched his neck. "Did the baby's autopsy reveal anything unusual?"

"There wasn't an autopsy. *At* the time, no one suspected anything. Especially when the licensed, delivering doctor said the baby was stillborn."

"You don't have much to go on."

"I know. But the mother of the first dead baby, delivered in that house, has been reported missing."

"Hell. She's not the first of the sisterhood of street workers to go missing. That kind of stuff goes back to Jack the Ripper. Those women go missing all the time."

The detective chuckled, "Maybe there's a serial baby killer running loose. Who knows?"

"Maybe that killer is Snow. If I'm right, we might be saving the life of another baby and a mother. Don't forget Snow might be connected to the death of that cable guy."

The detective warned, "Careful what you allege, King."

"Sorry but we've got to get Yolanda inside that house."

The detective rubbed his forehead. "That might be helpful but she's not an educated woman. If she had to give testimony, I'm not sure a jury would believe her."

"Leave that to me. I'll work with her—everyday if I have to."

"You're keen to do this aren't you?"

"I've never been more certain. My gut tells me 'something is rotten in Denmark.'"

"Okay. See what you can find out. But be careful. Don't go off half-cocked accusing a respected member of the community if you don't have an air tight case."

King returned to the interview room. He explained how he wanted Yolanda to take the job if offered. She would be the eyes and ears of the police department.

"Ya help me get the job, and I'll help you," Yolanda said.

"Deal." King cocked his head. "Have you ever had any run ins with police? Have a record?"

"No sir. I got a clean record. *Never* done nothing bad. No sir. Nutin'."

"Good. I'll do a record check about you. If it's clean, I'll give you a police report you can give to Doctor Snow

287

as another reference."

"Thank ya 'cause I want that job. I need the money."

"No problem. Come back tomorrow afternoon. I should have the report by then."

Police report in hand, Yolanda rang Doctor Snow's doorbell.

"Yolanda! I hadn't expected to see you so soon."

Yolanda held out a white envelope. "Doctor Mary, I want ya to have this police report stating I'm an upright citizen. No arrests, no thefts, no robberies, no reports of anything against me, and no jail time. Not even a driving ticket. Not here, not nowhere."

"My, you are thorough. I'm waiting to hear from your references so give me a few days."

"Yes, Ma'am. I'll be waiting to hear from you. Anything ya want me to do just for today?"

"Thanks, Yolanda. Not now but have a nice day."

"Mary. It's Irene. How are you?"

"Fine, thank you."

"Yolanda told me you had interviewed her. Think you'll be hiring her?"

"Not sure. I'm still checking references." *Why is she bugging me about Yolanda?*

"She has excellent references and a police report giving her a clean bill of health, so to speak. Did you see it?"

"I did."

"She'd be a great help to you, from what you've been saying about Tim's needs."

"I appreciate your concern, Irene. I'll get back to you

as soon as I complete my assessment of the references."

"Good luck, Mary. Keep in touch."

Shit. Why did I ever mention my need for a damn maid? What the Hell do I do now? Can't just brush Yolanda off. Damn it. I'll hire her for a few days and then let her go.

Yolanda answered her phone. "Yolanda speakin'."

"Yolanda, this is Doctor Snow."

"Mornin', Doctor. You made a decision about my working for you?"

"Yes. Can you start Monday?"

"I'd be pleased ta start Monday. Mind if I get there at eight o'clock?"

"That's good. See you then."

Yolanda made mental notes of everything she saw in Mary's house and reported to Officer King daily— often debriefed by him in his car while she waited at the bus stop near the Snow house.

One morning, Yolanda cleaned the second-floor hall as Mary walked toward Tim's room with a white towel over her left arm. On entering the room, Yolanda saw something black under the towel. Mary covered the item then closed Tim's door.

Wonder what that was?

Yolanda finished cleaning the hall, the second-floor rooms, and then knocked on Kashandra's door.

"Come in."

Yolanda opened the door. "Want me ta clean in here?"

"Sho, baby. Fraid I've made a mess."

Yolanda left the door open while cleaning. Midway

through the task, the door to Tim's room opened and Mary walked into the hall. For a second, Yolanda caught a glimpse of a black bra-like thing dangling from the TV's mounting bracket. *I seen black bras before, but they made of lace. That ain't lace. It's shiny like rubber, but what's a white woman doing with a black rubber bra?*

Mary entered Kashandra's room. "How's everything? Kashandra, you feeling better?"

"Baby, I'm feelin' much better today. I'll be able to care for Tim in a few minutes."

"Good," Mary said then addressed Yolanda. "Why don't you let Kashandra rest? Clean downstairs?"

"Sure, Doctor Mary."

Yolanda left the room, paused at the top of the stairs and listened.

Mary half closed Kashandra's door and said, "You are to say nothing about your work here. Do you understand? *Nothing.*"

"I understand, baby."

Yolanda thought, *Why did she want me outta that room? What she not want me to know or what she hiding?*

Yolanda moved down four steps, pretended to wipe the handrail, and then looked up. Mary had walked to the head of the stairs. "Doctor Mary, you want me ta first clean in the front or the back of the house?"

"Start in my office. I'll do something else while you clean. Later, I need to work in the office without being disturbed."

"Yes, Ma'am."

Mary went to the kitchen as Yolanda cleaned the office at the foot of the stairs.

"What was that?" Yolanda muttered, cocking her ear toward the stairs and listening hard. *Musta been nothin'.* She had returned to cleaning when she heard the strange sound again. *I'd better see what that is.*

She went to the second-floor hall and said, "Oh, my God."

Tim's door stood open and Kashandra, naked, held onto his door frame as she slid to the floor, vomiting.

Yolanda rushed to her side and helped her up. "Oh, Lordie, Miss Kashandra, what you doing here? You look like death."

"Help me ta my room," Kashandra muttered, "but don't let Doc Mary hear us."

"Don't worry. She in the kitchen." Yolanda put her arm around Kashandra's waist and helped her to bed.

"Quick. Get my bathrobe out of Tim's room then close his door." Worry colored Kashandra's words. "Sorry, but I didn't mean ta puke a mess for you ta clean up, baby."

"Ain't nothing ta worry about. You need anything?"

"No, but don't tell Miss Mary ya seen me like this."

"Okay, but what are you doing naked in Tim's room?"

"Just lookin' in on him. I take care of him."

"Takin' care is one thing, but honey, you is naked."

"Just parta the job."

Shocked, Yolanda asked, "What kinda job you got, Miss K? Why you working naked?"

"Nothing ta talk about, but you keep quiet, baby. Please. Can't say nothing ta Mary."

Yolanda fluffed Kashandra's pillow, cleaned up the mess, and then returned to cleaning the office.

Somethin' strange goin' on in this house.

Chapter Twenty-three

A week after Yolanda started her job, Officer King still met her daily to talk about activities in the Snow house.

"I'm going to record our conversation," King said, turning on a small recorder. "Hope you don't mind. This way I can listen to what you say and not worry about taking notes."

Yolanda chuckled. "Hope I don't have ta sing. I ain't no recording star." She told King her story but dwelled on the Kashandra portion. "There's somethin' weird going on. I don't know what, but it's strange." Yolanda fingered her purse as she stared out the car's window. "I still wonder what that rubber bra is for and why Mary spends two hours with Tim behind closed doors." For a moment, Yolanda stared at Officer King. "The room's padded, so ya don't hear nothing. I never heard or saw the TV going when Tim's door is open. I understand he don't talk much. Miss Mary say he gotta mind like a four-year-old, so I know they ain't talking highfalutin things. Mighty strange."

"I agree with the strange part," King said, "but keep talking to Kashandra. Get her to open up. Find out what she does in there. We know she's not a maid, so find out what she meant about taking care of Tim. Find out why she left her sickbed and went to his room—naked."

"I'll try, but she don't wanna talk about nothing. She seemed afraid ta talk."

"Did she look pregnant?"

"Not sure, but I think she is . . . could be a little fat."

"Keep an eye on her belly," King said. "One other thing. Keep an eye out for that rubber bra. Where is it stored? When is it moved? Who, if anyone, wears it? What is it used for?"

"I'll do my best."

"See you in a few days. Call if there's anything new or unusual to report."

Yolanda left the car as King started the engine. He pulled into traffic thinking, *I should follow up on this bra thing? Who the hell sells rubber bras. Better talk to a medical supply house.*

Officer King contacted several surgical supply houses, and much to his surprise, he learned none sold rubber bras. However, he got interesting information from one supplier. "Sex shops sell rubber bras as a fetish thing for weird people, but they called it *latex* not rubber."

"Thank you," King said to the supplier. "You've given me a great lead in my case."

Officer King sat at his desk. *My gut is telling me she played a role in the death of the babies. I need photos of Snow to show sex shop owners.*

King searched online for photographs of Doctor Snow. He spoke to the Division of Motor Vehicles, checked with the US Department of State for passport photos, the medical license board, medical school year book, and newspaper archives.

He found one, full face and one semi-profile photo acceptable for his task. The state police photo lab enlarged them. When they were ready, King took them on his visits to several sex shops.

Every shop reported selling the occasional latex bra,

but none stocked them.

One shop owner said, "I have an enormous rubber bra in stock, but it's a joke item. It would fit King Kong's wife."

While talking to another shop owner, King asked, "If I wanted a rubber bra, where would I get it?"

The shop owner said, "Baltimore. The Pleasured Chest."

King visited the shop with the erotic sounding name.

"It's a pleasure," the door alarm announced as he entered the Baltimore shop.

His nostrils burned with the mixed scents of leather, latex, baby oil, and a sweet-smelling perfume.

"Welcome to my shop," a young woman said, re-stocking a wall of neon colored dildos.

King admired the blouse-less fortyish looking shop owner. Her rubber bra supported "D" cup breasts.

He said, "I'm Officer King."

"I finished my time. Been clean for a year."

"Glad to hear that," King said, eyeing old needle marks on her arms. "I'm not here about you."

"Then what?"

"I wanna know who buys rubber bras."

"Like mine do you?" the woman said, pushing up her latex-restrained breasts.

"Nice specimens but I'm interested in your *buyers*. I understand you supply all the area sex shops."

"They're *not* sex shops. No one sells *sex*—anymore."

"Sorry!"

"We supply discriminating clients with personal latex items."

"Like what?"

"You name it, we have it, make it, or can get it. We also tailor."

"Pardon my ignorance but who has tailored rubber wear? Sorry, *latex*."

"Fat people, skinny people, and people who want something extraordinary for their special interests."

"Uh . . . I don't want to go there. What kind of items have you tailored in the past?"

"Everything I just mentioned. You looking for something special? Something for yourself?"

"God, no." King shuddered. "Not for me."

"We've made underwear, leggings, straps to hold butt plugs, ball binders, ball lifters, bras with and without holes to expose nipples. The list goes on and on. You got something special in mind?"

"I told you nothing for me. What records do you keep?"

"We're computerized, but our paper records go back twenty years."

"See if you have any orders for a Mary Snow?"

"That's privileged information. I couldn't divulge it, even if I had it."

Trying a bluff, King said, "You can either give me the information now, or I can get a court order to close you down—search everything. Who knows, I might find drugs. Then bye bye freedom. Hello jail."

The woman stared at King in disbelief. "Shit. You wouldn't? Not a 'plant.'"

"Wanna find out? I'm working a murder case, lady. Don't interfere with my investigation."

"Okay. Okay. Give me a minute, *Officer*. Go play

with a butt plug while I search the records. The *lube* is on me."

King wandered around the shop examining plain dildos, double headed dildos, crotch-less panties, rubber erection rings, enema nozzles and other unidentified items.

Ten minutes later, the shop owner waved a printed page. "Here." She slammed the page on the glass case displaying flesh colored vibrators. "This is a list of all bra orders for the last fifteen years."

King scanned the page. "Shit! Snow order a tailored black-latex bra."

"Read on, Officer. It's not only tailor made, but it's *specially* tailored. See there." The shop owner pointed to line eighteen. "Double walled. With *working* nipples—a first for us."

"What the fuck," King said. "Why would anyone want a double walled, rubber br—?"

"Latex!" the shop owner said. "She wanted it to hold something,"

"Okay, a *latex* bra but to hold what?"

With a look of disbelief, the owner said, "Give me a break. What do bras do?"

"Hold breasts?"

"Maybe."

"What do you mean?"

The shop owner sighed. "Maybe cover breasts or *simulate* breasts."

How disgusting, King thought. "If a woman wanted to simulate a breast, why wouldn't she buy a regular bra and stuff it with . . . socks? Or buy a medical prosthetic bra made of foam?"

"Officer . . . Stop. Think about the feel of a water-filled bra verses a foam-filled bra. Which do you think would feel most lifelike? The water filled one. Especially if it's filled with *hot* water."

"Okay. But who wants a water filled bra?"

"My first guess would be a man who wanted to feel like a woman. Maybe a drag queen, a transsexual, or an old-fashioned pervert."

"What kind of pervert?"

"Shit, man. Don't you have any imagination?"

"Not as perverse as yours or your customers."

The shop owner sighed. "I'll ignore that comment. It could be filled with urine. Some guys get off on feminine things like bras *plus* urine—female urine."

"How the hell can you deal with these . . . people?"

"Hell, they can be quite interesting, but honey, they pay the bills."

"I hadn't thought of urine," King said, rubbing his chin. "What else might someone put in a bra?"

With a look of disbelief, the owner asked, "If someone wanted to simulate a real breast, what do you think they might use to fill the bra?"

"Fat?" King asked?

"Shit! Think man. Think."

"Shit?"

"Noooo. For God's sake man—*milk*!"

"Milk?"

"Yes, milk. That's what breasts are meant to do, *Officer*—make . . . hold milk."

"Snow's bra had nipples?"

"Yep. And she wanted them to function. That took a lot of planning . . . to prevent leaks. See there. Read the maker's notes.

King moved his finger across the page. "Says here they made the nipples from a baby bottle nipple." He glanced at the shop owner then continued, "Those nipples must have been obvious if they were worn in public, under street clothes."

"If that's how they were used."

"What do you mean?" King asked.

Looking at the list of buyer's names, the shop owner said, "Mary may not have worn anything over it."

"You mean exposed? You think she didn't have normal nipples and wanted the look of real ones or as normal as a bottle nipple might be."

"Possibly. But remember, she wanted them to work like real nipples."

King looked at the order date. "It was made some years ago. Snow was no spring chicken then. Who would want or expect milk from her."

"My guess would be a sick boyfriend. Could be an old man wanting his mama, or it could be a lesbian wanting to be a mama."

"Wait a minute. Maybe Mary didn't wear it. Maybe someone else did. Maybe she sucked on the damn thing. Mary could be a lesbian and another woman wore the damn bra."

Smiling, the shop owner said, "Officer King, you're beginning to think like a pervert!"

"Is that a compliment?"

"Maybe."

"But why make it out of black rubber?"

"I don't know, but she specified it be black latex."

"Maybe she expected to use it with or on a black

woman," King said and rubbed his chin. *She has black women in the house.*

"I love your perverted mind," the shop owner said then smiled.

"Got to admit I've learned a lot today." King folded the page with the bra information. "I'm taking this page, but I promise to keep it confidential."

Officer King drove toward headquarters, but he had trouble concentrating on the road. He considered the permutations of possibilities for use of a rubber bra.

Maybe Mary is lesbian. Might explain the prostitutes in her house. They're known for doing anything for money, keeping their mouths shut. Honor among whores is mythic.

Suddenly, he heard a whirring bump, bump, bump on the right side of the car. "Shit! I've drifted over the rumble strips." *Better concentrate on your driving, Gary, or you'll end up in a ditch. Maybe Mary wears the bra for the prostitute's pleasure, or she likes to feel she's a mother to a black daughter she never had . . . That's it. She's breastfeeding a make-believe daughter but why a black daughter? Why not a white one? Black doesn't fit. Why drink breast milk? Does someone do it for money? Think, man, think. Were black women chosen or just a chance encounter? Better check their work sites.*

Officer King reviewed the arrest records of the women who had stillbirths. He correlated the twenty-three arrest records, and noted the arrests were made in Swamp Town. *Why would a high-class doctor go there?* "Better go through these records again."

"You talking to me?" the officer at the next desk asked.

"No, but all the arrests occurred between eleven p.m. and four a.m." *If Mary had visited Swamp Town, why would she be there when the whores worked the streets? Was she looking for whores, or did she just find them? If she found them, why was she there in the first place? Just passing through? If so, to what or where?*

King walked to a wall map, located Swamp Town, and then pinpointed Mary's house. He located her office and then the hospital where she had admitting privileges. The hospital lay on a straight line from her house.

It's possible she might go to the hospital at night, and the shortest route would be through Swamp Town . . . then her meeting the whores might have been accidental but why stop for a whore?

King leaned back in his chair, lost in thought. *Had Mary's desire to be a mother to a daughter reached a boiling point, and she acted on the impulse because of the availability of the black women? That's gotta be it. Opportunity.* "Shit! That's not a crime." *Kinky, maybe sick, but not a crime.* "Hmmm." *But what has that got to do with dead babies? Surely, the mothers didn't kill their babies—certainly not after delivery. It would be easier and safer to have an early abortion.* "Gotta think about this."

Officer King waited for Yolanda at the bus stop.

"Mista King. How ya doing?" she asked through his opened window.

"Long day," he said. "Get in. How was your day?"

"I'm fine. Nothin' exciting today. That Kashandra

spends a lotta time in Tim's room. She in and outta his room six times today. She in there about thirty minutes each time. His mama in there a lot too."

"Was Kashandra in there with her?"

"No, sir. She alone."

"Did you see that black bra again?"

"No, but I'm sure she took it in . . . under a towel."

"Did you see her bring it out?"

Yolanda shook her head. "No, sir."

"Think she left it in the room?"

"Can't say."

"Have you ever seen Kashandra do any work? Anything?"

"No, sir. She spends a lotta time in her bed and in Tim's room, and Doctor Mary takes Kashandra's food to her bedroom."

"Does the doctor spend much time in Kashandra's room?"

"Maybe . . . fifteen minutes."

"That's all?"

"Just minutes."

"Have you seen Kashandra naked anymore?"

"I ain't seen her naked. She wears a robe all the time."

"Can you tell if she wears underwear or a bra under that robe?"

"She don't wear no bra, 'cause I seen her titties. I don't know about underwear. That part is covered."

"You've done well, Yolanda. Keep your eyes open. We'll talk later. Oh yeah. Don't forget to peek at any papers you see in her office trash can or on her desk."

Chapter Twenty-four

Officer King sat in his unmarked police car at a red traffic light two blocks from his station. The light turned green, but his car didn't move. Several drivers honked their horns.

"Move it, bastard!" a driver yelled.

"Shit! I'm day dreaming."

King gunned his car through the intersection. He turned on the radio and listened as the announcer reported a fire in a local orphanage. Three children had died in the flames.

"God. I can't take any more bad news." He searched the FM dial and found a station with relaxing music. As if having an epiphany, he said, "That's it. Snow is an orphan. She takes in pregnant women so she can play mother to the woman and later mother to their children." *Damn. That doesn't make sense.* "Why their babies? Hell, she wouldn't need a bra for that scenario, but why does she and the prostitute spend so much time in Tim's room?" *Gotta find out about that.*

Four days later, King met Yolanda at the bus stop.

"Nothing much ta report," she said.

"We need to change our approach. We've got to find out what goes on in Tim's room. Is his door always locked?"

"Most of the time, but there's a key in the outside lock."

"Tomorrow, see if the door is locked or not."

"And if it ain't?"

"Open the door a little and leave it like that."

"That could get me fired, but why?"

"Hang around. See if you can hear or see anything unusual going on inside. Have a peek when Kashandra is inside."

"I could lose my job—"

"Possibly, but if that happens, I'll help you find another one."

"Promise?"

"Promise."

The next day, Yolanda carried a mop and bucket to the second-floor bathroom. She filled it with water, added floor cleaner, and then began mopping the hall farthest from Tim's room. With her first pass of the mop, Yolanda watched Kashandra exit Tim's room.

"Mornin', baby," Kashandra said, tying her bathrobe. She closed Tim's door, entered her room, and then closed the door.

Wish she hadn't closed Tim's door.

Yolanda tiptoed to Tim's room then turned the doorknob. She opened the door about three inches and peeked inside. Tim lay curled on his bed, thumb in his mouth as he slept. She scanned what little she could see of the room. *Nothing. Better get back to mopping.* Just then, she heard footsteps on the stairs. "Oh Lordie." *I can't close the door quiet enough. What am I gonna do?*

Mary stepped into the hall. Her forearm draped with a white towel.

Yolanda swung her mop across the floor, striking Tim's door. Startled by the thud, Mary jumped and retracted her arm. The abrupt motion jostled the towel,

304

revealing a plump black bra draped over her forearm.

"Oh, Lordie," Yolanda said, pointing at the door. "Look what I've done."

"Stay away!" Mary yelled. "Who left it open?"

"Sorry, Doctor Mary. I didn't mean ta hit it. Didn't know it was open."

"Damn Kashandra. If she wasn't feeling so bad, I'd give her a piece of my mind." Mary pointed toward the stairs. "Go work downstairs."

"Yes, Ma'am."

Yolanda collected her tools, so she could empty the bucket and store the mop.

"I said work downstairs!" Mary yelled. "Forget the damn bucket!"

"Sorry, Ma'am. Right away."

Shaken by Mary's outburst, Yolanda rushed downstairs then sat in a living room chair. *Don't know why she gets so worked up.*

Thirty minutes later, Yolanda thought she heard a noise at the front door. She looked out its window but saw nothing. *Nobody here. Guess I'm hearing things.*

Yolanda went to Mary's office to clean. She saw an opened letter on the desk. Across the top were large red letters—Second Notice. She read the letter without touching the paper. *Oh my. The water and electric department gonna cut her off. She ain't paid her bills.*

Seconds later, Yolanda heard the knocking sound she had heard earlier. She cocked her head and listened. "That's upstairs. Better check it out."

Stepping into the second-floor hall, a distant sounding thud came from Tim's room. Yolanda placed her ear against his door just as the thuds occurred again. "Somebody hit this door and they is talking." *It can't be Tim. Never heard him put three words together.*

Yolanda looked up and down the hall. *Maybe I should look inside.*

Yolanda turned the doorknob and then pushed the door inward. Suddenly, it flew open, startling her.

"Thank God you heard me," Mary said. "I didn't notice the outside lock was on when I closed the door."

"You alright?" Yolanda asked. *Lordie, that bra is hangin' on the chair.*

"I'm fine."

Yolanda shared the day's events with Officer King, as they sat at the bus stop.

"I seen that bra . . . when I opened Tim's door for Mary . . . on the chair."

"And you saw nothing unusual earlier when you peeked in the room?"

"Nothing but Tim on his bed."

"Could you tell if Kashandra wore a bra or underpants today?"

"I see she's not wearin' a bra, but I don't know about panties."

"How long after Kashandra left the room did Mary come up?"

"Maybe . . . twenty minutes."

"After you went downstairs, could you tell if Kashandra left her room?"

"No, sir. Not less she tippy toed."

"Well . . . thanks for the info. Be careful. Keep your eyes and ears open."

"Oh, I did see one more thing . . . on her desk. The

water and electric folks gonna cut her off cause she ain't paid her bill."

"That's her problem."

Boredom filled the Snow household. Mary went about her usual chores. Yolanda cleaned the house, never opening Tim's door again.

One day, Yolanda stood at the foot of the stairs, waiting to clean Mary's office. She heard part of Mary's telephone conversation. It had something to do with breast milk. ". . . for a deserving baby and a desperate mother," Mary said. "Fine . . . I'll be over with a breast pump tomorrow. Give me that address again."

Yolanda watched Mary scribble on a yellow pad then say, "I appreciate this." Mary tore the page from the pad. "See you soon."

Yolanda waited a moment then knocked on the door. "Want me ta clean in here?"

"Yes. Come in. I'm just finishing up."

Yolanda held the door open, letting Mary pass.

"Do a good job," Mary said, folding the yellow paper.

Waiting for Mary to get far away from the office, Yolanda dusted items on the oak bookcase. In the waste basket, she spied a crumpled list of names and phone numbers. *Better take that.* She picked up the pad on which Mary had been writing and examined it for indentations. *This is just like on TV. Clues. Officer King is gonna like this.* She tore off the top page and wedged it and the page from the waste basket in her bosom.

Anxious to share her findings, Yolanda finished her workday then rushed to the bus stop where King waited in his car. She hurried to the passenger side, got in, and waved the papers so hard they almost tore. "Look what I got."

"Calm down," King said, snatching the pages. "What have we here?"

"Doctor Mary been calling these women. Heard her talkin' about breast milk and pumps."

"Damn. She's putting human milk in that bra. That sex shop gal was right."

"What you talkin' about?"

"Your boss is putting women's milk in that black bra. The only question is what does she do with it. You did well today. Thank you."

Three days after debriefing Yolanda, Officer King rushed into his chief's office. "Sorry to barge in, but I have to talk to you about the dead babies and Snow."

"Doctor Snow?"

"Yeah, her."

"Whata ya got?"

"God, I don't know where to start."

"First, calm down," the chief said, "then get on with it."

"I did some snooping around in Baltimo—"

"What?" The chief asked, glaring over his reading glasses. "Who authorized you to go to Baltimore?"

"You did, Chief . . . well, you said I should do whatever I had to do."

"Yeah, but going to Baltimore, that's another jurisdiction?"

"So what. I got some good information."

"From who?"

"A sex shop owner."

"Have you lost your mind?"

"*No,* damn it. Oops! Sorry, *Chief.* Please, just listen."

The chief dropped a stack of papers on his desk and leaned back in his squeaking chair. "Okay, regale me, but it had better be good."

"Doctor Snow has a custom made black latex bra. It holds milk . . . human milk. The damn thing has working nipples, made from a baby's bottle. Not sure who wears it or why, but she and the bra go together. Today, I learned she's buying human milk supposedly to help a desperate mother who can't make breast milk for her starving baby."

"So far, you've told me nothing, King. Nada. Even if all you say is true, *where . . . is . . . the . . . crime?*"

"I was hoping you'd help me figure it out, Chief. There's gotta be some skullduggery in there somewhere. I know it."

"Better work on another case." The chief pounded his desk. "You're going nowhere with this one. I don't see how milk is tied to dead babies."

Dejected, King sulked toward the door. "Sorry to bother you."

"Drop it, son. You're wasting time and taxpayer's money."

All afternoon, King sat at his desk pondering his problem while moving a yellow pencil from space-to-space between his fingers. *This Snow stuff is getting me nowhere. Better talk to the women on that list.*

King called two women and mentioned buying

breast milk.

"Not interested," one said.

"Don't want to talk about it," another said.

"Damn," King said. "This isn't working." *Better do some face-to-face calls.*

Using Yolanda's list, he looked up addresses by last names and then cross-referenced the names with birth announcements in newspapers and searched birth certificate records. He selected eleven addresses for home visits.

King parked in front of the first woman's house, where a young man worked under the hood of a tan 1963 Plymouth parked in the driveway.

"Afternoon," King said, holding up his badge.

"Afternoon, Officer." The man wiped his hands with a rag. "How can I help you?"

"Has anyone asked your wife about selling breast milk?"

"How'd you know?" the man asked, mopping sweat from his brow with his sleeve.

"We've received some complaints."

"Why would someone complain about my wife?"

"Sorry. Didn't mean your wife was the subject of a complaint, but has someone asked her about selling her milk?"

"Yeah, she got a call from some doctor. The wife and I discussed it. I told her it was okay with me, but she'd have to make the decision."

"What did she decide?"

"She decided not to do it."

"Did the caller mention money?"

"Don't know, but Sidney, that's my wife, didn't

mention money."

"Think I could talk to her?"

"She's resting right now. Call later if you need to."

"Thanks. You've been helpful. Have a good day."

King visited the second woman on his list. He opened her storm door then knocked on the hand carved wooden door.

The sounds of running feet neared the door. It then opened inward. A little girl, with tousled blond hair, moved between the main door and the storm door. She had red jelly on her lips and her yellow dress.

"I have a new brother," she said, putting a finger in her mouth.

"Is your mommy home?"

"Mommy says I'm not suppos ta talk . . . uhh, to strangers."

"Ask your mommy to come to the door? Okay? Tell her a policeman is here."

Without a word, the girl stepped inside then closed the door.

Damn! King thought. *Now, what?* He knocked on the door. Again, the sounds of running feet emanated from inside. The door opened a few inches, and the same little girl said, "Hello."

Suddenly, the door opened wider. A tired looking woman peered out. She clutched her pink bathrobe over her chest.

Gary said, "I'm Officer King. Just want to ask a few questions about breast milk."

Appearing exasperated, the woman said, "Not you too?"

"What?"

"You're not wanting to buy my milk are you?"

"Gosh, no!" King said. "I'd like to know if anyone asked about yours."

"What's going on?" the woman asked, looking annoyed. "Is there some peeved milk cartel or something?"

"Far from it, ma'am. Just want to know if anyone has asked you to sell your breast milk?"

"Matter of fact, yes . . . a Doctor Snow. A nice lady doctor. Said some mother couldn't make milk for her baby. It was allergic to cow's milk and needed human milk. Doctor Snow said, 'she was trying to help the mother find breast milk for the baby.'"

"What did you tell her?"

"I said, 'Yes. Happy to help.'"

"Oh."

"I have just had my second child, and I make plenty of milk. With my last baby, I had to pump my breast just to feel comfortable."

"Anyone mention money?"

"Only in passing but I'm donating it. I make plenty. Who knows, I might be in the same boat someday."

"Thanks." King nodded. "You've been very helpful. Have a great day. You too, little one."

The little girl peeked from behind her mother and waved goodbye. "Bye, Mister Policeman."

King visited the remaining nine listed women. All had received calls from Doctor Snow.

Woman number eight had agreed to donate milk for the desperate mother.

At the time of King's visit, neither of the volunteers had been visited by Snow.

King asked each donor to let him know when Doctor Snow would be coming and not to mention he had been notified."

The women agreed to King's request.

Two days later, the volunteers notified King that Doctor Snow had called and had made appointments to instruct them about collecting and storing their milk.

Fortunately for King, the visits were scheduled back-to-back.

Anticipating Doctor Snow's arrival at the first house, King parked six houses away and waited.

Taking a cooler and pumping equipment from her car, Mary went to the front door then rang the donor woman's doorbell and waited. Seconds later, the door opened and Mary went inside.

Twenty minutes later, Mary left the house with less equipment than she took in.

Mary placed the cooler in her trunk then drove away.

"Hope she's going to the second mother," King muttered.

Allowing sufficient space between cars to avoid being noticed, King followed Snow to house two. She remained in the house about twenty minutes then left with just a cooler.

More milk, King thought. *Now, let's see where she goes.*

King followed her for twenty minutes. "Just as I thought. She's going home."

He stopped several houses away from Doctor Snow's driveway then edged his car to the back of a neighbor's house and watched Mary drive into her garage. *Better hang around. See if she makes another trip.*

King became restless. Every few minutes, he glanced at his watch. After an hour, he decided to leave. He didn't want a homeowner to find him blocking the alley or become suspicious of his presence.

King returned to his office and phoned the first donor. "How did things go with Doctor Snow?"

"Great!" She's a good woman. It didn't take much time, since I already knew how to use a pump. I filled two bottles quickly, and then she left."

"Did she mention the name of the mother who needed the milk?"

"Linda, I think. She didn't mention a last name. Said it was confidential."

"Thanks for your cooperation. It's greatly appreciated."

"Officer . . . has the doctor done anything wrong?"

"I don't know that she has done anything wrong, but please call me if you have another appointment. Again, thanks for your help."

The second mother told the same story but mentioned a Charlotte as the needy mother.

King went on seven stakeouts where he waited outside each donor's home while Mary collected milk. He then followed her. She always took the cooler with the presumed breast milk home and remained there the rest of the day.

This pattern held steady for weeks.

One day, mother number one called King. "Officer,

I wanted to let you know Doctor Snow called to say she didn't need my milk anymore. She's going to pick up the pump tomorrow."

"Really? When did she call?"

"A few minutes ago."

"Thanks for calling and thanks for all the cooperation you've shown over the weeks."

A couple of hours later, mother number two called to make the same report.

King wondered what has happened. *Better talk with Yolanda.*

Chapter Twenty-five

Officer King drove to the edge of Swamp Town. Having located Yolanda's paint-hungry frame home, he knocked on her door then waited.

Opening the squeaky door, Yolanda said, "Officer King. Shhh. Don't want my auntie to hear us. Thought you'd forgotten me."

"I didn't. Just busy with other cases."

"Ya must need something."

"I want you to peek in Mary's refrigerator. See if there are any small bottles of milk. If so, how many? Can you do that?"

"Sure. I can do that."

"Could we meet after you get off work today?"

"Usual place?"

"Yeah."

"Thanks for meeting me," King said as Yolanda got into his car. "What's going on in there?"

"Nothing much . . . except Kashandra be pregnant."

"Really? How far along is she?"

"From the size of her belly, I'd say about seven months."

"Seen any changes in her breasts?"

"I think they're bigger. Probably full of milk."

"Milk?"

Yolanda chuckled. "Yes sir. That's what pregnant women do. They make milk."

"Thanks, Yolanda. *That explains why Snow doesn't need donated milk anymore.*

Turning from his office window, the chief stopped chewing on his cigar butt and placed his hand over the mouthpiece of his phone. "Come in, King." The chief returned to listening. "And then what?" he asked the person on the other side of the conversation. The chief motioned for King to sit down.

Waving the chief's smoke away, King coughed then muttered, "Thanks."

The chief continued to listen to his caller. Suddenly, he yelled into the receiver held at arm's length. "Okay! After the next round of promotions." He hung up and glared at King. "Whatta you want?"

"Some help with my puzzle."

"Puzzles? You're playing with puzzles?"

"No. I meant the Snow case."

"Shit, son. You still wasting time?"

"I don't think so."

Looking frustrated, the chief knocked ashes off his cigar. "Then whatta ya got?"

"Doctor Snow told her milk-donors she doesn't need their milk anymore. That black woman, Kashandra, who lives with Snow, is pregnant and now makes milk. Snow is using her milk instead of the donors."

"Wait until I tell the milk commissioner about this," the chief said, rolling his eyes. He rose from his chair faster than smoke from his stogie and waved his arms overhead. "Better send in a SWAT team!"

"I'm serious Chief. Weird shit is going on in that house."

Sitting down and leaning back in his chair, the chief asked, "Who lives in that damn house?"

"Well, there's Snow and Kashandra—the prostitute. It's not her legal address, but she has been staying there for a long time. Yolanda, the maid, comes and goes every day, and then there's the son, Tim."

"Tim's the one," the chief said with a flourish of hands toward the ceiling.

"The one what?" King asked, confused.

"The one who's drinking the milk," the chief said, looking perturbed. "That's what babies do."

"Shit, Chief. The son is about twenty years old, maybe more."

"She got cats?"

"Haven't heard of any. Why do you ask?"

"Maybe they're feeding the milk to the cats."

"Why feed cats human milk?" King asked. "Cow's milk is easier to get, and it's cheaper."

"Yeah, but didn't you say she doesn't *pay* for the milk—it's free. Can't get any cheaper than free." The chief shook his head. "Son, you're supposed to give *me* answers. Not the other way around. Give it up! I told you before, and I'm telling you again. Give . . . it . . . up."

A week later, Yolanda gave King a debriefing as he sat in his car. "I ain't seen them milk bottles you asked about, but Doctor Mary is spending less time in Tim's room."

"Do you mean fewer visits or less time per visit?"

"Both. She in there two times a day, twenty minutes each time, except when she cleans the room."

"How do you know she's cleaning?"

"I seen her cleaning. She leaves the door open."

"Where is Tim while the room is cleaned?"

"On his bed."

"Have you seen the black bra again?"

"Not no more."

King frowned. "This isn't getting me anywhere, Yolanda. Keep me posted if you hear or see anything new or weird."

"Whats that thang, Doctor Mary?" Kashandra asked, staring at a TV-like silver box Mary wheeled into the
room.

"An ultrasound machine. It's used to see inside a woman's womb."

"Baby, you gonna look inside me?"

"Yes," Mary said, plugging the machine into a wall socket. "We need to know if your baby is developing normally. We don't want you, or it, getting into trouble without knowing about it."

"Not gonna hurt is it, baby?"

"Absolutely not," Mary said. "The only thing you'll feel is the cream I'll rub on your belly then a slight amount of pressure. Nothing painful just a little cold."

"What you expect ta see, baby?"

"The size of your baby, its sex, the status of its arms, legs, toes, fingers, back, head, and heart. And maybe some information we might use at delivery time."

"When you gonna do it?" Kashandra asked in a quivering voice.

"How about now?"

"Ya sure it won't hurt?"

"I'm sure." Mary pulled the sheet off Kashandra's

abdomen. "This will feel a little cold." Mary smeared a glob of clear cream on Kashandra's abdomen.

"Yeah, baby, it's cold."

Mary held up a six-inch long metal tube connected, by an electrical cord, to the machine. "I'm going to move the free end of this tube over that smeared cream. I'll be pressing a little, to produce a better picture of the baby on the TV screen. Are you ready?"

"Okay, baby. If ya gotta."

Mary turned the viewing screen toward Kashandra, so she could see the images of the baby.

"That's ma baby?"

"That's him," Mary said, pointing to the white outline of the baby.

"Is it a boy?"

"Yes. A boy." Mary pointed to the penis then moved the tube lower over Kashandra's abdomen to view other parts of the baby. "Hmmm," Mary said, stopping the tube over another area of Kashandra's belly. "Uh huh," she said several times. "Kashandra, this is not looking good." Mary pointed at some white lines on the screen. "That's the baby's backbone. See those dark spots. They shouldn't be there." With her finger on the screen, she pointed to the area in question. "The whole back part should be white like these spots."

Mary knew Kashandra had no idea what she saw on the screen.

"What that black spot mean, baby?"

"It's not good. I'm 99% sure your baby will be paralyzed from the waist down, due to that back problem. But there's . . . more bad news."

Mary pointed to the baby's heart as Kashandra

321

raised her head to get a better look. "There. His heart has a hole in it. The hole causes no problem while he is in your womb, but once he's delivered, he won't live more than a minute or two."

Kashandra stared into Mary's eyes. "O Lordie. My baby gonna die."

"I'm sorry." Mary shook her head and sighed. "I know you don't want to hear this, but the outlook isn't good."

"What we gonna do, baby? Tim, me, and you gonna lose this boy?"

"We could do nothing, and let the baby grow in your womb. Deliver him . . . and then watch him die within minutes . . . or—"

"Or what, baby?" Kashandra held her breath as if waiting to be reassured with alternatives.

"We could get the court's permission to do . . . an abortion."

"Abortion?" Kashandra asked, horror choking her voice.

"Yes, an abortion. The process would be easier on you than going through a full pregnancy, delivery, and then watch the horrible scene of his rapid demise."

Kashandra shook her head and rubbed her belly. "Oh, Lordie. I don't know what to do. Alls I know is I don't wanna talk about it." She struck the mattress with her fist. "Damn! Not now." A tear ran down her cheek. "I need ta pray on it."

"I understand. Get some sleep. We'll talk tomorrow."

The next morning, Mary left the kitchen with a cup of steaming coffee and an omelet for Kashranda.

"Sorry I spilled some coffee," Mary said, entering Kashandra's room then placing the breakfast tray on the bedside table.

"Don't worry, baby. I'll pour it back."

"Feel like eating?"

"Maybe . . ."

"I made one of your favorites . . . a Swiss cheese omelet."

"Thanks, baby, for takin' care of me."

"We're kind of family, now," Mary said, uncovering a plate.

"Yeah," Kashandra said. "My, that smells good."

Mary smiled. "Hope you like it." *You need protein to make Tim's milk.*

Kashandra picked up the fork and took a bite of the omelet. She dropped the fork and stared at Mary. "I can't eat, baby. I can't. I keep thinking 'bout our baby."

Mary bit her tongue. *Damn it woman, stop saying our baby! There's not going to be an OUR baby.*

"Have you made a decision?" Mary asked, patting Kashandra's hand.

"I've been praying all night. Prayin' for an answer."

"And . . ."

"I think it's better if God has our boy sooner than later, baby. Don't want him suffering."

"I know it's a hard decision, but I think it's the right one." *I don't want a baby using Tim's milk.* "I'll be back later with papers for you to sign. I'll need them for the judge."

"Do what you gotta do, baby, but I can't eat now." Kashandra pushed the food away. "Sorry ya went to all the trouble."

The next day, Mary entered Kashandra's room. "How are you feeling?

"Baby, my body's fine but my heart's heavy."

Gripping Kashandra's hand, Mary said, "I understand . . . I have those papers I mentioned. You need to sign each page where I placed an "X."

"Whatever ya say, baby." Kashandra scribbled her name on each page then handed them to Mary. The grieving woman wiped a tear and looked up. "Lord, help me get through this."

"I have to go to the office . . . to see some patients, but Yolanda is here. If you need anything call her. I'll tell her to clean just the first floor. That way you can feed Tim without her knowing. Whatever you do, say nothing to her about the abortion. Nothing. Understand? I'll give her the day off when we do the procedure."

"Nothin'. I promise, baby."

In her downtown office, Mary searched through files for an ultrasound record of a former patient.

Four years earlier, a patient had delivered a baby with the same spine and heart problems Mary alleged Kashandra's unborn son had.

"Good, the files are here."

She held a photograph toward the light. *I need to copy this.*

Mary copied the records in such a way as to omit the patient's name.

"That should do it," she said, examining the copies. "These and the signed authorization form should be enough for any judge."

Mary called home.

Yolanda answered the phone. "Doctor Snow's residence."

"Yolanda, its Doctor Snow. Everything alright?"

"Yes, Ma'am. No problems."

"Fine. I should be home in two hours."

Construction of the ornate court house occurred during the Public Works Administration era. Mary stood under its enormous dome, admiring the allegorical themed statues placed high around the rotunda. Voices, footfalls, and elevator bells echoed around the circular lobby. She headed for the judge's chamber whose name plaque hung to the right of the lobby entrance.

Acknowledging the secretary, Mary said, "I'm Doctor Snow. I have an appointment."

"Oh, yes. The judge is expecting you, Doctor. Please, have a seat. I'll let him know you're here. He's just finishing with an attorney."

Mary sat on a hard, wooden chair. She scanned the walls covered with photos of the judge shaking hands with governors, President Truman, and several senators and congressmen. The silence of the office gave way to what sounded like tiptoed footsteps in a library as the secretary returned.

"Doctor Snow, you may go in now."

The volume of cigar smoke left little breathable air in the judge's cavernous office. The smoke almost obscured his presence behind a wide mahogany desk.

"Thanks for seeing me, Judge Kean," Mary said then coughed.

"Glad to help," the judge said, knocking ashes off his cigar. "Nasty business this abortion stuff."

"Sometimes, they have to be done."

Nodding, the judge said, "What documentation do you have for me?"

"First of all, the ultrasound report." Mary removed a set of photographs from her briefcase then held them toward the judge. "These are the abnormalities. The incomplete spinal bones will leave the baby paralyzed. This hole in his heart is incompatible with life outside the womb. The baby would die a horrible death within minutes after delivery."

"Do you have the mother's consent?"

"Right here, Judge." Mary pulled papers from her briefcase. "See. The mother signed each page as required. She's a poor, uneducated black woman, but we discussed, at great length, the pros and cons of the procedure. She agrees it has to be done."

The judge flipped a page. "And who is paying for the procedure?"

"It's *pro bono*."

"No reason for the taxpayers to complain about that. You're leaving these photographs with me?"

"Yes, your Honor."

"Fine. Hand me the forms."

Mary handed the papers to the judge. As he signed them, he asked, "When will you do the procedure?"

"Day after tomorrow."

"Give the papers to my secretary, for notarization."

Chapter Twenty-six

Mary sat in her home office, listening to the phone ring six times for Sam Godsey. For years, Sam, a nurse anesthetist, had assisted Mary with surgical procedures at the hospital.

"Sam here."

"Sam, its Doctor Snow."

"Gosh! Haven't heard from you in a long time. Thanks for the call. Hope all is well."

"All's well, thank you, but I'm calling because I need a favor. A *pro bono* favor."

"For you, anything. What's up?"

"I'm doing some *pro bono* work with a poor black woman who needs a third trimester abortion."

"Ouch! Third trimester eh?"

"I know. I know. But I have the patient's signed authorization and a court order signed by Judge Kean."

"Judge Kean signed the permit?"

"Yep, the old guy himself."

"When do you want to do it?"

"Tomorrow. At my house."

"Your house? Are you *crazy*?"

"Hang on, Sam," Mary said. "The woman can't afford private care, and you know the public hospitals won't allow it. She can't afford to travel to another abortion site, so we have to do it—at my house."

"That'll be a first. Why not your office?"

"My docs are too conservative to permit an abortion there, and I don't want antiabortionists picketing the office because they heard I had done one in our building.

"I understand. Is she to have a spinal or general anesthesia?"

"A little of both. That'll keep us and her out of trouble."

"Okay if that's what you want. What supplies do you have?"

"Everything except the anesthetic, endotracheal tube and respirator."

"My, you are prepared, aren't you?"

"Always. Can you be here at eight in the morning?"

"Wearing bells."

"Please, don't wear scrubs. I don't want to draw the neighbor's attention. Jeans would be better. You can change inside."

"I hear ya."

"Oh, another thing. Drive to the back of the house. You can bring your equipment in through the garage."

At 8:00 a.m., Mary's kitchen doorbell rang. She opened the door. "Sam, glad you're here. I'll open the garage door. Bring your stuff in through the garage."

Mary had not seen Sam for a few years. The thirty-eight-year-old black man's sedentary lifestyle had added pounds to his short frame.

In the house, Sam asked, "Are you feeling okay. You don't look well."

"I'm fine." Mary pushed her hair from her face.

"Don't worry about me. Let's get started. You can change into your scrubs in my office. Follow me."

Sam moved his equipment to the foot of the stairs then changed clothes.

"Where's the patient?" he asked, exiting the office,

dressed in scrubs.

"She's upstairs. Come, I'll introduce you."

Kashandra lay in bed, eyes closed. Her mouth moved without emitting a sound.

She must be praying, Mary thought. "Kashandra, I want you to meet someone. This is, Sam, a nurse friend of mine. He'll be giving your anesthesia."

"A brother, eh? Sam, thanks for ya help, baby."

"You're welcome," Sam said, shaking Kashandra's hand. "Sorry you have to go through this."

"Me too."

Taking a folder from a drawer in the ultrasound machine, Mary said, "Sam, in case you want to see them, here are the ultrasound photos and the court order."

Sam held the photos to the light. "Uh huh. I see what you mean. Well, should we get started?"

"Ready?" Mary asked Kashandra.

"I'm ready, baby." Kashandra spoke in a thready voice and nodded from her pillow.

"Sam will put a needle in your arm, so we can start fluids."

Kashandra glanced at Sam. "That's okay, baby. I've had that."

"Then you know what to expect."

"Sho do . . ."

Sam placed a needle into a forearm vein then taped it in place. He attached an IV tube to a bag of fluids then adjusted the flow of the medication. Nodding to Mary, he took a syringe containing a yellow liquid and forced out its air bubbles.

Mary nodded and said, "Kashandra, this will make

you sleepy."

Sam injected an anesthetic into the tubing that delivered fluids into Kashandra's vein. "Everything is going to be alright."

Seconds later, Kashandra drifted off to sleep.

"Give me a second to get the airway in," Sam said, taking a laryngoscope from his bag. He used the "L" shaped tool to insert a breathing tube past the vocal cords and into the trachea.Using a syringe filled with air, he inflated the small balloon at the far end of the tube to keep it in place. "Okay. It's in. I'll attach the respirator and then we'll roll her onto her side so I can do the spinal."

Sam pulled and Mary pushed Kashandra onto her side. Mary swabbed her mid back with an anti-septic.

Pulling on a pair of sterile gloves, Sam then prepared the spinal needle and anesthetic.

"You ready?" Mary asked, straining to keep Kashandra in a semi-fetal position.

"Ready," Sam said, feeling the spaces between the bony projections of his patient's spine. "Here we go."

He inserted a spinal needle in the selected space then waited for a drop of spinal fluid to escape to indicate he had the needle in the right place. Attaching a syringe to the needle, he emptied the syringe of its anesthetic into Kashandra's spinal canal.

Sam and Mary moved Kashandra parallel to the long axis of the bed.

Looking at Mary, Sam said, "Start whenever you want."

Using a device to keep Kashandra's knees bent and a meter apart, Mary pushed one end of a plastic sheet under Kashandra's hips then draped the other end inside a bucket on the floor.

Sam checked her blood pressure, electrocardiogram, and respirations

"I'm ready," Mary said.

"She's stable," Sam said, giving a thumbs up. "Start when you want."

Mary inserted sterile instruments into Kashandra's vagina then dilated her womb opening. Mary opened the fetal membranes, releasing a gush of womb water that ran along the plastic sheet and then into the bucket.

After several minutes of scraping Kashandra's womb, it had been emptied.

"Even though it had to be done, I get a little uneasy about doing these," Mary said. *But not in this case.*

"I know how you feel," Sam said, "but . . . sometimes it has to be done."

Mary rubbed her itching nose with her sleeve. "I'll clean the instruments. You monitor her."

"Will do," Sam said, pointing to the bucket. "What are you going to do with the tissue?"

"Take it to the hospital for incineration along with tissue from their recent surgeries."

"Won't they ask questions?"

"Probably not. If they do, I'll show them the court order. That should do it."

Sam sat in a chair at Kashandra's side and monitored her vital signs as the anesthesia wore off.

After fifteen minutes, Sam called out, "She's not waking up."

Mary rushed to Sam's side. "How are her vitals?"

"A little unstable."

"Give her another few minutes."

Sam checked Kashandra's vital signs every two minutes. "They're stable, but she's not waking up."

"Oh, God. We can't have her die," Mary said wringing her hands.

"Should we call 911?"

"Not yet. Give her a few more minutes."

"Okay . . . if you insist."

"I have some naloxone somewhere. A sample. God, where did I put it?" *Think Mary!*

"We shouldn't wait too long," Sam said.

"Damn! Damn! Where did I put it?"

"If you can't find it soon, I am going to call an ambulance."

"The safe! Maybe it's in the safe," Mary said, striking her forehead.

"Then get it—quick!"

Mary left the room and soon returned waving a small bottle. "Got it."

With a syringe, Sam withdrew some of the clear liquid then injected it into the tube carrying saline into Kashandra's arm.

"Come on, girl," Mary said. "Wake up."

Sam took a deep breath. "Kashandra, open your eyes. "

Physically shaking, Mary and Sam waited for what seemed like a year for any signs of recovery. Suddenly, Kashandra took a deep breath on her own and blinked."

"Thank God," Mary yelled. "She's going to be okay. Who knows what we'd do if she wasn't?"

Between visits to Tim, Mary spent much of the

night at Kashandra's side. She required several inject-tions for pain and restlessness before falling asleep.

At 8:30 the next morning, she and Mary woke at the same time.

"How are you feeling?" Mary asked, rubbing sleep from her eyes.

Kashandra scrunched her face, frowned, and then whined. "Baby, I feel like I've been hit by a big Mac."

"A hamburger?" Mary chuckled.

"No, baby, the truck." Kashandra held her belly while trying not to laugh. "Oh, God it hurts."

"Then don't laugh. You rest. I'll be back at lunch-time with soup."

After two days of bed rest, Kashandra walked around the second floor.

"Kashandra, would you attend to Tim today?" Mary asked. "Wait too long and your milk will dry up."

"But I ain't feeling like it."

"Sorry, but you have to. He needs your milk."

"Okay . . . I'll start tonight, 'cause I need the money, but I don't know if I can keep doing this."

You will. Mary said to herself. *You'd better!*

Three days following the abortion, Yolanda knocked on Kashandra's half-opened door.

"Hi, baby."

"Okay if I clean in here?"

"Sure, go ahead."

"You lookin' awfully down. Feeling ok?"

"Sorta." Kashandra looked down and fingered the sheet.

"What ya mean, sorta?"

"I'm feelin' down, baby."

"Wanna talk 'bout it?"

"Can't, baby."

"Why?"

Kashandra gripped the sheet and started to cry.

"Oh, Honey. What's wrong?" Yolanda asked, leaning her broom against the side table and then hugging Kashandra.

"Not suppose' ta talk about it."

"Maybe you should if it got you so upset."

"Promise to tell no one what I'm gonna tell ya . . . especially Doctor Mary. Baby . . . I lost my boy."

"What ya mean you *lost* your boy?"

"He had problems in my womb. Had to get him out of me."

"He in the hospital?"

"No. They took him outta me right here in this bed."

"What ya mean, they? Here?"

"Baby, I had one of them abortion things . . . in this bed. Doctor Mary and a nurse did it."

"Oh, Lordie. When?" *I can't believe this.*

"Three days ago."

Yolanda stood then backed away. She looked Kashandra in the eye. "Oh Jesus. I'm so sorry. Anything I can do for ya?" *What a mess this poor woman got herself into. Who done got her pregnanat?*

"Nothin'. Just pray for me."

Continuing to stare at Kashandra, Yolanda said, "Oh Lordie." She shook her head, got the broom, and then returned to cleaning the room. *Poor woman.*

Yolanda returned several times that day to check on

Kashandra.

Late in the day, Yolanda called Officer King and requested a meeting at the bus stop.

"Mista King, I got bad news." Yolanda said."

"Something new in the Snow house?"

"Kashandra, poor woman, done had an abortion. A nurse and Doctor Mary did it in the house. Kashandra said her baby had problems inside her womb."

"In Kashandra's house?"

"No! Doctor Mary's house."

"Shit!" King slapped the steering wheel. "Sorry." Kashandra must have been close to her due date. The baby's problem must have been really bad to do a late abortion. Did she seem sick before the abortion?"

"Not that I could see."

"Anything else unusual?"

"Not that I seen."

"Wow." Officer King shook his head. "Thank you. Keep me posted."

King sat at his desk staring at a stack of papers when his chief walked in.

"Gary, you seen Harry Jackson? Wondered if he had anything new on the Murphy Park case? The press is giving me a hard time about not closing it. Is he ready to make any arrests?"

"He's still working it, Chief. Say, do you know if a late second or early third trimester abortion is legal in Maryland?"

"It can be legall. Why do you ask?"

"Not sure—yet."

335

"What've you got, son?"

"Now, don't yell at me but that Doctor Snow did a third trimester abortion, on a prostitute—*in* the doctor's house."

"Oh, God. You're not still milking that Snow case?"

"I know. You asked me not to, but Snow's maid, Yolanda, told me Kashandra, the prostitute, told her that Kashandra had an abortion because her baby had problems."

"That's not so unusual."

The chief pushed papers aside then sat on King's desk.

"Maybe, maybe not," King said. "Remember, this is the third time a prostitute has lost a baby at the doctor's house, and all the mothers were street girls."

"There's no evidence of a crime, son, unless you can prove the doctor did an illegal abortion but check it out."

"You giving me permission?"

"Hell, I guess so."

"Thanks, Chief."

King did an online check of court papers and found no record of permission being given to Doctor Snow to perform an abortion. In fact, he found no records of any abortion in the county over the past eight months. *Better let the chief know about this.*

"Chief, if a third trimester abortion occurred, done at the doctor's house, it was probably illegal because there's no court record of its approval."

"Let's assume the hooker had an abortion—third trimester. Without a court order, it was illegal. Better look into it, but first find out how long it takes to get court reports posted online.

Anxious about what he might find, King drove to city hall. He parked his unmarked car in a spot designated COURT POLICE.

On entering the grand Art Deco building, he approached a woman behind the information desk. "How long does it take to get court records posted online?

"Officer, I don't know." The receptionist pointed to her left. "Ask in the County Court Clerk's office. Second door on the left."

"Thanks."

King entered the clerk's office, took a numbered ticket, and got in line to wait his turn for assistance. He looked at his ticket. *Number seven. I can't wait that long. Better pull rank.*

He walked to the head of the line and spoke to the clerk. "Police officer. Pardon me, but I need your help right away. How long does it take to post court reports online?"

"Varies," the clerk said. "Could be a day, if the case has great importance, otherwise it could take up to three months."

"What about permission for third trimester abortions?"

Several women in the line gasped at the mention of the word *abortion*.

"Depends on the judge," the clerk said. "Some take weeks. Some take months."

"How many judges can give permission?"

"For the past year—three."

"Who are they?"

337

"See those three doors across the lobby. Any one of those judges could."

"Thanks. You've been very helpful."

King headed for the office of Judge Hammond. Inside, he asked the secretary if the judge had granted permission for a third trimester abortion in the past three months.

He had not.

King went next door to Judge Kean's office. "Has the judge granted a court order for a late term abortion in the past three months?"

"Yes," the secretary said. "He granted one a few days ago."

"May I see the file?"

"I think it's still on his desk." The secretary left and then returned waving a folder. "Here it is."

"Thanks."

"You may sit at that table to review the files."

"Thanks." King pulled out a chair and sat down. "Could you show me a copy of the law concerning third trimester abortions?"

The secretary went to a bookcase that dominated the far end of the room and fingered several large, leather-bound books. "Here we go," she said, pulling a book from the shelf. "Law was changed last year. This is the current law."

King scanned several pages, stopping to make notes. His finger moved down the lines of small print until he found what he needed—three requirements for a third trimester abortion: evidence of a major anatomical problem(s) likely to cause serious physical or mental problems for the baby or mother; a licensed specialist who states the abortion is medically necessary; a signed consent form from the patient, and husband / father if available . . .

Better see if these requirements are mentioned in the judge's folder, "Is this everything to do with abortion law?" King asked, waving the folder.

"That's it."

King took photographs from the folder and held them to the light. "Hmmm." *Looks like a baby's skeleton. Wish the hell I knew what to look for.*

"Ma'am, may I borrow these photos?"

"You'd need the judge's permission."

"Is he here?"

"He's in court. Won't be back until around four."

King looked at his watch. *It's three ten. Think I'll wait.* "May I wait until he returns?"

"Make yourself comfortable."

At 4:05 p.m., the secretary's phone rang. "Yes, Judge. And there's a policeman waiting to see you. May I send him in?" Seconds later, she said, "Very well."

King leaned forward hoping to hear he could go in, but the secretary said nothing.

Minutes later, the secretary's buzzer sounded.

"The judge will see you, Officer."

King knocked on the judge's office door.

"Come in." Judge Kean lit a cigar butt as King stepped inside.

"Your Honor, I'm Officer Gary King. I'm working on a case and needed to see these records. Your secretary allowed me to examine them."

"Which case?" the judge asked then puffed on his cigar butt.

"Case involves Doctor Mary Snow."

"I remember her." The judge knocked ashes from his cigar into an already full ashtray. "Nice lady doing gruesome work."

"Judge, were you convinced she presented all the necessary documentation?"

"Better watch it, Officer." The judge wagged his finger at King. "I wouldn't have signed the order unless she had met the requirements of the law."

King cleared his throat. "Sorry, Your Honor. Would you give me permission to have these records examined by an independent expert?"

The judge glared at King. "What's going on, Officer?"

"Not certain. But I'm pretty sure Doctor Snow is involved in some strange things that might involve murder. Maybe illegal abortions too."

"Does your chief know about this investigation?"

"Yes, Judge, he does."

"I don't have time now to go into the details, but I'll grant your request to have them reviewed by a specialist. He or she will have to be someone on the county's list of recognized experts. See my secretary for names, but I want to hear from you, or your chief, about this matter within four weeks."

"I promise, Your Honor. I'll speak to your secretary now. Thank you."

The secretary handed King a page of names. "Here are four names of obstetricians, two names of perinatallogists and four names of radiologists who perform or read ultrasound tests. You may choose any three." She handed King three papers. "Have each of your chosen specialist fill out this form and mail it to me. I need it to pay the doctors."

"I can't use the first doctor. He's in the practice of the doctor in question. I'd like to use the second obstetrician, the first perinatologist and the first radiologist."

"Fine. I'll set up an appointment for each and let you know when they're available."

"Thanks," King said. "Here's my card."

Chapter Twenty-seven

Two days later, Officer King squirmed on a chair in the waiting room of his consulting obstetrician. *God, this is one busy doctor. Didn't know there were so many pregnant women.*

An elderly woman, sitting beside King, said, "My granddaughter has been having lots of problems with her pregnancy. It's her first."

"Sorry to hear that."

"How's your wife's pregnancy coming along," she asked.

"Oh, my wife isn't pregnant."

The woman moved her head back and stared at King. "You look too young to expect a grandchild."

King cleared his throat. "You're right. I am."

The woman appeared ready to ask another question but stopped. "Sorry to bother you."

A nurse approached King. "The doctor will see you now, Officer."

King shivered as he sat on a chair in front of the doctor's desk. *Damn, this office is cold.* Stacks of medical journals and medical records hid most of the desk workspace.

Seconds later, the doctor entered, donning his lab coat. "Officer, how may I help you?"

"Thanks for seeing me, Doctor. I need your input about these images."

King took photographs from a manila folder. "I'd like to know if there's enough information here to lead a doctor to believe a late term abortion was necessary."

"Third trimester, eh?" the doctor said, furrowing his brow. "May I see what you have?"

The doctor took the photographs, turned on a desk lamp, and examined each picture.

"My. This baby certainly has problems."

"Like what?" King asked.

The doctor pointed at several areas of the pictures. "Part of the spine is missing. This baby would most certainly have been paralyzed below the waist—if he had lived. Secondly, he has a hole in his heart. He would not live with that after birth."

"So a mother would be within her rights to have it aborted?"

"Absolutely!"

"Thanks, Doc. I appreciate your input."

"Glad I could help."

"Oh. I almost forgot. Judge Kean's secretary asked that you complete this form with your assessment of the case. It's needed to pay you."

Laying the form on his desk, the doctor said, "No problem. I'll complete it in a few days."

Later that day, King consulted the perinatalogist, a specialist dealing with unborn babies who have problems requiring frequent monitoring.

After examining the photos, the specialist said, "I agree with your consulting obstetrician. This baby could have lived through a normal delivery, *but* he would not have survived *beyond* that. The mother did the right thing by having an abortion."

King presented the report and billing forms and left the office.

The next day, King visited the selected radiologist

for his interpretation of the photos.

"Officer, this baby was a sick one. Look here." The doctor pointed to the image of the baby's back. "Part of the spine is missing, and the second photo reveals a hole in his heart. He wouldn't have survived beyond birth."

"So, you agree the mother was right in having an abortion?" King asked, replacing the photos in the court folder.

"Definitely. No question about it."

"Thanks, Doc. Would you complete this form and mail it to the judge's office? It's needed to pay you for your consultation."

"Sure, but where's the patient's name? I have to put it on the payment form. Wait a minute. Let me see those photos again."

King handed the files to the doctor.

"There's something strange here. The patient's name should be on the photos. Usually at the bottom, but it's not there."

Puzzled, King asked, "How would it get there?"

"The ultrasound machine has a keyboard. The person doing the examination should type in the patient's name, date, and the name of the ordering doctor. If the test was done in a hospital, the name of the hospital would be entered as well."

"You would expect that information to be *on* the images?"

"Absolutely. It's needed to insure the report gets filed properly, the right patient gets the right report, and for legal reasons."

"Is there any way of tying these photos to the written reports I showed you?"

"Not really. Just because the documents and photos are in a named file, doesn't mean the documents and photos are of the same or named patient. If the mother had some unusual abnormality that showed up on ultrasound, we might correlate it to an abnormality on an x-ray. Otherwise, it would be difficult to associate the findings with a given patient. Certainly couldn't use these images in court."

Shocked, King jerked his head back. "What?"

Shaking his head, the doctor said, "These photos can't be used in a legal hearing. Without identifiers, they're legally worthless."

"But the abnormalities are real?"

"Absolutely. The abnormalities are real, but we don't legally know to whom they belong."

"Is it possible a technician forgot to add the identifiers?"

"Anything is possible, but technicians are so drilled in these matters it is highly improbable they would forget to add the name on *all* the photos. Oh, another thing. Some machines won't let the technician proceed without entering the patient's information."

"Who does ultrasounds?"

"Doctors do them all the time, sometimes a specially trained technician, but patient identifiers are usually entered for us by a nurse, technician, or an aid. I always make sure the information is entered before I proceed."

"But it's possible a person could do the test and not enter the patient identifiers?"

"That would be considered bad medicine, but yes."

Sitting on the edge of his seat and waving the folder, King asked, "If a doctor wanted to do an abortion and presented this information to a judge saying the pictures belonged to a certain deformed baby but didn't, the judge might grant the abortion request. That is if he didn't suspect something foul."

"Hate to say so, but yes—especially if the judge did not check for identifiers."

"So, a judge could grant an order to abort a normal baby and not know it?" King asked then thought, *Oh, God!*

"Are you okay, Officer? You look pale."

"I'm okay, Doctor. Just imagined a worst case scenario."

The doctor shook his head. "I don't think I want to know what you're thinking."

King barged into his chief's office. "Chief! We have to talk."

The chief frowned and shrugged. "King, you're beginning to get on my nerves. What the hell do you want now?"

"Please, don't yell, but it's about Doctor Snow."

"Not again." The chief rolled his eyes and dropped several papers on his desk. "Who'd she kill today?"

"Not today—three days ago."

"You got evidence?"

"Kinda."

"Damn it, man! Either you do or you don't. Which is it?"

"Please, just listen."

King patted the air, hoping to calm the chief.

"Son, your blood pressure must be up. You're red in the face. Sit down, take a deep breath, and dump it."

"Doctor Snow submitted false evidence to Judge Kean to get his approval for a third trimester abortion.

Certain things she presented had no identifiers. Unfortunately, he overlooked the missing informati—"

"So? The judge is responsible if he didn't do what *he* should have done. Can't hold the doc responsible for the judge's mistake."

"Chief, you don't understand. There's *no* mistake. The doc intentionally omitted the identifiers because she wanted to abort a baby—but not the one seen on the photos she shared with the judge."

"You're not making sense, son."

"That street walker, who lives with the doc, was pregnant. The doc didn't want her pregnant. The doc wanted to get rid of the baby so she faked the documents to get a court order to abort it."

"Why the hell would she wait until the third trimester to abort it when an abortion could have been done in the first trimester—and would require no legal permit?"

"I'm not sure, but it has something to do with breast milk."

"You think the doc aborted the prostitute because the doc didn't want her making milk? Ridiculous."

"Yes! Well . . . something like that."

"Okay, mister smart guy. If she did an unnecessary abortion, somewhere there has to be baby parts. Find them. See if the baby had any abnormalities."

"Where do I look?"

"Start with Planned Parenthood. Ask them what a doctor or clinic would do with . . . aborted stuff."

"Thanks, Chief. I'm on it."

King gripped his steering wheel as he waited for an opening in the line of shouting, placard-toting protesters, so he could drive onto the Planned Parenthood parking lot.

As he drove past them, several protesters banged their fists on his car and shouted, "Baby Killer."

At the reception desk, King said, "I'd like to speak to your director."

"Certainly, sir."

The receptionist made a phone call then smiled.

Moments later a tall woman, wearing a pink plastic halo hair band, approached King and extended her hand. "I'm Buffy Kennedy, the Director. How may I help you, Officer?"

"Could we speak in your office?"

"Surely. Follow me."

Closing her office door, Buffy said, "Now, how may I help you?"

"I'd like to know how you dispose of tissue from an abortion."

"Uh huh," Buffy said, walking behind her desk and gesturing that King should sit down. "Depends on the law in question."

"This state."

"This clinic has a special license. We incinerate. That is, we use a company that specializes in those services."

"Any steps in between?"

"Not for us. However, a hospital might have the tissue sent to their pathology department for an examination by a pathologist. He would dictate a minimal report, which would be filed with the mother's medical record."

"Would the doctor do an autopsy on the tissue?"

"I would imagine that happening *only* if the baby was suspected of having some horrible problem, a medical rarity. Might want to use the tissue for research purposes."

"So, the stuff is simply disposed of."

"Yes, but a small sample might be taken for genetic investigations if a genetic abnormality was in question."

"So, if a question arose about the necessity for an abortion after the fact, chances are there would be no tissue to evaluate."

"You're correct, but I hope you don't suspect this clinic of doing anything unethical. Do you?"

"Absolutely not. Would you give me the name of your service provider?"

"Certainly, I'll get it for you."

With the phone number in hand, King said, Thanks. You've been most helpful."

King sat at his desk and stared at the notes he had taken while in the clinic. *Should I call the disposal people, or is this idea too crazy to pursue? Hmmm. Hell, I'd better call.*

He dialed the number and waited.

"Professional Services. How may I direct your call?"

"Director Harry Grant, please. Police Officer King calling."

"One moment, sir."

"Officer, this is Harry. How may I help you?"

"Mister Grant, have you ever been asked to dispose of aborted tissue collected at a doctor's office?"

"Never heard of such a thing, Officer."

"If such an abortion occurred, how would the doctor dispose of the tissue?"

"All depends if the doctor has something to hide. If the abortion was illegal, the tissue could be quietly buried, scattered somewhere . . . thrown in a dumpster. If you have a vivid imagination, you might come up with other ways of disposal."

"If the abortion was legal, would you get a call?"

"So far we haven't."

"Then what happens to the tissue?"

"I guess it might be taken to a hospital. Hospitals incinerate lots of tissue. Tissue from surgical cases and autopsies."

"Hospitals uh? Thank you, sir, you've been very helpful."

Officer King drove to Memorial Hospital where Doctor Snow had admitting privileges. After introducing himself, a hospital guard escorted him to the pathology department in the bowels of the building.

"Not often I get visitors down here," the pathologist said.

"I know why," King said. "We had trouble finding our way here. I'm working on a case that might involve an illegal abortion."

"Illegal? Not in this hospital, I hope."

"Definitely not here."

"Thank God for that."

"If one of the hospital doctors were to perform an abortion in their office, could that doctor bring the tissue here for disposal?"

"First of all, office abortions are rare in this day and age; secondly, we don't ask if the tissue was obtained legally, and thirdly, we would accommodate a doctor if they were on our hospital staff."

"What if the tissue was from a third trimester abortion? Would you ask about a court order?"

"Probably. If we *knew* it was third trimester."

"Have you had any third trimester tissue in the past few months?"

"I doubt it, but I'd be the last to know. Those matters are handled by the morgue staff."

"Could you check with them?"

"Surely, I'll call Jim. He heads that staff."

The doctor dialed Jim's number and waited. "Jim, this is Doctor McKinley. Can you come to my office right away . . . Good."

Moments later, Jim walked into the director's office. "What's up, Doctor?"

"Jim, this is Officer King, Towson Police. Have we had any tissue, from a *doctor's* office, for incineration during the past three months?"

"Yes, Sir. Two cases. I remember because we don't get many."

"Do you remember which doctors?" the director asked.

"Doctor Linden removed a big fatty tumor from a patient's abdominal wall. Doctor Snow was the other. She had done a third trimester abortion"

"And you just took the tissue?" King asked, feeling

anger rise in his voice.

"She showed me the court order," Jim said. "I had no reason not to take it."

King asked, "Jim, did you see the tissue Doctor Snow brought in?"

"No, sir. No need to. Besides, it was in a black plastic bag. Couldn't see inside."

King shook his head and sucked air through his teeth. "I guess it was incinerated within a few days."

"Same day," Jim replied.

"Well, gentlemen," King said. "Thanks for your time."

King sat in his car assessing the information. *Snow housed a pregnant prostitute . . . did she slip out of the house for late night liaisons? Snow did a third trimester abortion. Permission obtained under questionable circumstances. The judge didn't look for identifiers, which were intentionally omitted. Tissue was incinerated. Can't be examined for abnormalities—if they existed.*

Squirming on his seat, King dropped his head in his hands. *That prostitute performs no obvious service, but she spends lots of time in the son's room. She's been naked, leaving the room and wears a bathrobe without a bra. Panties—in question.* King righted himself and took a deep breath. *Snow has a double-walled, black rubber bra that may hold breast milk. She takes it in Tim's room. She and the prostitute aren't in the room together. What the fuck is going on? Gotta sleep on this shit.*

King slapped the snooze alarm for the third time. *I*

should call in sick. I don't want to get up.

An hour later, King got out of bed. He called in sick then made a pot of coffee. He filled his favorite mug displaying palm trees on one side and the motto, "Another shitty day in paradise" on the other. He reached for a milk carton with the photograph of a missing young black girl. "Shit!" he yelled as though lightning had struck. "Pregnant women make milk, but when do they start?"

Moments later, Gary had his consulting obstetrician on the phone. "Doctor, this is Officer King. Remember me?"

"Certainly. How may I help you?"

"When does a pregnant woman began to make breast milk?"

"Some do it earlier than others but somewhere about the seventh month."

"Seventh, eh?"

"Could be that early."

"Thanks, Doc."

King paced, muttering, "Snow bought breast milk until Kashandra reached her seventh month then Snow stopped buying. Was that because the prostitute made milk? If so, for whom? Mary is a grown woman. She doesn't need it. Kashandra doesn't need it, even though her baby would have, and a grown man like Tim doesn't need it. Shit! Who needs it? Is there some kind of weird cult stuff going on in that house or is Snow taking milk baths?"

Chapter Twenty-eight

King was unable to find any information on modern milk cults, but he had information about ancient pagan rites and fetishes. A few ancient, wealthy women did bathe in breast milk, for beauty or to enhance fertility, but that would be impossible today because of its ineffectiveness, costs, and difficulties in acquiring the required volume.

From Yolanda's description of Tim's room, there was no tub for milk baths, and there weren't enough people to be a cult.

He took a sip of Scotch and then sighed. "I've got to get away from this shit for a few days. Clear my head."

King watched the evening TV news broadcast. It ended with a commercial for Baltimore's cultural events. Information about an art exhibit scrolled across the screen.

That sounds interesting, King thought. *Maybe Wanda would go with me. Hope she'll speak to me.*

Wanda, a short blond woman, and King had met a few months after his wife died in chilbirth. Wanda mirrored his wife's, boundless energy and interests in sports—observing and playing. She liked art, the theater, classical music, and travel—always on the go—the opposite of him, but he liked her. Wanda and he got along well. So well, she had hinted at marriage, but he busied himself in work as a way of avoiding commitment.

Gary phoned Wanda and waited through nine rings. "Hello," Wanda answered.

"Wanda. This is Gary King. Thought you weren't

going to pick up."

"Well, well. Officer Gary King. You're still alive?"

Gary laughed. "Last time I looked."

"It's been a long time. Thought you might have been shot, moved away, went into a witness protection program, or joined a monastery."

"Almost wished I had—moved away. Been busy as hell. How's everything with you?"

"Same old same old. Working, going to school, volunteering."

"Still working at the soup kitchen?"

"Once a week. Helps keep me grounded."

"That's why I'm calling. I need some grounding."

"What? I never thought I'd hear you say that."

"Well, it's true. The reason I called is I saw a TV ad for an art exhibit at the Walter's Art Museum. When I saw the ad, I thought of you."

"Me?"

"Yes. You always liked art. How about we see the exhibit?"

"I saw the same ad. Sounds good. When do we go?"

"How about Sunday. First lunch then the exhibit."

"I'd love to."

"Good. I'll pick you up at eleven.

Wanda tugged at the Walter's bronze door. "Why do art museums have to have such heavy doors?"

"Let me," Gary said, opening the door. "They cost a lot . . . gives the building status. Today, they'd cost a fortune."

Gary bought the tickets then said, "Let's visit the permanent exhibit before we go to the special one."

"Why not?" Wanda said. "I haven't been here in a year. Can't remember the permanent ones."

For an hour, Gary led Wanda on a wandering tour through the permanent exhibits. "Got to admit," he said, "I think I like the Van Gogh stuff better than this modern crap."

"I agree. The early 1900's stuff makes more sense. Cezanne and Picasso's work speaks to me. Wish I could afford one."

Gary laughed. "I'd use the money to buy a tropical island. Ready to see the special exhibit?"

"Yeah. Let's go."

They walked to the second floor and explored the special offerings.

After studying a few canvases and perusing others, Wanda waved to Gary. "Come here. Look at this. It seems out of place in a museum. It's almost pornographic."

"What are you talking about?"

"This one." Wanda pointed at the painting *Mortal Comedy. "*It was painted by Paul Matthews from Bucks County, Pennsylvania. Says so on that card."

Gary stared at the canvas for a few seconds. "So."

"Gary! Are you blind? Look there." Wanda pointed toward a white splotch of paint in the upper right-hand corner of the painting. "That! Right there."

Gary squinted and scanned the upper portion of the canvas. "On my God! I think that's a woman's tit, and that old man is sucking it. Damn. It does look a little pornographic doesn't it?"

"That's what I said. And it's in *this* museum."

Gary's heart seemed to stop. "That's it! That's it!"

"That's what?" Wanda asked, a look of astonishment twisting her face.

"A case I'm working on."

"You know an old man who sucks on a young woman's tit?"

"No, a young man sucking an old woman's tit."

King slapped his forehead. "Why didn't I think of that?"

Wanda shook her head. "I have no idea what you're talking about, but it sounds weird."

"It is. Believe me. I'm sorry, Wanda, but I have to get to the office. Someone's life may be in danger."

"Uhh . . . go! Do whatever you have to do but give me a call. Thanks for Brunch."

"You're welcome," Gary yelled, running down the wide marble steps. "I'll call." *I need to cross reference everything there is in the records on Snow, even the little stuff.*

In the police station, King discovered two Snow records he had not seen. They were written by a detective who worked on a different floor. Detective Jackson had started the investigation of the cable installer's death.

The file information did not relate to the death of prostitutes or babies. However, there were two entries regarding the park case and Doctor Snow. One open entry had to do with bicycle tires and the other with shoe prints.

Better follow up with Jackson, I know it's Sunday, but I'm going to call him anyway.

"Harry Jackson?" King asked the person on the other end of the call.

358

"Speaking."

"Harry, this is Officer Gary King. We both work in Towson."

"Working on Sunday, eh? How can I help ya, Gary?"

"I'm working a case involving Doctor Mary Snow. I found records where you interviewed her about a cable installer's death. His body was found in Murphy Park."

"Yeah. I remember her. I don't know what, but there was something strange, even weird about her."

"I hear ya," Gary said. "There are things mentioned in your reports that haven't been closed out. One has to do with bike tires and another with shoe prints. Did you ever hear anything about those?"

"Not yet. Been so busy with other cases, I haven't followed up. Got new information?"

"Not on the cable guy but I'm working another case involving Snow."

"Gary, I'm grilling hamburgers right now, and lots of guys sucking down beer. Could we talk tomorrow?"

"Oh. I'm sorry. Didn't mean to interrupt. Yeah. Monday would be great."

Gary looked up as Detective Harry Jackson approached King's desk.

"So, you have an interest in the Snow case," Harry said.

"You bet." The men shook hands. "Thanks for stopping by. Have a seat. I hope this makes sense, but I suspect Snow killed the cable guy found in Murphy Park. I also think she had something to do with a couple of baby deaths and a missing person. Your report mentioned some evidence that *might* bring our cases together."

"You mean the tires and shoes? Harry asked. "How do you think you can wind up this case?"

"I can't. Not until we get your requested information. Mind if I go after it?"

"Hell no. Go ahead. It'd save me time and lots of work. I'll send my files down. Promise you'll fill me in before anyone else about anything new."

"Deal."

Later that day, a clerk delivered a package to Gary's desk. "Harry Jackson sent this."

Gary tore through Harry's file with the eagerness of a starving man handed a lunch bag. *God, these companies have taken forever with the requested information. I'd better call.*

King phoned the manager of the Victory Tire Company.

"Officer King," the manager said, "I'm sorry no one got back to you guys. The report has been available for some time, but we dropped the ball. Sorry about that."

"What did you find?"

"The tire was made between 1935 and 1942. After 1940, the tires were differentiated from a winged ⁻V⁻ on the earlier tread to a wingless V."

"So, the tires are really old?"

"Yeah. I'm surprised they're still rolling. Someone must have taken very good care of them."

"Do you have any information about their distribution back then?"

"They were distributed only along the east coast. Most were sent to the DC, Baltimore area."

"Do you know who distributed or sold them?"

"Sorry, not after all these years."

"Well, thanks for the information. Would you please send the report to my attention, so we can close this part of the case?"

"Will do."

King thought, *That guy raises another question. Could the tire imprints have been a plant from just a part of an old tire? The tires, or fragments, are old, and the user may have known they would be difficult to trace. But why use a bike? Why didn't the perp drive, walk, or use skates? The location of the imprints makes me think the killer was not aware either bike or shoe imprints were left.*

Pensive, King ambled around his office fingering various items. *Who uses tires that old? Maybe some old person had the bike from their youth and hadn't used it much, or someone had a newer bike but used old tires to distract us. I'd better check for other cases of assault or robbery with related tire prints. Maybe the bike was used because the distance to the killer's destination was too far for walking or they didn't own a car.*

Gary phoned the internal records department. "Officer King here. I need a traffic map. Can you get one to me right away on the fourth floor."

King rapped his desk while waiting for the map.

Buddy dropped the requested map on Gary's desk. "Don't tell me you're lost, Officer."

"Hell no. I want to map some destination distances a killer might travel from Murphy Park. The perp might have ridden a bike, but I'm looking for average walking distances a killer might have considered. Outside those areas might have been bicycle or car riding areas."

"What if the perp transported a bike in a vehicle and then rode it away?" Buddy asked.

"Yeah, that's another possibility. Thanks."

King scoured office records for assault or robbery cases in Murphy Park. *Shit, nothing in the past year. There goes that theory.*

Gary phoned Detective Jackson and filled him in on what he had learned from the Victory Tire Company.

"Unfortunately, that's not much to go on," Harry said, "but thanks for the update."

"I noticed an entry about another detective talking to area distributors about bikes and old tires, but there's nothing's in the file. Did they get anything?"

"Damned if I know. Give the state lab a call."

"Thanks. I will."

"State lab, Timothy Banes speaking."

"Officer Gary King here. Anyone in the lab remember working on a murder case in Murphy Park dealing with old bike tires?"

"Yeah. That'd be Bob. He's the bike enthusiast. He volunteered for the task."

"Can you transfer my call?"

"Hang on, Gary."

"Gary. Bob here. I remember that case. What do ya need?"

"Did you find anything about those old bike tires?"

"Maybe." Bob said.

"What do ya mean, *maybe*?"

"I remember a local bike shop owner who thought he had seen an old bike with those kind of tires, but he couldn't remember where or when."

"That information isn't in the files," Gary said.

"No, it isn't. Sorry, but I couldn't say someone *thought* they remembered an old bike with old tires and have that mean anything, so I didn't put it in the report."

"Who gave you that *maybe* info?"

"Would you believe a former winner of the big bike race in Europe? He owns a chain of bike shops—one is downtown. If I remember, his name is Hank. Can't remember his last name."

"Thanks. I'll find him."

King pulled out the phone directory and scanned the Yellow Pages for local bike shops. "Here it is," he muttered. *The ad boasts the owner being a Tour de France winner.* "Gotta visit him."

Inside the Spinning Wheels bike shop, King shifted his weight as he waited for the shop owner to finish talking with a customer.

"Hank, I'm Officer King, Towson Police Department. Nice shop. Never seen so many bikes. Never heard of half these brands."

"Great stuff, eh? We try to appeal to a wide range of customers."

"I'm following up on a case about a presumed Schwinn bike—maybe old, maybe new—with very old tires."

"Yeah, I remember discussing that with a policeman, but I told him I couldn't recall when or where I had seen it. I get lots of bikes in here, from all over. It's hard to remember one from the other or who owned it."

"Can you remember if it was a man's or a woman's

bike?"

"Gee, I can't be sure. I think it was a woman's, but I wouldn't swear to it."

"Thanks. If you remember anything, give me a call. Here's my card."

King listened to "hold" music while waiting for the detective to return to the phone.

"What ya got, King?"

"Spoke to that pro biker, Hank. He thinks the bike was a woman's, but he can't be sure."

"You trying to rule out a male perp?"

"Could be. It certainly would help if we could focus only on women."

"Well. That leaves only 150 million other people to consider," Harry said.

"Yeah. Know what ya mean. I'll keep you posted."

Joan struggled to get her bike into the back of her station wagon. She closed the rear door then went into the house and dialed Spinning Wheels, her husband's bike shop.

"Spinning Wheels," the receptionist answered. "We pedal butts."

"See you're still using that horrible greeting, Ellie. This is Joan. Is my husband available?"

"I think he's with a customer. Please hold."

Joan thought, *If that butt pedaling shit plays one more time, I'll scream.*

"Hey, what's up, hon?" Hank asked.

"Nothing. It's what's *down* that has me calling."

"What are you talking about?"

"My tire. It has been weeks since you said you would fix my flat and you haven't."

"Honey, I'm sorry. I promise I'll get right on it."

"I know you will. I have it loaded in the wagon, and I'm bringing it down there—now."

"Okay. Okay. Drive round to the back. I'll have Andy get it out. You can wait—No, we'll go to lunch while he takes care of the tire. How does that sound?"

"Sounds good. See you in a few minutes."

Hank unloaded the bike then he and Joan headed to Le Sur for lunch.

Looking up from his menu, Hank said, "Hon, I'm sorry I hadn't gotten that damn tire fixed."

"You're forgiven, but I just couldn't ask to borrow Mary's bike again. Besides it's old, and I felt embarrassed riding it while the girls rode their fashion wheels."

"I know how you feel . . ." Hank stared into space. "Hmm. What was it?"

"What was what?" Joan asked.

"The type of bike? Mary's bike."

"It's a girl's bike. I think it's a . . . Schwinn. Yes, an old Schwinn."

"You know, I think I've seen her on that damn thing. A really *old* one."

"You said it. It's an antique. It's probably worth some money."

"Shit!" Hank said. "Honey, I have to call the police. They've been asking about an old bike. Hers may be the one they're looking for."

"What?"

"Later," Hank said, leaving the table.

He asked to use the restaurant phone and then called Officer King.

A department secretary answered the phone. "Sorry. Officer King is out. May I take a message?"

"Do you know when he'll be back?"

"Sorry I don't. Want to leave a message?"

"Guess I'd better. Ask him to call Hank at Spinning Wheels. Tell him I have information about an old bike."

Officer King returned from lunch and received the message that Hank had called. King phoned him and was told that Doctor Snow owned an old girl's Schwinn bicycle.

King then phoned Detective Harry Jackson. "Harry, I think I know where you can find an old Schwinn bike."

"You do? Where?"

"Doctor Snow's house."

"Now that I think of it, I believe I saw one in her garage. I accidently knocked it over when I was there."

"You're kidding me?"

"No," Harry said, "We've got to get a look at the damn thing."

"You're the experienced detective," Gary said. "Invent a story to get in the house. A search warrant would be hard to get based on what we have, and we don't want to tip her off with an overt search."

"Makes sense. I'll think of something."

Harry Jackson rang Doctor Snow's doorbell.

"Detective Jackson, it's been a long time," Mary said. "Do come in."

"Thanks for seeing me, Doctor. I'm still working on

the cable guy case. I'd like to see the cable he installed. I want to know if he installed the same cable here as he installed at another house the day he disappeared."

"On to something are you?"

"Not sure."

"Where would you like to start?" Mary asked.

"First, I'd like to look at the backyard pole and then the cable in the house. It's possible there's a junction box somewhere that has a different cable than the entry cable."

"Go on out back. I'll open the garage door so you can get in the house when you're ready. I'll be in my office, right over there, if you need me."

"Thanks. I'll try not to intrude too much."

Harry followed Mary through the dining room to the kitchen then out the backdoor. He crossed the deck, the backyard, and then walked to the pole anchoring her TV cable.

Harry thought, *I'd better pretend to examine the cable before I go in the garage.*

He walked under a length of cable, often staring up at it as if looking for something specific. He took a photograph of the pole and cable then took a notepad from his jacket pocket and feigned making notes.

Appearing to be in deep thought, he ambled toward the garage and wondered if the bike still leaned against the wall near the interior kitchen door. He ducked under the half-raised garage door then squeezed past Mary's car.

Thank God, the bike is still here. Damn! It is a girl's Schwinn and an old one, and there's dried mud on the tires. Better take some of that. I may not be able to use it in court, but I can check to see if it matches dirt from Murphy Park.

He took several photos of the bike and then broke a clump of dried mud from a rim. Putting the crumbly dirt in his coat pocket, he examined the tread. *Oh God, the tires have 'Vs.' Stay cool, Harry. Stay cool.*

He took several photos of the tires then let himself into the kitchen.

He called to Doctor Snow, "Okay if I go to the basement?"

Mary walked into the kitchen. "It's this way. Let me turn the light on for you."

Harry followed her down the steps then examined the cable stapled to the ceiling and joists.

"May I ask what you are looking for?"

"Sure." Harry pulled a short length of cable into view. "See these numbers. I'm comparing these and the cable's texture to some we have downtown." He took a close-up photo of Mary's cable.

"I hope this is helpful," Mary said.

"Very helpful, thank you. Well, I've seen enough, Doctor. Thanks for your cooperation."

"Anytime, Detective. I'll show you out."

Excited about his find, Harry turned on his siren and ran two red lights on the way to the state lab. Once there, he scurried to the lab to find Jim Bonavista.

Breathless, Harry said, "Jim, compare this sample to your dirt database. Give it an exhibit number for the Murphy Park case and that cable guy." Harry held out his camera. "Take this. See what you can do with the photos inside."

"Got something hot, eh?" Jim asked.

"I'd like to think so," Harry said, looking back as he

exited the lab.

Back at headquarters, Harry rushed off the elevator and hurried to Gary's desk. "Guess what, Gary? Doctor Snow killed that cable guy."

"You think so?"

"Absolutely," Harry said, striking Gary's desk. "I got a look at her bike. It's an old Schwinn, *and* it has 'V' tires. I don't think she's cleaned the bike since the murder. I took photos of the tires and got a sample of dried mud from its rims. As we speak, the mud is in the state lab being compared to dirt samples in the data base."

"Well, I'm glad Hank's wife jogged his memory about the bike because she had ridden it with a group of neighborhood women on one of their tours."

"Did you ask Hank if his wife and friends ever biked to Murphy Park?"

"I did, and he said no. The park is too far away for them to do their one hour ride."

"Thank God," Harry said. "Looks like we won't have to rule out female neighbors as killers."

"If the soil test is positive, do you think we should arrest Snow?" Gary asked.

"How can we be sure the mud didn't get stuck to the tire while Joan rode the bike?"

"That's a consideration. However, I don't want to interview those women bikers now, so let's hold off on the arrest until I track down the remaining info from Liberty Shoe. I want as much evidence as possible when we request a warrant."

Chapter Twenty-nine

Tim's growing hunger suggested Kashandra's milk production had slowed.

Mary expected her to stop lactating someday but did not expect that time had arrived so soon. Mary hated to search for women willing to sell, or donate, milk, so she needed Kashandra to keep producing as long as possible.

Mary called John, one of the doctors in her office.

"John, I need some information from a doc still active in obstetrics."

Chuckling, John said, "That's me. Ask away."

"What's the latest hormonal product for stimulating lactation?"

"Gosh, there're several new drugs since you quit obstetrics. I'll have Terri collect some of the package inserts the pharmacy reps left. They'll be on your desk when you arrive tomorrow."

Mary scanned the information sheets then chose the product that had the best record of maximizing breast milk production. She took a sample bottle of the medication from the office supply closet. *This should keep Kashandra producing for a while.*

Smiling, Mary entered Kashandra's room.

"You're sho looking happy, baby," Kashandra said and winked.

"I am. I have a new medicine for you."

"For me? Why?"

"When women stop making milk, they sometimes

have problems. This new medicine will help prevent breast pain and lumps as your milk production tapers off."

"Ya think I need it?"

"It's a matter of making sure you *don't* have problems. I prefer not to treat you *after* symptoms develop."

"Lord knows I don't need problems, baby, especially if they can be prevented."

Mary opened a small box and removed an information sheet. She placed it on the bedside table then removed a vial of clear liquid. She held it up for examination. "Thank God I get free samples. This would cost $300 if you had to buy it."

"You know I ain't got that kind of money, baby."

"Oh, it's free to you, but I need a syringe. Can't do an injection without one. Be back in a minute."

Mary went downstairs. As she reached the bottom step, the phone rang.

Kashandra heard part of Mary's conversation. *My, she's talkin' a long time*, Kashandra thought.

Kashandra picked up the paper from the box then scanned the information sheet. *My. Lotta big words here. Hmm. There's a word I know. 'Stimulation.' This stuff makes ya make milk. Why she want me to do that?*

Kashandra heard Mary climb the steps.

"I wanna know more about this stuff," Kashandra said under her breath.

She tore off the part of the page concerning stimulation and tucked it under her pillow. As Mary entered the room, Kashandra stuffed the rest of the information sheet into its box.

"Trying to read that doctor stuff?" Mary asked.

"Too many big words for me, baby."

Mary used a syringe to draw medication from the small vial then dropped the emptied vial and its box into the wastebasket. "Roll onto your right side so I can inject your left hip."

"If ya gotta, baby."

"We do." Mary made a quick injection. "There, that wasn't too bad was it?"

"Not yet but is it gonna hurt later?"

"Maybe a little . . . Okay. Now relax. See you in a while."

Yolanda mopped the hallway outside Kashandra's room.

"Hi, Miss Ka."

"Hi, baby. You okay?"

"Sho am," Yolanda said as Kashandra motioned for her to come in.

"Come here, baby," Kashandra whispered.

"Why ya whispering?" Yolanda asked as she moved to Kashandra's bed.

"Baby, I might be in trouble."

"What kinda trouble?"

"Not sure. Kashandra pulled the paper from beneath her pillow. "See this? Find somebody that knows what this means, baby."

Yolanda stuck the paper in her cleavage. "What's it about?"

"A medicine. Doctor Mary done give me a shot of it. I think she lied about why I need it."

"Sorry, Miss Ka, but I don't know no doctor to ask."

"Maybe a nurse or one dem guys in the white coat at the drug store, baby."

"Wait. I know who I can give it to."

"Good, but be careful."

Near the end of her work day, Yolanda called Officer King. "I gotta see you right away."

"Can we meet tomorrow?"

"No sir. We gotta talk tonight."

"Okay, I'll come by your house. Is seven okay?"

"That'd be good."

Yolanda stood by her front window, peering past tattered lace curtains held aside by her shaking hand. *Where can he be?*

Seeing his car pull up, she said, "Thank God."

As King strolled up the walkway, she opened the front door. "Hurry, Mista King!"

"You look worried. What's up?"

Yolanda waved the drug information sheet. "I need ta find out about this."

King took the sheet. "What is it?"

"It's got ta do with a shot Doctor Mary gave Miss Ka. She thinks she don't need it, but she took it. She thinks Mary lied 'bout her needin' it."

King scanned the information sheet. "Lots of technical stuff here, but it looks like a medicine given to women to stimulate breast milk production."

"Why she need that?"

"I don't know, but before we jump to conclusions, I'm going to talk to a doctor I know. Thanks for getting this."

"Can ya call me before eight o'clock tomorrow?"

Yolanda asked. "Let me know what ya find out?"

"I'll try."

Sitting in his car, King contemplated calling his consultant. *I know it's late, but I had better call on that payphone.*

"Doctor, sorry to bother you," Gary said.

"Officer, my service said you have an emergency."

"I do but in a police way."

"How may I help?"

"I can't pronounce the name of this medicine, so I'm going to spell it for you. I'd like to know what it's used for." King spelled the name of the medication. "It's for injection."

"I know it. Use it in my practice from time to time. It's a hormone. Stimulates a woman's milk production."

"Why would you do that?"

"Sometimes a woman makes too little milk to feed her baby. Many times, the hormone will stimulate her breasts to make milk, so the baby can continue to breast feed."

"Doc, let me run this past you. If a woman loses her baby, let's say by abortion, why would she need this medication?"

"Officer King, does this have anything to do with the baby whose ultrasound exam you showed me?"

"Can't say. But would a woman who loses her baby need the shot?"

"No. She wouldn't have a baby to feed—unless . . ."

"Unless what?"

"Unless she wanted to make milk for another woman's baby—to be a wet nurse."

"Oh, my God!" King said.

"Officer, are you okay?"

"I'm fine, but someone else might not be. Thanks Doc."

King walked back to Yolanda's door and knocked.

"Comin'," Yolanda opened the door. "Oh, it's you. Thought you'd left."

"Nah. I called a doctor I know. We talked about that medicine. Just as I thought, it's used to help a woman make breast milk when they make too little for their baby."

"But, there ain't no babies in that house."

"I know," King said. "But a man there drinks breast milk."

"You kiddin' me. Men don't need breast milk."

"One does—and it's Tim."

"You jokin' with me? Yolanda asked, her eyes widening.

"No. Kashandra has been breast feeding Tim, and Mary uses that rubber bra to feed him breast milk she gets from donors. He thinks she's really breastfeeding him. I'm thinking Mary caused Kashandra's baby's death so there would be no baby needing her milk—just Tim."

"Why? That's like . . . murder!"

"You might say that."

"Why she do it?"

"Perhaps some warped sense of obligation or love. I'm not sure why Kashandra is involved, but money probably plays a role."

"But Doctor Mary—"

"She's sick, Yolanda. Maybe she's . . . what do they call it . . . psychotic.?"

"But she's a doctor."

"That doesn't make her immune to mental problems."

"You sayin' she's crazy?"

"Maybe."

"What we gonna do?"

"I need to talk to my people about this, but I want you to go to work tomorrow. Act like nothing has happened. Tell Kashandra she has to get out. The sooner the better. Once she's out, she should call me. Give her this card. It has my number."

"I can do that, but what about me? I don't wanna work there no more."

"Tell the doctor you have a new job. Say it's closer to your house and pays more. Let her know tomorrow is your last day. Apologize for the short notice and tell her you need to start right away, or you'll lose the new job."

"What if somethin' goes wrong?"

"Then get out of the house."

"Mista King, I'm scared."

"I'll wait in my car near the house. You hightail it out of there at the first hint of trouble. Understand?"

"You bet. Lord, help me."

Walking into the chief's office, Gary asked, "Who is our psychiatric consultant?"

The chief chuckled. "Police work driving you crazy, King? Need a shrink?"

"Not me, but I know someone who does—a criminal."

"Then you need a forensic psychiatrist? Who's the crazy one?"

"It's that—"

"Don't tell me. Doctor Snow?"

"Yep. I think she's one sick gal. Responsible for a

377

murder and an illegal abortion."

"Call Professor McDonald at the medical school. He's our psych guy. Get back to me in an hour. I'll get his direct number. I'll approve your talking to him but don't do a damn thing with the info until we talk. Understand?"

"Professor, thanks for making time to see me," King said, looking around the psychiatrist's office. "Don't you guys use Victorian couches anymore?"

"They're only used for sleeping these days."

"Well, thanks for seeing me."

"I had to," Doctor McDonald said. "I'm on retainer."

"I guess that's good. I need your insight about a case."

The professor pulled out a pad and pen ready to take notes as if interviewing a patient.

King explained the happenings as he knew them then waited as the doctor gathered his thoughts.

"I'm thinking the obstetrician has mental problems but so does the prostitute," the doctor said. "Who do you think is most dangerous and why?"

"The doctor," Gary said. "I think she promoted the prostitute's pregnancy, maybe more than one, and an abortion or abortions. She did it so the prostitute would produce milk for the doctor's son. What do you think, Doc?"

"With this limited information, I would presume the mother, the obstetrician, had a disturbed childhood. I would not be surprised to learn she had been abandoned or lost her parents, maybe in an accident, when she was very young. She either feels unwanted, abandoned, unloved, or all three. It's possible she has compensated by doting on her son. She probably thinks he's the only person who loves or needs her."

"Sounds awful."

"The mother's continued breastfeeding is unusual, but many babies don't like being breast weaned—often causes problems. Some babies have to be forced to take bottle milk. Breastfeeding promotes a strong emotional mother-baby bond, which is a physically and emotionally satisfying activity for both. It can be as hard for the baby as the mother to break that bond by giving up breastfeedings. She gives him what he wants, and he gives her what she wants."

"Strange, but why?"

"I think your doctor-mother sees her son as a surrogate for herself. What she's doing for him, she's doing for herself. She sees him as herself as a child. In loving him, she's loving herself. In taking care of him, she's taking care of herself—the child. In other words, she perceives him as being her when she was a child feeling helpless and un-loved."

"That's horrible."

"If I'm right about her losing her parents, then she is acting the role of the lost mother caring for her son who she sees as herself, either as an unwanted or orphaned baby."

"She's the absent mother *and* the abandoned child at the same time?"

"You got it," the doctor said.

"How could a woman like that become a doctor?"

"Officer, doctors are like everyone else. As a group, we have the same problems as the general population. Doctors can and do have mental health issues. Mental problems can progress over time. Some people slowly become insane. Other cases more quickly."

"Are you saying this obstetrician is insane?"

"That would be difficult to say without interviewing her, but she wouldn't have to be to act the way she does. She may have a severe neurosis, depends on whether or not she knows right from wrong, but she's compelled in her actions. Are you going to arrest her?"

"Probably."

"If it comes to that, I would very much like to interview her."

Trembling with fear, Yolanda crossed the back deck and approached Mary's kitchen door. She did not want to enter the house, but she had to talk to Kashandra. She took a deep breath, composed herself, knocked on the door, and entered the kitchen.

"Good morning," Mary said, looking up from the morning paper.

"Mornin' Doctor Mary," Yolanda said in a faked upbeat voice. "Okay if I start upstairs?"

"Fine. That would give me time to finish paper work in the office."

Yolanda started cleaning the second floor. Minutes later, she tiptoed into Kashandra's bedroom then shook the sleeping woman's shoulder.

"Uh," Kashandra said, rubbing her eyes. "Yolanda. What you doin' here, baby?"

Putting a finger to her lips, Yolanda whispered, "Shhh. You gotta get outta here, girl. Police say ya might be in danger. That medicine Doctor Mary give you is ta make you make more milk longer."

"Why she do that, baby?"

"Officer King said it's to keep ya making milk for Tim. If ya do, Mary don't have to get milk from women who lost their babies and that includes you."

"What you sayin', Yolanda?"

"Doctor Snow may have caused you to lose yer baby, so Tim could have your milk."

"Who told you that?" Kashandra asked, looking perplexed and propping herself up on her elbows. "I don't wanna think about this. It's awful!"

"You gotta get out of this place," Yolanda whispered. "I'm gonna give my notice at the end of the day. I don't wanna work here no more."

"How I gonna get outta here? I only got this robe. After she washed my clothes, they kept in the closet near her office."

"You run outta this place naked if ya have ta."

"Maybe you could slip my things to me, but don't you let Mary know ya done it."

Yolanda pondered the situation. "Maybe I could bring a piece at a time, under my clothes. We could hide 'em in your closet."

"That'd take too long, baby."

Yolanda cupped her ear. "Shhh. I think I hear her coming. I gotta start cleaning. We'll talk later."

"Everything alright up here?" Mary asked, stepping into the second-floor hall.

"I'm fine," Kashandra said. "Just sharin' a joke with Yolanda."

"Okay, but Kashandra, it's time to care for Tim. Get along, Yolanda."

Yolanda busied herself mopping a second-floor room

while worrying about what her new friend did behind Tim's closed door.

Later that day, Yolanda entered Kashandra's room. "You gotta get dressed and run outta this house today."

"Honey, I got bunions. I can't run with no shoes, and what am I going ta do with no taxi money or no bus fare? Baby, I got nothing. My pay gets mailed to my mama.

"You get out of here today, and you go to Mr. King's black car parked at the bus stop." Yolanda emptied her pocket of small change. "This ain't much, but it's good for bus fare or a payphone. Call Officer King if he ain't there. He wants ta talk to you." Yolanda dug in her pocket and pulled out King's business card. "Take this but hide it."

"What time you leaving, baby?"

Yolanda looked over her shoulder. "At five."

"Maybe we could meet some place and go off together," Kashandra said.

Yolanda whispered, "Girl, you're a strong woman. You gotta take care of yourself."

"Watch out, baby, 'cause I might be right behind ya."

"Maybe I can get Mary out of the house," Yolanda said. "Then you go downstairs, get dressed and get outta here."

"How ya going to get Mary outta the house?"

Yolanda grinned. "I'll think of somethin'—somethin' about her flowers out front while you go out the back."

"Lordie, baby, I hope she don't shoot us," Kashandra said, frowning.

"I gotta clean, or she gonna think something strange goin' on."

Yolanda added extra pine oil to the mop water as if it would kill the evil she felt lived in the house.

Mary called from downstairs, "Yolanda, you about ready to clean down here?"

"Five minutes, Doctor Mary." Walking past Kashandra's room, Yolanda whispered, "Be careful, girl. Let's talk tonight."

As Yolanda carried the mop bucket down the stairs, Mary said, "That pine oil smells good. Clean the office first."

"Yes, Ma'am."

Yolanda cleaned the office then went to the kitchen. "Doctor Mary, I'm through with the office. Gonna start in the living room if that's okay."

"Thanks," Mary said, looking up from the newspaper.

Yolanda whistled as she cleaned the living room. Her tune wavered as nervousness intruded on her plan. *Gotta get Mary to the front yard?*

In deep thought, Yolanda slumped into a living room chair and stared at the floor. She suddenly sat upright. "That's it. I'm gonna do it."

Yolanda went to the flower bed under the living room picture window. She stomped a section of flowers then hurried back to the living room.

"Doctor Mary, come look!" Yolanda yelled, looking out the window. "Your flowers is ruined."

The shout echoed throughout the house—a signal for Kashandra to ready her escape.

"What's ruined?" Mary asked, walking into the living room.

Yolanda pointed to the flowerbed below the window. "Look at them poor flowers."

"Oh, God,' Mary said.

Mary, followed by Yolanda, went to examine the crumpled flowers. Yolanda slammed the front door closed behind her to alert Kashandra that she and Mary were outside.

"Who could have done this?" Mary asked. "And why?" She examined the downed blossoms and broken stems, trying to get them to stand upright. "They're done for. Might as well use them as cut flowers. Yolanda, will you get the scissors from the kitchen junk drawer?"

Yolanda went for the scissors and caught a glimpse of Kashandra getting dressed outside Mary's office. "Better hurry, girl."

"Baby, I'm outta here."

Yolanda handed the scissors to Mary as she kneeled amid the plants. She cut the downed flowers then took them to the kitchen while Yolanda returned to cleaning the living room.

After the flowers were trimmed and arranged in a vase, Mary took them to her office. Walking past the closet where Kashandra's clothes were stored, Mary thought *Why is the closet door ajar?* She used her hip to bump it closed.

Mary placed the vase on her desk and sat down, admiring the flowers. *I'm sure I closed that door.* She went to the closet door and opened it. "Shit! Her dress is gone. Yolanda! Come here!"

Yolanda entered the hall. "Yes, Doctor Mary."

"Where are Kashandra's clothes?"

"I don't kno nothin' about her clothes."

Mary felt dizzy as if she had seen her own funeral.

"Kashandra!" she called and walked to the foot of the stairs. "Kashandra! Where are you?" The only reply was Mary's echo. "Shit! She's run out on me."

Mary struck the banister, sending a thud rumbling around the room. She stared at Yolanda. "You had something to do with this didn't you?"

"I don't know what you talkin' about, Miss Mary. Last time I seed her, she was in bed."

"Don't lie to me. Where is she?"

"Lordie, Doctor Mary, I don't know. Believe me."

"Out! Get out of my sight!"

Trembling, Yolanda returned to mopping.

Mary sat at her desk, feeling assaulted. After regaining her composure, she started to write a check but stopped. "Damn utility people." Mary sat still for a moment. "Why did she leave?" Mary threw her pen at the wall. "Damn her!"

Two hours later, Yolanda finished her workday and stored her cleaning supplies. She paused at the office door and said, "Good night, Doctor Mary."

"Night," Mary replied gruffly.

Yolanda walked toward the bus stop. *Glad both us are outta that house.*

Officer King tooted his horn and waved at Yolanda.

She thought she would see Kashandra in his car but didn't.

King lowered his window. "How did things go today?"

"The important thing is did Miss Ka get out? Thought she'd be in your car. Have ya seen her?"

"No."

"Oh well. The bus is comin'. I'm going home. You got my number; let me know when she calls.

At home, Yolanda cooked supper for her auntie. Watching her frail aunt slurp mushroom soup, Yolanda's innards felt knotted from her not knowing what had happened to Kashandra. *Better call Officer King. See if he's heard anything.*

"Mista King?"

"Yes. Is this Yolanda?"

"Yes sir."

"What happened to Kashandra?"

"Not sure. I thought she got out the house, but I ain't heard from her. Did you?"

"Not a word. Did you tell Doctor Snow that you were quitting?"

"No. I was afraid, but I'm thinking I gotta go back tomorrow. See what's going on. See if Ka is there."

"I can't ask you to return, but I sure would like to know what happened to her."

"Then I'll go back."

"I should be talking you out of this, but . . . okay. Stay safe."

Mary placed a chicken in the oven then turned around. "My God. I didn't expect to see you again."

Kashandra smiled, pulling at the bosom part of her dress. "Why not?"

"Your clothes were missing from the hall closet. I assumed you had sneaked out—gone."

"Well, as you can see, I haven't. I got tired of wearin' that bathrobe all the time. I wanted ta feel normal again, so I got my clothes on and went for a walk. Hope ya didn't mind."

"Uh . . . no. Not at all. You didn't see any of my neighbors did you?"

"Not that I know of."

"Hope you're hungry? I'm baking a chicken."

"Baby, I love chicken."

"Have a seat. I was about to have a beer. Want one?"

"Make it a lite one." Kashandra laughed and rubbed her belly. "I'm watching my figure."

Chapter Thirty

Yolanda arrived for work as usual. Worried about the unknowns she might confront, she had to know if Kashandra had stayed behind, and if so, why?

"Morning, Doctor Mary," Yolanda said, smiling.

Mary held up her cup of coffee. "Good morning." She took a sip then said, "Start upstairs, will you?"

Heading for the stairs, Yolanda replied, "Yes. Ma'am."

Yolanda saw Kashandra asleep on her bed. *Lordie, why is she still here?* She shook Kashandra and whispered, "Why you still here?"

Shaking sleep from her head, Kashandra sat up. "You back, baby?"

"Of course, I'm back. I had ta know what happened to ya."

"I lost that policeman's card, and I couldn't remember his number, so I didn't wanna leave without it. I did not want ole Mary ta find it."

"Oh, God,' Yolanda said. "We gotta find it. If she finds it, she's gonna know I brung it in the house. She'll kill both us."

"What are we going ta do, baby?"

"We gonna look for it, that's what we're gonna do."

"You gotta do most of the looking, baby. She ain't gonna think anything strange if you move things. She'll think you're just cleanin'."

"Okay, but you search this room."

Yolanda cleaned as usual, but she looked under and around everything, for King's missing business card. It had to be on the second floor but where? *What am I missing?*

A short while later, Kashandra went into Tim's room. Twenty minutes later she left.

Yolanda smiled at Kashandra as she left Tim's room.

Kashandra smiled, tied her bathrobe and thrust her hands into the robe's pockets as she asked, "Have you found—?" Kashandra's face went pale.

"What's the matter?" Yolanda asked.

Giggling, Kashandra pulled her right hand from her pocket. "It's the card, baby. I guess I hid it here."

"Thank God, Miss Mary didn't wash that robe."

"Yeah. Now, I can get outta here."

"Good. I'm givin' notice at the end of the day."

"I don't know when, baby, but I'm getting out too."

"Good. I'll wait for ya at the bus stop where Mister King waits. It's at the end of this block—at the traffic light."

Yolanda finished cleaning the first floor then knocked on Mary's closed office door. "Excuse me, Doctor Mary. Could I please speak to ya?"

"Come in."

Yolanda opened the door then stared at the floor. "I hate to do this, but I gotta tell you that today is my last day. I got a job near my house, and it pays more. I have ta start tomorrow, or I don't get the job."

"Don't fret. I understand. You have to do what you have to do. I'm happy for you. Good luck."

Yolanda thought, *My, she don't seem upset about my leaving.* "I appreciate yer understandin'."

Yolanda gathered her things then hurried to the bus stop to meet Officer King. Panting, she said, "I quit. I

390

ain't her cleaning girl no more."

"Relax. Did Kashandra get out okay?"

"She's suppose to done left and meet us here."

"Take a deep breath," King said. "Try to relax. We'll give her a few minutes."

Yolanda kept glancing at the car clock. "It's takin' her a long time to get here."

"Does seem like a long time since you left," King said. "I don't want to break in there without a reason, but how about you going back? Go in and say you left something upstairs. You could look in on Kashandra to make sure she's okay and retrieve your stuff. If there's a problem, hightail it out of there. I'll be parked here, just out of sight."

"Mista King, I ain't cut out to be no cop. Besides, I got no gun."

"All you need is a scream and fast feet. Will you go back?"

"Lordie, I guess I gotta, but I'm shaking so bad inside I might get discovered. Look at my hands. They shaking."

Yolanda removed her wristwatch and placed it in her pocket. Trying not to look nervous, she headed for Mary's kitchen door.

Yolanda knocked on the door, opened it, and yelled, "Doctor Mary. It's me."

Mary walked into the kitchen. "What are you doing here?"

In a shaky voice, Yolanda said, "I think I left my watch on the second floor. I'd like to get it."

"Certainly. Go on up."

Dashing up the steps, Yolanda rushed to Kashandra's room. "What the hell ya doin' in bed? Thought you were going ta meet me at the bus stop."

"I wanted to, but I remembered I get paid tomorrow. Mary mails my check then. I didn't wanna leave until the mailman picks it up a two o'clock. If I left now, I'd lose my due money."

"Woman. You crazy."

"Maybe, but I need that money. I'll leave tomorrow."

"Lord be with ya, honey."

Going downstairs, Yolanda held her wrist watch toward Mary. "I found it. Musta taken it off before I mopped."

"Glad you found it," Mary said. "Good luck with your new job."

Sitting in his car, King listened as Yolanda explained what had happened.

"She's a big girl," King said. "She's got to do what she's got to do. Guess I should come back tomorrow, be here when the postman picks up the mail."

"I sure hope she gets out okay."

"Maybe there is something we can do," King said. "Did Kashandra ever talk about her family?"

"Not much, but I think she lives with her mama."

"Her mother," King said, rubbing his chin. "Hmmm. Tomorrow, after the mail is picked up, call the Snow house. Disguise your voice and say you're a cousin of Kashandra and that her mother is sick. Tell Doctor Snow that Kashandra is needed at home right away. That would give her an excuse to get out of the house. Can you do it?"

"Ya know I wanna help."

"Then meet me here, tomorrow, one o'clock."

"I'll be here."

#

Minutes after King parked his car near the Snow house, a bus arrived. The driver opened the doors to let Yolanda out.

Entering King's car, she asked, "What's goin' on?"

"I just saw the postman pick up the mail," King said. "He's early. Here's a quarter. Go to that corner payphone and call Doctor Snow. Hold your nose to change your voice. We don't want her suspecting anything."

King stood by Yolanda, ready to listen in on the conversation. Yolanda took a deep breath and then dialed the number. Her whole body shook as she waited for Mary to answer.

"Hello."

Yolanda pinched her nose. "Doctor Snow. This is Shanilla. Kashandra's cousin. Can I speak to her? Her mama's sick and needs her home."

"How did you get this phone number?"

"Kashandra gave it to her mama when she started workin' fer you."

Yolanda knew Mary would let Kashandra speak to the caller, so no one would become suspicious.

"Shanilla, give me a minute to get her to the phone."

Kashandra placed her book in her lap and stared at Mary. "You say my cousin is callin' 'bout my mama?"

"That's what the woman said. You want to use the phone in the hallway?"

"Sure."

Kashandra followed Mary to the phone. Mary handed the receiver to her and stood nearby.

"This is Kashandra." She listened, nodded and then

said, "Uh huh. Tell momma I'll be right there. I'm coming as fast as I can."

Mary said, "Sorry your mother is ill. How long do you think you'll be gone?"

"Not sure. I'll be back as soon as I can. I need the money."

"Hope you're back in a day or two. We need you. Make sure you milk your breast twice a day. Can't have you drying up." Mary muttered, "Guess I'd better start phoning mothers just in case."

Sitting in King's car at the bus stop, Yolanda said, "Here she comes, Mista King."

"Get in," Yolanda said. "This is Officer King. He's workin' on the case about Doctor Snow."

"Pleased ta make your acquaintance again," Kashandra said. "What's going on in there that makes you wanna get involved?"

"I can't talk about it now, but do you know if there were any other women involved with Tim?"

"Musta been some, but I know only one and she missin'."

"Who was she?"

"My friend, Quickie."

"Did she have a baby while working there?"

"Only heard a rumor . . . from my bar friends about her having a baby. Some said she went on a long trip, but I wondered if she be pregnant and didn't want nobody ta know. Pregnant is bad for a girl workin' the streets. Johns get scared, baby."

"What do you mean?" King asked.

"If a girl can get pregnant, she not using protection,

and that means she can get diseases, baby. She ain't safe for sex. No sex, no money."

"Any other information or rumors from the bar?"

"My friend, Puss, the bar owner, says Quickie done got mixed up with a weirdo and she's dead."

"I need to ask more questions, and that might take a while. Would you mind coming with me to the station?"

"I *gotta* go home ta see my mama."

"Yolanda made that call," King said. "Your mother is fine."

"I'd still like ta see her. Maybe see ya tomorrow?"

King nodded. "I understand. Can you come to the station in the morning—at ten?"

"I'll be there."

"Don't let anyone answer your phone for the next few days. You don't want Snow discovering you're home with a well relative."

At the police station, Kashandra pushed her way through a group of policemen then stopped at the reception desk. She asked for Officer King.

Moments later, King entered the waiting area and greeted her. "Thanks for coming. Would you follow me? We're going to an interview room."

"Sorry ta say but I've seen them before."

"I forgot," King said as they entered an eight by eight-foot room containing a table with a worn green top, a large mirror, and two aluminum colored chairs. A bright ceiling light shown on the center of the table where Kashandra placed her faux Louis Vuitton handbag.

"I need to ask some embarrassing questions, but I want to know what went on in that house. What did you do there?"

Kashandra took a deep breath, bit her lower lip, and then exhaled. "Mr. Tim, he's Mary's son. He gotta thing for titties. Likes ta play with 'em. Suck 'em." Gaze downcast, Kashandra said, "Mary hired me, so Tim could play with my titties. Said she wanted him ta have fun just like other boys his age, so we did."

"How often did you . . . take care of Tim?"

"Baby, He played with my titties four or five times a day but we only did *it* once a day."

"How did you get pregnant?"

"Mary said Tim is allergic to condoms. So, I couldn't use 'em."

"Did that bother you?"

"Yeah, but I needed the money. I liked the steady work—safer than workin' the streets. Paid good plus being with just one guy. I liked it better than being with who knows what in dark corners. No more weirdoes, baby. I thought I could judge my monthly, but I missed."

"Looks that way." King smiled.

"Do you know anything about a black rubber bra?"

"Yeah. I seen it."

"When?"

"When she was wearing it."

"And when was that?"

"When she coming outta Tim's room."

"Was she naked?"

"No. She had on panties."

"Have you ever seen anyone else in the room, besides Tim when she wore the bra?"

"Not that I seen. My door is mostly closed."

"So, it was just the two of them? You knew she got

breast milk from women who had recently had a baby?"

"Yeah. She wanted me to call some of 'em, but she didn't like the way I talk on the phone, so I don't do it. But I was supposed to say it was for some lady needing milk for their baby."

"Did you ever see little bottles of milk in the refrigerator?"

"From time to time."

"Did you see what Snow did with the milk?"

"Nope."

"Were those bottles missing from the refrigerator when Snow was in the house?"

"Couple times . . . when I'd slip a beer, but, baby, I don't know what happened to 'em, but I didn't bother 'em."

"After you delivered your baby, did you see Doctor Snow do medical things to get him to breathe?"

"I saw her moving her arm around."

"You could see your baby?"

"Well, not direct. A sheet covered my legs. But I seed the baby when she lifted him to slap his butt."

"Hmmm," King said, making notes on a small pad.

"You think she killed my baby?"

King put down his pen. "That's all for now. I'll be in touch, but I suggest you lay low."

Kashandra left the station thinking something was being withheld. *I know she done killed him. She's not goin' to get away with it.*

That night, Kashandra had a nightmare—horrible scenes of torture where people and demons tortured a baby. Despite its cries of pain, the baby received no mercy. Doctor Snow stood in the background and watched the horror. She did nothing to stop it.

Kashandra woke in a sweat. She sat up and shook her head as if nightmares could be shaken from consciousness. *Somebody gotta stop her.*

For the first time in many months, Kashandra could go about life without caring for Tim. She attempted to push thoughts about her son's death from her mind, but horrible images intruded on her consciousness. *Who gonna stop her? She's a big, highfaluting doctor. Ain't nobody gonna get her.*

Kashandra finished lunch at her kitchen table when she suddenly sat erect. "I know what ta do." She looked at the kitchen clock. *Twelve fifty. She gonna feed Tim at three. I gotta get there.*

After dressing, Kashandra headed for the bus stop. Forty-five minutes later, she arrived at the stop near the Snow house. She exited the bus and stood on the sidewalk for a moment. *It's gotta be done.*

Won't these cramps ever stop, Mary thought, rubbing her belly. *I'll never again order burritos from that Montezuma place.*

Mary went to the medicine chest and removed a bottle.

"A little Lomotil should stop this diarrhea." *Don't want to get dehydrated.* She washed the tablet down with a glass of water and rubbed her belly. *God, another cramp.* "Pill, do your thing."

Kashandra walked to the back of Mary's house. She looked about for anyone who might see her. "Thank the Lord ain't nobody around."

She crept up the steps to the deck, tiptoed to the kitchen door window, and looked inside. *Nothing.* She peeked in a side window. *Nothing. She must be feeding Tim.*

Kashandra tried the kitchen doorknob. "Thank God it ain't locked." She entered the kitchen, removed her shoes and put her purse on the table.

After rummaging through a kitchen drawer, she found a chef's knife. She turned it over in her hand and stared at the shiny blade. She cleaned the handle with a dish rag then wrapped the handle with the rag. *Get on with it, girl.*

Kashandra crept to the foot of the stairs, looked into the office. *Empty.* She cupped her ear, listening for sounds from upstairs.

Kashandra heard Mary say something about "Mama's baby."

She's caring for Tim.

Gripping the knife, Kashandra crept up the stairs. She paused in the second-floor hall and took a deep breath.

Mary continued to talk to Tim. "Mama's baby is a good boy. Yes, he is, and she loves him very much. Yes, she does. Mama loves Tim."

Kashandra tiptoed toward Tim's open door. She stopped midstride when Mary said, "Hold on Tim. Mama has to turn on her side. Her back is in a strain. There . . . That's better." Mary turned her back to the hall. "Okay. Feel this breast, okay?"

Kashandra crept closer to the open door. *Girl, don't make a sound.* She moved to the frame of the open door and raised the knife to a striking position. Just then the floor creaked. *Damn!*

Mary turned her head toward the door. "Kashandra,

what are you doing . . .?"

The sound of Mary's voice trailed off as Kashandra pulled the door closed. "Damn. She saw me."

Kashandra barely heard Mary's shouts through the door's padding.

"Open this door," Mary yelled. "Do you hear me? Open this door, now!"

Kashandra backed against the door. She felt the buffered thumps of Mary's fists striking the door as she yelled.

"Nobody hearing you, woman, nobody. You ain't going nowhere. Ya can't open it from inside."

Kashandra went to the kitchen. "Glad I didn't stab her."

She placed the knife back in its drawer then pulled on her shoes. She stared out the window, recalling Tim's room had no phone. *She can't call anyone; the windows don't open, and they got no break glass. Nobody gonna hear her. The light switch is outside, so she can't signal with the lights. Could make sparks with the TV electric cord or burn the padding, but fire or smoke would kill her and Tim.* "Better turn off the electricity to that room in case she tries funny things with the ceiling light."

Kashandra wandered around the basement until she found the fuse box. She used the hem of her dress to unscrew the fuse labeled "Tim's room."

She returned to the kitchen and got a beer. *Better stay 'til dark. Don't want no one see me leave.* She made a meal then waited for nightfall.

With nightfall at hand, she switched off the kitchen lights then turned the tab of the kitchen doorknob to the locked position then headed to the bus stop.

"Let's see you get out of there, baby."

The next morning, a water department employee rang Doctor Snow's doorbell. No one responded. He rang the bell again. No response. He went to the kitchen door and rang the back doorbell. Nothing.

Back at his truck, he removed a four-foot long iron rod from a storage box. The rod had a "T" handle at one end and an upside down "U" at the other. At the grass-covered water box, near the curb, he brushed aside the grass, removed its lid, placed the inverted "U" end of the rod over the valve, and turned it.

"There." he said, "Water's off. When she pays up, it'll get turned on."

Chapter Thirty-one

Four days following Kashandra's visit to Officer King's station, the chief entered King's office carrying a box. "This special delivery came while I was downstairs. Thought I'd drop it off since it's addressed to you."

King took the box and searched the label for the shipper's name. "It's from that shoe company." He smiled then said, "You know, the shoe that made the imprint we found in Murphy Park. Remember, the dead cable guy?" King pulled at the paper tape binding the box.

Opening the box, King lifted a plaster cast from the shredded packing paper. "This is what the state lab sent to the manufacturer," he said, looking at the chief. "Ah. Here's an envelope. Hmmm. It's marked: Confidential for Officer Gary King."

"Well," the chief said. "Open it."

Gary opened the envelope, removed a letter, and silently read it.

"For God's sake, what does it say?" the chief asked.

"The shoe imprint matches Mary Snow's shoes." King looked up from the page. "She did it. She murdered the cable guy. We've got our man—I mean woman."

"Better get an arrest warrant," the chief said. "Contact the DA's office. Take William and George with you and contact social services. Someone has to take care of her son. They'll probably hospitalize him for a while. I doubt anyone will accept him as a foster child."

King yelled across the room to William and George. "Want to make an arrest?"

"Love arresting people." William said, "Is there going

to be any shooting?"

"God, I hope not."

"When do we leave?" William asked.

"Give me an hour. I have to contact Social Services to see if they can send someone to take care of the son and also get a warrant."

King contacted Towson's Social Services. Their supervisor agreed to have an unmarked car, driver, and a chaperone for the son.

The social service officers parked to the north of Mary's house where he could not be seen by her.

The driver, Jake, looked at his watch. "I thought the cops would be here by now."

"Don't be so impatient," the chaperone said. "Maybe they stopped for donuts."

Jake turned on the radio, tuned in the five o'clock news, and then lit a cigarette.

"For heaven's sake, Jake," the chaperone yelled, "Smoke outside."

"Damn nonsmokers," Jake muttered under his breath, exiting the car. He walked a few feet away then took a drag on his cigarette. He glanced up and down the street, enjoying his smoke and looking for cops.

A contaminated chilli burrito, eaten two days before Mary and Tim were locked in, had caused her persistent and worsening diarrhea despite medication. She looked out Tim's window. *What am I going to do?* Feeling weak, she thought, *I need antibiotics and water. Can't go on like this.*

Just then, she caught a glimpse of a man pacing the

sidewalk, smoking a cigarette.

"Thank God there's someone around." She mustered her failing strength and yelled, "Help! Help!" *I've got to get his attention. Got to get him to open this door.*

She tried to yell but emitted only a squeak. She had little strength to wave much less strike the window with enough force to get the man's attention.

"Look up man. For God's sake look up here!" Mary whined and struck the glass with the energy required to smash a marshmallow.

What little sound escaped the window died on the wind.

Jake watched a squirrel cross the street then run up an Oak tree. His gaze followed its path as it jumped from limb to limb in front of a second story window of the Snow house. *Oh to be able to jump like that.*

Jake crept closer to watch the antics of the squirrel, but the sun's reflection from Mary's windows made it difficult to see the animal.

"He's a cute little thing," Jake mumbled.

The squirrel jumped to a large limb in front of another window. Jake squinted to watch it munch on an acorn.

What was that? Jake asked himself, squinting to see if something other than the squirrel had moved. *Damn sun doesn't help. Did someone wave from that window? Nah. It's the squirrel's tail.*

Mary slumped to her knees, fists against the glass. She struggled to strike the window as she wept. "Don't leave. Get me out of here. Out of here . . . out of here. Don't . . . leave." She slumped to the floor crying, "Get me out . . ."

Jake walked toward his car, puffing his cigarette. He looked at his watch. *It's five twenty-five. I don't think they're coming.* He crushed his cigarette on the pavement then got in the car. "Let's find a pay phone and call those cops."

Driving away, Jake listened to a radio commentator announce a three-car pileup a few blocks away. "Better head in a different direction," the social service driver said. "We don't want to get caught in that mess."

Jake found a pay phone and called his office.

"Supervisor please . . . Joe, this is Jake. We went to the Snow house, but the police never showed up."

"Glad you called," Joe said. "They won't be there."

"What? After waiting all this time."

"They were involved in an auto accident near you. They're on their way to the hospital. I understand they're hurt pretty bad. One died."

Jake stood motionless for a moment. "Should we do anything at Doctor Snow's house?"

"Not without the police. Come on back to the office."

The police chief grabbed his cap, headed for the door, and yelled to his secretary, "King has been in an accident. William and George were with him. I'm going to the hospital. Hold all my calls. Get the phone numbers of the guys' next-of-kin and call me."

The chief's light bar flashed and his siren screamed as he raced through seven red lights before arriving at the hospital.

Three ambulances, along with a police escort car,

were parked at the entrance to the emergency department. Their lights still flashed. The front doors of the police car were wide open. A policeman, standing at the entrance, saluted as the chief approached.

"What happened?" the chief asked.

"Seems an eighteen wheeler ran a stop sign," the officer said, sadness tingeing his words.

The chief hurried inside where another policeman had finished giving information to a nurse.

"What's up?" the chief asked the nurse.

"Not good," she replied. "One officer was DOA. Two others are in bad shape. One's in surgery now; the other is in X-ray and will be going to surgery shortly."

The chief asked, "Which one is . . .?"

"I believe his name is George—"

"Oh, no," the chief said. "What about Gary and William?"

"Gary King is in surgery," the nurse said. "He's thought to have a ruptured spleen, fractured arm and leg, and a closed head injury."

"Did his doctor mention a prognosis?" the chief asked.

"He didn't, but he looked concerned."

"Thanks, nurse . . . Do you know when William will be back from X-ray?"

"I'm not sur—Oh. Here he comes now." The nurse pointed down the hall.

William wore a neck brace. There were scrapes, cuts, and crusted blood on his face, arms, and a leg, which pro-truded from beneath a sheet. His eyes were closed. IVs ran in each arm.

The chief reached out to touch the officer's arm, but

the nurse pushing the gurney brushed his hand away.

"Sorry," she said, steering the gurney into an elevator. "Got to get him to surgery. The doctor is waiting."

The chief walked to a corner of the waiting area, removed his cap, rubbed his brow, and then dropped into a chair. He held his head in his hands then motioned for a policeman. "Check with my secretary. See if she's found the contact information I asked for?"

"Anything else?" the policeman asked, fidgeting with his cap.

"Pick a man who can spend time with the men's families when we notify them of the accident. That man is to stick with the family. Give them anything they want, do whatever is asked of them—understand?"

"Will do, Chief."

An elderly man, sitting two seats away, looked at the chief. "Sorry to hear about your men."

"Thanks. And you?"

"My wife. She's in surgery—emergency—vomiting blood."

"Hope she's going to be alright."

"Thanks. Me too."

The chief stared into space, oblivious to the turmoil around him. *God, don't let anyone else die. Not my boys.*

Reporters filled the waiting room. They accosted the chief for details about who had been injured or killed.

The elderly man left the crowded room.

The chief regained his composure and quieted the crowd. "I can't identify anyone until next of kin has been notified. See me in an hour. If I can, I'll give you more information then."

Several reporters pressed the chief for information.

"I told you—later!" He then whispered, "Remember, you're in a hospital. There are sick people here. Keep it down. Go wait in the coffee shop or outside. Now get."

A police officer pushed and shooed the crowd out of the waiting room door. He then spoke to the elderly man who waited by the door. "Please, come back in, sir."

"Sorry about your loss," the elderly man said.

"Thanks," the officer said, his voice breaking.

For two days, the chief spent long hours with the injured men's families in the intensive care waiting area and visiting the injured officers. Later he spent a few unsettling hours in the surgical waiting area when Officer King had to return to surgery because of internal bleeding.

King improved and later shared a hospital room with William. At the end of the fifth hospital day, Officer King inquired of the chief. "What became of Doctor Snow?"

"Nothing yet. I was too worried about you guys to think about her, but I'm going to send two guys tonight."

"So, she's still in the house?" William asked.

"Yes," the chief said, glancing at King. "A guy is watching the house."

"I'll feel better when her case is closed," King said.

The next morning, the chief sent seven policemen, arrest warrant in hand, and a social service detail to the Snow house.

The policemen surrounded the house while one officer, Mark, rang the front doorbell. Hearing no response, he rang again. Still no response. He went to several windows on the front porch and peered inside. "Nothing." He walked to the back of the house and spoke to another officer. "There was no response at the front. Anything going on back here?"

"Nothing here," Gregg said.

"Nothing? Let's look inside," Mark said looking through a kitchen window. After a few seconds, he said, "You're right. Nothing here."

Suddenly, a loud clap of thunder rumbled overhead.

"A storm is brewing," Mark said. "That cloud is going to darken everything."

"There's a car in the garage," Gregg called out. "Try the back doorbell."

"It's ringing, but no one is responding," Mark said, "I can hear it. It's a loud one."

"Better check with the chief," Mario said.

Mario went to the car and radioed the chief. In a few minutes, Mario reported to his colleagues. "Chief says break in if we have to. Let's tell the social service people of the situation."

Gregg went to the back door.

Mario rang the front doorbell and pounded on the door. He got no response.

Gregg could be heard knocking at the backdoor.

"Mark, we're going in," Mario said. "Tell Gregg."

Mario broke the window in the front door, reached inside, and unlocked it. The darkened house yielded no sounds, except for glass shards being crunched under foot.

"Police!" Mario yelled. "We have a warrant. Come out. You can't get away."

Mario crunched his way toward the center of the house, gun drawn. Light from flashlights moved about the house as the men searched the first floor. Mario opened closed doors and looked behind open ones.

"Gregg, check the garage," Mario said. "See if there is a basement. Mark, come upstairs with me."

Mario and Mark crept up the stairs, flashlights scanning the dark area ahead.

"I hope that's a dead rat," Mark said, sniffing the air.

"Yeah. Me too," Mario said, his voice fear filled. His tongue almost stuck to the roof of his dry mouth.

Ready for anything, Mario stepped into the dark second-floor hall, illuminating the space with his flashlight. He saw a light switch and flipped it, but nothing happened. "Damn! No Power?"

"Police!" Mark yelled. "We have a warrant. Come out. You can't escape. Make it easy on yourself."

What a stench!" Mario said.

"Yeah. Bad news . . . and it's too damn quiet," Mark said.

Mario opened a door to a bedroom, scanned it with his flashlight, and then flicked the light switch, but the lights did not come on. He rescanned the room and looked under the bed. "Clear."

Gregg arrived at the top of the stairs. "Garage and basement are clear. This is the house with that dungeon. Remember the story about that old man?"

"What are you talking about?" Mario asked.

"The torture dungeon where the old pervert who used to own this house was found chained up years ago. His so-called girlfriend did it. Nearly killed him."

"Really?" Mario asked.

"There's a key in the lock for the room opposite the one I just cleared," Mark said.

Mario tried the knob below the key, but it did not turn. He turned the key and retried the knob. It turned. He opened the door then peered inside. "What the fuck?"

The men covered their noses while Mark felt for a light switch. "No switch in here." Mark scanned the room with his flashlight. "Oh, God!"

"I'm calling the chief," Mario said, lifting the receiver from the hall phone. "Gregg, check the basement for a blown fuse or a thrown circuit breaker."

"What the . . .," Mario exclaimed, shining his flashlight into the dark room. "Shit!" He gagged and backed into the hall.

"I don't think I want to look," Gregg said.

Mario placed his hand over the phone's receiver and yelled, "Gregg, light's on!"

"Look," Mario said, "there's a naked male on the floor just beyond the bed."

"Withered looking isn't he," Mark said. "Wow. He's covered with a lot of blood?"

"Wonder if that's Doctor Snow on the bed?" Gregg asked.

"They've been here for a week or so," Mario said scanning the blood-smeared floor, padded walls, a corner shower, and window glass.

"Looks like somebody was trying to get out," Mark said, holding his nose. "What a mess."

"Mark," Mario said, "check the rest of this floor, but the chief want us to wait in the hall until detectives and forensics arrives."

Chapter Thirty-two

A week after police had entered the Snow residence, the police chief visited Officer King in his hospital room.

"How's my favorite police officer?" The chief asked, shaking Gary's hand.

"Fine, except for hospital food." Gary pushed away a food tray. "Doc says I should be able to go home in a day or two."

"Well, that's good news. Speaking of news, I thought you'd want to see the report filed by the guys who raided the Snow house."

"Sure would," Gary said, accepting the report.

He opened the envelope, pulled out several stapled pages, and then read in silence. His widening eyes conveyed his shock. At one point, he put his hand over his gaping mouth and shook his head.

"Oh, my God," he said, turning a page. "Has the coroner finished his report yet?"

"Not yet. He's waiting for the toxicology report, but he said he didn't expect to find anything."

Gary handed the report to the chief. "So, Doctor Snow and her son had been dead for a week or more. Dehydration."

"Yeah." The chief fidgeted with his hat. "Looks like it. Too bad she didn't live. She deserved a trial."

"Yeah. Appears the son died after his mother, otherwise he couldn't have gnawed off her breasts."

Chapter Thirty-three

A black Rolls Royce limousine stopped at the entrance to the Baltimore County Morgue. A man in his mid-forties, wearing a classic chauffer's suit, hurried from the driver's seat to open the left rear door.

An elderly lady, dressed in a full-length mink coat, exited the car with the assistance of the driver. An elderly man exited the right rear door then joined the woman.

Hanging on to each other's arm for support, the couple followed the chauffer to the morgue's entrance where he opened the door for the pair. The elderly man said something to the chauffer who then returned to the Rolls.

"There's the information desk," the elderly man said. "Let's inquire there."

"Pardon me, young lady," My name is Benjamin Goldberg. With whom do I speak about claiming a body?"

"That would be Doctor Potts. His office is down that hall, fifth door on the left."

Shuffling down the hall, Benjamin said to his wife, "Hope this goes well. The doctor might think we're crazy."

"Come in," someone said from behind Doctor Potts' closed door.

Benjamin opened the door to greet a man wearing a long white coat. He approached the couple. "Hello. I'm Doctor Potts. How may I help you?"

"Doctor, I'm Benjamin Goldberg. We're here to claim two bodies."

"We don't have anyone named Goldberg. Are you sure you're at the right morgue?"

"Yes. The police directed us here," Benjamin said.

"What are the names of the deceased you want to claim?

"It's Mary Snow and her son Tim."

"You have a different last name than the deceased. I understood Doctor Snow never married. Are you related?"

"Yes. My wife, Carol, and I are the estranged parents of Mary, and Tim is our grandson."

"Strange, police didn't mention any relatives."

"For decades, we knew nothing of Mary, or Tim. That is . . . until we saw the newspaper article about . . . Mary's, shall we say, *life*. Something in the report piqued our interest. We investigated, and . . . we wind up here.

Carol and I have regretted giving up Mary when she was an infant, but circumstances were what they were. We felt we had no choice. Claiming their bodies and burying them is the only thing we can do to make amends."

The End

Frank Barham is a retired physician, a former hospital administrator and a bioethicist. He has published: *Saving the World One Dog at a Time*; *The Religious Right is Wrong - the Ethics of Religion*; *Why Republicans Are the Way They Are*; *Puppy Love; Mayan Dolls Don't Die*; *Sweet Heart, and* two short stories: *Rain* and *The Gift.*